THE LONG, HOT SUMMER

KATHLEEN MACMAHON

ISIS
LARGE
PRINT

First published in Great Britain 2015
by
Sphere
an imprint of Little, Brown Book Group

First Isis Edition
published 2016
by arrangement with
Little, Brown Book Group
An Hachette UK Company

A catalogue record for this book is available
from the British Library.

ISBN 978–1–78541–284–4 (hb)
ISBN 978–1–78541–290–5 (pb)

Published by
F. A. Thorpe (Publishing)
Anstey, Leicestershire

Set by Words & Graphics Ltd.
Anstey, Leicestershire
Printed and bound in Great Britain by
T. J. International Ltd., Padstow, Cornwall

This book is printed on acid-free paper

THE LONG, HOT SUMMER

The MacEntees are no ordinary family. Determined to be different from other people, they have carved out a place for themselves in Irish life by the sheer force of their own personalities. But when a horrifying act of violence befalls television star Alma, a chain of events is set in motion that will leave even the MacEntees struggling to make sense of who they are. As media storms rage about them and secrets rise to the surface, Deirdre, the flamboyant matriarch, is planning a birthday party for herself — and with it one final, shocking surprise . . .

SPECIAL MESSAGE TO READERS

For Des

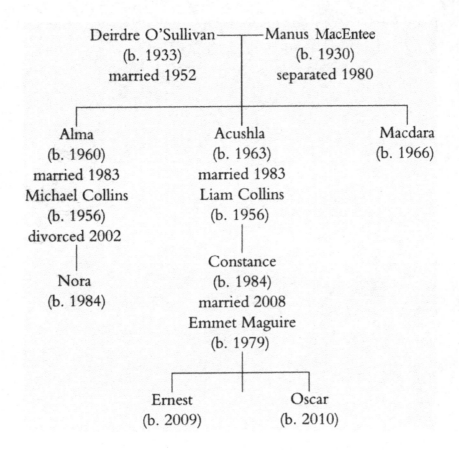

Prologue

The story of their lives was all there.

Sandwiched between two battered green leather covers, on a hundred pages of charcoal paper, a bulging patchwork of newsprint, starting on the first page with the engagement notice Deirdre had snipped out of *The Irish Times* six decades ago, the paper tobacco-coloured now with age, the typeface a faintly quaint relic of a bygone age.

Mr M. MacEntee —
Miss D. O'Sullivan

The engagement is announced be-
tween Manus, only son of David and
Eleanor MacEntee of Kildangan,
Co. Kildare, and Deirdre, youngest
daughter of Eamonn and Mary
O'Sullivan of Ennis, Co. Clare.

That was the first time Deirdre's name had ever appeared in print. A brief mention, and one that for most of the women of her generation would be the only newsworthy event of their lives. An event as frivolous and short-lived as a single firework on a summer's night, falling somewhere between the announcement of their birth — if indeed anyone had bothered to announce their birth — and that of their death, however many decades later. In between the two, a farmhouse somewhere along the road. A husband, rising up out of the bed before dawn and not returning until after dusk. A clatter of children and a couple of hospital stays. A new hat for each special occasion.

So it was for Deirdre's sisters, but not for Deirdre. Deirdre's life was always going to be different, something her father seemed to see in her from the start. "The world is full of boring people," he used to say to her, and Deirdre's heart would squirm with the secret pleasure of knowing that he was referring to her sisters.

The youngest of five girls, Deirdre was separated by six years from the next sister up. And while the other four were one prettier than the other, with their neat little noses and their dancing brown eyes, Deirdre always stood apart from them. With her long-boned face and her wide full mouth — a mouth with hardly a dip in the bow of the upper lip — she was unusual-looking, or so her father kept telling her. "I'll let you in on a secret," he said to her, when she was no more than six or seven. "You're not a pretty little thing, like your sisters. You're something far better than that. You're *unusual*-looking."

"You must promise me you'll never be afraid to be different," he told her, on more than one occasion. And because Deirdre loved her father more than anyone, because she never for one moment doubted the wisdom of what he told her, she made it her life's work to fulfil that promise. When she left home for Dublin at just seventeen, it was her father who walked her to the train. He found her a carriage with a nun sitting in it, and before he left her there he presented her with the scrapbook as a parting gift. "All you have to do now is fill it," he said to her, his voice brisk and brusque. "Not a bother to you, Deirdre O'Sullivan." As the train pulled away, Deirdre looked back to see him standing on the platform, his arm raised in a rigid salute and tears raining down his cheeks.

That was the morning after the old Abbey Theatre burnt down. The smell of it in the air as Deirdre's train pulled into Heuston station, the news on everyone's lips. The Abbey, gone up in flames! Deirdre rushed up the quays and stood with the crowd gathered to peer at the smouldering remains of the national theatre. As the Dublin fire brigade hosed down the rubble, as the players and stagehands did everything they could to salvage precious relics from the wreckage, Deirdre looked on in despair, imagining that she had arrived in the capital too late to fulfil her dream of becoming an Abbey actress. In fact the fire would prove to be her opportunity.

As she stood on the street outside, a man in shirtsleeves leaned out of an upstairs window and started flinging costumes out on to the street. Deirdre was among the onlookers who helped salvage them, spending the rest of the afternoon pegging wet gowns and uniforms on to a clothes line that had been strung across the empty auditorium. Before the day was out, she had the stage manager on a promise to get her an audition for the Abbey School of Acting; on the day of the audition, he was the one who schooled her in the flowery Irish she would need to impress the theatre's director.

It was as a student of the Abbey school that Deirdre secured her first walk-on part just two months later, playing a nurse in the production of *The Silver Tassie* that marked the start of the theatre's long exile on Pearse Street. By the following spring she had her first speaking part, as Nellie the Post in *The Righteous are Bold*, a play that scandalised her mother as much as it delighted her father. When the notice appeared in the following day's *Irish Independent*, Deirdre's father sent the hotel porter out for five copies, one of which Deirdre pasted into her scrapbook, using her fountain pen to draw a wide loop of violet ink around the salient sentence:

> Deirdre O'Sullivan delivered a
> vivid performance as Nellie the
> Post . . .

Deirdre leaned in to squint at the small print, but she couldn't make out the letters. Blurry discs across her eyes; the first one had appeared a year ago in the corner of her left eye and slipped across her eyeball. A partial eclipse that affected both eyes now, so that everything was steeped in sepia, as if the whole world was ageing with her.

"You have cataracts," the doctor had said, when finally she was persuaded to see one. Turning off his miner's torch, he wheeled backwards on his chair with something like glee. "Nothing whatsoever to worry about," he said. "It's extremely common at your age. I'm going to refer you to an eye surgeon."

Spinning his chair round to face his desk, he dropped his chin to his chest and started tapping on his keyboard. Using his middle finger in a stabbing motion, as a pianist would to hit a final, definitive note, he set the printer in motion. It spat out a page, which he handed over to Deirdre with deadly gravity.

"You know what this is?" Deirdre said to him, once she was standing.

He looked up at her expectantly, waiting for her to answer her own question.

"This," she said, waving the piece of paper at him. "This is the thin end of the wedge."

The paper she was holding in her hand was a ticket to everything she had always feared. A summons that sooner or later would see her sitting in an ugly armchair in a triple-glazed sunroom in an overheated nursing home, surrounded by other old ladies, and nothing to separate her from them, nothing to make her different. The possibility that her entire personality, and the life she had built on the strength of it, the prospect that all of it might turn out to be nothing more than a notion she had taken upon herself, this was something Deirdre could not bear to contemplate.

As soon as she was out on the street, she slipped the referral letter into the nearest bin. Giddy as a schoolgirl, she sailed along the pavement, holding her umbrella out imperiously to bring an approaching bus to a stop. She climbed on board, brandishing her free travel pass like a police badge, aware of a mischievous sense of her own power. Not since she had boarded the bus from Ennis to Dublin all those years ago, with her money sewn into her knickers for fear of the criminals she might encounter in the city, not since then had she had such a drunken sense of freedom. The fact that she had found a way to escape the ordinary, at this late stage of her life, it was almost like being immortal.

She was only a week in Dublin when she met Manus. Six weeks later they were engaged, and by the following summer they were married. A photograph of their wedding appeared in the *Irish Independent*'s Wedding Bells column; looking at the clipping now, Deirdre had to bite her bottom lip to stop herself from smiling. Manus looked so camp, it was ridiculous. "How did you not know he was gay?" Deirdre's daughters had asked her many times over the years. "Darlings," she had told them, "if I'd known what a homosexual was, I might have recognised him as one. But we neither of us would have had a notion what the word meant. You have to understand how innocent we were. Nobody ever told us anything."

Manus was a Protestant, which was scandal enough in those days. Of course, he had to convert to marry her. In a gesture of reciprocity, their wedding reception was held not in her home town but in the long-overgrown walled garden of the estate his father managed in County Kildare. To the horror of Deirdre's mother, there were no chairs, only rugs laid out on the grass for the guests to sprawl on. When Manus left Deirdre for another man — twenty-eight years and three children later — Deirdre's mother claimed not to be in the least bit surprised. After what she'd seen of their wedding day, she had long been prepared for the worst.

When Manus left Deirdre, it was a point of pride with her not to react the way everyone expected her to. Everyone expected her to be heartbroken, and humiliated, and of course she was both of those things, but she was damned if she was going to show it. "Manus and I were always more like friends than lovers," she told everyone she met, aware that she needed to subvert the unspoken suggestion of some sexual inadequacy on her part that might have provoked her husband to seek his thrills elsewhere. "All is fair in love and war," she told other people, hinting at a broader dimension to her marriage than might have been outwardly apparent. "It's a great relief to me," she said, "not to have to put up with him stealing my face creams any more."

Such was the force of Deirdre's ability to create a part for herself, such was the gusto with which she reprised the role year after year, and decade after

7

decade, that she nearly came to believe it herself. What she almost entirely succeeded in obfuscating, what not even her children guessed at, was the fact that she had never not been in love with him. She had spent her entire life loving a man who could not love her. It was too big a thing to contemplate.

Oh, Manus, Manus, Manus. Every cutting of his was pasted into her scrapbook with such naive pride. Reviews of his novel, and feature pieces written with all the genteel reverence of another age. A black-and-white photograph of Manus sitting at his desk in this very study at the top of the house, with the light from the window falling in on him. In the photograph he has an upright typewriter before him, a sheet of paper primed to receive his next novel, a novel that would never come to be written.

Deirdre was sitting at that same desk now, with the same wintry light falling in through the window, only less of it. In the fifty years that had passed since that photograph was taken, the wisteria she had planted as a young bride had stealthily climbed three floors, immersing the back of the house in a deep green sea of leaves, so that even on the top floor you had the sense of being in an underwater cave. A green gloom over everything, it had the advantage of disguising the dust. The patches of dry rot climbing down out of the ceiling cornices. The bucket in the corner to catch the drip from the leaking roof. Deirdre had long ago given up pouring money into that bloody roof.

She turned the pages of the scrapbook impatiently, passing over articles so well known to her that she didn't need to read them; they were like familiar fields flashing by the window of a train. The piece about Manus from *The New York Times*. The photograph of them both posing on the tarmac at Idlewild, he wearing dark glasses and she a ruby-red turban to match her coat; they looked for all the world like movie stars, which was what they almost were.

Turning the next page, she came upon a publicity photograph of herself, and stopped. A photograph of her standing alone on stage in a flowing gown, her chin lifted slightly to display her long, pale neck to advantage. Her eyes were open wide and artfully vacant, as if she were just an empty vessel aching to channel all the great parts that still lay in store for her. The beauty of her, undeniable by then. Not a small-town beauty like her sisters, but a beauty capable of commanding the national stage. Capable perhaps, even, of conquering the world.

Had she known then that she stood balanced on the brink? Review after review, pasted lovingly into her scrapbook, attesting to her triumphant position as the queen of the Dublin stage. There was talk of movie parts, perhaps a move to Broadway, until the beginning of the end was announced in the form of a tiny patch of newsprint no bigger than a postage stamp; it was attached to the page by a piece of Sellotape as dry and yellow as a flake of old skin.

MacEntee — 4 July 1960, at
Stella Maris Nursing Home.
To Deirdre, wife of Manus
MacEntee, a daughter, Alma.
Deo gratias.

Alma, who arrived in a flurry of numbers. Talk of inches, then ounces. Weeks, then months. All Deirdre wanted to know was when she could go back to work. "See that scar on my head?" Alma would joke in later years, pointing to a chickenpox dent on her left temple. "That's the mark my mother's heel made when she was climbing over me to get back on to the stage." And for a year or two it seemed that motherhood had done nothing to slow Deirdre down. It was only when she fell pregnant again, and sick this time with a morning sickness that lasted all day, only then were her ambitions finally derailed. Reluctantly, she passed up on the part of Brigid in *Shadow and Substance* (a part she was a little long in the tooth for, truth be told) and took to the bed to await her deliverance.

Deirdre suffered a collapsed lung giving birth to Acushla, and it took her a long time to recover, and although Manus did insert a birth notice, nobody thought to save the paper when it appeared, so no record exists of Acushla's birth, much to Deirdre's regret. There is no record of her father's death either, an event that occurred on the same day Acushla was born. Deirdre was too weak to attend his funeral. She cried for a year afterwards, two years maybe; she began to think she would cry for ever. "Why didn't you ask

10

anyone for help?" asked Acushla once. "Why didn't you go to the doctor?" Oh, it was hard to explain. You didn't ask for help back then. It just wasn't something you did. "What got you out of it?" asked Acushla, even though she already knew the answer. "Your brother did," said Deirdre with a smile. "It was your brother got me out of it."

> **MacEntee** — to Manus and
> Deirdre (née O'Sullivan), a
> son, Macdara.

Macdara, who is Deirdre's favourite, according to the girls. As evidence, they cite the fact that the PIN for Deirdre's bank card is the year of Macdara's birth. "Don't be ridiculous," Deirdre says. "I love all my children equally." Even though that's not strictly true. She loves all her children in equal measure, certainly, but not all at the same time, and not in the same manner.

Her firstborn Deirdre loves with a mixture of awe and pride. Alma, who arrived in the world fully in charge of herself; no sooner did she open her eyes than she took command of her surroundings, a command she never once let go. Sometimes it seems to Deirdre that she loves Alma precisely because Alma never asks for her love, and never indicates that she needs it.

Acushla, on the other hand, was born crying out for attention. A fretful baby, she would wake in the middle of the night in need of comfort, a comfort Deirdre did not have it in her to give. Many was the night Deirdre

11

spent walking Acushla around the house in the dead of night, her own helpless tears pooling with her daughter's to form a puddle of sticky grief in the hollow of her collarbone. The legacy of that awful time is a tenderness between Deirdre and Acushla, a tenderness verging on pity for the misery they shared. It is nothing more or less than another strain of love.

By comparison, Deirdre's love for Macdara was always miraculously straightforward. From the moment she set eyes on him in the hospital, she loved him with a love that was as uncomplicated as it was unexpected. By then, she had ceased to hope for anything out of motherhood, but with Macdara's arrival, after a birth as easy as a bump in the road, she was transformed overnight into an earth mother. Macdara was breast-fed from the start, where the girls had been bottle-fed. Where the girls had been left with nannies, Macdara went everywhere Deirdre went, nestled to her chest in a sling, and at night he crept into the bed between his parents, something the girls would never have been allowed to do.

After Macdara was born, Deirdre did not even contemplate returning to work, determined not to miss a moment of her belated joy in motherhood. It was only when he was dispatched to boarding school that she relaunched her career, enjoying a brief but glorious three years back in the footlights. She was just preparing to go on tour with *The Gigli Concert* when Macdara's crisis came, a crisis that occurred three weeks into his scholarship to the University of Provence (for some reason never entirely understood by Deirdre,

12

the crisis was triggered by a picture of a hermaphrodite he saw in a book). Macdara's breakdown was so severe, and the challenge of helping him back to full health so enormous, that Deirdre dropped out of the tour, an act of career sabotage from which there would be no way back. Thirty years later, mother and son are still shuffling around the same space, brushing up against each other's foibles with a mutual acceptance and an ever-increasing endearment that baffles everyone but themselves. "You're enabling him," Alma said to her once. "We enable each other," Deirdre replied, cutting her off at the pass.

"Mum!"

It was Macdara's voice, calling up to her. "Do you want tea?"

By the sound of it, he had climbed as far as the return.

"Please, darling!" answered Deirdre, rising out of her chair to shout her answer, only to feel the familiar lick of pain racing down her right leg. "Sciatica," the doctor had said. "Again, perfectly normal." The bladder incontinence Deirdre did not deign to mention to him, certain in the knowledge that this too would be written off as a normal consequence of ageing.

Lowering herself carefully back down into her chair, Deirdre began to speed through the scrapbook, looking for Macdara's only item of news, after his birth. She skimmed over Alma's first article for the college newspaper. Alma's first article for a national newspaper. A front-page photograph of Alma's wedding to Michael

Collins (much was made of the fact that the groom was the youngest sitting deputy in the nation's parliament. Much too of the name he bore, a name passed down to him by his father despite the irony of naming your son after the dead hero of the opposition — oh how they laughed at the notion of a Fianna Fáil Michael Collins!). The pages that followed were plastered with coverage of Mick's early political career. His media appearances fast became so numerous that Deirdre had been forced to stop saving them. She took to keeping only those clippings that featured Alma. Alma photographed side by side with Mick at a state dinner. Alma pictured at the edge of a media scrum, microphone in hand. Alma in a full-page interview about the new generation of women making a name for themselves in television.

There was the odd article about Acushla too. A morsel in a gossip column about her engagement to Mick's twin brother Liam. A picture of her wearing a large hat to Ladies' Day at the Spring Show. An appearance in a list of Ireland's best-dressed women. The only time Macdara's name made it into any form of publication was an entry in his school annual noting that he had triumphed in the spellathon. Deirdre had cut the piece out and dutifully pasted it into her scrapbook, confident that it would be no more than a prelude to greater things. In retrospect, it might have been better to leave it out.

Hearing Macdara's tread on the landing, she flipped the page.

"Here's your tea," he said, coming into the room without knocking. Hunched, the way very tall people often are, he bore the mug of tea forward with all the practised care of a butler. He was wearing a freshly ironed shirt, as always, and one of the hand-knitted ties he had learned to make in occupational therapy — he'd been making them for people as Christmas presents ever since. A V-necked lambswool sweater and camel-coloured cords, and on his feet a pair of Ugg boots. Macdara was very prone to cold feet.

"Scrapbooking?" he asked her, as he set the mug down on the worn leather surface of the desk.

"Yes," she said, wafting her hand over the open pages. "I was just going to paste in an article on your sister but I got carried away."

She glanced down at the page in front of her.

"My mother's death notice," she said. And there was silence for a moment as they both stared down at it. Macdara was standing on the far side of the desk, so he had to twist his neck so as not to be looking at it upside down.

> **O'SULLIVAN**, Mary. In her
> 95th year. Widow of the late
> Eamonn . . .

"When was that?" asked Macdara, looking up at her. His eyes grey and guileless.

"Nineteen eighty-four."

He was in France when she died. Both of them know this but neither of them mentions it.

"Thirty years ago," he says, with surprise.

"Yes," she replies, but she's not sure whether he's referring to his grandmother's death or the ill-fated stay in France. Or indeed both.

"Well," he says, cocking his head as if he's about to say something else. He drifts towards the door with his head still tilted, and the conversation is left hanging. The next thing he's gone, and whatever it was that he was going to say, it remains unsaid.

Once Macdara is gone, the room seems emptier than it was before he entered it. Deirdre sits for a moment searching the air for some visible change, but there is nothing but a faint hum.

She makes a conscious effort to summon a memory of her mother. A desperate desire in her, to remember her mother as a young woman — all that comes to mind are frozen images from photographs. The living, breathing memory is that of a bag of bones in a bed. A pair of angry staring eyes. A smell that remains on Deirdre's breath — despite all the money they spent on the nursing home, there was always that greenhouse smell of human rot. The memory of it horrifies Deirdre. It frightens her, and try as she might, she cannot supplant it. The fact is that her mother lived too long. She outlived even herself.

> . . . deeply regretted by her
> daughters Margaret (Peggy),
> Mary, Catherine (Kitty), Maeve
> and Deirdre.

All of them still alive. Peggy must be ninety-three by now, and Mary ninety-one. Kitty on the verge of ninety. Even Maeve must be eighty-six, which makes Deirdre eighty at her next birthday. A fact that has been passing through her head with increasing regularity since the start of the year. The number is puzzling to her; it seems incorrect.

"I don't fancy the idea of it," she confided to her ex-husband recently, thinking that he of all people would understand.

Infuriatingly, Manus just laughed.

"I've always been younger than everyone else," Deirdre went on, anxious to make herself understood. "I can't see myself as an old person. I don't even *like* old people."

"Nonsense," he said. "You have the makings of a magnificent old lady. You were born to be an old lady."

Oh it annoyed her no end when he said that. It trespassed upon her vanity.

"You're going to live to be a hundred," he said. And she became aware of a great and petulant desire to prove him wrong.

"Let's face it," he told her, with a tease in his voice. "You come from a long line of survivors."

"Oh, Manus," she said. "That's the problem. It fills me with dread, the thought of getting old."

"Indeed," he said, with a grim chuckle. "And yet you must admit, it's better than the alternative."

Deirdre had smiled at him, and nodded, but in her head she had started churning a slow-moving thought. Turning over the words he had used until she had extracted the meaning out of them. What had caught her attention was not her ex-husband's cheerful fatalism in the face of the ageing process. What had taken hold of her was a notion that he had unintentionally planted in her head, the notion that there was an alternative.

"You can't kill yourself just because you've developed cataracts," said her doctor. "Sure, you're as fit as a fiddle. You're in better nick than I am."

"Don't even *think* about patronising me," she said. "I've given this a lot of thought. I'm going to be eighty in October and I feel I've had a good innings. I've decided to quit while I'm ahead."

"I wonder could you be suffering from depression?" he asked her, peering at her more closely.

"Do I look like I'm suffering from depression?"

"You're not suffering from a terminal illness," he said, ticking another box in his head.

"Of course I am! I'm suffering from the onset of old age, which in all cases that I know of has proved to be fatal."

He didn't even smile.

"You do know it's illegal for me to help you?"

"I'm not asking you to help me. I'm simply asking you to provide me with my medical records and confirm that I'm of sound mind."

"Oh, this is all most unusual."

"Exactly," said Deirdre, happily.

"I would strongly urge you to inform your family of your plans."

"Of course," she said, although of course she had absolutely no intention of telling them. That was all part of the fun, the surprise they would get when she sprang it on them. Manus in particular she delighted in surprising. She couldn't help wishing she would be around to see his face when he heard. It was Manus, more than anyone, who would appreciate the supreme stylishness of this thing she was planning to do.

"I wonder have you stopped to consider the effect this will have on your children?" asked the doctor.

Deirdre looked at him, wondering how on earth he could be so maddeningly stupid.

"Don't you see? I'll be doing them a favour."

And really, that did seem to Deirdre to be the case. By releasing them from any duty of care to her as she got older, by dividing between them the not insignificant sum of money she had scrimped and saved over the years before it was swallowed up by doctors' bills and nursing home charges, it did seem to Deirdre that she would be doing her family a huge favour.

Once the decision was made, there was a great falling away of her fears. The things that had worried her before — the cataracts and the sciatica, the dilapidated state of her house — these seemed no more than mere irritations to her now. The clouds she had seen gathering — the cancers and the dementia, the incontinence and the immobility — they had miraculously cleared, and for the moment at least, Deirdre saw nothing but blue sky above her. A frothy sweetness to everything, it was as if her life was made of nothing but sherbet. She found herself prone to unexpected bursts of happiness, singing as she went about the house, songs she had not sung since her girlhood.

When the old house creaked at night, Deirdre rolled over in the bed and went straight back to sleep. When winter storms tore a long portion of guttering from the back wall, she picked it up and tossed it into the flower bed. When the weathermen predicted flooding as a consequence of global warming, and wet summers in perpetuity, she didn't pay a blind bit of attention, because she wasn't going to be there to worry about it.

"I've decided to throw a party for my birthday," she told her children. "I thought it would be nice to gather us all together under the one roof."

"Why would that be nice?" asked Alma, with a disdainful expression that was most typical of her.

"We could combine it with your fiftieth if you like?" Deirdre suggested to Acushla, in a moment of rather rash generosity.

"Why on earth would I want to go advertising the fact that I'm turning fifty?" asked Acushla, appalled.

"It's going to be a proper party," said Deirdre doggedly. "We'll have champagne, and canapés, and printed invitations."

"It sounds more like a wedding," said Macdara, in a morose tone.

And Deirdre giggled, giddy as a young bride. Because Macdara was right! This was not at all unlike a wedding, what with its focus on the fripperies rather than the momentous step into the unknown that would follow.

★ ★ ★

Deirdre had an image in mind of her party, an image that drew on a painting she had always loved. The painting was by Sir John Lavery, and it had been hanging for many years in the National Gallery; for many years Deirdre had been in the habit of dropping into the gallery to visit it, as you might visit an old friend. The subject of the painting was Lady Lavery, and she was depicted seated in a vast and grand room, wearing long, rich robes of satin and silk. On her head she wore an elaborate feathered turban, and her daughters and a dog were arrayed around her, with a servant bearing a tray aloft in the background. In the painting, Lady Lavery's long, pale face was luminous, her posture serene, her eyes sadly knowing.

Deirdre fancies that she used to look like Lady Lavery, a resemblance that was pointed out to her once by a drunk at a party. "Look," said the drunk, "it's the lady on the face of the old pound note!" And while Deirdre had brushed off his ramblings with a self-deprecating laugh, while she had pretended to be embarrassed by him, really she was flattered. Ever since then it has formed a private but important part of her image of herself, this notion of a resemblance to Lady Lavery, so that when she thinks back on herself as a young woman, it is Lady Lavery's face that comes to mind, clearer than any memory of her own.

In imagining her party, Deirdre has an image in her mind of that particular painting. She visualises herself seated in similarly theatrical attire in her own living room, with her family arrayed around her. In planning the party, she is constructing a subtle *tableau vivant* in her head. It occurs to her fleetingly that the desire to create this tableau might be the only reason for having the party. If she were to dredge her soul, she might find this to be true. But Deirdre has been playing a part for so many years that she has long since given up on trying to find the place where her own personality ends and the pretending begins.

In Her Own Words:
Alma MacEntee
in conversation with Dara Lynch

What's your favourite film? *La Dolce Vita*.

What's your favourite book? *Love in a Cold Climate*, by Nancy Mitford. She makes my family seem almost normal, by comparison.

What part of your body do you like best? My breasts. If I say so myself, I've great tits.

Part of the body that you like least? My teeth. I come from a generation before perfect teeth.

What is the trait you most deplore in yourself? Slovenliness.

What is the trait you most deplore in others? Humourlessness.

Which living person do you most admire, and why? My father, because he has never lost his sense of innocence.

What is your greatest regret? I don't believe in regrets.

What's your favourite smell? The smell of rashers being cooked for me.

Who's your favourite fictional hero/heroine? Scarlett O'Hara.

And your hero/heroine in real life? Hillary Clinton.

Have you ever said "I love you" and not meant it? No.

What is your most treasured possession? My waistline.

What beauty product could you not live without? My factor 50 sunscreen.

Who would you choose to play you in the film of your life? Julianne Moore.

Who's your ideal dinner guest? My ex-husband (I'd poison him).

Motto? Be yourself; everyone else is already taken.

Alma

Alma MacEntee. Five syllables that, when spoken out loud (as they often are), tumble into each other with an energy that seems to come from within. Almamacentee. A bubbling stream of a word that, in the time it takes for it to travel through the locks and sluice gates of your brain, calls to mind a slew of images, slabs of information, half-remembered snippets of gossip. A gash of red lipstick, a helmet of unashamedly red hair. That hair that seems to get redder all the time, heightening the effect of the china-white skin and the always-amused eyes. In your head you can hear that oh-so-familiar voice, with its almost inappropriate suggestion of intimacy.

Alma MacEntee. In the less than three seconds it takes for you to hear her name, you have her whole history in your head, and with it your own. You remember her beginnings, how she spilled out of the continuity studio and shouldered her way through the dandruff-smattered suits on election night, an oversized microphone in her hand, the questions she asked famous now for their fearlessness. In her next incarnation she was standing on a small, round podium in a pool of artificial light, a dark, murmuring crowd at her feet. The silver gown she wore fell from her hips like an oil spill and her hair was styled into two shining chestnut wings that swept off her painted face. "And now for the results of the Belgian jury," she said. "*Royaume-Uni, dix points*. United Kingdom, ten points. *Irlande, douze points*. Ireland twelve points." As the crowd went wild, Alma MacEntee allowed herself a smile. Of course, nowadays her eyes wrinkle when she smiles, which is why she is careful not to do it so often. Nowadays she is more often seen with her eyebrows disdainfully raised, her elbow resting on the studio table as if in preparation for a bout of arm-wrestling, one manicured fingernail poised to signal an interruption to this or that politician.

She was married to a politician, once. You remember their whirlwind romance. You remember the front-page photos of their wedding and the kiss for the cameras. You remember the divorce, back when divorce was a scandal. (Was it even legal to get divorced back then? It seems that Alma MacEntee was a divorcee before divorce existed.) She was the lover of a prominent businessman, the lover of a famous actor, the lover of a newspaper owner, long before the word "lover" was ever spoken out loud. She was a woman before her time. And while all the Marys and Anns of the small screen were spoken of with their surnames attached, to distinguish them from all the other Marys and Anns out there in the world, while the Eileens and Sharons were sometimes confused with or mistaken for other Eileens and Sharons, Alma MacEntee required only four letters to define her.

Alma.

On the first day of April — a day she always considered the first day of spring, treating as a bad joke the notion that spring arrived in these parts in February, or even March — Alma woke at seven, as she always did, to the sound of the radio. She lay in her vast empty bed, as was her practice, while she listened to the headlines, suppressing a growl as she heard the morning newscaster mispronounce Barack Obama's name again. No matter how many times Alma lobbed angry rants into General Mail, no matter how many times she raised the issue with the subs, the newsreaders persisted in mispronouncing his name, placing the stress on the first syllable instead of the second. Was the man himself not authority enough on the pronunciation of his own name? Was his wife not to be trusted to get it right? All you had to do was listen to them, for Christ's sake. Swinging her feet out of bed, Alma fought the urge to ring in.

"I'm a crank," she said, even though there was no one there to hear her. She nodded, as always, in agreement with herself. "I know. I'm a crank."

Pulling her black velvet robe off the back of the bedroom door, she made her way down into the kitchen, where another radio was tuned in to the same station. She turned on the coffee machine, and while she waited for it to heat up, she stared out of the window into the small back garden, where her daughter's bicycle lay abandoned against the wall, a garland of plastic flowers wound around the handlebars and a threadbare tarpaulin of cobwebs hanging over it. Across the skyline the neighbour's washing swayed in the breeze, underpants and shirts hanging upside down like a row of dead cats strung up by their front paws.

Alma turned away from the window to make her coffee. In her mind she was already running through her agenda for the day, careful not to get anything out of sequence. The hairdresser's first. Then the dry cleaner's. And she had better stop by the paper for a minute on her way in to work, just to cut off any trouble at the pass.

For that, she'd be needing some war paint.

"Well," said Jim, when she walked into his office without knocking.

He was sitting at his desk with his jacket off, wearing a lemon-yellow shirt (cotton-polyester mix, Alma would be willing to bet) with a Cross pen in the breast pocket. A cheap red tie curled up in his in-tray like a sleeping snake.

"I got your message," said Alma.

Jim propped his feet up on the desk. He leaned back in his chair and intertwined his hands behind his head, revealing the underarms of his shirt, dark and wet.

Alma's expression did not waver.

She advanced into the room, walking from her hips. She ignored the two chairs that sat facing the desk, weaving her way round to sit on the edge of it instead. She had one bum cheek on the surface, one in mid-air, her pencil skirt riding high above her knees. She wrapped her left ankle around her right leg, balancing herself on a single three-inch heel. (Men like Jim aren't used to having beautiful women flirting with them. This

28

was something that Alma understood. Flirt with a man like Jim, and he's yours for life.)

"I'm listening," he said, his eyes bulging as he looked at her. Alma allowed the faintest touch of a smile to tug at one corner of her lips.

"I thought it was funny. Go on, Jim. Admit it. You thought it was funny too."

He sighed.

"People seem to have taken offence."

"Oh," she said. "People."

Eyebrows raised, she waited for him to say more.

"The earthworm analogy, in particular, seems to have upset them."

She shrugged.

"I thought the earthworm thing was quite mild, actually. I've said way worse stuff than that in my time."

And she had. There was the piece about Ladies' Day at the races (Crufts for humans), the one about West End musicals (strictly special needs, she had suggested, and was forced to apologise a week later, to special needs people and West End musicals both. It was the first of many apologies).

"Personally, I think the obesity piece was my most offensive to date."

He put his hand over his face.

"Don't remind me."

She had him now. She knew she had him. But he still had to put up the pretence of a fight.

"Alma," he said, throwing his arms out wide. "You know as well as I do. I pay you to be provocative. People read your column *because* it's provocative. But there's a line there, and we need to stay on the right side of it."

"So what are you saying? The earthworm thing was the wrong side of the line?"

"Forty-six e-mails, twelve letters and nineteen phone calls."

Alma planted one hand on the surface of the desk. The other hand she propped on her hip, and like a teapot, she tipped herself forward.

"Jim," she said, in her deepest, throatiest voice. "People have no sense of humour any more."

"These are serious times. Call it evolution."

"In that case, we're the dinosaurs, darling."

He laughed. It was the use of the word "we" that was warming him up. The thought of him and her, wrapped up together in that one little word.

"We're not extinct yet," he said, his raw, doughy face flushed with his own fumbling flirtation.

"No, darling," said Alma, narrowing her eyes at him. "We're not extinct yet. And we must not go down without a fight."

The phone on Jim's desk rang and he reached out to pick it up, winking at her with his left eye, while his greedy little right eye slobbered all over her. She hopped down off the desk and sashayed towards the door, enjoying the knowledge that he was watching her arse as she went. At the door, she turned to blow him a kiss.

His secretary was sitting outside, watching her with heavy eyes.

"You know yourself," said Alma, pausing to lay a hand on the secretary's desk. "A girl has to make a living."

Eight hours later (after three more cups of coffee, two interminable editorial meetings and a marathon session in make-up), she was sitting in the studio. Her hair was sprayed to the texture of dry bark, and she was wearing a creamy white jacket that set off her colouring perfectly. A skimpy black tank top revealed her milky cleavage. Thirty seconds to air and she took a cosmetic purse out from under the table, opened it up and started applying a fresh layer of lipstick.

"Jesus," said the programme editor, in the control room. "I wish she wouldn't do that."

"I wouldn't mind," said the studio director, "but that shade of lipstick she insists on wearing? It's completely inappropriate for a news programme."

"I'll tell you what. Why don't you be the one to tell her?"

Sniggers from the shadows, interrupted by Alma's voice, amplified through the gallery.

"Where are we going first?"

The programme editor went into a spasm, grappling at the heap of papers in front of him.

"Jesus! Does she not have the running order?"

This tendency of Alma's to wander into the studio without her notes was the stuff of legend. Legendary also was her ability to manage without them. She had been known to present an entire programme without so much as glancing down at her scripts. She had sailed through the first segment of an election special once with her constituency guide sitting on top of the coffee machine in the corridor; when at last the ad break arrived and a broadcast assistant dashed in with it, it was only to be stared at by Alma as if to say, what would I need that for? She had winged her way through the peace process, presenting programmes late into the night from outside Hillsborough Castle, or Stormont, without so much as a handwritten lead-in. She had done outside broadcasts from rain-sodden piers and muddy fields, or on bridges over flooded rivers, with no more equipment than a powder puff and a golf umbrella. When the autocue went down on budget night 2010, she had not even raised an eyebrow, because she had all the figures in her head.

So if Alma was a picture of calm fifteen seconds to air and flying the studio blind, then this should have been no surprise to anyone. What was surprising was the panic in the gallery. The gallery had never learned not to panic. The programme editor was standing up, gripping his skull with his hands to contain his stress. A broadcast assistant was standing at the studio door with Alma's scripts, her little heart pounding with fear as she waited for the opportunity to slip inside.

The director leaned in to the talkback.

"Straight to Government Buildings," she said, holding the button down. "You should have Simon McFeeley in vision."

"Simon!" said Alma, as if she had just bumped into him on the street. "How are you, my darling?"

Her voice shattered the sanctity of the empty studio.

"Hi, Alma," came Simon's voice in return, delayed by a two-second lag.

"Ten seconds to air," said the broadcast co-ordinator.

Alma gave her hair one last little pat. She dropped her chin a little, to disguise the wrinkles on her neck, as the broadcast co-ordinator began the countdown. The sting began to roll, graphics tumbling through splintered space. Alma appeared on the monitor, face full square to the camera, blue eyes twinkling. Her perfect symmetry lent her a luminescence on screen that was not apparent in the flesh. She looked, quite simply, magnificent.

"Good evening," she said. "And welcome to *Headline*. Coming up on tonight's programme, the latest on the talks between the Troika and the Department of Finance. A rude awakening for the drinks industry. And the abolition of the Senate: we debate the pros and cons. But first I'm joined from Government Buildings by our political editor Simon McFeeley . . ."

"Sweet Jesus," said the programme editor, leaning back into his chair. "That woman puts years on me."

The lights were still on in the stadium when Alma's taxi swung into the square.

Bloody waste of electricity, she thought, wondering to herself was this the seed of a column. Not enough, she decided, and let the thought sink to the bottom of her mind.

The taxi driver slowed to a crawl, bending low over the steering wheel as he peered up at the stadium. The place was still relatively new; it had been named after the insurance company who sponsored it, and while at first the city's residents had vowed never to use this new name, it was slowly slipping into the lexicon in much the same way as the stadium itself had ingratiated itself into the city's affections. From a distance, it had a curiously transparent appearance, like a great glass bubble on the skyline, but up close and hovering above the forty dark houses of the square, it looked like a spaceship. A great glowing ship of steel and glass.

The taxi driver was gaping out of the window at it. An Indian man, or Pakistani perhaps, he had a laminated picture of his children on the dashboard.

"Anywhere here is fine," said Alma, impatient to get out of the cab.

The driver stopped at the corner of the square, but he continued to look up at the stadium. "You are very lucky," he said. "You are so lucky, to live beside this magnificent stadium. I would be very happy to live beside this stadium."

It was something that Alma found impossible to understand, the devotion of sports fans to this secular temple. From far and wide they came, posing for photographs in front of it. ("It's a *football stadium*," Alma had written in one of her columns. "It's not the Taj Mahal.")

"I'll sign for that," she said, desperate to be out of the cab. The arches of her feet were aching and her mouth was dry. She was longing to take off her shoes. Longing for a drink, and the ritual post-programme cigarette; it was the only one she allowed herself these days.

The driver turned round to face her. "On my day off, I am going to come back here. I am going to bring my son to see your gorgeous stadium."

The word "gorgeous", spoken in a Dublin accent.

"It's not really my stadium," said Alma, leaning into the gap between the seats. "Now if you don't mind, I'll sign your docket for you."

"Of course," said the driver. "Sorry." He rooted about in the glove compartment until he found the docket book. Rooted again until he found a pen. Alma signed her name, adding a hefty tip as she always did.

As she climbed the steps to her house, the square behind her was in shadow. A small enclave of forty red-brick Victorian villas, at one time these would have been solid working-class homes, but then people like Alma started moving in, attracted by the relatively reasonable prices and the proximity to town. Barely twenty minutes' walk to Grafton Street, Alma didn't even need to keep a car, choosing to make liberal use of taxis with impunity instead.

She raised her knee to her chest to prop up her handbag while she fished around for her front-door keys. By the time she was finally turning the key in the lock, the taxi was sliding out of the square. She pushed open the front door and tossed her keys on to the table inside. She stepped out of her shoes, and with her stockinged foot she gave the door a shove to close it, but the shove didn't take. It didn't take because there was someone standing behind her, holding the door open with his boot.

HORROR ATTACK ON JOURNO was the banner headline in the evening paper the next day. BRAVE ALMA REFUSED TO GIVE THIEVES HER RINGS said a smaller headline on the inside page. And in even smaller print there followed the gory detail: TV STAR LOSES TWO FINGERS IN HORROR ATTACK.

"It's the familiarity with which they use your first name," said her mother. "That's what I'd have a problem with."

Alma's mother had a peculiar talent for tangents. She could discover tangents that no one else knew were there, seizing on them with a single-minded zeal, as if she alone had the power to see through to the heart of the matter.

"Whatever about the fingers," she said. "The fingers you can live without. It's the familiarity, don't you see? They're on first-name terms with you. That's what I'd have a problem with."

Alma looked to her brother first, then to her father for help.

Macdara was standing over by the window. With his eyes roaming the ceiling, it was hard to know if he'd heard. Macdara was often adrift like this. No matter what room he was in, he seemed always to be looking for a way out.

Alma's father was sitting to the left of her bed in a padded chair that doubled as a commode. He was wearing his customary daytime outfit. A nautical blazer, shiny from over-wear, with a hand-made shirt that was thirty years old and scuffed at the cuffs and collar. A pair of white cotton trousers that rode high enough on his ankles to reveal a natty pair of turquoise socks. With his shock of white hair, he looked like an ageing Captain Sensible: all he was missing was the parrot on his shoulder. He was sitting bolt upright in the chair, but his head had drooped to one side. A lick of hair had fallen across his forehead and his eyes were closed. Poor old boy, Alma thought. He had been the first to arrive. Woken by the early-morning call, he had burst into the hospital room barely twenty minutes later, unshaven and wild-eyed, the nurse trailing after him star-struck. If this was a test of love, then Alma's father had won it hands down.

It had taken her mother a good hour to arrive (even though her house was nearer, as the crow flies), and when she did come she was dressed for a performance. Her long grey hair was swept up off her face in great swirls that came together in a huge bird's nest on top of her head, and she was wearing her trademark black riding skirt with a purple silk blouse buttoned high up her neck. Thrown over it all was a black wool cape. She looked like she was going to a Bloomsday event.

"Darling," she said, as she bent over her daughter's bed.

Alma found herself drowning in Yardley's Lily of the Valley. So her mother had even taken the time to douse herself in perfume.

Maman, nul points.

"Who would you like me to ring?" the nurse had asked Alma, as soon as she came out of the anaesthetic.

"There was no ICE contact on your phone. We didn't know who to ring."

Thirst was Alma's first thought. Her mouth was so dry she couldn't swallow. Her next thought was that she was cold. A terrible cold, as if she'd been refrigerated from the inside out.

"Cold," she said. "Very cold."

The nurse came and covered her with some extra blankets. She gave her a sponge stick to suck, which relieved the parched mouth but not the cracked lips. As her physical discomfort crashed over her like a wave, Alma became aware of her right hand, bulkier than it should be and swaddled tight by her side.

"How did I get here?" she asked, noticing the curtained cubicle she found herself in. The large empty window to her left, with the daylight just starting to leach through the clouds. From somewhere outside the cubicle she became aware of noises. A clattering of tin; by the sound of it, someone was shaking a sack full of saucepans. The nurse was checking a bag of fluid that was hanging by Alma's bed. She bent down to write something on a chart, answering Alma's question without looking at her.

"You were brought in by ambulance."

As soon as she said it, Alma remembered. She remembered the ambulance men in their astronauts' boots traipsing across the bloodstained floor of her kitchen. She remembered worrying that they'd walk the blood into the hall carpet on their way back out. "Darling," one of them had said to her, once they'd strapped her into the wheelchair. "Now, darling," he had said as they lifted the chair down the front steps. Alma remembered being touched by the way he said it, as if she was his daughter, or his sweetheart even.

"Who called them?" she asked.

But the nurse didn't answer. She was copying numbers down on to the chart from a digital monitor by the bedside.

"Any pain?" she asked, and she paused to scrutinise Alma's face.

"No. No pain."

"It was Mr Maguire who operated on you," said the nurse. "He's gone home to get a few hours' sleep, but when he gets back he'll come and talk to you. In the meantime, is there anyone you'd like us to ring?"

The first person who came to mind was Mick. Mick was the one to ring, naturally. Why did they even have to ask? She was just about to tell them when she remembered that she was no longer married to him. Hadn't been married to him for fifteen years. As she retraced the steps in her mind, it was with a vast sense of loss. She missed him, all of a sudden, as she had never missed him before. She could have cried with the pain of missing him.

The next person she thought of was Nora, but as soon as she thought of her daughter, she thought also of her absence. Pointless to even try and contact her.

"My mum," she said to the nurse. "In my phone you'll find numbers for my mum and dad."

Thinking, Great! Fifty years old and my next of kin are my mum and dad.

★ ★ ★

So here they were, Alma's parents. Sitting on opposite sides of her bed, like an old married couple settled into their armchairs around the fire on a winter's evening. (Macdara had disappeared without anyone noticing.)

"Is he asleep?" asked Alma's mother, nodding towards Alma's father.

"Who?" said her father, snapping himself awake. "Not at all. I was just dozing."

"It's the narcolepsy," said her mother, speaking to Alma. "It's genetic. His father had it before him."

"Nonsense," said Alma's father, yawning. "You're just jealous of my ability to fall asleep at will."

Alma's mother sat up even straighter in her chair and without comment began to nudge any stray hairs away from her forehead, using spidery fingers. That famous hair; it lent her an air of theatricality that was by no means accidental. She liked to think she still belonged to the theatre, even though it was thirty years since she'd been on a stage.

Mad old bag was the general impression she gave, whereas Alma's father was a *wonderful eccentric*. An inequity that was apparent to nobody more than to Alma's mother herself. "Your father," she would say, "seems to have achieved a kind of cult status in his old age. But I, on the other hand, remain a mere curiosity." And while all of his eccentricities seemed effortless (the disco dancing and the eye make-up, the clapped-out old Jag); while his multiplying oddities seemed more an unpeeling of his personality than an adornment to it, hers had a somewhat forced air about them, as if she

40

was just hashing over a part she'd been playing for years.

"Oh," said Alma's father. "I forgot. I have something for you from Sam." Shifting his weight, he began to feel around in the pockets of his jacket. "I know I put it in here somewhere."

At last he located what he was looking for, tucked inside his breast pocket. A small, much-folded parcel made out of a single sheet of paper, which he passed across to Alma. Painstakingly using her left hand, she unfolded it and revealed a perfectly round coin of golden foiled paper; painted on the surface of it, in black ink, was the silhouette of a small bird in flight.

"Oh," she said, clamping it to her heart. "I love it. Tell Sam I said thank you."

Sam, who you couldn't help but love, even though Sam, just twenty-four years old at the time and fresh out of Tangier, was the reason why Alma's parents' marriage had broken down. ("Oh, that's rubbish, darling," Alma's mother had said once. "It wasn't the affair with a younger man that ruined our marriage. It was your father's vulgar addiction to Hellmann's mayonnaise.")

"How is he?" Alma's mother asked now, with genuine concern.

Cheerfully, Alma's father bobbed his head.

"Oh, he's much the same. Although he's not happy with the new regime I have him on. I'm feeding him mackerel three times a day. Apparently it has miraculous healing powers."

"You make him sound like a sea lion," said Alma's mother, her eyes wide and startled. "Of course the fish oil seems to be the cure for everything nowadays. That and the blueberries." She pronounced the word with great suspicion, as if it was a trick.

"Oh, yes. Sam and I are all for the blueberries. We eat them for breakfast, with granola."

"It's well for you," said Alma's mother, "that you can afford to live on blueberries."

Never did she let an opportunity go by to remind him of her impecunity. Alma laid her head back against her pillow and closed her eyes as they continued to bat back and forth across her bed.

"I'm afraid Sam's diet isn't the problem. It's the climate. He wasn't bred for this ghastly climate."

"We were none of us bred for this climate. If we were, we'd have fins."

"What was that Seamus Heaney poem?"

And so their conversation meandered from superfoods to Seamus Heaney. From Seamus Heaney to Yeats and from Yeats to book tokens and on to Greene's bookshop and the dapper little man who used to deliver their books for them, what was his name?

As Alma listened to them, it seemed to her that their conversation was like a deck of cards that had been well and truly shuffled and then dealt out, each card appearing at random but still familiar. The whole time she lay there listening to them, the one thing they did not discuss was the thing that had happened to Alma.

"Remember that scene in *Reservoir Dogs*?"

Alma's visitors nodded nervously.

"Well, it wasn't a bit like that."

She was sitting up against a bank of pillows, a black satin kimono jacket draped elegantly over her shoulders and the wounded hand lying discreetly by her side. She had managed to style her hair with some hand cream, which, incredibly, someone had brought her as a gift, but in the absence of her regular, ruthless blow-dry, her hair was taking its first tentative steps back to nature. Thicker and frizzier, it had the effect of softening her face. She had contrived somehow to apply some make-up, using her left hand and without the use of a mirror. The action of painting on her eyebrows, for so long a reflex, now had to be performed with careful deliberation. Even the application of lipstick, which with her right hand she could have done in her sleep, felt weirdly new. It was as if she'd been turned inside out.

Alma's visitors were gathered around the bed, sitting in an assortment of ugly hospital chairs filched from other, less visited rooms. The air was thick with the fug of tiger lilies. The windowsills, the ledges, the surface of the bedside locker, all crammed with expensive floral arrangements. What with the heat in the room and all that foliage, it was like being in one of the greenhouses at the Botanic Gardens.

"Get a bottle of Prosecco out of the fridge," Alma told her visitors when they arrived, gesturing with her good hand towards the small fridge in the corner of the room. "I've decided that Prosecco is going to play a key role in my recovery. Declan, you can do the honours."

Declan, who had started out in the newsroom on the same day as Alma. She remembers him, straight out of

The Tuam Herald, with his cowlick and his confirmation suit. He was head of news now, and therefore Alma's boss. Were she and Declan friends? She thought not. And yet he had come to visit her, all the same, out of duty most likely. And Pat Deacon and Mary O'Malley had volunteered, or more likely been volunteered. A reluctant delegation, they bore with them bags of small gifts sent by those lucky enough to be spared.

Declan poured the Prosecco into four ribbed plastic cups that he found in a stack on top of the fridge. Awkwardly, they all toasted Alma, keeping their eyes on her face so as not to look at the hand. They sipped at the Prosecco, with the plastic cups buckling in their hands, each of them secretly determined to leave their drink unfinished (Declan because he was driving, Pat because she had to chair the afternoon news conference and Mary because she had to read the two o'clock bulletin).

The door opened. A head poked around it, a head that for some reason always called to Alma's mind a raw chicken, or a lanky turkey. Free range, with that yellow tinge.

"You all know Jim," said Alma. "Long-suffering editor of my newspaper column."

Jim was holding a bunch of pre-packed flowers, clearly from the Spar. ("Follow the crowd," the nurse had said, when he asked her which room.)

"Hiya, Jim," said the others, shifting in their chairs to acknowledge his arrival.

"Well," said Jim, looking around for somewhere to put the flowers.

"Just put them in the sink," said Alma. "They've run out of vases."

Jim settled himself against the scorching-hot radiator as Alma continued her story.

"I'm afraid I was unlucky in my attacker. I'm not sure he'd severed many fingers before. He made quite a meal of it. Funny, the bone was the easy bit. I suppose when you think about it, it makes sense. You know when you chop up a chicken? It's easy enough to cut through the bone, if you have a sharp knife. The skin is the tricky bit. There's always a bit of skin that just won't break."

A horrified silence in the room.

"Oh, dear," said Alma. "Is this hard to listen to? I'm so sorry."

She took a sip of her Prosecco, and flashed them a smile.

"Actually, I'm not a bit sorry. Pity about you."

They set down their plastic cups, glanced at each other to synchronise their departure and, like a flurry of startled birds, took off. Declan made the first move, but Mary and Pat jumped up after him and they walked out together, taking grateful gulps of the cold air outside. Conscious, each of them, of their ten movable fingers.

"She's got balls," said Pat. "You have to say that for her."

"Ah, she's some woman," said Declan. "She'd be great in a war."

"Nonsense," said Mary. "All that bravado, it's the drugs talking. She must be up to her eyeballs in morphine. I hate to think how she'll feel when it wears off."

"God help her," said Pat. "What a horrible thing to happen."

The morphine was heaven for the first twenty-four hours.

After that, Alma began to feel imprisoned by it. She was struggling to distinguish between day and night. She was too high and she wanted to climb down. Whereas before she had thrilled in this soaring pain-free elation, now she wanted rid of it. She needed to face up to reality, whatever reality was. When her surgeon came by on his rounds, she asked him to take her bandages off. She wanted to see the damage to her hand.

"Are you sure?"

Alma was sitting on top of the covers, with her white La Perla nightdress pulled up high on her thigh to reveal two long and shapely legs. She was confident he would not notice the stubble on her calves, the plum-coloured polish on her toenails that was starting to chip.

"Come on, Luke," she said. "I'm a big girl. How bad can it be?" (She had met him at a dinner party once and was determined to continue their relationship on the same footing, as a social acquaintance rather than a patient.)

She shifted herself up in the bed and he sat down on the edge of it. He looked her in the eye and Alma felt something unfurl inside her, something she recognised belatedly as a rustle of panic. She forced herself not to blink.

"Okay," he said, and without turning he spoke to the nurse who was hovering behind him. "Jean, can you get me some scissors, please. I'm going to change Miss MacEntee's dressings for her."

"Careful," croaked Alma. "That could be misinterpreted."

Even to her own ears, the attempt at flirting fell flat.

The bandages came off easily, exposing first of all an entirely normal-looking thumb. Next to emerge was a relatively unscathed index finger; the only evidence of any injury was the crust of dried blood that had settled into the wrinkles on the finger, like the sediment left at the bottom of a glass of red wine. The fingernail had black blood caked into the cuticle, as if she had been digging in soil. Carefully, he peeled back the gauze to reveal what was left of the middle finger. It had been severed just above the first knuckle and the stump had been sewn up with what looked like barbed wire, the rounded tip of it blackened, as if the fingertip had been burned off. The ring finger, too, was blackened and criss-crossed with barbed wire. It had been severed just below the knuckle.

Alma noticed that she was breathing out through her mouth. In through the nose, out through the mouth, the way they teach you in pre-natal classes.

"I warned you it wouldn't be pretty."

She nodded.

He removed the last bit of bandaging, and a perfectly intact, precious little finger emerged. Alma felt a rush of pity for it.

"Poor little finger. He's been left out on a bit of a limb, hasn't he?"

The joke fell out of her, mis-spaced. Misjudged. Maguire didn't even smile.

"We had a job tidying it up," he said. "Most of the amputations we see are power-tool-related, which makes them fairly straightforward, but yours was a bit trickier than that. We were three hours in surgery trying to reattach the fingers."

He reminded Alma of a mechanic discussing a tricky problem with an engine. She gave up any hope of flirting with him.

"You're as well off, actually," he was saying. "Reattached fingers tend to be a bit troublesome. "Believe it or not, you're as well off without them."

It was not true that Alma had refused to give her attackers the rings. She would have given them the rings in two seconds if she'd only been able to get them off her fingers. She'd have thrown the bloody things at them, and good riddance to them. They were a relic of her marriage, those rings. An ugly, oversized ruby that came down from Mick's grandmother, and an ostentatious clutch of diamonds he'd bought her with some cash he didn't want the tax man to get his hands on. When they'd split up, she had transferred the rings to her right hand rather than give them back to him. If she'd been wearing them on her left hand, her attackers would have chopped those fingers off instead and Alma would have been left with the use of her right hand. She'd have been able to put her make-up on properly. She'd have been able to write, for God's sake. In a way, she decided, this was all Mick's fault.

Two days since the accident — why did everyone insist on calling it an accident? Two days since the *attack*, and not a squeak out of him. He must have heard about it by now. He was in Brussels, for God's sake, not Ulan Bator. There was no way he wouldn't have heard. More than a year since she had spoken to him, but she imagined that maybe now, because of this, he would break the silence. What was she expecting, flowers? Who was she kidding? Even at the best of times Mick had never been a great man for the flowers. The first time he took her out to dinner, he ducked under the table to look at her legs. That was the most romantic thing he ever did.

Even when Nora was born, there were no roses. No "push gift" — isn't that what they call it now? A revolting notion, and anyway, Nora was born by C-section because she was lying breech. Alma had banned Mick from the operating theatre, mortified by the notion of him seeing her with her belly sliced open. Mick had been relieved that she had taken the decision out of his hands. He waited in the pub around the corner until they sent for him, the phone ringing behind the bar; he said it was the only time he ever left a pint half drunk. Alma remembers how the midwife handed Nora to him, an awkward manoeuvre of the elbows, as if between them they were trying to make a cat's cradle. Mick bent down low over the baby and whispered something in her ear, something Alma couldn't hear. It was the start of a long father-daughter conversation, one that might on the face of it have seemed to be driven by their differences. To Alma's eyes, they were more alike than either of them realised. The same stubbornness in each of them, even if it found a different expression.

She was always between them, Nora. Driving them apart, keeping them together. Hard to know which. For as long as Nora was a child, they were attached by their mutual attachment to her. And even after they separated, even after Mick went to Brussels and the house they had shared was sold, after Alma and Nora had moved into their new little house and the furniture was divided up, even after all of that, they managed to co-operate in a semi-civilised fashion on the parenting of Nora. But now that Nora was grown up, now that there were no more school reports to discuss, no parent-teacher meetings at which to present a ham-fisted united front, no graduation ceremonies to attend (one of them on either side of her, with Nora's arms binding them from behind, like a tight chain), now that Nora had drifted out beyond all the milestones, into the murky world she had chosen to inhabit, there was no reason for Mick and Alma to ever speak.

Thinking about Nora gave Alma an uneasy feeling, but she could not have said why. Her daughter was occupying her mind with an insistence that was almost physical. Not the Nora of recent times, but the Nora of long ago. Nora at twelve years of age, with her school kilt and her embarrassing budding breasts, and her big sad eyes. Had Alma noticed at the time that Nora was sad? It seemed to her now that her daughter had needed her then, and that she had not been there for her.

Oh, she'd been there, of course, she'd been there. She had driven Nora to school every morning and she had come home from work every evening, and they had sat down together to eat whatever meal the child-minder had prepared for them. The child-minder was like an aunt to Nora, she was like a granny to her — Nora was better off with the child-minder, that's what Alma used to tell herself. Anyone could see that Alma wasn't cut out for the job.

"How do you manage as a single mother?" she was often asked, in interviews for the lifestyle pages of the papers. And Alma had a stable of stock phrases that she rolled out in reply. "Oh, I have lots of help," she would say, or "It's a team effort."

"It takes a whole village to raise a child," she would say. "I have the greatest admiration for anyone who manages to stay home with their children. I know I couldn't do it."

As she lay in her hospital bed, it occurred to Alma that what she was feeling was guilt. A guilt she had never before stopped for even a moment to entertain, it had her in its grip now and it wouldn't let go of her. With the light outside her window hovering between night and day and the hospital room cast in a bruised blue shadow, with her own voice ringing phrases from the past in her ears, phrases that ran loose in her head, banging the walls as they went and raising echoes to the rafters, Alma realised with great sorrow that she was alone in her hour of need, with no one to blame but herself. She could not call on her daughter now, no matter how much she might feel in need of her. She could not call on her because she had long ago forfeited the right to do so.

"I've been trying to track her down," said Connie, falling into the wing-backed chair beside Alma's bed, with her oversized handbag at her feet and her suede wedges turned inwards at the toes. A green felt cloche hat sat on top of her beautiful Modigliani head. The hat's wisp of green netting hovered over her fabulous eyebrows. "I think she might be on a ship, headed for Gaza. That was her plan, the last time I spoke to her."

"Oh, Jesus," said Alma. In her mind she was seeing a headline sequence. A ship at night, with a helicopter hovering overhead. Camouflaged figures wearing night-vision goggles, dropping down on to the deck. The crackle and flash of gunfire. Grenades, louder and brighter again. How many people were killed? Eight? Ten? What were the chances of it happening again?

"I think they may have sailed from Cyprus, or Greece. Nobody seems to know."

Alma pictured a big top-heavy boat, bobbing about on the waves with no radar, no communications, no defences.

"I've been trying all the numbers I have for her," said Connie. "Her Irish mobile seems to have been disconnected. The last number she gave me was for a Greek mobile, but I've been ringing and ringing it and I keep getting some guy who doesn't speak any English. I'll try e-mailing her this evening. She may be checking her e-mails."

"Actually," said Alma. "I'd prefer if you didn't."

Connie turned her mouth upside down, as she always did when she was dubious about something.

"I don't see any point in telling her, Connie. If she's on a boat in the middle of nowhere, there's no point in her being told."

Connie tilted her head and drew a breath in. She was about to speak when Alma stopped her.

"Connie, you're going to have to leave this to me. Nora is not to be told."

Connie pursed her lips and knitted her eyebrows at Alma, to show that she was unhappy. Like a mime artist, her every feeling played itself out on her face.

Connie of the stolen name, a name Alma had hoarded since childhood, stashing it in a secret place in her heart for the daughter she would one day have (at no point did Alma ever consider the possibility that she would have a son). The only person she confided the name to was her sister, and her sister stole it from her. When Acushla's daughter was born, three months to the day before Alma's, Acushla named her Constance. Furious and hurt, feeling betrayed and blindsided, Alma was forced to go back to the drawing board, and the name she came up with was Nora. In time her sister was to commit worse crimes against her (one crime in particular was far, far worse), but it was the theft of the name that rankled still, long after everything else had ceased to matter.

It seemed to Alma now that the theft of the name was a crime of lasting consequence. With that name went everything she would have wanted for her daughter, as if the name carried within itself the blueprint of a life. For it is Connie now, who is constant. Connie with her house and her husband and her two little boys. It is Connie who is here at Alma's bedside, while her own daughter is nowhere to be found. It is Connie who is even now unloading bottles of Prosecco from her voluminous handbag and stashing them in the fridge. Connie whom Alma loves, with an easy camaraderie that she has never been able to muster for so much as a single moment with Nora.

"Has my mum been to see you?"

"Oh, yes," said Alma. "She came yesterday. Briefly."

Alma knew that Connie had a great desire — a pathetic, childish desire — for her mother and her aunt to be friends again.

"She brought that orchid," said Alma, gesturing with her freshly bandaged hand towards the window, where a spindly black stalk threw out perfect little bursts of magenta flowers.

It was so typical of Acushla to bring an orchid. She had brought a scented candle too, and a tray of out-of-season peaches, all from Marks & Spencer. Dressed in soft shell-pinks and mauves, she had perched on the edge of the visitor's chair, with her knees falling to the side and her handbag in her lap, like a woman in a waiting room. The space between the chair and the bed may as well have been a vast canyon; as the two sisters spoke, they were both afraid of falling into it. The air between them swirling with all the things they couldn't say to each other.

"The orchid shouldn't be in the window," said Connie, and she went to move it. "Where will I put it?"

For a moment Alma was tempted to tell her to take it home. But she stopped herself.

"Here," she said, clearing a space on her bedside locker. "Put it here. It's so beautiful, it deserves pride of place."

Pleased, Connie set the orchid down on the surface of the locker.

"Well," she said. "I'm afraid I have to dash. I've to collect the gruesome twosome from Mum's."

"All right, doll. Thanks for the supplies."

"No worries. I'll be back tomorrow. Let me know if you need anything."

On her way out of the door, she had to sidestep to avoid bumping into a small Oriental man walking behind an enormous bunch of roses. A jumble of different colours, there were yellow roses, and pink roses, and roses as red as cherries; peach-coloured roses, and roses the colour of Christmas clementines. The man deposited them on the table tray that hovered over Alma's bed and Alma foraged among the stems with her awkward left hand until she unearthed the florist's envelope. Ripping it open with her teeth, she found a small card bearing a four-line message, typed out in tiny letters.

You must turn your mournful ditty
To a merry measure.
I will never come for pity,
I will come for pleasure.

Alma let her hand drop down on to her lap, with the florist's card still in it. She knew who the flowers were from, even though there was no name. She recognised in the gesture, three days late and already overblown, all the hallmarks of the film director she had been sleeping with, on and off, for the past few months. The very absence of his name, that was a vanity. The extravagance of the bouquet, that was another one — he would have wanted to be certain that his flowers dwarfed everyone else's. The use of the second-hand sliver of Shelley from *Out of Africa*, that was a vanity heaped on vanities. So she was Karen Blixen to his Denys Finch Hatton, was that what he was suggesting? Or was she Meryl Streep to his Robert Redford? The old Alma would have loved the comparison. The old Alma would have respected the lack of sentiment. But the last few days had changed her, and this was a new Alma, one who was saddened by the flowers, and made lonely by them. She would have preferred that he come and see her, instead of sending her more bloody flowers.

For the first time in as long as she could remember, for the first time since she was a kid, perhaps, Alma laid her head down and cried wet tears of self-pity that left skid marks of black mascara across the starched white surface of the hospital pillow.

After three days in the hospital, Alma was told she could go home. Three days that had been provided to her more as a favour than a necessity — the private wing of the hospital was half empty, so nobody was in a rush to send a fully insured patient home.

"I'm not sure I'm ready to go," she said, panicked at the thought of it.

"I can't justify keeping you here," said Maguire, sitting down companionably on the edge of her bed. "Your hand is healing well. You've seen the physio, and the pain specialist. I'll see you in a week's time, in my private clinic. In the meantime, I'd recommend the liberal use of painkillers, whenever you need them."

"Couldn't I stay another day or two? I'd like to get some value out of that bloody insurance I've been paying all these years."

"Alma," he said, dipping his balding head and looking her sternly in the eye. "You need to go home."

After he was gone, she turned her head and stared out of the window. From six floors up, she had a view of the city below her. She could pick out the landmarks of her life, from the water tower at the college where she had once been a student to the transmission mast at the television station where she had spent her whole career. For all its familiarity, there was something about the scene that wasn't quite right. As if there was a kaleidescope inside her head, one that since the attack had been twisted ever so slightly by an unseen hand, altering the patterns and colours that up until now Alma had been accustomed to seeing. In some weird way that she couldn't yet describe, the entire landscape of her life had become strangely unfamiliar to her.

After the attack, all Alma's old columns came back to haunt her. There was the one about the Neighbourhood Watch scheme (a licence for men with small penises to exploit their vigilante tendencies). The one about Meals on Wheels (shoot me if I'm ever forced to eat an overcooked stew out of a tupperware container). The demands of friendship (what's so awful about solitude?). After the attack, Alma was afraid to be alone after dark in her own home, but the men on her square were so well informed about her views that they resisted the temptation to check on her, for fear of causing offence. Alma found herself dependent on ready meals because none of the neighbouring women dared to darken her door with a casserole. She was desperate for company, but most of her friends and colleagues assumed she'd prefer to be left alone while she recuperated. She found herself stewing in an isolation that was entirely of her own making.

On her first full day home, she forced herself up to Sandymount village, on the pretext of buying some firelighters. Although it was well into April by now, the temperatures were still low and Alma felt in need of the comfort of an open fire. As she made her way up Sandymount Road, she was as wobbly as a newborn foal. The air that swirled around her was strangely threatening, every sound sharply heightened. When she saw an old lady bearing down on her, bent almost double under the weight of two supermarket bags, she felt a curious stirring of fear at the prospect of an encounter. The old lady drew level with Alma, and paused for a moment.

"Good to see you out and about," she said approvingly, straightening her head but not her body.

"Thank you," said Alma, buoyed up by a pride that was out of all proportion, like a child who has been praised by a teacher.

"Now, my love," said the weary-looking lady behind the counter in the café, when Alma went in on a whim to order a cup of coffee. "You sit down there and I'll bring it over to you." Alma unwound her scarf from her neck and slipped out of the sleeves of her coat, letting the warm clouds of steam from the coffee machine wrap themselves around her as she sat and waited.

There was a young woman sitting at the table next to her, with a baby asleep in her lap. The young woman was holding her cup of coffee out to one side to avoid any danger of spilling it on the baby, and she was staring into space, her eyes dull with a tiredness the coffee would not relieve. The baby was sleeping with his arms thrown out either side of him, back blissfully arched, belly rising and falling with his breath. Alma was reminded of when Nora was a baby. Nora used to fall asleep just like that, with her arms stretched out either side of her and her head thrown back, mouth open. For a moment it seemed to Alma that the baby might have been Nora, so deeply was her memory resurrected. She found herself overcome by nostalgia, a yearning in her for the sheer ordinariness of being a young mother again, until it occurred to her that she had never been an ordinary young mother. Determined to be extraordinary, she had gone back to work when Nora was three weeks old, with barely a thought for what she was leaving behind.

"Best time in your life," she heard someone say, and looking up she realised that the weary-looking waitress had arrived with her coffee. She too was gazing at the baby.

"Best time in your life," she repeated wistfully. "When your children are small."

Alma stared at her.

"You don't feel it going, do you?" said the woman.

"No," said Alma. And it seemed to her all of a sudden that it was the truest thing. The truest and saddest thing.

The woman put a plate down in front of her.

"I thought you might like a scone, on the house. I've sliced it for you, to make it easier."

Alma was about to decline the offer — normally she would never eat a scone with her coffee — but the comforting smell of the baking soda made her tummy hollow out with hunger, so instead she said thank you.

"You're very kind," she said, blinking her eyes several times in quick succession to stop them from welling up. The kindness of people, that was something Alma had never noticed before. She was profoundly affected by it.

"I've decided to give up my column," she told Jim that evening. She had phoned him rather than going in to see him. The thought of walking through that newsroom filled her with dread. She'd have sooner walked through a snakepit.

"Now don't rush into any decisions," he said. "You're only just home. It may take you a while to get your strength back."

"It has nothing to do with my strength," said Alma. "Physically, I feel fine. It's just that I can't bring myself to say anything nasty about anyone any more. I feel like going to live in a bloody Amish community."

How could she explain it to anyone? In order to say all the mean and amusing things that she was expected to say in her column, it was necessary for her to feel that she was different to other people. But since the attack, it had begun to dawn on her that there was nothing different about her at all. She was just the same as everybody else.

"Come on," said Jim. "Give it time. You'll soon be back to your wicked old ways."

"I wish I could be so sure," said Alma. "Things were much easier for me before I discovered I was human."

After the attack, or the incident as her mother insisted on calling it, Alma took six weeks off work. (Whenever she felt guilty about it, she reminded herself of that curtailed maternity leave.) Dawn broke earlier every morning, and the evenings were getting longer, but to Alma's surprise, she found that she had no trouble filling her time. She would rise early, making herself a mug of fresh coffee as usual, but instead of standing by the kitchen counter with the radio on as she drank it, she took to sitting beside the French windows in the quiet to savour it. The quiet was new to her and she found it surprisingly pleasant, the absence of all that noise.

Summer had arrived, and with it a burst of colour. After the longest winter anyone could remember — a winter that ran right through the month of April and into May, so that people still had their heating on and their fires lit throughout the May bank holiday weekend — the weather changed overnight. The sudden rise in temperatures caused all the summer flowers to bloom at once so that in the space of a single week you had the first tulips bursting open, along with the lilac and the early roses.

In Alma's garden, two little robins were building a nest where two walls met under the protection of a small weeping cherry tree. Alma found that she liked to sit and watch as the she-robin fussed about at the nest. The he-robin would make occasional trips from the nest to the wall, or from the nest to the top of the shed, returning with scraps of ivy in his beak, or small twigs, which he handed over to the she-robin. The division of labour, while unequal, seemed harmonious. There seemed to be no question between them but that she was in charge.

"Fair play to you," said Alma, raising her mug to them. "You've got it all ironed out."

After she'd watched the robins for a while, after she'd drunk a mug or two of coffee, Alma would go about opening the mountain of mail the postman delivered every morning. Day after day she received cards from complete strangers, cards that told of people's hardships and wished her fortitude in dealing with her own. There were letters from people she came across in the course of her work; the politicians in particular emerged as very diligent letter-writers. Some typed their letters, while others hand-wrote them; it was the fact that they had taken the time to write at all that Alma found so moving. It turned out they were all human beings after all.

Some days Macdara came for lunch, bringing with him curious delicacies he'd unearthed in Lidl or Aldi, or in the Polish section of the local supermarket, delicacies like venison sausage or smoked eel. He would deposit them without explanation on the kitchen counter and Alma would unwrap them with all the discomfort of a cat owner who's been honoured with a present of a dead mouse. But where the old Alma would have expressed her disgust in lurid language, the new Alma accepted these offerings in a spirit of quiet martyrdom, rather than risk hurting her brother's fragile feelings.

He and Alma would sit on either side of her impractical little kitchen table, with their strange lunch set out on a platter between them, and they would talk about small things. A sense of something delicate and tentative unfurling between them, something that, given time, might slowly take root in this space provided by their mutual unemployment. For the first time in a long time, Alma asked herself no questions about the mystery that was her brother's life. For years she had bombarded herself and anyone who would listen with angry queries about him. (What on earth does he do all day? How does he survive? Where's he going to live if we ever have to sell Mum's house? I hope he doesn't think we're going to look after him when she's gone?) Now, in her isolation, she found herself accepting her brother for what he was. A sweet if somewhat unexplained presence.

Acushla came by with lunch other days, bringing enough expensive salads to feed an army. She never could stop; she was always rushing off somewhere else, with some other good deed to do. Alma tried to get her to take some of the salads away with her again, but Acushla wouldn't hear of it and Alma didn't have the energy to be arguing with her.

Her mother was the other extreme. Bringing a leftover piece of salmon for the two of them to share, or a chicken leg that had been languishing at the bottom of her fridge, she would breeze in without warning, like a gust of wind that comes in through a briefly opened door, jumping up again just as suddenly to go. In her wake she always left a lingering smell of Elizabeth Arden face powder and mothballs, a smell that reminded Alma acutely of her childhood.

Alma's father could not visit her for long, because of Sam, but once or twice a week, following a touchingly formal invitation, she would venture out to see them in their "little shoebox" (Alma's father refused to use the word "apartment", on the basis that it was vulgar — when his imagination failed him, he would revert to calling his place "the flat"). "Would you join us for a spot of lunch in our little glass eyrie?" he would say, checking always with Sam before he gave Alma a time. Alma was shocked to find how grateful she was for these invitations. During the daytime particularly, it was good to get out. Any invitations for the evenings she made a rule of turning down.

She would eat her evening meal at the kitchen table with a novel spread open on a wooden Prop-It, which allowed her to read while she ate. She would drink one or two glasses of red wine with her meal, so that by the time the light had begun to drain out of the garden she would be feeling mildly sedated. She would draw all the curtains in the front room tight against the night and put the chain across the front door, locking the door carefully with the new triple lock system she'd installed after the attack. Then, taking her mobile phone with her, and the rest of the bottle of wine, she would move upstairs, using the sound of the TV to drown out the night-time noises in the house. All the footfalls and the tappings, the human and inhuman sounds that filtered through the walls from the houses on either side of her. Alma had never noticed them before. Now they scared the life out of her. She took to leaving the TV on all night.

Six weeks Alma was off work, and in all that time she did not go to the hairdresser. She did not go for her customary weekly pedicure — the manicures, for obvious reasons, she also cancelled, allowing Connie to cut the nails of what fingers she had left. She watched with morbid fascination as, slowly but steadily, her toenail polish grew out with her toenails. Her hair lost its chestnut sheen as the colour bled out of it and she studied her roots every day in the mirror, fascinated to learn — for she had long ago forgotten — what her natural hair colour was. By the end of the six weeks she had a clump of dull brown hair, every third strand of it silver, and at the crown of her head an inch of brave new growth as shocking and white as snow. She studied this new growth in the mirror every day with a protective pride. She was like a man who, for the first time in his life, decides to grow a beard. She was fascinated by this as-yet-unexplored aspect of herself.

"Good God!" said her hairdresser, when at last she appeared. "You've gone snow white!"

He scrabbled with his fingers in Alma's hair, looking up at the mirror every so often to gawp at her. He couldn't disguise his excitement.

"It must have happened overnight!"

"Is it any surprise?"

Tenderly, he cupped her head with his hands. "Poor baby," he said, talking to her through the mirror. "But don't worry. We'll come up with a plan of attack."

Alma shook her head.

"No plan of attack. We're going with it."

His eyes flew wide.

"No!"

She smiled. For the first time in weeks, she was enjoying herself. Stirrings of freedom moving through her. ("A woman's hair is her crowning glory," Alma's mother used to always say. It gave Alma great pleasure to think what her mother would say when she saw this.)

"We're going for a crew cut," she said, addressing herself in the mirror. "And the colour stays the way it is."

Looking at herself in the mirror, there was no doubt in her mind but that she wanted to do this. She could not go back into the world looking the same as she used to. What had happened to her had changed her so profoundly that she needed her appearance to reflect that change.

"Okay," said the hairdresser, looking at her with new-found respect. "Okay. You go, girl!"

Slowly, and with great aplomb, he pulled the scissors out of his belt. With a bullfighter's flourish, he draped a plastic cape around her shoulders. "Let's do it," he said, looking up at her one last time, just to check that she wasn't having second thoughts. "Okay," he said, and he began to snip. Snip, snip, snip. Snip, snip, snip. "Omigod," he said. "I can't believe we're doing this."

And when it was done, "Omigod. You look STUNNING."

"Oh. My. God," said Nora. "What happened to your hair?"

"Nora! Where on earth are you? We've been worried about you."

On the screen, Nora was all distorted. Her face was too small, her eyes too big. She looked like a woodland animal who has stumbled upon a secret camera and is inspecting it, oblivious to its purpose.

"Nora!" said Alma. "Can you hear me?"

Nora's face froze, disappeared, and then appeared again in a slightly different position.

"What happened to your hair?"

"Oh, I had a bit of an accident."

There she was again, using that word.

"What kind of an accident?" asked Nora. "An accident to your *hair*?"

"No," said Alma quietly. "No, no. An accident to my hand."

Nora seemed confused.

"But you're all right?" she asked.

And Alma wanted to say, No! No, she wanted to say. No, I am not all right! But watching Nora's waiting face, she could not bring herself to do it.

"I'm grand," she said. "You know me. I'm pretty tough."

Like a dieter who refuses a chocolate they have been offered, or a teetotaller turning down a drink, Alma had a deeply satisfying sense of her own self-restraint. A sense of pride that she had not told her daughter what had happened. A sense of regret, too, that the moment was gone and could not be brought back.

Nora nodded, relieved.

"You look good," she said. "The hair suits you."

It was hard to tell in the darkness, but Nora looked sun-tanned.

"Where are you?" asked Alma. "You look like you've been out in the sun."

Nora tilted her head to one side and her hair fell across her forehead. Using a gesture of her father's, she pushed it away.

"I can't tell you where I am," she said. "But don't worry, I'm perfectly safe."

"Well when are you coming home?"

"Soon," said Nora. "I just have to do something first, and then I'll be home."

Alma had a sudden urge to cry. She felt a swell of tears rising up in her like vomit. She had to gulp to force them back down her throat.

"Nora!" she said, unable to keep the panic out of her voice. "You mind yourself, all right? I want you to promise me that you'll mind yourself."

"Don't worry," said Nora. "I'm fine. Look, I'll talk to you soon. Give my love to everyone."

And Alma was about to send a message of love to Nora — it was in her mind to tell Nora that she loved her, but the connection was already lost.

"Alma!" said her boss. "Jesus."

She kept forgetting what a shock it was to people to see her without her hair. Without her hair she looked like a different person. Her skin tone had changed, that was the first thing. Whereas before it had had a pale, ethereal quality in relation to her hair colour, now it looked positively pink. Her eyes were brighter, their blue more intense, and she had taken to wearing less make-up. The effect of this was to make her look younger. Of her old look, the only thing she had retained was the red lipstick.

"Alma," said Declan, jumping up out of his chair and sticking his hand out to grasp hers before realising his mistake and whipping it away. ("Use the hand as normally as possible," the doctor had said when he took her bandages off, but Alma found this was easier said than done.)

"Alma. You look great!"

He leaned forward to kiss her. His mind would be whirring, she knew. Wondering could he put her back on the telly looking like this? Wondering could he stop her going back on the telly, or would that constitute discrimination? Poor Declan — since he took on this job he'd had an employment appeals tribunal always biting at his heels. The old Alma would have revelled in his misery.

"Welcome back," he said, with his head stretched back on his neck as he opened his arms to her. "It's great to have you back."

She allowed him to hug her, hoping he wouldn't notice that she was shaking.

"Declan," she said, as she sat down. "Here's the thing. I can't go back to being on TV. I want a move to radio."

Fair play to him, he made a decent fist of disguising his relief.

"I don't think you should make any rash decisions," he said. "Why don't you settle back in first? Take a few days to catch up."

She cut him off with a shake of her head.

"I don't want to be in front of the camera any more," she said, trying to be as direct with him as she could without giving too much of herself away. "TV's a young person's game, you know that, Declan. I've held the line for long enough, but it's a losing battle and I don't have the energy to fight it any more."

He looked at her with a puzzled expression on his face.

70

"Are you trying to tell me that TV's no place for an older woman? You're the very last person I would have expected to say that."

She held his gaze and smiled.

"Yeah, well, vanity prevails," she said. "I don't want the nation to watch me ageing under those studio lights." (When the truth was that she was afraid the nation would see something else — something she would not be capable of disguising for the cameras. She was afraid she would not be able to conceal her poor, bruised soul.)

"Look, Declan. The truth is, I'm too fragile for the telly. What happened to me is written all over my face. I can't hide it." She could hear the wobble in her own voice and it terrified her. She uncrossed her legs, leaning forward over her knees and fixing her eyes on his. "Believe me, you don't want me on the telly. I'm like Princess bloody Diana. Too much empathy. It's not pretty."

This was supposed to make him laugh, but it didn't. The expression on his face was one that Alma didn't recognise at first, so unfamiliar was it to her. It was the one thing she could not bear, to be pitied. She reached down deep inside herself and tried to access something of her old, lost bravado.

"Come on, Declan, it's not like anyone died. I'll only be moving across to the other side of the newsroom."

He nodded. His expression funereal.

"Sure," he said. "It just feels like the end of an era."

"Ah, now. Let's not get too dramatic. Why don't you buy me a cup of coffee in the canteen and we'll come up with a plan for the next stage of my career."

He stood up, fumbling his coins around in his pocket. Already his mind had turned to plugging holes in his rosters.

"Actually, it so happens that I'm short a newsreader for the radio bulletins this afternoon. But of course, if it's too soon . . ."

Very quickly she made the calculation that she would be better off getting it over with as soon as possible.

"Why not?" she said. "I'll have to get back on the horse sometime."

But no sooner had she said it than the panic began to rise in her. A lump of nausea formed in the back of her throat and she swallowed it back down, moving ahead of Declan towards the door of his office. Swinging her handbag over her shoulder, she planted one high-heeled foot in front of the other with exaggerated precision. She let her hips swing from side to side, attempting to muster a display of her old swagger. Without her hair to toss around, it just didn't feel the same.

All morning a steady stream of people made their way over to Alma's desk to welcome her back. Tentative some of them, intrepid others, they all avoided looking at her hand, admiring her hair instead, with varying degrees of conviction. Mary O'Malley arrived into the office with a small bunch of pink roses she'd picked from her own garden, their stems wrapped in damp kitchen paper. She settled them in front of Alma's computer, using an empty smoothie bottle as a makeshift vase. One of the young radio reporters brought her back a Kit Kat from his coffee break, laying it down beside her keyboard without a word as he passed. And Ray O'Donnell — fellow news anchor and long-time nemesis of Alma's — he came in the door backwards, carrying a wet umbrella and a laptop, and the first thing he did was walk over and kiss her on the top of her head.

Before the attack, none of the young reporters would have dared to approach Alma, no colleague would have dreamed of kissing her. There could have been no clearer indication of how it had changed her, not only in her own eyes but in the eyes of everyone else too. She felt miserably undeserving of people's kindnesses, like someone who has arrived without a present at a party but is made to feel welcome nonetheless. In the gentle attentions of her colleagues. Alma saw only reflections of her own unworthiness. It was a relief to her when the time came round for the afternoon news conference.

She arrived just as the conference was starting, making for the last empty chair at the far side of the table. As she sat down, the news editor pushed a news list towards her. Was she imagining it or did he look at her nervously? She glanced around the table but everyone had their heads buried in the list.

"Okay," he said. "We've got unemployment figures out today. The Minister is available. Likewise all the usual suspects."

Alma kept her eyes on his face. Once or twice, as he rattled through the list (ward closures in one of the capital's main hospitals, a gangland murder, another rise in the jobless figures), he looked up at her, as if in anticipation of something — but what?

"Brussels," he said, reading the next slug off his list. "This is a story about our European Commissioner, Michael Collins."

There was a shift in the air pressure inside the room. All those lungs full of carbon dioxide that everyone was afraid to breathe out. A current of excitement like the atmosphere inside a classroom when the monotony of the day is about to be broken by a pre-planned prank.

Valiantly, the news editor ploughed on.

"Someone has posted a video on YouTube that appears to show the Commissioner stealing a pepper grinder from a restaurant table in Brussels."

Oh, the pleasure in the room; it was like a sudden release of gas. Legs were uncrossed, spines unfurled, shoulders rolled back. An atmosphere of lip-smacking malice was unleashed.

"Hang on now," said the news editor, with his hand up to still the room. "We need to think this one through carefully."

All eyes on him.

"What's to think through?" asked one of the programme editors.

"Well, we need to be fair about this. We need to check the authenticity of the footage. Make sure it wasn't a set-up."

"Where did it come from?"

"Someone with a mobile phone."

"And we're sure it's him?"

"Oh, it's him all right."

"Well feck it, I don't know about anyone else, but I'm running it."

Despite a few minor quibbles, there was general agreement. What with everything else that was going on, everyone agreed that the nation could do with a bit of light relief.

Alma watched the footage, for the umpteenth time, on the nine o'clock news. She was tucked up in bed, the dregs of a glass of wine beside her on the bedside table. Fair play to Ray O'Donnell, he managed to read the intro with a straight face.

"Ireland's European Commissioner, Michael Collins, finds himself at the centre of a media storm tonight following the publication on a video-sharing website of mobile phone footage that appears to show him removing a pepper grinder from a table at a Brussels restaurant."

The footage showed a pavement café. White tablecloths, with wicker chairs under blood-red umbrellas. Mick was sitting alone at a table with a coffee cup in front of him. He was wearing a dark-coloured overcoat, a yellow wool scarf doubled round his neck. (That's what a decade in Brussels does to a man, thought Alma. Before he went to Brussels, Mick would never in a million years have been seen dead in yellow.) The footage showed the waiter approaching the table with the bill on a small steel tray. Mick dug into his pocket and handed him some notes. The waiter dipped into his apron and gave Mick some change, then moved off to another table and Mick was alone again. He leaned forward, elbow on the table, and lifted the pepper grinder an inch off the surface, using his hand as an upside-down claw. He turned the head of the grinder around once, twice, three times, with his free hand cupped underneath it to catch the pepper grounds, which he examined closely. He looked up briefly to check if anyone was watching. Then, with a shifting of the shoulders, one up and the other down, as if they were scales, he slipped the pepper grinder into his pocket.

Alma watched as the TV showed exterior shots of Mick's apartment, with the curtains drawn. They showed the gate to an underground car park, resolutely closed. They showed a close-up of a doorbell, and next to it a small typewritten label: *Monsieur M. Collins*.

"Every attempt has been made to contact Mr Collins," went the voice-over. "But so far all our efforts have been unsuccessful. The Commissioner's whereabouts are this evening unknown."

Alma reached for the remote control and turned the television off. The quiet that followed had a sound of its own, which she found herself listening to. It was the sound of her house making its presence known to her. The sound of her own blood pounding in her ears. As she lay there listening, she heard another sound, one that it took her a moment to recognise. It was the sound of her doorbell, winding its way through the dark and empty rooms downstairs.

WIKIPEDIA

Michael "Mick" Collins (born 9 March 1956) is the European Commissioner for Internal Market and Services and a former Irish government minister. He was first elected to Dáil Eireann in February 1982 and held his seat in Tipperary North until 2002, when he was nominated by Taoiseach Bertie Ahern to serve as Ireland's European Commissioner. A brother of the politician and former minister Liam Collins, he was married to the Irish television presenter Alma MacEntee, with whom he has a daughter, Nora. They separated in 1998 and subsequently divorced. In April 2013 he became a YouTube sensation when mobile phone footage showed him removing a pepper grinder from a table in a Brussels restaurant. The footage went viral and within twenty-four hours had been viewed by more than twenty million people.

Contents

Mick

It was hard to know which of them was the more shocked.

She was sitting on the edge of her armchair, her velvet robe bound tightly across her chest, her bare feet balancing on the points of her toes. Mick kept looking from her face to her hair, her hair to her face. The face, he knew. Even without her make-up, he knew her face. But the hair belonged to someone else, and he couldn't get used to it. On the doorstep he had wondered for a second had he arrived at the wrong house. Until she said, "Mick! Jesus. What are you doing here?"

Her face was thrown into shadow by the glare of the lamp she'd turned on in the corner of the room. She had offered to light the fire and he'd said, "Ah, no, sure it's not that cold. I'd kill for a glass of wine, though." She had handed him the bottle first, then the opener.

"So," she said to him, once they'd settled themselves on either side of the barren fireplace. "Why here?"

He'd been asking himself the same question.

"The truth?"

Even as he said it, he was wondering did he have it in him to be truthful. He could tell her that she was the first person he'd thought of, except that wasn't true. He had thought of his brother first, and then he had thought better of it. His brother would not welcome him arriving on his doorstep.

"The truth is there was no one else."

She came down off the points of her toes, crossed one leg over the other and sat back into the armchair.

"I'm not sure whether I should be amused by that, or annoyed."

Mick leaned forward, resting his forearms on his knees, so that he was looking up at her. He adopted his most earnest expression.

"You were the only one I could trust. I figured you wouldn't have the heart to turn me away."

"Trust," she repeated, following the word up with an inward hiss of her breath. He liked the way she did that, the sharp intake of breath, as if she was taking a drag on one of the cigarettes she had long ago given up.

"You invited me in," he said. "You could have turned me away."

She let a reluctant laugh out of her, a laugh like a yelp.

"And miss out on hearing the story from the horse's mouth? Are you mad? You knew my curiosity would get the better of me. You old bollocks."

He laughed himself now. Leaned his head back against the headrest, content just to watch her. She had drawn her legs up on to her chair, her bare feet tucked in under her, like a praying saint. She reached her right hand out for her wine glass, gripping it by the stem with her thumb and her index finger.

"Does that cause you pain?"

She hesitated, and he found himself wondering why. The question wasn't difficult. Maybe she was thinking that he didn't deserve an answer. Maybe she was thinking, Fuck you, it's a bit late now to be asking.

She transferred the wine glass to her left hand and held the right hand out in front of her, studying it. From where he was sitting, it looked like she had her two middle fingers clenched in towards her palm — that old trick you play on a child to let on that you're missing a finger.

"The pain I can live with," she said, in a voice that sounded a little distracted. "The pain can be solved, with enough painkillers. The look of it is a bit unsightly, but I'm getting used to that too."

She turned the hand over and looked at it from the other side, as if she was seeing it for the first time.

"It's the fear," she said. When she looked up, her eyes were surprisingly unguarded. "The fear is very bad."

"I'm so sorry," he said. And really, he meant it. He felt an awful swell of guilt rise up in him as he contemplated the ordeal she had been through. He had heard about it, of course, he had heard all about it. But he had not thought about it, not beyond his initial revulsion. He had not thought about the effect it would have on her, imagining that she would weather it with her usual resilience, that she would scorn his sympathy. But a thing like that would change you, how could it not? What was wrong with him that he hadn't been in touch with her?

"Did they catch them yet?" he asked. "Any arrests? Any idea who they were?"

She shook her head. Over and over again she shook her head at the questions he asked of her, but she did not make so much as a single sound.

"I'm so sorry this happened to you," he said.

She continued to shake her head impatiently as she tried to explain.

"Do you know, I never used to notice the sound of sirens before? When I was in the hospital, I started hearing ambulance sirens day and night. And I thought it was just because I was in hospital that I was hearing them. But I still hear them now; there seem to be sirens going off all the time. And every time I hear one, I can't help thinking about the poor person inside. I'm like one of those old ladies who bless themselves whenever an ambulance goes by."

She was looking not directly at him but somewhere off to the side of him. Her attention seemed to be focused on something inside herself, and it was only when she had it in her sights that she turned her eyes on him.

"You see, you become aware of all the bad things that are happening out there, and the worst of it is that you know for a fact that the bad thing can happen to you. I will never again be able to live under the illusion that the bad thing won't happen to me."

He stared at her, struggling to take in this new version of the woman he'd married. In his mind he had a vision of her on the night they met. Twenty-one years old and precociously fearless, in her knee-high boots and her white skirt suit, an old cravat of her father's knotted tightly around her neck. She had interviewed him at the count centre, the two of them standing high above the crowds on a platform of bare boards, supported by builders' scaffolding. Once the camera lights had been turned off he had leaned in and whispered in her ear, "Let's pray the cameraman shot us from the waist up. We don't want the whole nation knowing that the new TD for Tipperary North had a boner for his interviewer." She'd thrown her head back and laughed out loud, a shameless laugh that convinced him then and there that she was the woman for him.

"Jesus," he said, looking at her now. "I'd string them up for doing this to you. I swear to God, Alma, I'd hold them down and cut off their balls, one by one."

She smiled and rolled her eyes at him.

"Thanks, Mick, but I suspect you're in enough trouble as it is."

He nodded. Allowed her the opening.

"So? What have you got to say for yourself?"

"I don't know. What do you want to call it? A moment of madness?"

"Ah, now. What is it you earn? Two hundred grand? Three hundred grand? What possesses someone who earns three hundred grand a year to steal a five-euro pepper grinder? That's what all the papers are going to be asking. You might want to come up with a half-decent answer."

He adopted his most reasonable voice.

"It's not that easy to find a decent pepper grinder. The one I have in the flat is broken. I keep meaning to buy a new one but I never seem to have the time to get to the shops."

She was shaking her head in disbelief.

"You're going to have to come up with something a bit better than that, Mick."

With the knuckle of his index finger he began to worry at his lip. Nudging the lip with his knuckle, it was a tic of his. An indication that he was rattled.

"I know," he said. "I know."

"They're going to have a field day."

He squirmed in his chair. He put his hands over his face and began to stretch the skin away from his forehead, as if his face was a latex mask that he could pull off. He was talking through the gap between his hands.

"You might try not to sound quite so pleased."

"It's not that I'm pleased. I feel sorry for you, Mick, just as you feel sorry for me. So here we are, feeling sorry for each other. Who would have thought?"

He took a long slurp of his wine, resting the glass on his knee while he studied her. "You're looking good, girl. Despite everything, you look good."

And she did. To him, she looked bloody good.

"You're a dirty liar. I look old, is what I look. I look like a washed-up old wreck."

"You're barely fifty, Alma, for God's sake. You're looking pretty good for fifty."

"Fifty-three."

"Ah, come on. You were always able to take a compliment. Don't stop now."

He reached out and picked the bottle of wine up off the cold hearth. Poured the last of it out between their two glasses.

"What about Nora?" she asked him. "Have you heard from her?"

"Not a whisper. And you?"

"The last time I spoke to her, she wouldn't tell me where she was," said Alma.

"Oh, I know where she is all right. I make it my business to know where she is. She's in Egypt. Having failed to get into Gaza by sea, she's now trying to tunnel her way in through Egypt."

"Don't they bomb those tunnels?"

He shrugged.

"From time to time."

He did not mention that the tunnels had been bombed as recently as December. He did not mention that the tunnels collapse, too. That the plywood that holds up the walls sometimes comes crashing down in a rain of rocks and rubble and shoddy building materials and that people get buried alive under there and that they die that way, unless someone can dig them out in time. None of this did he mention to Alma, even though he had made it his business to know it.

"I take it she doesn't know what happened to you."

Again, she shook her head.

"We're not in the habit of telling each other much."

"No," he said, by way of agreement, and they lapsed into silence for a moment.

"Do you think she's planning on ever forgiving us?" he asked suddenly.

"For what?"

"For fucking up her life. Isn't that what this is all about? She's punishing us for what we did to her."

"I'm relieved to hear there's two of us in it," she said. "I always thought it was just me she was punishing."

She sighed, and he saw something he had never seen in her before. A weariness of spirit; it was the first time he had ever known Alma to be tired.

"I miss her," she said simply.

"Yeah," he said. "So do I."

She rose out of her chair. "Well, her room's empty. I'm sure she won't mind you sleeping there. Top of the stairs, it's the door straight ahead of you. Bathroom's on the landing. There's a spare toothbrush in the cupboard under the sink. Don't even think about using mine." (That was always a bone of contention during their marriage, her suspicion that he used her toothbrush.)

She yanked her robe even tighter across her chest in a matronly display of modesty. What did she think he was going to do, try and jump her?

"All right," she said. "I'm off to bed. Good night, Mick."

He stood up. Leaned in and gave her a peck on the cheek, careful not to lay a hand on her.

"Good night," he said. "And Alma . . . thanks for letting me stay."

She turned out into the hall and, using the banisters to support her, climbed the stairs. The smell of her perfume stayed in the room behind her — or was it just the memory of her perfume?

Mick sank back down into the armchair. He let himself fall against the back of the seat and closed his eyes. It was a long time before he opened them again, and when he did, he realised that his fingers and toes were numb. Barely able to summon the energy to move, he hauled himself up out of the chair and crept upstairs, anxious not to disturb her.

He woke early, not knowing where he was. The bed was harder than the one he was used to, the pillows softer, and he wondered for a moment was he in a hotel? So many hotels in his life. Hotels and planes, hotels and trains; sometimes he had to check his location on his BlackBerry just to remind himself where he was.

Oh, fuck. Now that he remembered, he wished he hadn't.

He turned over and buried his face in the pillow, enjoying the sensation of smothering himself. His airways blocked, his eyelids forced shut, he listened to the sound of his own struggling breath, heard from inside his own head. At last, gasping for air, he flipped himself over so that he was lying on his side, facing the window.

The curtains were open and the day was dawning a pale, powdery pink. From this angle, the stadium was in profile. The great western rim of it like the edge of a gladiator's helmet, its glass tiles angled to reflect the sky. Seen from this perspective, it was a beautiful sight.

Outside the window, a telephone wire bounced up and down in the breeze. A row of small birds gathered along it, one of them tilted this way, one tilted that way.

Every so often one of the birds would fly away and then return to the wire. Watching them, it seemed to Mick that they were holding a wordless conversation, a dialogue they were acting out without sound. From behind the stadium a train appeared. It crept along like a mouse scurrying under a giant's sleeping head. A moment later it had disappeared, leaving a new stillness in its wake.

Mick rolled over on to his back and studied the posters on the wall in front of him. There was one of *The Motorcycle Diaries*, Che Guevara riding pillion with his arms stretched out either side of him. A poster of *Alive*, which was Nora's favourite film when she was a kid. She must have watched that film a hundred times, and forced Mick to watch it with her. Staring at the poster, all Mick could think was that he missed his daughter. He missed her not as she was now, but as she was then. He missed all the moments that he had missed of her life, this room of hers that he had never even seen, and this view from the window that was her view every morning when she woke up. He missed all the things that he had missed and that could not now be brought back, no matter how much he missed them.

The smell of coffee brought him downstairs. Alma was standing by the open French doors, coffee cup in hand, facing out into the back garden. She gave no indication that she'd heard him come into the room — for a moment he wondered had she not heard him — but then she started talking, without so much as turning her head.

"I've a robins' nest in my garden," she said, in a faraway voice. "Yesterday there were only three eggs in it but today there's a fourth. If you stick your head out the bathroom window you can see them. I don't like to go out there in case I disturb them."

He pulled out a chair and sat himself down at the kitchen table. He was wearing trousers and a shirt, no sweater, no socks. The tiles were cold on his bare feet and he nestled the sole of one foot against the other for warmth.

"Good morning," she said, turning to face him and speaking in an entirely different tone of voice.

"Good morning," he said.

"I'm afraid there's no waitress service in this house. Coffee's on the hob. Bread in the bread bin. Butter and jam on the counter."

He smiled in recognition of an old pattern. Any tenderness that ever existed between them by night, it would have vanished by daylight. He stood up, poured himself a cup of coffee, and sat back down at the table.

"I've some light reading for you," she said, throwing a copy of *The Irish Times* down in front of him. "Bottom of the front page."

He scanned the headline and let his head flop down on to his chest.

"Listen, you don't have a BlackBerry charger, do you? My phone's gone dead."

"Probably just as well. You might want to think twice about turning it on."

"Sure, but I need to ring my office."

"Here."

She passed him her own phone. "Now," she said, carrying her cup and saucer over to the sink. "I need to get into the shower."

He made himself two slices of toast that he slathered with apricot jam, the sound of the power shower in the bathroom upstairs like the roar of an aircraft taking off overhead. He had to wait for the noise to stop before he rang his special adviser. It was only when he went to dial the number that he realised he didn't know it. Didn't know his office number either, didn't know any of the numbers. He had them all in his BlackBerry.

"Fuck," he said, trying to remember how people used to find phone numbers before they had mobile phones, trying to remember how he used to do things before he had advisers. He looked around the room and spotted an iPad on the kitchen counter. He powered it up and with a fumbling forefinger stabbed the icon for the internet connection. It took him ten minutes to navigate his way through the Commission website to a number for his own office. Another five to negotiate the call answering system. Noises upstairs as Alma moved from room to room.

"Jesus," he muttered. "How the hell are people supposed to contact us?" Until it occurred to him. Sure, that was the whole point.

"*Bonjour*," said a woman's voice at last. "*Bureau du Commissaire Européen pour le marché intérieur et les services.*"

It was a point of pride with Mick never to speak French. Fucking Frogs; it was bad enough to have to march to their tune without speaking their bloody language too. At least the Germans spoke English.

"Good morning," he said, with all the authority he could muster. "This is Commissioner Collins speaking. I need to speak to Feargal McCarthy immediately."

"*Un instant.*"

She put the call through straight away. That in itself was suspicious. It was as if they were waiting for him to call in. He imagined the whole office falling silent, everyone frozen in motion as Feargal picked up the phone.

"Mick! Where are you?"

"Never mind that. Now, what's the score?"

"Well. We're under siege. We've had every media organisation in the world on to us already this morning. We've had requests for interviews from every TV and radio station on the planet. We've got our own government looking for an explanation. And we've got the Commission president breathing down our necks."

Nasal at the best of times, at moments of excitement Feargal's sinuses tended to seize up on him and his voice took on a distinctly adenoidal pitch. Mick moved the phone away from his ear just a fraction to lessen the impact. The difference this made was surprising and extremely pleasant. Rather than coming out of the handset loud and clear, as if he was in the room with him, Feargal's voice now seemed much further away and therefore less real.

"We're putting out a holding statement. You know, it was all a misunderstanding, et cetera et cetera . . ."

"Good," said Mick. "Good man."

"You've no public engagements today or tomorrow, so that buys us a bit of time."

"Good stuff."

"If we could meet up maybe, somewhere other than the office —"

"Ah, fuck it, I think the battery on my phone's about to go . . ."

"Is there another number —"

"What's that? No, can't hear you. I think the phone must be running out of juice. I'll tell you what. I'll try you again later. In the meantime, just keep on doing what you're doing, good man."

"But wait —"

Taking the phone away from his ear altogether and using his thumb as you would to flick a switch, Mick closed the call down. When he looked up, Alma was standing in the kitchen doorway in a belted black dress. With her high heels on, and her red lipstick, she looked almost like her old self.

"This thing seems to be gathering a bit of momentum," Mick told her. "It might be as well if I lay low for a day or two. How would you feel about harbouring a fugitive?"

Knowing her well enough to know that the idea would appeal to her.

As soon as the door was closed behind her, as soon as he'd seen her taxi reverse out of the square (waiting a few seconds in case she had to come back for something), Mick set about checking out the house. He patrolled the front room first, taking in objects both familiar and unfamiliar. The print above the fireplace in the dining room, that was one of Sam's. Mick recognised the motifs immediately — spindly minarets against a midnight-blue skyline, and the outline of a bird in flight etched out in Sam's signature gold leaf.

He wandered into the dining room, taking stock of the highly polished antique mahogany table and its matching mahogany chairs, their seats upholstered in a deep pink velvet. He wondered who had chosen the table and chairs. Alma had never shown any interest in antiques when he was married to her. Could it have been one of her many lovers? That actor fella she was seeing at one stage struck Mick as a suitable candidate, pretentious fucker that he was, and him out of a butcher's shop in Mullingar. Mick had met him a few years back, at an arse-licking session in the embassy, and he'd made a point of establishing a bond with him as a fellow Midlands man. Your man couldn't get away from him fast enough. Oh, he had Mullingar well and truly in the rear-view mirror, that fucker. And Alma too, by the sound of it. Last Mick heard, he was gallivanting around with some young one out of an Australian soap opera.

Mick swept forward to study the photographs on the mantelpiece. There was one of Nora as a baby, looking exactly like herself, her eyes wide with indignation. There was a picture of Alma's mother on the Abbey stage, a spotlight pooling at her feet. There was a formal portrait of her father at his writing desk, the same portrait that had appeared on the back of his book. At the edge of the mantelpiece was an old snapshot of

Alma herself. It showed her sitting on a low stone wall, wearing a white sundress and a pair of huge sunglasses. Mick identified it as one of their honeymoon photographs, and he was as certain as he could be that it had originally been a photograph of the two of them, but now it showed only Alma. Looking closer, he saw the evidence. A blue knee jutting into the picture from the right-hand side. She must have cut him out of the picture and had it reframed.

He headed upstairs, bypassing the bathroom and making straight for her bedroom. The bed was unmade, a pile of pillows on one side, dented still by her head. There were clothes heaped on the ottoman, clothes piled up on the armchair by the window, high-heeled shoes scattered around the floor. It had always been a mystery to him how someone so particular about some things could be so slovenly about others. ("But I *like* being a slob," she had told him once.) Before he left the room, he had a peek into her underwear drawer. He had to know did she still wear the same satin underwear. He was thrilled to find that she did.

He stripped off on the landing, taking a visceral pleasure in wandering naked through his ex-wife's house. Leaving his clothes in a puddle on the carpet, he headed to the bathroom and ran the shower, waiting until it was steaming hot before he stepped in. Afterwards, he helped himself to a clean white towel that he found on the heated towel rail. He collected his clothes from the landing, putting the underpants on inside out for the sake of hygiene. He put on the same shirt he'd been wearing yesterday, and the same trousers, for want of anything else to wear. On his way downstairs he stopped off at the bathroom again and gave himself a generous all-over spraying with a deodorant he found on the bathroom counter. An old trick, from his student days, it almost made him feel young again.

He made himself a mug of tea and settled down in front of the TV in the living room, feet on the coffee table, mug on the arm of the sofa. With some difficulty he managed to steer the channel to Sky News. They were showing pictures from Syria, but the crawl at the bottom of the screen made reference to him: *Spokesperson for Commissioner Collins says pepper grinder incident was "a misunderstanding"* . . .

As Mick watched, the newsreader appeared full screen.

"You're watching Sky News," she said. "Coming up this hour, new footage shows the European Commissioner Michael Collins stealing a *pen* from the Russian president Vladimir Putin."

"Oh, fuck it," said Mick, sitting up so fast that his tea slopped all over the arm of the couch.

On the screen, he saw himself in Moscow last year, Putin to the right of him. The Russian president was talking and Mick was listening, or pretending to listen, to the translator in his ear. As he watched, he saw himself reach out and lift Putin's pen off the table in front of him. He turned the pen around in his fingers and then, unmistakably, he could be seen tucking it into his breast pocket.

"Oh, fuck, fuck, fuck!"

He clutched his head with his hands and, sinking back into the couch, let his legs float upwards. Like an upended beetle, he grappled at the air with his feet.

"Oh, fuck, fuck, fuck, fuck, fuck," he said. Then he righted himself and went looking for his phone, which he had plugged into Alma's charger.

"It's a free-for-all," squealed Feargal. "The things they're tweeting about you, you would not believe. Former employees, ex-girlfriends, they're all coming out of the woodwork. I'll tell you one thing, you've really managed to make some enemies over the years. It looks like this is payback time."

Mick listened, the sound of static filling the air inside his head. He was having trouble concentrating.

"So, what do we do now?"

"Well, wherever you are, we think it's best if you lie low for a day or two. Where are we now? Thursday. The hope is this will all have blown over by next week."

"Any word from on high?"

"They're suggesting the best way out of this may be a treatment programme."

"Treatment for what?"

"Well," said Feargal, "according to the psychiatrist who's just been interviewed on BBC 24, it's a classic case of kleptomania. What did she say? I'm paraphrasing here, so bear with me. The irrational urge to steal things regardless of economic necessity belongs on the spectrum of obsessive — compulsive disorder."

"For fuck's sake," said Mick. "Did it never occur to them that I just fancied the bastard's pen?"

He spent the rest of the afternoon avoiding the news channels. He hopped around the lower reaches of the remote control, finding nothing but cookery programmes. Who would have thought there was so much cookery on the telly? You could spend your whole afternoon just watching people cook. He imagined a whole continent, morbidly obese and fed on fast food, sitting on their couches and watching cookery programmes on daytime TV.

He discovered that his favourite was a programme called *Come Dine with Me*. He watched with perverse fascination as five strangers cooked for each other in their own homes, night after night, competing for a prize of a thousand pounds. A thousand pounds? he thought, puzzled. Why would anyone want to expose themselves and their pathetic homes for a paltry thousand pounds? He watched, struggling to understand, as they snooped around each other's houses, making fun of each other's possessions for the cameras. He watched, appalled, as they cooked meal after gruesome meal for each other. He found himself marvelling at the awfulness of people. The niceness of them, too.

He had the dinner ready for her when she got home, a menu constructed on the basis of what he had managed to find in her kitchen.

"This is all very domestic," she said, as she deposited a large paper bag on the kitchen counter. He peered into it and saw multiple packs of black socks, white underwear, white T-shirts. He was overcome by nostalgia. She used to always shop for his clothes when they were married.

"Thank you," he said, touched.

She ignored him.

"So, they're staking out your apartment. They've someone camped outside your office. They're even keeping an eye on your brother's house."

Mick chuckled.

"I'd be tempted to pitch up there just for the hell of it."

He was standing at the cooker. A tea towel slung over his left shoulder, he was putting the finishing touches to the meal he'd prepared for her with some prawns he'd salvaged from the bottom of her freezer.

"So, when did you learn to cook?" she asked. She was standing against the kitchen counter, holding the glass of wine he'd poured for her.

"When you threw me out. It was either cook or starve. Has Nora not told you about my culinary prowess?"

"Nora tells me nothing, about you or anything else. I always assumed you lived on restaurant food in Brussels. I imagined you surviving on truffles."

He laughed.

"Yeah, there's a bit of truffling in Brussels all right. Brussels is all about the truffles and the mussels. Bit of a culture shock for a country lad like me."

When he met her, he had never even tasted an avocado.

"So, what are they saying?"

"Jesus, Mick, you've no idea. It's taken on a life of its own."

He upended a pot of boiled rice into a colander, and the steam rushed up at him.

"Come on. Tell me the worst."

"Oh, it's open season. Anyone who ever worked for you, they're spilling the beans. Some press officer with the Commission says you made an inappropriate comment about her legs. The waitress in the café near your office, she says you used to hassle her to go out with you AND you never left her a tip. Oh, and what about the secretary who used to pick up your dry-cleaning for you? She says you didn't pay her back."

He had two plates out on the kitchen counter and he was serving the rice up in little mounds, the way he'd seen it done on the telly.

"The dirty cow!" he said. "Once, maybe twice, I forgot to pay her back. But don't you worry. She used to tape the receipts on to my desk, to remind me. I used to buy her chocolates from Pierre Marcolini, for Christ's sake. I did everything to cosy up to that bloody woman, bar riding her."

He paused in ladling out the prawns to look up at her.

"Ah, don't look at me like that. You know what I mean."

He carried their plates over to the table, pulling out a chair for her before he sat down himself.

"Prawns flash-fried with butter and brandy," he announced.

98

Tentatively, she speared a prawn with her fork and put it in her mouth.

"I don't know why you're looking so nervous. It's not like I'm about to poison you."

She smiled.

"Not bad for someone who used to eat his dinner in the middle of the day."

That was something she had teased him about when they were first married.

"Tomorrow's going to be more challenging," he said. "Tomorrow I'm down to frozen peas and four eggs."

"I suppose you want me to do some shopping?"

"Ah, no. That would spoil the fun. I'm quite enjoying this. It's like that programme on the telly. What's it called? *Ready Steady Cook.*"

"It's like the diary of Anne Frank, that's what it is."

He raised his glass to her.

"And you, my girl, are the heroine of the Resistance."

"If they knew you were here," said Alma, shaking her head at the thought of it. "If they knew you were here, Jesus Christ, Mick. I'd be hung out to dry."

For two days, Mick was happy enough to hang around the house. Not for forty years had he had a pyjama day, not since he was a child and his school had been closed down for a week because of a burst pipe. He lay on the couch for hours on end, eating Alma's biscuits and drinking tea as he watched back-to-back editions of *Come Dine with Me.* In his mind, the notion that this was a welcome, albeit temporary, reprieve from the world.

On day three, everything changed. He woke, and before he even opened his eyes, he knew that the buoyancy of the past two days was gone. It was as if the world had turned while he was asleep and now everything was cast in a different light. Outside the window the telephone wire hung in the air, motionless and bereft of birds. The sky was a dense flat white, the tiles on the edge of the stadium sullen and unreflective. Mick lay in the bed, steeped in gloom.

Whereas initially he had chosen to view his predicament as a comical one (the adventures of a sane man in a crazy world), now it began to take on a less cheerful complexion. What at first had seemed a bit of an escapade — a lark, an adventure — now began to take on the appearance of a crisis. His career, everything he had worked so hard to achieve, it was all hanging in the balance. And all because of a fucking pepper grinder. He found himself raging against the injustice of it.

Swinging his legs out of the bed, he reached for his phone and put a call through to Feargal.

"Okay, Feargal," he said, "I've had enough of this. I'm coming back."

"Oh, I don't know if that's a good idea, Mick." Feargal's voice squeaked with protest.

"Hold on a second. Don't you think this whole thing is getting a bit out of proportion? I filched a fucking pepper grinder. I'm happy to pay for it. The Putin thing, that was just a mistake. I didn't realise what I was doing. What would I want with Putin's fucking pen anyway? Jesus, Feargal, what's the world coming to when a man gets subjected to a public bloody flogging just because he steals a bloody pen? It's not like I'm Dominique Strauss-Kahn, for fuck's sake. It's not like I'm fucking Berlusconi. All I did was pocket a bloody biro."

Silence on the other end of the line.

"There's a bit more to it than that, I'm afraid."

"What do you mean?"

"This doesn't reflect well on the Commission, Mick. Surely you can see that. What with everything else that's going on — people going hungry in Greece, half of Spain out of work — the Commission needs to be seen to take this seriously."

"What are you trying to tell me, Feargal?"

"They're putting you on paid leave while they decide what to do with you."

"What!" He couldn't believe what he was hearing. "You know what this is, Feargal? It's a fucking witch hunt!"

"Mick," said Feargal. "Can you please stop bombarding me with expletives. I've had about enough of listening to your foul language."

And that was the moment. When Feargal McCarthy — Feargal fucking McCarthy, whom Mick had hired as a spotty kid straight out of UCD — when Feargal fucking McCarthy pulled the PC card on him, that's when Mick knew it was all over.

He ventured out wearing his overcoat and his dark glasses, a woolly hat of Nora's pulled down low over his ears. The first person he met was Alma's next-door neighbour, bald as an egg, in a bulging diamond-pattern jumper.

"Howrya," said the neighbour, coming out of his house.

"Howrya," said Mick, wondering had the neighbour recognised him.

"Grand day," said the neighbour. And he pulled a rolled-up towel out from under his jumper.

"Thinking of a swim?" asked Mick.

The neighbour stood for a moment looking up at the sky. Then he turned to Mick.

"That's what I was thinking. High tide's about now."

"Looks like we're in for some rain."

"Ah, sure that won't hurt me if I'm wet already."

The neighbour turned and looked at the upstairs window of his house.

"Don't go telling on me now. If she found out, she'd kill me."

Sure, who would I tell? wondered Mick, walking with the neighbour towards the corner.

"Your secret's safe with me," he said, as he and the neighbour parted ways. "Enjoy your swim now."

The neighbour put his index finger to his lips to reiterate the need for discretion. And Mick thought, hang on a minute, who's the fugitive here?

In the Spar, he filled a basket with groceries. He scanned the front pages of the papers, afraid to bend down to study them properly in case he aroused any suspicion. With his sunglasses on he could hardly see, but he was afraid to take them off for fear of being recognised. He placed himself in line for the checkout, looking straight ahead of him. When his turn came, he marched forward and hefted his basket up on to the counter.

"Hiya," he said to the young man at the till. A stocky, mahogany-skinned man, he was Malaysian by the looks of him, or maybe even Mauritian. Mick prided himself on being able to guess these things.

"Where is it you're from," he asked. "Malaysia?"

"Me?" said the young man, surprised. "I'm from Brazil." He jerked his head to the man working at the next till along, "He's from Malaysia," he said, laughing as if it was all a big joke.

"Good stuff," said Mick, wondering to himself when it had come to pass that the only people doing an honest day's work in Ireland were the foreigners.

"Do you have a loyalty card?" asked the young man.

"What?" said Mick. "A loyalty card? No. I don't have a loyalty card."

"Would you like one?"

"No. No, you're all right, I don't need a loyalty card."

"You should get one," said the young man, his brown eyes full of concern. "It doesn't take long. You fill out this form."

Already he was producing the form from under the counter.

"Honestly," said Mick, waving it away. "I don't need a loyalty card. I'm not here for long."

"Okay," said the young man, putting the form back under the counter. He looked disconsolate, as if he'd just failed to save a soul. Even as he was scanning

Mick's groceries, he was ruminating over it. "You can save a lot of money if you have a loyalty card."

Mick emerged from the Spar with a plastic bag weighing down each arm. The rain had started and he had no raincoat. No umbrella either, and no means of holding one. There was nothing to save him from getting a wetting. He lingered in the doorway, looking hopelessly out at the rain, and it was then that he spotted Alma's father's car. It was definitely Manus's car, a powder-blue 1962 Mark 2 Jag — sure, who else would drive a car like that? It was stopped at the traffic lights, with Manus's mad head in proud silhouette above the steering wheel. Mick stepped out on to the street, ready to wave him down, a sudden rush of affection unfolding inside him for his former father-in-law.

The lights changed and the car began to move, prowling through the intersection.

"Manus!" called Mick, arm in the air.

The car cruised towards him, and Mick had to jump back on to the pavement to avoid being mowed down. Alma's father was in profile now, detached from the world like an old sea captain at the wheel of a great ship out on the open sea. Oblivious to the furious wake he was generating, he splattered Mick with mud as he passed.

"Manus," called Mick again, setting his shopping bags down so that he could wave with both hands.

The car moved slowly past the Spar, blithely occupying the centre of the road so that other cars were forced to pull in just to let it pass.

"Manus," called Mick, a third time. Even though by now it was clear that Manus hadn't seen him.

Majestically, the car moved off down the avenue, cresting the bridge and disappearing the other side of it. Mick picked up his shopping bags again and continued on his journey, feeling sadly invisible.

"Are you the fella from the Corporation?" asked a very old woman he met at the corner of the square. She was wearing a transparent plastic scarf knotted under her chin, and a large transparent raincoat, even though the rain had stopped and the sun was out again.

Mick put his shopping bags down and pointed at himself.

"Who, me?"

"Yes, you. The Corporation said they were going to send someone round to look at the drains. The drains is all blocked, I've been trying for weeks to get them to send someone round."

"No," said Mick, sorry to disappoint her. "No, I'm afraid I'm not the man from the Corporation."

The woman took a step towards him.

"Only, there's more rain forecast and I'm worried those drains is going to flood. They don't clean out the drains," she said, confiding in him now. "Years ago, there used to be always fellas out cleaning the drains, but nowadays you never see them."

Mick could feel dried mud splatters caking on the skin of his ankles. His clothes were damp and hung heavy on him but still he had a desire to linger. A desire for human contact.

"How long are you living on the square?" he asked her.

"Oh, I'm here all my life."

She turned and pointed to a house behind her. Mick wasn't sure if she meant the one with the yellow door or the one with the white door.

"I was born in that house," she said. "My mother had six of us in that house and then she died. My father only lasted three months after her. It was my grandfather who reared us."

Mick found himself surprisingly affected by her story.

"How very sad," he said.

"Ah, sure that was the way of it in those days. Times was harder then. People had to manage as best they could."

"Yes," said Mick thoughtfully, and his own misfortunes suddenly seemed very feeble to him.

"Well," said the woman, "we live in hope."

"Of what?" asked Mick, thinking for a moment that she had some answer to offer him, something that would show him the way out of the predicament he was in.

She looked at him like he was simple.

"We live in hope," she said, "of the man coming about the drains before the place gets flooded."

"Oh, that," said Mick, bending to pick up his bags. "Yes, indeed. We live in hope."

With the shopping bags weighing him down, he made his way along the last stretch of the square.

"You wouldn't do me a favour?" asked the bald neighbour. He was standing out in front of his house.

"You wouldn't take me towel? Stick it on a radiator for me. I'll get it back off you later."

"Sure," said Mick, putting his shopping bags down again so he could take the towel. "Afraid you're going to be busted?" he asked, weighing the wet towel in his hand as if he were trying to guess how heavy it was.

"Something like that," said the neighbour. "It's the cancer," he said, by way of explanation. "I'm in the middle of me chemo. If the wife knew I'd been in for a swim, she'd kill me."

Mick nodded, not sure what to say.

"I'll throw it in the dryer," he said. "Come and get it whenever you want."

"Nice one," said the neighbour. And he slipped into his house, pulling the door shut quietly behind him.

Mick took Alma's spare keys out of his pocket and tackled her new triple-lock system. Two Chubbs, one Yale, all of them put in the day she'd come home from the hospital, she'd told him. Just as he was losing his patience, the door gave in.

He unpacked the shopping, humming away to himself happily. He was thinking about the people he'd met, and the feeling it gave him to talk to them. He liked talking to people. That was something he'd missed, all the years he'd been living in Brussels. It only occurred to him now how much he'd missed it. Now that he was back among his own people.

"I met some of your neighbours," said Mick, once they were sitting down to dinner.

Risotto with baby peas; before adding the stock to the rice, he had thrown in a generous glass of a fine Spanish sherry he'd found in Alma's drinks cabinet. The result was sublime, a dish that was more than the sum of its parts. The peas as sweet as gum drops, the stock neither liquid nor solid, and the rice offering just the right resistance on the teeth.

"Don't tell me you've been drawing them down on me," she said. "I've spent years studiously avoiding them."

Rain falling on the skylight, like handfuls of small pebbles striking the glass. It had been raining for hours.

"Well, I met the man next door," said Mick. "The man with the cancer."

"I didn't know he had cancer."

"He's doing chemotherapy. He still swims in the sea, though. He doesn't want his wife to find out."

Alma sighed.

"That pair," she said. "They drive me mad. He insists on sticking a parking cone outside his house so no one will take his space. On Sunday mornings they cook cabbage and the smell of it seeps into my house through the fireplace."

"There's an old lady across the square. I got talking to her too."

"Not Dolores?"

"I didn't get her name. Nice old lady . . ."

"Invisible hairnet, lipstick on the teeth?"

"As I said, a nice old lady. She's concerned about the drains."

Alma smiled. Very slowly she began to shake her head from side to side.

108

"You're unbelievable! You're canvassing my bloody neighbours! Where are we? Three years from the next election? So what are you thinking? Time to reinvent yourself?"

She was still shaking her head.

"I know exactly what you're thinking. You're thinking you'll snatch that seat right out from under your brother's nose."

He stared at her, shocked that she had guessed what he was thinking before he had even formulated it himself. His brother's seat, lost at the last election, it would be ripe for the picking next time round. The thought had been percolating at the back of his head. Not even a thought yet, more like mild vapours, conspiring to take a hold of him.

"Ah, come on," he said. And he lowered his face to look down into his risotto. "Come on," he repeated, digging around in the rapidly congealing rice with his fork. "What do you take me for?"

When he looked up at her again she was still staring at him. She had one eyebrow raised, her eyes twinkling at him and her lips clamped shut to suppress a smile. She saw right through him — always had done — and yet she liked him all the same. That was the thing about himself and Alma, he thought, they had always liked each other.

"What happened to us?" he asked her. "We were so good together. We brought out the best in each other."

She snapped her head to the side, looking out into the garden. In her throat she sounded a dry little laugh, or an expression of indignation, he didn't know which.

"You know what happened, Mick."

But did he? It seemed to him that they had never talked about it. Not then, and not since. Not properly.

"The thing with Acushla," he said. "I still don't know if you believe me. You can ask me a hundred times and I'd give you the same answer over and over again. Nothing. Happened. Between. Me. And. Acushla."

"It wasn't just that," she said, looking down at her plate now. "It was all the others, too."

"They didn't matter." Was there a way of saying this without making it sound like a broken record? He tried to put extra feeling into it, tried to make every word ring true. "Not a single one of them mattered to me, Alma."

She looked up at him as she answered in a throwaway voice.

"They mattered to me."

Suddenly he felt very, very bad. Not just because it had cost him his marriage, not just because it had cost him his home and his daughter, but because he had hurt her.

"I didn't take it seriously enough," he said, and it was a revelation to himself as much as it was to her. "I took it for granted, what we had. I was a gobshite."

"In fairness," she said, softening, "we neither of us did. We neither of us knew what it was we had."

And it was typical of her, thought Mick, to be so just.

He dropped his shoulders forward, lowering his head so that he was looking up at her. Eyes narrowed, he ventured to ask, "Do you think you'd ever be able to give me another chance?"

She grimaced, the way you do when you're breaking bad news to someone.

"I don't know, Mick. The honest answer to that is, I simply do not know."

The flood came at nightfall.

A wet, dark, silent thing, it slithered out from under the gates of the stadium and coiled itself around the gutters, expanding until it had filled the streets right up to the top of the kerbs. Noiselessly, it spilled over, flooding the pavements. It seeped into the grass and began to rise like a sponge cake, the water levels steadily climbing the inside walls of the square. It crept up the pathways of the houses, slipping under their front doors without anyone noticing. Its stealth was a living, breathing thing, silent in the night.

The first Alma and Mick knew of it was when the neighbour banged on their door. Two dull thuds that bore the sound of a fist rather than a row of knuckles. Alma and Mick were waiting for the start of the nine o'clock news, when they heard it.

"Jesus," said Mick. "What the hell was that?"

He looked over at Alma. She had not moved from where she was sitting. Hands in her lap, head held high, she had closed her eyes, as if by doing so she could make herself disappear. For a second, Mick had a memory of Nora as a child. Whenever they played hide-and-seek, Nora would put her hands over her eyes, imagining that if she couldn't see him, then he couldn't see her either.

"Stay here," he said. "I'll get it."

When he opened the door, the flood poured in. The neighbour was standing outside in his pyjamas, his wellies deep in the water. The street outside was moving but the sky was still. The rain had stopped, leaving behind an eerie silence.

"What is it?" asked Alma, coming up behind Mick.

"It's the river," said the neighbour. "The river's gone and burst its banks."

Behind him Mick could make out dark figures wading through the water with buckets and flashlights. On the doorsteps, backlit by their brightly painted front halls, children stood in their pyjamas watching. Above them loomed the stadium, dimly lit from within. It looked sheepish, as if it was trying not to draw attention to itself.

"Hold on a second," said Mick. "I'm coming."

He reached back into the hall for a raincoat, grabbing a bright yellow mac of Nora's that was hanging on the coat rack. He just about managed to squeeze himself into it. There were no wellies in his size so he took his shoes off, rolled his trousers up over his knees and stepped out into the flood waters in his bare feet. He was thinking about broken glass. About rats and Weil's disease. Underfoot, he could feel sharp stones. Uneven tarmac. A manhole cover.

"You stay here," he shouted back to Alma. "Get a brush and try to sweep the water out. I'll find out if there's anything we can do to stop it rising any further."

Together with the neighbour, Mick waded out into the middle of the street, up to his knees in the cold black water.

"Where does the water drain to?" he asked the neighbour.

"It doesn't. The drains are all blocked up."

"All right. We'll need to open a manhole, so. Has anyone got a crowbar?"

"I do, in the house. I'll go and get it."

"Wait," said Mick. "I don't know your name."

"Maurice," said the neighbour. "My name's Maurice."

He held out his hand to shake Mick's.

"Maurice, I'm not sure whether you should be out here. I'm worried you might catch something."

"Ah, well. It's a bit late for that," said Maurice. "And anyway, nothing this exciting has happened round here for years. I'm not about to miss it now."

Maurice waded back into his house, his pyjama bottoms sagging under an inadequate drawstring. A moment later he returned with a crowbar.

"I came across the manhole cover here somewhere," said Mick, walking around in the pitch-black water. He was scoping out the ground with the soles of his feet. Every so often he would touch on something slimy, or something that moved. At one point something scurried between his feet and he scrambled, comically, to lift his legs off the ground, hopping first on one foot and then the other. At last his right toe made contact with the dimpled metal surface of the manhole cover.

"Here it is!" he shouted. "Here it is, Maurice, I have it!"

"Good man," said Maurice, and he waded over to Mick with the crowbar. Taking it from him, Mick blind-guided it in through the opening on the cover of the manhole and leaned on it with all his weight. The cover didn't budge.

"Give us a hand here."

Maurice came around behind him and together they grabbed on to the crowbar.

"All right, are you ready? One, two, three."

The two of them leaned down on the crowbar and gradually, with great reluctance, the manhole cover lifted. Carefully, Mick hefted it to one side, and he and Maurice stood peering down into the black flood waters. In both of their minds was the possibility that whatever was down there might make its way up — a geyser of raw sewage — to add to their troubles.

As they gazed into the impenetrable depths, slowly but steadily the manhole began to draw on the flood water. From all around them it was being sucked downwards until, unbelievably, the water levels began to fall.

"Sweet Jesus," said Mick. "It's working."

"I don't believe it," said Maurice, looking up at him. His strangely hairless face was shining in the moonlight. "We did it," he said, and he slapped Mick on the back.

The water was hovering around Mick's ankles, and still falling. A festival air about the place, all around the square people were squelching about in the puddles. Children had ventured out, dressing gowns lapping around the rims of their wellies. The old lady Mick had befriended came out of her house in a quilted robe. Plastic bags tied around her feet, she began handing out mugs of tea that she poured from a giant flask.

Someone else passed around biscuits and they all stood about in the dull glow of the stadium, enjoying a neighbourly midnight feast. And into this happy atmosphere, into this almost magical gathering of people brought together by their combined efforts to avert disaster, arrived Mick's brother. With his rain jacket open at the neck to reveal a shirt and tie, and his suit trousers tucked into his wellies, he peered down into the open manhole, just as the last slops of the flood waters were being swallowed up.

"You might want to put the cover back on that," he said. "That's a danger to small children the way it is."

"You should have seen your face." Even now Mick was heaving with childish laughter; he had to clutch a hand to his ribs to contain it. "Fuck me," he said. "It was worth anything to see your face."

"You looked like Paddington Bear in that raincoat," said Liam drily. He picked up his water and sipped at it.

"Would you not have a pint?" Mick had asked him.

The two of them were standing at the bar; Liam was looking anxiously around him, alert to the potential damage of being seen in his brother's company. Three years out from the next election, but already he was shaping up for it. Even after the beating he'd taken, even after the ritual humiliation of his recent defeat, he couldn't wait to get back in the ring. Mick could see it in his eyes.

"Ah, have a pint with me," said Mick.

"I'm happy with the Ballygowan," said Liam. "I'm watching my glucose levels. You know yourself."

Mick looked at him. Noticed that he was thinner. He looked older, too. His cheeks slack, like an empty hammock, his complexion grey in the yellow light of the pub.

"What prompted this?"

"Ah, I've been seeing this dietician. She has me off gluten. Dairy, you know, the usual."

"And when you say *seeing*?"

"Jesus, Mick. Is that all you think about? I'm seeing her for my cholesterol levels. I'm trying to get the cholesterol down. Our father died of a heart attack at fifty, or had you forgotten that? It's time we started minding ourselves."

"Well in case you hadn't heard, Liam, my cholesterol is the least of my fucking problems."

So there they were, back to square one. Fighting each other for space in the back of the car. Measuring their MiWadi glasses against each other, using an upended ruler to mark out the slightest discrepancy in the levels. Setting the alarm to be the first to wake on Christmas morning so as to plunder the other one's stocking. From the moment they arrived into the world, seventeen minutes apart and roaring the both of them, from that moment on they had been out to get each other.

They collected their drinks from the bar and carried them over to a table in the corner.

"So, are you not going to ask?"

Liam shrugged. Took another sip of his water.

"I don't have to ask. I saw it on the telly."

"Oh, and that's it?"

"What more could there be?"

"Well, you might let me try and explain."

Liam dipped two fingers into his water glass and drew out an ice cube. Putting it into his mouth, he crunched on it.

"I don't need to listen to you explain. I'm your brother, Mick. I know you. You're the guy who used to steal robins' eggs out of their nests just for the crack. You're the guy who used to nick bottles of milk off old ladies' doorsteps. You're the fucker who robbed my hurling medal, for God's sake. You robbed it out of my school bag and you let Tommy Mangan take the blame."

Mick let a deep breath out of him.

"I did not rob that medal."

And in so far as he knew, it was true. He had no memory of ever robbing that bloody medal.

Liam was staring at him, staring right into his eyes.

"I'd still love to know what you did with it. You must have hidden it away somewhere, somewhere you knew I'd never find it. It had my name engraved on the back of it, so you couldn't even go showing it off to anyone. Why would you bother? That's what I never understood. Was it just for the pleasure of knowing that you had something that belonged to me?"

Listening to him, Mick found himself wondering was it possible that he *had* robbed the medal? Was it possible that he had robbed it and didn't remember?

"This is ridiculous," he said. "I don't even remember the bloody thing. It seems only to exist in your memory."

"You see? You're still denying it."

Mick picked up his pint and took a gulp, trying to keep a lid on his rage. It was ridiculous for them to be fighting over this. Jaysus, it was embarrassing at their age.

"Would you listen to us," he said. "And us in our fifties."

"Yeah," said Liam, but he was determined not to let it go. "Fifty-seven years old, but some of us still have some growing up to do."

And it was a mark perhaps of the doldrums that Mick found himself in that he let his brother have the last word.

"Well," he said. "None of this has turned out exactly how we planned it, has it?"

Liam shrugged, his face grim as he answered.

"We've been thrown a few curve balls all right."

"Ah, come on. We dropped the fucking ball, Liam. We stood on the shagging thing and burst it. We took it and stuck a pin in it."

Liam's eyes took on an opaque quality.

"It's been a tough time, I'm not denying that. It's been a tough time for the whole country. But we need to look on our present troubles as an opportunity. There's a great opportunity now for a fresh start."

"Jaysus," said Mick, with a bark. "You're starting to sound like a fucking politician."

118

Liam turned his face to look at his brother head on. Defensive now. Accusatory.

"What else am I going to do, Mick? What else *can* I do? Head up a charity? Go and write a crime novel? Politics is my trade, Mick. It's what I do. It's the only thing I know how to do. I don't see any other options out there for me. There isn't exactly a queue at my door for my services. I can hardly retire at fifty-seven. I have to find some way of filling the next ten years."

There was panic in his voice and Mick almost felt sorry for him.

"I hear you," he said. "Sure, aren't we in the same boat, the two of us? Two washed-up old farts."

But Liam didn't like that. He didn't like to think their predicaments were in any way comparable.

"Speak for yourself," he said, the fucker.

Mick let it go.

"So, what's your plan?" asked Liam.

"I don't really have one," said Mick. "Sure, my term was up soon anyway. They were only dying for an excuse to get rid of me."

Liam weighed that up.

"Yeah," he said. "But at least while you were in Brussels you were still inside the tent, instead of outside it pissing in."

Mick laughed, a laugh that stayed trapped inside his chest.

"Have you not heard?" he said. "The tent has been blown away in the storm. There is no fucking tent!"

"So, we pitch a new one," said Liam, with grim determination.

Where was he getting this shit from? Some counsellor? Some overpriced life coach? Some change-management guru that he'd signed up to?

"Do you know what, Liam? I think I'd prefer to sleep out in the open."

Mick picked up his pint and drained it, his eyes on his brother the whole time. He beckoned to the barman for another.

"Tell me," said Liam, as they waited for the pint to arrive. "How's Alma doing?"

Mick dropped his head to the side. Thought about it for a minute.

"Physically," he said, "she's grand. She went and chopped all her hair off, but otherwise she's grand. Mentally, though, I think she's very fragile."

Liam raised his eyebrows.

"That's not a word I'd ever have associated with Alma."

Mick laughed.

"Fierce, yes. Fearless. Ferocious. All the F words. But not fragile."

"Yes, it was always Acushla was the fragile one."

And they were both of them silent for a moment, thinking not of Acushla as she was now, but Acushla as she was when they first met her.

Mick remembers her in her pale pink bridesmaid's dress and her gold strappy sandals walking across the lawn at his wedding. She was holding her sandals by their straps in one hand, the way a poacher carries a brace of game birds. Later, when she was dancing barefoot, he saw that the soles of her feet were stained green by the grass. He saw his brother watching her and he knew instantly what was going to happen. Two brothers marrying two sisters: it seemed like it was meant to be.

"How is she?" asked Mick. "Acushla."

"How's Acushla?" repeated Liam. "The truth is, Mick, I'd be the last person to know. We live in the same house but we hardly have a word to say to each other."

Mick looked at his brother as if he was only seeing him for the first time.

"I'm sorry to hear that," he said. "I really am."

And it was true, he *was* sorry. He was surprised at how sorry he was. He had assumed that Liam and Acushla were happy. Despite everything, he had imagined their marriage to be a success, holding it up against the very public failure of his own. To find out now that it was not what he had imagined it to be, there was no satisfaction in it for him. He felt only sorrow.

As his brother looked back at him, Mick made a conscious effort to hold his gaze. Eyeball to eyeball for five seconds. Eyes open wider. Six, seven, eight, nine, ten. Just like that game they used to play when they were kids: the first to blink would lose. Staring into Liam's steady blue eyes, it seemed to Mick that he could see his brother's feelings moving like dancers behind a screen. Resentment, self-pity, suspicion.

Liam blinked and Mick spat out a laugh in triumph.

"You fucker," said Liam, picking up his water glass.

In the far corner of the pub, unbeknownst to either of them, a man was holding his phone up in the air to take a photograph of them. Bending down low over his lap, the man posted the photograph on Twitter, wondering with a happy burp of warm hops how long it would take someone to pick up on it.

Acushla MacEntee At Home

Her name is synonymous with understated glamour, so it's no surprise to find Acushla MacEntee Collins immaculately clothed in a grey silk shirt-dress and simple gold jewellery on a Monday morning in early summer. Welcoming *Style* magazine into her home in Dublin 4, the 45-year-old wife of the former Minister for Justice says the key to her look is simplicity. "I think the most important thing is to dress for yourself. At my age, I don't care what anyone else thinks. I'm very comfortable in my own skin."

Acushla has a grown-up daughter and two small grandsons but she hardly looks old enough to be a mother, let alone a grand-mother. So what's her secret? "If you're asking me whether I've used Botox, then the answer is no," she replies, with disarming candour. "I'm afraid I'm too squeamish to allow anyone near me with a needle. I'm terrified of going under the knife. So the only alternative is to grow old gracefully. I try to drink a lot of water, and I stay out of the sun. Apart from that, it's all down to genes. I have my mother to thank for that. She's about to turn eighty and she still has the complexion of a teenager."

Of course, Acushla's mother is none other than Deirdre O'Sullivan, star of the Abbey stage and a legendary figure in Irish theatre. "From an early age, my mother instilled in us the importance of presenting your best face to the world. We were always taught to walk with our heads held high and our shoulders well back. You might be wearing rags, but if you walk like a queen, then that's what the world will take you for."

It's salutary advice for the times we live in. And Acushla MacEntee is no stranger to hardship. Two years ago, she was the wife of a senior member of the Cabinet. Now her husband is fighting to win back the seat he lost in the last election. "Politics is such a tough game," she says, "and it's very hard watching someone you love take a knock like that. But Liam is a remarkably resilient person. I'm so proud of the way he has picked himself up and started again. He really cares about the future of this country and he wants to be a part of it."

For her part, Acushla is content to support him. "I've always been more comfortable playing the supporting role than the lead. Even when my sister and I would put on little plays as children, she always took centre stage and I was left with all the bit parts! Since I married Liam I've been very happy to let him occupy the limelight. My job is in the wings, but it's an important job, the job of wife and mother. Now I'm a grandmother as well, so I find I've plenty to keep me occupied!"

Acushla

Acushla stood at the kitchen window and watched as Connie unloaded her grandsons from the back of the car. She was short of breath, her heart beating too fast in her chest, like a distressed bird. Instinct and counter-instinct battling it out with each other. She was looking forward to the morning ahead of her — she always looked forward to these Friday mornings with the boys — just as a part of her was dreading it. Already she was anticipating the droop of their heavy little heads over the kitchen table. Their pudgy fists clutching the crayons, and the frantic windscreen-wiper motion of their hands across the page. The voracious appetite for fresh paper.

She had it all ready for them — a neat stack of foolscap pages in the centre of the table, and on top of it, acting as a paperweight, the tub of crayons. The Ribena was already mixed, the plastic beakers standing by on the kitchen counter to receive it. The boys would knock the beakers over, of course. They would spill the Ribena all over their artwork and Acushla would be forced to hang the pages out like wet laundry, draping them over the backs of chairs and radiators. Later, the dry drawings would flutter to the floor, enjoying a moment of flight before coming to land under the kitchen dresser, or the Aga, from where Acushla would gather them up and stash them outside in the green bin.

Oh, she was tired just thinking about it. She was tired and apprehensive at the same time. As she watched the boys tripping along the gravel path towards the kitchen steps, her heart was in her mouth. The way they walked, with the weight of their bodies thrown out over their feet, it was inevitable that one of them would fall. And sure enough, as Acushla watched, Oscar went tumbling down. Connie swept up behind him with Ernie hanging on to her right hand, a huge shoulder bag acting as a counterbalance on her other side. With a scoop of her free hand she set Oscar on his feet, and with the same tipping motion he began to tumble forward again, tripping over his own toes. Acushla watched him spill down the stairs and wondered should she have taken a whole Valium this morning instead of a half?

She opened the kitchen door and stood aside as Oscar stormed in, his brother following fast behind him. They kicked their shoes off and together they made straight for the far side of the kitchen, pulling a stool alongside the counter so they could climb up to the biscuit tin.

"Boys!" said Connie. "Are you not going to say hello to your granny?"

They turned around, just.

"Hi, Ganny."

126

A biscuit in each hand, they scrambled back down, leaving the lid off the tin. Helplessly, Acushla stood and watched them. She'd be the whole afternoon cleaning up.

"Oscar needs to take his antibiotics," said Connie. "And I'll leave you some Calpol, in case the fever comes back."

Her daughter was rooting around in her handbag, the loose waves of her hair falling down over her long, thin face. She was wearing a vintage raincoat, open on to a short green dress that had the look of a charity shop about it. The matching green leather gloves she wore made it difficult for her to negotiate her way around the inside of the handbag. Impatiently, she pulled one glove off with her teeth and dipped her naked hand back inside. She unpacked half a dozen loose nappies on to the table, along with a blister pack of Calpol fastmelts and a small brown bottle of medicine.

"How much Calpol should I give him?" asked Acushla anxiously. You'd think she would know this. She was a mother herself; surely she would know this? When she became a grandmother, it was as if everything she had once known about babies had been wiped clean and she was forced to start over again. She was as nervous minding Connie's boys as she would have been minding a complete stranger's children. More so, maybe. She was terrified she would let something happen to them.

"Give him five mil of the antibiotics," Connie was saying. "And one fastmelt every four hours."

Acushla was sorry now that she'd taken the Valium. She was struggling to absorb Connie's instructions. A breeze blowing through her head, it picked up the words and swirled them round inside her skull.

"Shit," said Connie. "Look at the time."

"Where do you have to be?"

"Oh, I've to do a feature piece for the *Indo* about this abortion thing. I've found a woman who's willing to talk about it. They need the piece by tomorrow, so I'll have to write it up tonight when the boys are in bed. These people think that freelancers have no lives . . ."

Connie was still talking, but Acushla's head had emptied of everything but that one word. A word that was on the radio every time she turned it on these past few weeks. On the front pages of all the papers, again. On her daughter's lips, even now, as she rooted around in her handbag, her voice muffled by a tumble of hair.

"This woman was raped, but she had to go to England earlier this year for an abortion because she couldn't get one here. I swear to God, there are times when I think this country is still in the Dark Ages."

Acushla didn't answer her, but Connie didn't seem to notice. She had her head in her handbag. A reporter's notebook coming out on to the table, and a hooded fleece. A freezer bag bursting with Lego.

"Finally," said Connie, pulling out a glossy magazine, its spine doubled back on itself to reveal a photograph of her mother sitting elegantly balanced on the arm of the drawing-room couch.

"I thought you might want a spare copy. For Grandmother's scrapbook." (From the moment Connie

128

had arrived in the world, it had been made clear to her that her grandmother's title was not to be abbreviated. Under no circumstances was anyone to call her "Granny", or "Nana". Nothing short of "Grandmother" would do. Whereas Connie's mother delighted in being "Ganny" to her boys.)

Acushla made an effort to smile.

"The photo's nice," said Connie, leaning in for a second to plant a kiss on her mother's cheek before rushing for the door. She paused and looked back, with a wink. "I have to say, you're looking pretty good. For *forty-five*."

As her daughter swept past, Acushla swayed, and for a moment she feared she might topple over.

"You're an angel, Mum. I don't know where I'd be without you."

Her head disappeared past the kitchen window. Looking up at the clock on the wall above, Acushla saw that it was only two minutes past ten. That left two hours and fifty-eight minutes before Connie would be back. It seemed like an awful long time.

By eleven o'clock, they were in Accident and Emergency.

"He's got a piece of Lego stuck up his nose," Acushla told the nurse. "I don't know how he managed it. I was with him the whole time." She was desperate not to appear negligent.

"Let's have a look," said the nurse, dipping down to see.

Obligingly, Oscar tipped his head back for her. This was not the first time he had stuck things up his nose, so he knew the drill.

"Well, I can see it up there," said the nurse. "But we're going to have to wait for the doctor to take it out."

Oscar whirled off to join his brother, who was pulling a stream of tickets out of the dispenser.

"Lads," growled the nurse, her index finger raised.

Acushla kneaded the handbag on her lap.

"How long do you think the wait will be?"

The nurse shrugged, unsympathetic.

"There's a few people ahead of you. You're looking at an hour at the very least."

Wispy thoughts floated unbidden through Acushla's mind. The thought of the amount of money she'd raised for this hospital over the years. The thought of the fund-raising dinner that was taking place this very night. She had the hospital CEO's number in her phone. In a matter of hours he would be sitting across the table from her; she could ring him right now if she wanted to. The thought roamed around her head like an unwanted guest. Of course she would not ring him! Not in a million years would she ring him about something so trivial. But it would make a good story for later, the story of her morning in Accident and Emergency. She pictured herself regaling the table with it. It gave her great buoyancy to think that she had this story to tell.

She picked herself up and moved towards the row of plastic seats in the waiting area. The boys were kneeling on the ground, making imaginary pancakes on a brightly coloured plastic stove. Acushla picked up a tattered copy of *Hello!* magazine and sat down to read about Kate Middleton's pregnancy, but the words kept jumping around on the page. Pressing in around her, the presence of the other people in the waiting room.

There was a fevered baby screaming. A toddler pedalling a plastic tractor up and down the corridor in a frenzy. There was a little girl in pink pyjamas curled up on her mother's lap, her eyes silently roaming the room. The mother looked young and poor. She kept petting the little girl's head, planting kiss after kiss on her threadbare skull. Acushla felt guilty looking at them. With her designer handbag in her lap, and her expensive coat folded inside-out across her knees — with her boisterously healthy boys and their frivolous medical emergency — she felt overprivileged and unworthy by comparison. She vowed to cede her place in the queue to the woman if her ticket happened to be called first.

She thought about ringing Connie, but, heroically, she didn't. Every five minutes she thought about ringing Connie, but she resisted the temptation each time, proud of herself every moment that went by for holding the line. Anticipating already the pride she would take in telling her daughter there had been no need to ring.

"Oh, we managed just fine," she would say. "Didn't we, boys? We managed just grand."

From her handbag she produced two bags of popcorn to keep them going, and dipping into the inside pocket she fished out a Valium for herself. As she broke the little yellow pill in half, she saw that the polish on one of her fingernails had chipped away. She felt a rising sense of despair at the thought that she would have to do her nails again before the dinner tonight. She still had her dress to collect from the dry-cleaner's, and she had promised to stop by the hotel to check the flowers. The goodie bags would need to be stashed under the chairs, the chocolate favours distributed around the tabletops. What had seemed on paper a simple list of chores now began to take on a nightmare complexion. Too late, Acushla realised that she had taken on too much, again.

The dinner was in aid of the children's hospital, one of half a dozen charities that Acushla patronised. The venue was a five-star hotel barely a mile from her home. A brand-new, purpose-built palace, its completion had coincided with the high-water mark in the country's fortunes. No sooner was the red carpet rolled out, no sooner was the first Rolls-Royce pulling up outside than the nation's finances were in free fall.

"We'll have a job getting money out of people tonight," said one of Acushla's fellow committee members as they moved around the tables checking place names. An angular beauty by the name of Laura, this woman had been a model in her past life. Small-town stuff, standing around Stephen's Green in a skimpy bikini, covered in fake tan and goose bumps. She'd gone on to become the wife of a well-known cardiologist. The mother of a child with cancer, she was a tireless fundraiser for the children's hospital. Acushla couldn't help but feel inferior to her, as if her suffering had earned her extra points in the game of life.

"You look gorgeous," said Acushla, surveying the simple satin gown, the effortlessly twined hair, the barely there make-up.

"So do you," said Laura. "But then you always look lovely."

"Oh, I don't know about that," said Acushla breathlessly. "I had to throw myself together. You know yourself — one of those days."

She had not had time to put rollers in her hair and she had been forced to patch her chipped nails rather than redoing them from scratch, little chinks in her armour that left her feeling horribly vulnerable.

"That's a great dress," said Laura, as they moved on to the next table.

"Well, the sleeves do wonders for the bingo wings," said Acushla, with deliberate self-deprecation.

"Oh, get away out of that," said Laura. "You don't have a pick on you."

Was Acushla imagining it, or was Laura's tone a little impatient? Irritated, even?

"Your sister was very good to honour her commitment to us. Everyone would have understood if she hadn't felt up to it — under the circumstances."

"Oh, Alma's a real trouper," said Acushla. But the words sounded a big hollow clang in the air. She tried them again, like a showjumper coming around for a fresh attempt at a fence. "She's an absolute trouper," she said. "She wouldn't dream of letting us down."

As soon as Alma's name was announced, there was an explosion of applause. Heads turned to see, arms draped over the backs of chairs. As she stood up and weaved her way towards the stage, a low outbreak of commentary rose from the tables.

"Fair play to her," said the man on Acushla's right. "That's courage for you."

"Oh, she's got mettle," said someone else. "I'll say that for her."

Acushla twisted from the waist, clapping with what she hoped looked like genuine affection.

Alma reached the podium and paused, expertly adjusting the microphone while she waited for the applause to die down. She was wearing a simple black tuxedo suit with a pair of ankle-strap stilettos. The double-breasted suit jacket was fastened by a single button, and she was wearing nothing under it.

"She looks ay-may-zing," mouthed the woman to Acushla's right.

Acushla gave a nodding smile, crinkling her eyes in agreement as her sister's voice, familiar as a shiver, slunk around the ballroom.

"You're too kind," said Alma into the microphone, quelling the last of the applause with the power of that beautiful voice. A voice like honey in the sun, as one columnist had famously observed; it was a voice with the power to make a man lie down at her feet and lick them, he had written. For years Alma had kept that clipping tacked up on the door of one of her kitchen cupboards, along with a letter from another fan who wrote to tell her that he liked to close his eyes and jerk off to the sound of her reading the news. She took great pride in that letter, much to the horror of her sister.

"There is no more worthy cause," said Alma, her voice all the more powerful for its unsentimental tone, "no battle more worth the fighting than the battle to provide state-of-the-art health care to our sickest children. Among us tonight are some of the doctors and nurses who work at the coalface of our hospitals, as well as the dedicated volunteers who support them in their mission. Truly, this is the work of the angels."

Already the waiters were going round the tables topping up people's wine glasses, the committee members rising out of their chairs and gathering at the foot of the stage, ready to bear the auction items around the room.

"Never has the funding of our hospitals been a more critical issue," said Alma. "Never has the task of fund-raising been more arduous. But rest assured, never has your generosity been more gratefully appreciated."

By the end of the night the auction had fetched forty-nine thousand euro. Which was good money, everybody said; it was a great result for the times that were in it. But it was a far cry from the night that someone paid a hundred and fifty grand for a round of golf with Pádraig Harrington.

"I have one remaining item to auction," said Alma, leaning in to the microphone in conspiratorial fashion. She took something out of her jacket pocket, a small, transparent object that she placed on the podium in front of her.

135

"For those of you who can't see, this is an unremarkable but rather infamous glass pepper grinder. Now, can I start the bidding at a hundred?"

"That was a bit of a show-stopper," said Acushla, when she ran into her sister in the powder room.

Alma was sitting in front of the mirror touching up her foundation. Acushla slid on to the seat next to her and took out her own make-up bag, delving into it for her concealer.

"Sorry," said Alma unapologetically, as she dabbed at the side of her nose with the index finger of her maimed right hand. She was looking at Acushla through the mirror. "I'm afraid I couldn't resist it."

Acushla avoided looking at her sister's reflection. She had always been squeamish, and the sight of her sister's wounded hand was more than she could stomach. It seemed to her a little inconsiderate of Alma not to be more discreet in her use of it. She could easily have used her left hand to do her make-up.

"I don't know why you're apologising," she said coldly. "It brought the house down. It'll be the talk of the town tomorrow."

Sitting poker straight on the upholstered stool, she sucked her cheeks in and swept a slick of fresh blusher across her cheekbones, the reflection of her sister's face hovering at the edge of her peripheral vision.

"Are you annoyed with me?" asked Alma, brandishing her uncapped lipstick in mid-air. She appeared bemused by the idea.

"Why would I be annoyed with you?" said Acushla, still without making eye contact. She was shaping her eyebrows with her index finger now, licking the finger and smoothing. "No," she went on, in a tinny voice. "It's just it would have been nice to know that Mick was staying with you. I seem to be the only person in the room who didn't know, that's all."

"Sure it's all over Twitter," said Alma, her eyebrows hoisted high. "And anyway, I assumed your husband would have told you."

Acushla felt as if she'd been backed into a corner.

"Yeah, well, I haven't seen him," she said, aware of what this revealed about her marriage. "We're both so busy these days, we hardly ever see each other."

She zipped up her make-up bag and combed her hair back with her fingers. She looked across at her sister's reflection in the mirror. Alma was looking back at her, with no effort to disguise her humour now.

"Don't tell me you're jealous. I swear to God, I think you're jealous that he came to me rather than to you."

"Don't be ridiculous," said Acushla, stretching out her spine.

"After all these years," said Alma, "you're still trying to steal my husband!"

"Oh, for God's sake," said Acushla, and for want of anything else to say, she stood up and made for the door.

Outside in the corridor, a photographer stopped them and asked them to pose for a picture. Without a word, the two sisters draped their arms around each other's waists and inclined the crowns of their heads a little towards each other, to catch a flattering angle. Too late, it occurred to Acushla that she'd been caught on the wrong side of the picture. Her left-hand side had always been her bad side, but she couldn't swap places now. As the flash erupted, she was drowning in the certainty that her sister had stolen a march on her, again.

"Poor Acushla," Acushla's mother liked to say. "She spent her entire childhood trying to catch up with Alma. She used to follow her around like a lost puppy. Oh, it was painful to watch."

And it's true, Acushla's earliest memories are all of Alma moving ahead of her like a figure in a dream. Alma in the playground, making for the empty swing. Alma on the street, chasing after the ice-cream van. Alma on the beach, heading for the waterline. In her memory, Acushla is always running after Alma, calling out to her but never catching up.

When Alma started school, Acushla took it so badly that her mother had to buy her a school bag too, and a lunch box just like Alma's. When Alma started swimming lessons, Acushla was so determined to prove she could swim that she jumped into the deep end and nearly drowned. When Alma started wearing a bra, Acushla stuffed socks inside her vest to make it look like she was wearing one too, and when Alma got her period, Acushla lay in bed and willed hers to come, to no avail. When Acushla's own milestones did eventually come around, in their own good time, they brought her no satisfaction, coming so long after her sister's as to have no value to her at all.

Acushla was fourteen when she faced up to the fact that she was never going to catch up with her sister. No matter how hard she tried, Alma was always going to be smarter than her at her schoolwork, better at sports, more popular with the boys. And it occurred to Acushla how futile it was for her to continue trying to beat her sister at her own game. Instead of focusing on Alma's strengths, Acushla adjusted her sights, forcing herself to study her sister's weaknesses instead. In everything that her sister was not, she carved out a whole new personality for herself.

The new Acushla would be gentle where Alma was rough. Meticulous where Alma was careless. Thoughtful towards people where Alma was casual. With absolute determination, Acushla sat down and designed a new style of handwriting for herself. She acquired a watch and took pride in her new-found punctuality; she even started making lists, to overcome her tendency towards forgetfulness. She remembered people's birthdays, and made cards for them, something Alma would never have dreamed of doing. When Alma was drawn into the debating club at school, Acushla volunteered for the benevolent society. While Alma was launching a school newspaper, Acushla was preparing to accompany a group of handicapped people on a pilgrimage to Lourdes. In her final year of school, Acushla was chosen to be head girl, and there was an added satisfaction to her achievement because Alma had never even made prefect.

That was the year their father left home, moving in with his as-yet-nameless Moroccan lover in a scandal that was passed around the country and parsed with glee, bringing a splash of much-needed colour to the otherwise drab winter of 1980. Their brother was sent off to boarding school in a disastrously misguided attempt to insulate him from the jibes of his contemporaries. And while Macdara had done nothing but irritate Acushla when he was in the house, once he was gone she found that she missed him. She missed the physicality of their horseplay. A bump of the shoulders as they passed each other on the stairs, a shin kick under the table at dinner. When Macdara was living at home, he and Acushla had played at hating each other, but without that game to play she was strangely bereft. She missed him most at breakfast time, when they would set up the box of cornflakes as a wall between them so they wouldn't have to look at each other; with Macdara gone, there was no need for the box of cornflakes.

Alma was in college by then and seldom surfaced until midday. Acushla's mother took her breakfast in bed, to recover from the exertions of the night before. She had chosen that winter to relaunch her stage career, with a triumphant run as Grace in Brian Friel's *Faith Healer* at the Abbey — a part that one critic said was made for her. She dined out most nights after the show, with the result that Acushla ate alone every evening as well as every morning, with the exception of Sunday.

140

She was supposed to be studying for her Leaving Cert. Everyone had assumed that she would go to college, perhaps to study Arts, but Acushla was brewing a different plan, one that she had stored up secretly and nurtured during those long winter evenings with the food of her family's neglect. When she should have been memorising the life cycle of the liver fluke, or committing Cordelia's words to heart, she was filling out application forms for Aer Lingus, and rehearsing for her interview.

"You're going to be an *air hostess*," her mother repeated, when Acushla made the announcement. "What do you mean you're going to be an *air hostess*?"

They were all of them gathered round the dining table to celebrate Macdara's sixteenth birthday. It was the first time he'd been allowed home from school for the weekend. The first time they'd all been together since their father had left. Sam had been included in the party, purely it seemed to Acushla because it gave her mother such pleasure to think of the fuss it would cause when people heard that she'd invited her husband's gay lover to dinner.

"I've been offered a job by Aer Lingus," announced Acushla. "As soon as I've finished my Leaving Cert, I'll be starting my training."

"You must like to travel," said Sam, agreeably.

Deirdre gave him a withering look.

Oh, what a scene there was that night. One parent a draper's daughter from Ennis, and the other the son of a penniless estate manager from County Kildare, they had their snobberies in common and they were agreed on one thing. No daughter of theirs was going to become an air hostess. They would have preferred her to announce that she was joining the circus, or the chorus line at the Folies-Bergère; they would have seen the glamour in that. They wouldn't have minded her falling pregnant outside of marriage, or running off with some dissolute poet, if only he had an ounce of talent. But for her to become an air hostess? God, no. There was absolutely no question of it.

By the time September came round, Acushla was safely enrolled in First Arts in UCD. She staggered through two years of college, each summer sacrificed to the misery of repeats, until a reprieve came her way in the form of Liam Collins. They were married the Christmas of Acushla's final year and Connie was born the first week in May, providing Acushla with the perfect excuse not to sit her finals. And while the lack of any letters after her name never caused her a moment's regret, while it never once occurred to her to go back and finish her degree, she always felt a pang of something not unlike pain whenever she caught a glimpse of an Aer Lingus uniform. The sight of that petrol-blue coat, with the leather gloves and the sensible low-heeled shoes, never failed to stir something in her. It seemed to Acushla that there was another life that she might have lived, a life beyond that uniform. She could imagine that there existed a house somewhere full of rowdy children and a handsome pilot husband. A laughing version of herself dressed carelessly in a pair of jeans and a sweater, with her hair tumbling down her back in effortless, unkempt curls. It seemed to Acushla that all of this could have existed for her, if only she had managed to defy her parents' prejudices.

The house was in darkness when she got home, the windows staring out at her, large and black and empty. She went into the kitchen and switched on the kettle to make herself a cup of valerian tea, lining up her vitamins on the counter while she was waiting. Two multivitamins for her general health, extra calcium for her bones, and Siberian ginseng for the stress. She washed it all down with a double dose of soluble vitamin C. The fizz of the orange flavouring gave her an instant feeling of well-being, like the comfort a child takes in a sucky sweet.

At least she has her health, that's what she tells herself. She has friends who've had chronic back trouble, friends who suffer from diabetes. Friends who've had emergency hysterectomies, and double mastectomies — their bodies papered over again but still bearing the scars. Alone among the women she knows, Acushla remains miraculously unscathed. Her belly is flat and trim, her breasts still small and upright. Her nipples in particular are triumphantly youthful, suckled as they were by just the one baby. Such scars as Acushla bears are all on the inside, and invisible to anyone but herself.

"Would you describe what you feel as guilt?" a therapist asked her once.

And Acushla has been thinking about that ever since. Can you feel guilty and still have no regrets? Can you be remorseful even though you wouldn't have done anything differently?

"I would suggest that what you're feeling is grief," suggested another therapist. "Grief that has never had a chance to find its expression."

"Betrayal," said another. "You were betrayed by the very person you should have been able to trust."

And of course they were right. They were all right, every last one of them. Acushla does feel betrayed. She feels sad and guilty; she feels full up with grief. But it's anger that she feels more than anything. Anger like the stagnant water in a pond, or the toxic liquid that's left behind in an old mine tailings dump. For twenty years it has been seeping silently out into her life. Poisoning her slowly, without anyone noticing.

Of the five people who know, it was her mother she told first. Her sister, who took care of all the arrangements. Her husband, who imposed a rigid code of silence on the whole thing, as if the silence were paramount and not the thing itself. Her father was away at the time and only found out after the fact; it was Acushla who told him, spilling the story out of her in spite of her husband's directive. Over and over again Liam said that no one must know and Acushla never thought to defy him. Not at the time, and not since — only once in all the years that followed did she ever tell another soul what had happened to her, and that was when she told Mick. Mick is the fifth person who knows — something that in Acushla's mind creates a bond between them that can never be broken. Mick's kindness to her, and the sweet, brief friendship that grew out of it, this is a holy thing to Acushla. A memory that she treasures, despite all the trouble it brought down on them. Mick salvaged her faith in men.

It was three male doctors who broke the news to her — all of them middle-aged, all of them wearing pinstripe suits. They leaned away from her as if it was radioactive, this thing that she had inside her. One doctor was sitting, the other two standing. Arms behind their backs, they kept looking at each other rather than at her. Talking in sentences that trailed off in the middle. The words they used seemed to form some kind of a code, but Acushla was not able to make out what it was they were trying to say. They seemed to be circling something, but before they got to the centre of it, the consultation was over. They sprang to action, one of them jumping up to grab her coat for her as his colleague dashed to hold the door open. Out in the corridor a nurse slipped her a torn-off piece of paper with an English telephone number written on it in blue biro. "I could be fired for doing this," she whispered.

When Acushla told her husband, he said the same thing.

"I could lose my job," he said. "I'd have to give up my place in Cabinet. I'd never be re-elected."

His career was riding on Acushla's silence. A silence that she maintained through election after election. Through abortion referendum after abortion referendum — referenda that convulsed the country for weeks and months on end, filling the streets with protesters and the airwaves with rage and outrage. Acushla took to turning the radio off during those times. She started switching the TV channel away from the news. She avoided buying a newspaper or answering the door, rushing away from shop counters without her change and standing back from the other mothers outside the school gates so as to stop herself coming into contact with this one word that could not be spoken.

A word that in Acushla's head reverberates even now with hard consonants, bouncing off the walls of her skull like a small ball bearing, rolling around in her head with no way of escaping. A word that is never spoken between her and Liam — if ever they refer to it, which they seldom do, they speak of when she "lost the baby". The other word is deployed only in the context of the legislation that Liam voted against time and time again over the years, in line with his party whip. In line with the views of the majority of voters, views that were carefully calibrated in poll after poll, while what happened to Acushla was submerged in a dense solution of secrecy. Even now that Liam's career is in tatters; now that his reputation is on the floor with the nation's finances and any hope of ever salvaging either of them hanging by a frayed thread — even now the secrecy remains.

Acushla was sitting at her dressing table when she heard him come in. The silver raw silk curtains were only partially drawn, and outside, the stadium occupied the night like a huge paper lantern. Stars speckled the sky above it, surprisingly bright for the city; their presence made Acushla feel very small.

146

She sat and listened as her husband closed the front door behind him. She heard the sound of a light switch being turned on, and a pause while he checked the post on the hall table. Then his footsteps moved across the wooden floor, and she heard creaking treads as he climbed the stairs.

"You're up," he said as he came into the room, his shoes moving noiselessly over the thick-pile carpet.

She didn't answer. She removed her pearl earrings, dropping them one by one into the crystal ashtray that she kept on her dressing table for this exact purpose.

Liam crossed the room behind her, the mirror reflecting only the middle section of him, from the shoulders to the knees. Acushla gave no indication that she had seen him.

He removed his jacket and draped it carefully over the garment butler. His trousers he took off and folded neatly along their crease, sliding them legs first into the trouser press and letting the waist fall over the edge. With his hand cupped in the manner of a man rolling a pair of dice, he dropped his cufflinks into a small silver bowl on his dressing table and rolled his shirt into a ball, stashing it in the laundry basket beside the window, along with his socks.

"Jesus," he said, "that was a long day."

Acushla watched him in the mirror as he moved across to the bed and slipped his hand under the pillows, where he found a pair of pyjamas that had been neatly folded and stowed there for him. He put them on, taking the time to fasten all the buttons. He got into bed and plugged his phone into the charger before switching on the lamp and taking his reading glasses out of the case that he kept on his bedside table. Putting on the glasses, he reached out for a copy of a satirical magazine he subscribed to. He didn't seem to have noticed that she wasn't speaking to him.

"I saw Alma tonight."

"Oh?"

"She was doing the auction for us."

"Oh, right."

"I gather Mick's staying with her."

No answer.

"I hear you met up with him for a pint."

At last he lowered his magazine and looked up at her. Their eyes met through the mirror, and his reflection started talking to hers.

"Do you know what kills me? He's wandering around like he doesn't have a care in the world. He doesn't seem to have any idea of the impact this has had on the party. It's the last bloody thing we need."

A high-pitched wobble in his voice, as if his brother had given him a shove and he was struggling to retain his balance.

"I wouldn't mind, but we were just starting to see a bit of a bounce in the polls. We were just starting to alter people's perceptions of us. We'll be back to square one again after this."

When she didn't say anything, he sighed and raised his magazine again, leaving their conversation hanging in the air.

Acushla stood and turned off the overhead light, then hung her robe on the hook on the back of the

148

door. Wrapping her nightdress around her legs, she climbed modestly into the bed, staying as close to the edge as she could. Without saying good night to him, without saying anything to him at all, she turned to lie facing the door. She reached a hand out for the small plastic pill jar that she kept on her bedside table; taking the lid off it, she tipped out a Valium, popped it into her mouth and washed it down with a swig of water. As she waited for the tranquilliser to take a hold of her, it seemed to her that she could not survive another second of the silent scream that was her marriage.

"Why did you marry him in the first place?"

That's what a therapist had asked her once. And Acushla had paused on the question, pretending to puzzle over it. She had sighed, and fiddled with her wedding ring, and said it was hard to remember.

"I think I was trying to get one up on my sister."

"Seriously?" asked the therapist.

"Oh, I don't know," she said wistfully. "We were young. We hardly knew each other. We neither of us had a clue what we were getting ourselves into."

It was at Mick and Alma's wedding that she met him. Six foot two and lean as a greyhound, with his hair falling down over his eyes and his face tanned the colour of a ripe red apple from the hay harvesting, he was the image of his brother, only better-looking. As soon as she caught sight of him, Acushla became acutely aware of him, and everyone else in the room disappeared. A feeling more like danger than love, although at the time she did not distinguish between the two.

"Watch out for that fella," Mick warned her. "He's a cool customer." To Acushla's ears it sounded like he was giving her his blessing.

Acushla was the bridesmaid and Liam the best man. Liam was supposed to ask her up to dance, but he didn't. He stood against the bar instead, smoking cigarette after cigarette and watching her on the dance floor. When she drifted out into the garden, she could feel his eyes on her back and when she came back into the room there he was, still watching her. By dawn the next day, his face drained pale and deadly serious from the night's drinking, he had announced his intention to marry her.

"We'll see about that," she said, and she whirled away from him, determined to test the measure of his love. The measure of her own she did not think to take, so giddy was she with the notion of being loved.

He started phoning the house every day; when Acushla came on the phone she found he had little to say to her, but somehow this only made his persistence all the more touching. "It's him," her mother would say, with her hand over the mouthpiece, and her eyes thrown up to heaven. "The poor eejit."

"He's out there again," she would say, looking out the front window to where Liam had taken to standing under the branches of the acacia tree, lighting one cigarette off another as he waited for Acushla to come out and give him her answer. Crouched on the threadbare rug in her mother's darkened bedroom, peering out over the base of the window frame, Acushla could see the burning tip of his cigarette glowing orange in the shadows of the garden.

"Away with you," her mother would shout, leaning out of her bedroom window with her hair falling down over the front of her nightgown like some middle-aged, never-rescued Rapunzel. "Away with you now," she would say, as Acushla peered out from behind her shoulder. "This is no time to come calling on anyone, sure it's after midnight."

Through the gap in the curtains her mother would monitor his eventual retreat with all the satisfaction of a conquering general. It played to Deirdre's sense of vanity for her daughters to drive young men to lose the run of themselves. It played to her insatiable appetite for drama.

"It all sounds very romantic," ventured one therapist.

"Oh, I don't know if I'd describe it as romantic," said Acushla, racking her brains for a more accurate word. "It was thrilling all right. It was very flattering. But I don't think I'd call it romantic."

"I was starting to feel like the boring one in the family," she told another therapist. "There was my dad, shacked up with a Moroccan man half his age. My mother was in the Trocadero half the night being serenaded by opera singers. My sister was just married and fast becoming a TV star. And I was still stuck in college. I was impatient for something to happen to me."

"And that's when he came along?"

"That's when he came along."

In a way, it was funny.

"He thought he was getting a younger version of my sister. And I thought I was getting a more handsome version of his brother. And by the time we both realised our mistake, it was too late."

"Well," said her father. "Never a dull moment."

He was studying the newspaper Acushla had brought him. The photograph on the front page was a picture of Alma standing at the auction podium brandishing the famous pepper grinder. A wing of white hair fell down over her face; her neck was as long and pale as a swan's.

STOLEN PEPPER MILL SELLS FOR THOUSANDS AT CHARITY AUCTION.

Her father chuckled.

"I'll say one thing for her. She certainly knows how to throw the cat among the pigeons."

He was fumbling with the coffee pot. He insisted on using one of those tin Italian espresso makers that you have to assemble and place on the gas ring. The Nespresso machine that Acushla had bought him for Christmas was sitting gathering dust on the kitchen counter.

"I hear Mick's staying with her?" said Acushla.

"So I hear."

Acushla took the pastries she'd brought out of their paper bag and arranged them on a plate. This was their regular Saturday-morning ritual. He made the coffee; she brought the pastries.

"Naturally, she wouldn't admit it, but I gather she's quite pleased to have him back."

Acushla studied the things on his shelf. There was a disturbing number of jars of Branston Pickle. Various chutneys and unopened pots of English mustard. He seemed to be stockpiling them, but for what?

"She has him in Nora's room," he said, as the coffee began to hiss and splutter on the cooker. "But I predict it's only a matter of time before he makes the journey across the landing."

Acushla became aware of a pain in her side. Clamping her hand to her belly, she made a pretence of studying the collage on the kitchen wall. A patchwork of postcards and photographs from all the places they had been over the years, it told the story of a life of travel and culture, a life of love. There were opera tickets from Verona and La Scala and matchbooks from Raffles in Singapore and the Algonquin Hotel in New York. There was a cartoon of Sam sketched in around the margins of a Los Angeles restaurant menu by David Hockney and a snatch of verse by Seamus Heaney written in seeping fountain pen on to a white paper napkin and dedicated to Manus. Here they were standing on the terrace of the Peggy Guggenheim museum in Venice, both of them wearing black polo necks and dark glasses, while another photograph pictured them on a Tokyo street in a snowstorm. From the evidence on the wall, it seemed they had been to every country in the world. The only place they had not been to was Morocco. Once Sam made the decision to move in with Acushla's father, the country of his birth was the one place in the world he could never visit.

"How's Sam?" Acushla asked, glancing towards the open kitchen door.

"Oh, you know Sam. He's as sweet as ever, thank God. He may be losing his marbles, but he still has his lovely temperament. Now. I'll carry the tray, if you'll follow with the pot of coffee."

Acushla trailed after him into the living room, her head struggling to keep up with her heart. She was overwhelmed, as she often was, by the richness of her father's life. The love that was vested in every word he spoke about Sam. The tenderness, even the tragedy of it, was all thick and rich. Every time she visited her father and Sam in their home, Acushla felt like a lonely little cold-water fish who has ventured into the tropics. She didn't know whether to be pleased for them that they had found this happiness, or sad for herself that she hadn't.

"Sam," said her father, as he set the tray down on the dining table. "Look who's here. It's Acushla."

Sam was sitting over by the vast glass wall of the apartment, his armchair angled to face out, a pack of Marlboro Red and an overflowing ashtray on an occasional table beside him.

"Oh," he said, getting to his feet. "Acushla." As if he had just heard her name for the first time.

She came forward to kiss him, first on one cheek, then on the other.

"It's almost warm enough to sit out on the balcony," said her father. "But I'm afraid it's not safe. Those

154

bloody seagulls seem to think this is a cliff. You're taking your life in your hands venturing out there. Poor Sam got a nasty cut on his head the other day when one of them made a dive for him."

"Isn't there anything you can do about it?"

"Short of shooting the bastards?"

"I was thinking more along the lines of an awning, or a sun umbrella. I could get one for you, if you like."

"Your sister suggested we hang up some old CDs. Apparently the seagulls are repelled by their own reflection."

"When was Alma here?" asked Acushla, trying to keep her voice breezy and light.

"Yesterday," said her father. "She brought Michael with her."

There was no getting away from it, she had that stitch in her side again.

"I always said those two would get back together," said her father, oblivious to the pain he was causing her. "They're much too well suited to be apart."

And Acushla said nothing, even though she had thought many times over the years that it was Liam and Alma who would have been better suited to each other. It was Liam and Alma who should have been married, they would have been perfect for each other. And Acushla would have been perfect for Mick.

The amazing thing was how two men who had emerged from the same womb, at the same time, could be so very, very different.

The cartoonists got it straight away — the difference between them — and they delighted in exaggerating it. Whereas Mick was always depicted as fatter and more jovial than he really was, Liam was leaner and more menacing. Mick was the bon viveur, always holding a bottle of wine and a fat cigar. Liam was the worrier, with his pinched face poring over the latest polls. "Mick Collins is too likeable to be party leader," wrote one newspaper pundit at the time of a party heave, "and Liam Collins isn't likeable enough."

Poor Liam! The moment that line was printed, it came to define him. No matter what he did after that, no matter how hard he worked, and what political points he scored, he was never able to throw off the notion that there was something lacking in him, some essence of charm that was a prerequisite for the top job and that was inexplicably absent in him. When the final meltdown came, on the night the electorate rose out of its stupor and punched the party of government full square in the face, Liam Collins earned himself another epithet, one he would never live down. He showed himself to be a poor loser.

The night Liam lost his seat, he stormed out of the count centre without speaking a word to the waiting media. Without shaking the hand of the young woman who had displaced him. Without stopping to accept the commiserations of his election workers, or to thank them for their efforts. He climbed into a waiting car and went straight home, where he walked wordlessly past Acushla and straight up the stairs to bed. The next morning he wouldn't get up. It was three weeks into his collapse before she managed to persuade him to see a doctor.

She drove him to the appointment, and waited for him while he went in. On the way home, she left him sitting in the car while she filled the prescription the doctor had given him. Incomprehension in his eyes, and desperation with it, he was more like a sick animal than a man. And heartbreaking as it was to see him like that, Acushla found herself hoping that this illness was the chance she had been waiting for, the chance at last of a fresh start.

There was one evening in particular when they sat up late and talked. They opened a bottle of wine, and before they knew it, they had finished it. They opened another, and for the first time Liam talked to her about his humiliation. He told her about the panic attacks, how for days after the election he had woken in the dead of night with the weight of a concrete block on his chest. The first time it happened, he thought he was having a heart attack.

"Why didn't you tell me?" she asked, her head inclined towards his in sympathy, her hand on his freckled, feathery arm.

"Oh, I don't know. I suppose I didn't want to admit to you that I was scared."

"Oh, Liam . . ." she said. And it seemed to her in that moment that something was opening up for them, a tiny crack through which, in time, the love might pour.

He cried that night, big wet baby tears that slid out of him without a word. She cradled his head to her chest and stroked his hair. She kissed him on the forehead, and for the first time in a long time she felt strong. For the first time in a long time they made love, and after they were finished, they wrapped themselves up face to face in each other's arms, like they used to do when they were first married. And Acushla remembered something that she had long ago forgotten, something that had existed between them before everything went wrong. She remembered that they were once allies.

When she woke the next day, she was curled in towards the centre of the bed, with her face up against her husband's back. She slid in closer to him, snaking her hand around his waist and nestling the fronts of her knees into the backs of his. It seemed to her that morning, as she breathed in the familiar smell of his skin, that the past twenty years had been left behind them and they could pick up again from when last they had a chance of happiness.

That evening Acushla prepared fillet steaks for them, as a treat. She pulled the cork on a bottle of wine, leaving it on the kitchen counter to breathe. She freshened up her make-up and reapplied her lipstick, and when Liam came in the door from his counselling session, she turned expecting a kiss.

He walked straight through the kitchen and into the living room, bending down to pick up the remote control off the coffee table.

"There's a poll out," he said.

He stood in front of the TV, pointing the remote at the screen.

"Jesus. It's even worse than I thought."

The lowest poll ratings since the foundation of the party, the future of the very organisation was now in doubt. The penalty to be exacted for their role in the country's economic collapse, this ruthless mob vengeance.

"Like it was all our fault," he growled.

"Here," said Acushla, moving towards him with a glass of wine. "Have a drink."

He turned and looked at her as if she was a stranger.

"You know I'm not meant to be drinking, with all the medication I'm on."

"Oh. I just thought . . ."

His jaw was clenched as he spoke to her, his eyes cold.

"I shouldn't have drunk that wine last night. I can't afford to be doing that, in my situation. I can't afford to let my guard down."

So it was a mistake, that moment of weakness. It was a regret to him how he had unburdened himself to her. That brief oasis of tenderness they had happened upon, that little patch of warmth in the cold waters of their marriage, he was determined not to venture into it again.

The next thing he had himself going to a dietician who took him off gluten. He took up Pilates on the advice of Connie, and meditation on the advice of the Pilates teacher. He gave up coffee and tea, and slowly, over the course of the next year, he constructed a new narrative for himself. A narrative of recovery and rebirth. Through sacrifice and self-discipline Liam would build himself up again. He would become a tougher and wiser person and, like the country itself, he would live to fight another day. What saddened Acushla most, what she could not bear to watch, was the complete success with which he managed to rehabilitate himself. By the end of the year he had made a full recovery; if anything, he was harsher than he had been before, and more brittle. He had the added arrogance, too, of a man who has battled his demons and won, where another less capable creature might have lost. To her infinite sorrow Acushla was forced to accept the fact that the man who had hauled himself out of the wreckage of her husband's career was not going to turn out to be a nicer man than the one he had been before.

Acushla was coming out of the nail salon when she met Macdara.

Hands held out either side of her, with her fingers splayed to keep her newly painted nails clear of danger, she was just wondering how she'd get her car keys out of her handbag when she saw him. Unaware that he was being observed, Macdara was waiting at the pedestrian crossing, dressed in his usual gentlemanly fashion, in corduroy trousers with a slightly-too-small tweed jacket and a wide wool scarf wrapped several times around his neck. There was an innocence about him as he raised his face to check for the green man. Something of the little boy he had once been. Acushla was overcome by a wave of tenderness towards him. A wave of love for this brother whose world had drifted so far away from hers.

"Acushla!" he said, when he reached her.

"Macdara."

She would have liked to hug him but she didn't want to smudge her nails, so instead she reached up to kiss him, bumping her cheek against his clean-shaven chin. Her lips brushed against the soft-coiled wool of his scarf. A smell of extra-strong mints off him, he had a brown paper bag tucked under his arm in a way that suggested something clandestine. Briefly, Acushla thought of pornographic magazines, of discount double packs of chocolate biscuits, before her imagination ran aground.

"I was planning on taking the bus," said Macdara. "But if you have your car with you, I might take a lift."

This curious directness of his, it was a result of his spending so much time alone. Acushla knew this, but even so it struck her as odd.

"Would you like me to drop you home?"

Macdara paused, studying her with his steady eyes.

"Are you not going down to the court hearing?"

Acushla began to grow concerned for her brother's state of mind.

"What court hearing?"

"Haven't you heard?" he said, speaking with great gentleness. "They've arrested someone for the attack on Alma."

"Really?" said Acushla, struggling to regain her grip on the conversation. "That's great news."

"He's going to be charged this afternoon."

"But it's Saturday . . ."

"There's a special sitting."

"I had no idea." (Later she would find a clutch of missed calls on her phone, and a message on her answering machine from her father, but for now Acushla was under the impression that she had not been informed.)

"The court appearance is at two," said Macdara, slowly stretching out his left arm to check his watch. Everything Macdara did, he did slowly. "If you're happy to give me a lift, we can go down there together."

"Oh, I don't know," said Acushla, shy all of a sudden at the thought of going, and a little petulant at not being told. "Do you think she'd want us there?"

In her mind she was still nursing the sting of last night's brush with her sister. The offer Acushla had made her of a lift home, Alma had refused it out of hand. Acushla couldn't help thinking of all those salads she'd bought Alma when she was off work — salads Alma had invariably tried to return to her as she was leaving. The orchid she'd bought her — the colour chosen so carefully to cheer her sister up — Alma had dumped it in her dark downstairs loo. And back, and back, through all the little hurts her sister had inflicted on her over the years, not a one of them ever forgotten.

"I'm not sure she'd want me there," she said, wary of incurring yet another wound.

"Of course she would!" said Macdara.

And he spoke with such emphasis, and such conviction, that Acushla couldn't but be drawn into the beautiful orbit of his innocence.

They arrived late because of the traffic and got caught up in a one-way system that brought them in a wide loop around the Four Courts; it was only when they'd finally found a parking space on the quays that they realised they should have been in the new courts building, and by the time they walked up there it was all over.

Rain falling down out of a strangely cloud-free sky, they arrived to find everyone gathered in a small circle out on the street. The circle wobbled on sight of them, with Mick shuffling in closer to Alma, and Deirdre stepping back to make space for Macdara. Acushla squeezed in under her father's umbrella, his free arm pulling her in so close that she could smell Pears soap off him, and burnt toast. A dry gloom prevailed under the canopy of the umbrellas.

"Well," said Deirdre, with a grim expression.

"Well?" said Macdara, his transparent eyes roving from one to the other of them. "What happened?"

"He got bail."

Acushla ventured to look across at Alma. Alma raised her eyebrows and glanced around at them all. Everyone seemed to be waiting for her to speak.

"Well, I don't know about the rest of you," she said, using her left hand to fasten the buttons of her raincoat all the way up to her neckline. "But I could do with a drink."

The circle splintered as the family drifted in twos and threes across the slick wet street towards the nearest pub. Mick yanked the door open, standing out on the pavement to let them all through. First Deirdre, stamping her boots and shaking out the dripping hem of her cape, followed by Macdara, who bent his head down low, like someone entering a cave. Then Alma, on three-inch heels, with her raincoat tightly belted in the manner of a spy, or a stripper. Manus stumbled after her, managing to right himself again just inside the door. Acushla was left until last, with Mick holding the door open for her. Placing the palm of his hand briefly on the small of her back, he ushered her into the pub, and Acushla closed her eyes briefly as a memory ran through her. A shiver of a memory, it served to remind her how much she had once desired him.

Nothing happened between them.

She had assured Alma of this, at the time and many times since, indignantly at first, then with impatience and finally tears. Nothing had ever happened between them, that was the honest-to-God truth; they just had lunch together. A lunch that came about entirely by accident — Acushla had been in town shopping, and she was on her way back to fetch her car when she ran into an anti-abortion demonstration. Old men bearing placards with photographs of dead foetuses. Young women brandishing buggies with healthy babies in them. She found herself trapped among them and she panicked. Holding her hands up in front of her, she began to push her way out, her eyes squinting to block out the images, her head shaking the sounds away. She fell out of the crowd and straight into the path of her brother-in-law, who was slipping out the side gate of the Dáil. He took one glance at her and grabbed her by the arm, steering her up the street and in through the doors of the Shelbourne Hotel.

The air inside was a comforting hush. The pile of the carpet a thick bed of grass under her feet. Acknowledging the doorman with a nod, Mick guided Acushla to a low table in the corner of the lounge. The trees of Stephen's Green filled the enormous window. A piano in the corner, its notes little more than a watery trickle.

"The baby had no brain," she said. "Did you ever hear of such a thing?"

His face crumpled, as if she'd kicked him.

"Ah, Acushla. He never told me."

"And Alma didn't tell you either?"

She had always assumed that Alma would have told him.

He shook his head.

"When did this happen?" he asked her.

"Last year."

He nodded slowly and she could see that his mind was working on multiple tracks, as always. The personal and the political.

"Was it Liam who went to England with you?"

She paused, ashamed of the answer. Not so much for Liam as for herself.

"He let you go alone, the fucker!"

"My mum came with me," said Acushla quietly. "But that's not the point. The point is that this happens to people. That's what you need to understand. This happens to people you know."

"Can you tell me about it?"

Leaning forward in his chair, he made a steeple of his fingers and held it to his lips, and Acushla had the impression that never in her whole life had anyone ever listened to her so intently. It gave her great strength to be listened to like that. It gave her eloquence.

"Thank you for telling me," he said when she was finished. "I'm very grateful to you for telling me that story."

As they were leaving, he placed his hand on the small of her back and guided her out through the revolving door. A gesture that flooded her with longing. She had a great desire to be close to this man who had shown her such kindness. ("He has the Mickey gene," Liam always said. "He never met a woman he didn't want to sleep with.") At that moment Acushla found herself imagining what it would be like to be one of those women.

Out on the street, Mick drew her into a fierce embrace. Once he'd released her, he gripped her upper arms with his big bear hands, as if he was about to pick her up.

"You know where I am," he said with great seriousness. "If ever you need anything, you know where I am."

Then he took her face in his two hands and bent down to kiss her. A kiss that was aimed at her forehead perhaps, or the bridge of her nose; it was Acushla who angled her head back in order to receive it on the lips. The kiss lasted only a second or two, no more than that, but it was long enough all the same for each of them to be aware of a terrifying and thrilling possibility. The possibility of something more.

The kiss was witnessed by Alma as she passed by the hotel in a taxi. She told the taxi driver to go around the block but by the time they had passed the hotel again, her husband and her sister were gone. Nothing that Acushla said to Alma afterwards succeeded in convincing her that the encounter she had seen was entirely innocent.

"I saw you!" she said. "I saw you with my own two eyes."

"You won't tell Liam, will you?" said Acushla. An unfortunate reaction, and one that seemed to imply guilt where there was none. From that moment on, it was a losing battle. "It's not my fault if you can't trust your husband," she said to Alma, unwisely choosing to mount an offensive instead of defending herself. "Oh, for God's sake," she said when it came up again. "How many times do we have to go over this? Nothing happened." Until the time came when she was reduced to tears of frustration at being so endlessly misunderstood.

"He was just being nice to me," she said plaintively. "Nobody in my whole life has ever been that nice to me."

Inside the pub, Mick ordered whiskeys for Deirdre, Manus and Alma. A pint for himself, and a white wine for Acushla. For Macdara, he called up a ginger ale. (Macdara always was a useless drinker.)

"Let me give you a hand," said Acushla, while the others made for a corner seat. Coats and raincoats stacked behind their heads, they settled on to the plush velvet banquette. The feeling of a railway coach about it. Something of the rain was still present in the air inside the pub.

"Well, kid," said Mick, as they waited for the barman to assemble the drinks. "You look a million dollars." (From the night he first met her, in her mother's kitchen, he had always called her "kid".)

She looked down at herself, as if to check, and saw the camel cashmere coat she was wearing. The hem of her burnt-orange silk skirt peeping out from under it. She had one tan leather boot planted up on the brass foot-rail under the bar, the other on the red tiled floor.

"You don't look too bad yourself," she said, tilting her face up to his. "Despite everything."

He laughed.

"Ah, you know me. I thrive on adversity."

"Seriously," she said, lowering her voice. "Are you all right?"

"Sure," he answered lightly. "I'm having a grand time. The life of leisure suits me nicely."

Acushla nodded, not sure whether to believe him or not.

"What about yourself, kid?"

"Oh, you know. I'm grand."

She caught his eye, hoping he might see just by looking at her that she was lying. But he was distracted. He was pulling banknotes out of his sagging trouser pocket to pay for the drinks. Reaching along the bar, he corralled the three glasses of whiskey, one finger inside the rim of each, so that he could pick them up together. With the other hand he grabbed Macdara's ginger ale.

"Just take your own glass of wine," he said. "I'll come back for the pint."

168

Approaching the table, Acushla realised that something was wrong. For a moment she wondered was it something she had done, but then she saw that they were all looking off to one side, their eyes rooted to the spot where two men had taken up position on high stools at the bar.

"What's going on?" she whispered, as she slipped on to a low seat beside Macdara.

Her father was the first to speak.

"It seems your sister's assailant is celebrating his freedom by treating himself to a drink."

Acushla turned her head briefly to the side. One of the men had his back to her, but she could see the other clearly. In the second or two that she had him in her sights, she formed an impression of a round white face. A pair of restless little eyes.

"It's unacceptable that he can just walk in here," Manus was saying. "It's simply unacceptable."

With his knees all knobbly inside his thin cotton trousers and his knotty old hands lying clenched on his thighs, he looked very old all of a sudden. Old and vulnerable; a gust of wind would be enough to topple him over. Deirdre was sitting next to him, bullish by comparison. She was looking in the direction of the two men. She had her eye teeth gritted on one side, as if she was biting off a loose thread.

"I've a mind to go over there and have a word with them," she said, in a loud voice.

You and whose army? thought Acushla, wondering even as she did so where she had heard that phrase before.

"Perhaps we had better leave," said Manus tentatively. The electric blue of his eyes sparking with alarm.

"The fuck we will," said Mick. "If anyone's going to leave, it's him."

"We can't just sit here and ignore him," said Acushla, horrified at the thought.

Before anyone knew what was happening, Alma had picked up her whiskey glass and drained it in one go. She took her raincoat in her poor right hand, and slid out along the banquette. Raising herself out of the seat and on to her heels, she walked slowly and deliberately towards the bar. The two men turned on their stools to face her, their backs rounded, knees splayed. Alma drew level with them and stopped. Ignoring one, she stared the other straight in the face. Standing four feet away from him for one second. Two. Three. Then, without a word, she walked on towards the door. Her attacker turned back to his companion and muttered something inaudible, his head bent down over his pint.

In the stunned seconds that followed, Acushla jumped up and ran for the door.

There was no sign of her sister on the footpath outside. Acushla looked left and right, twice, before she spotted her on the far side of the road. Alma was leaning back against the river wall, three lanes of traffic passing between them. Acushla stepped into it, giving the cars no choice but to stop.

"Alma," she said, when she got to the other side. "Are you all right?"

Alma's face had drained of all colour. The bones of her jaw were rigid, and her mouth was slightly open, her breath coming out in shallow gasps. She had her raincoat draped over her shoulders and Acushla saw that great shudders were passing through her, as if she had just been rescued from a cold sea.

"Oh, Alma," said Acushla, in surprise more than anything, and she opened her arms up wide. Her sister stepped towards her, and Acushla wrapped her in tight and whispered into her hair. "Alma, sweetheart. It's going to be all right. I promise you — it's going to be all right."

As the others spilled out of the pub behind them, their familiar voices bubbling above the sound of the traffic, Acushla held her sister in her arms. Aware of Alma's birdlike bones under her clothes. Her sister's skull against her cheekbone. A stray strand of her hair streaking her lips. Alma's heart was thumping against Acushla's chest. Her breath hot and wet against her neck. Her perfume raising dust-cloud memories in Acushla's mind of the perfume they used to make as children by crushing rose petals and water in an empty jam jar. Not since they were children had they been this close.

At dinner that night, Liam sat, as he always did, at the head of the long dining table. A table they had bought early on in their marriage in the expectation of having a clatter of children. Acushla sat as always to his right, facing the empty chair Connie had once occupied. When Connie left home, Acushla had suggested to

Liam that he take Connie's place, so they would be looking across the table at each other as they ate instead of sitting at right angles to each other, with Acushla staring at the wall. But Liam dismissed the suggestion out of hand, determined to retain his position at the head of the table. And while Acushla never mentioned it again, it never ceased to bother her. Every time she sat down, it was with a stirring of anger that she was forced to sit to one side of him at the table while he occupied the head. Day by day that anger gathered, like drops of rain falling one by one into a bucket until suddenly the bucket was full to the brim and threatening to spill over. Sometimes Acushla feels like she's waiting for it to spill over.

"I presume you heard what happened in court today," she said.

"I heard he got bail."

He had his fork in his right hand, using it as a shovel to scoop up a load of mashed potato. Acushla couldn't bear it when he did that; in her mother's house it would never have been considered acceptable to take your fork in your right hand.

"He came into the pub while we were there," she told him.

"Really?" he asked, looking up at her now.

"How can it be," she said, "that he can just walk into the same pub as her like that? Surely that shouldn't be allowed."

He raised one shoulder and dropped the other as he weighed it up.

172

"I suppose if he was allowed out on bail, without restrictions . . ."

"But how can it be," she said, "that she has to go on with her life now, knowing that he's out there."

"Well hang on, he hasn't been found guilty of anything —"

"I swear to God," said Acushla, without allowing him to finish, "this country does my head in sometimes."

He sighed.

"We do have a justice system." In his voice was that air of weary exasperation he liked to use with her, as if he was tired of always having to explain things to her. "It may not work perfectly, but —"

"Nothing ever changes," she said, and her voice was shrill now with her own barely understood rage. "Nobody in this bloody country ever does anything to bring about change."

"What are you talking about?" he asked, his impatience getting the better of him.

"Oh, forget it," she said, shaking her head.

He placed his knife and fork together and stood up, his chair making a loud, angry sound as it scraped against the kitchen tiles. Without saying another word, he went into the living room, where he picked up the remote control, turned on the TV and flopped down on the couch. Through the open double doors Acushla could see the large flat-screen, with the graphics whirling for the nine o'clock news. As she picked up his plate, she heard the newsreader starting in on the headlines: "Protests in Dublin city centre as the Dáil prepares to hear submissions in relation to abortion legislation."

With the plate in one hand and his dirty cutlery in the other, Acushla turned to face the TV. On the screen she saw shots of people bearing placards — some printed, others home-made. A close-up of a young woman with WOMEN'S RIGHTS NOW written in blue marker on the skin of her cheek. Another woman had an empty buggy with her, a placard propped where a baby would normally be. The reporter's voice ran over the pictures: ". . . more than twenty years after the constitutional referendum on the X case, and Ireland still has no legislation on the circumstances under which doctors are permitted to terminate a pregnancy."

Acushla took a few steps forward, so that she was standing on the threshold between the kitchen and the living room. Liam was slumped on the couch with the remote control on his knee, his expression perfectly impassive. When the story came to an end, and the newsreader introduced a report from Syria, he didn't even blink. He remained motionless on the couch, the images on the screen reflected in his stubbornly opaque eyes.

For a second Acushla contemplated flinging the plate she was holding to the ground. She imagined it crashing against the kitchen tiles, a projectile of china splinters flying through the air. She imagined Liam turning towards her in shock. "What the bejaysus?" he would say.

Her fingers tightened on the steak knife she was holding, and for one terrifying moment she contemplated

174

stabbing him with it. She imagined herself closing in on him, her hand raised high over her head. By the time Liam realised what was happening, it would be too late. She would have brought the knife down on him in a single stab, driving it into the soft spot between his shoulder blades. She had seen a TV chef kill a lobster that way once.

This is how murders happen, she thought, as her thoughts spun out of control. Like a washing machine with its transit bolts loose about to enter the spin cycle, or a space shuttle malfunctioning as it left the launch pad, something seemed to have come unstuck inside Acushla's head, some small thing that nevertheless had the potential to cause a catastrophe.

She turned and walked back into the kitchen, where she forced her fingers to release the knife into the dishwater. She let the plate she was holding slide into the limp suds, drying her hands on a tea towel that she found on the kitchen counter. As she climbed the two long flights of stairs to her bedroom, she felt that her skull might explode, splattering blood and brain matter all over her spotless paintwork.

Reaching her bedroom, she walked to her dressing table. She sat down in front of the mirror, but for once she did not look into it. She did not unscrew the lid of her cleanser, as she normally would, to go about the task of removing her make-up. She did not brush her hair, or change her diamond earrings for sleepers. She did not reach for the little jar of Valium she kept hidden in her cosmetic bag. Instead she opened the right-hand drawer and took out a pad of ivory writing paper. Locating a biro at the back of the drawer, she began to draft a letter. Imagining for a moment that it would be a difficult letter to write, she was surprised to find how easily the words came tumbling out of her. It was almost as if she had it written already, inside her head.

Dear Sir,

Like many women in Ireland, I have been taking a personal interest in this week's Oireachtas comittee hearings on abortion.

Twenty years ago, I was forced to travel to England for an abortion because I could not get one at home. The baby I was carrying had no chance of surviving outside the womb, but my doctors said there was nothing they could do to help me, so I went to England.

I was heartbroken to lose my baby and I felt very let down by the doctors who were supposed to be looking after me. I was also angry with the politicians who were responsable for making the laws that turned women like me into common criminals. Twenty years later and nothing has changed.

Shame on them all.

Yours sincerely,
Acushla Collins

Connie

"Oh, Mum," said Connie. She was about to ask if it was true. It was on the tip of her tongue to ask, but she stopped herself just in time. By the silence in her grandmother's kitchen she knew, by the look on her mother's face, and the loopy convent-girl handwriting. Connie had only ever seen her mum's handwriting on shopping lists before, or on birthday cards, never in a letter, and it was the spelling mistakes that broke her heart. She had always suspected that her mother was dyslexic, a suspicion she had never had the courage to voice for fear of hurting Acushla's feelings. It reared its head again now as she looked down at the letter in her hand.

"Oh, Mum," she said, grasping at a small handful of words among the millions and millions that were at her disposal. There was a vast world of words out there, and Connie wanted to pick the exact right ones. It seemed tremendously important that she say the right thing.

She looked down at the letter again, not because she had failed to understand it the first time, but because she needed to buy herself some time. She leaned in over the table, tilting the page backwards to catch the light, but the words scrambled in front of her eyes, and the longer she stared at it, the less sense she was able to make of it.

"It's a good letter," she said, looking up again. "It's a really powerful letter."

The kitchen was lit by a single pendant light that hung down low over the large round table. Encircled by a black linen shade, the bulb threw a small spotlight over the table, leaving the rest of the room in darkness. In the corners, piles of books rose from the floor in spindly towers, while spider plants spilled down from the side tables and cobwebs older than Connie formed a canopy overhead.

Connie's mother, her grandmother and her aunt were sitting opposite her, their faces pale. Three versions of the same face, carved in white stone out of the darkness; Connie had never noticed before how alike they all were. As they waited for her to say something, she had the sense that she was at a job interview. A formality hanging in the air, she found herself suddenly deprived of her fluency.

"I never knew," she said. But even as she said it, the memories were raining down on her. Little morsels of memories, like feathers, or snowflakes falling down out of the skies, they settled into the empty spaces in the story of her mother's life. Spaces Connie had never even noticed were there, until now.

A memory of the day Ernie was born. Connie was sitting up in her hospital bed and her mother was leaning in over the bedside cot where Ernie was swaddled in a blue blanket. Acushla was wearing an oversized pair of sunglasses, which she did not remove, and behind the sunglasses Connie could see that her eyes were swimming with tears. At the time Connie had thought her a little overwrought by the experience of becoming a grand-mother.

"You've been carrying this around with you all these years," she said, as the understanding of it continued to fall down on her. "All these years, you've been carrying this around without telling anyone."

Her mother nodded, and Connie watched in amazement as Alma rubbed her back in a gesture of support. Self-conscious as a mourner at a funeral, Connie reached across for her mum's hand. She took the brittle fingers in her own and held on to them, so that they were chained together across the table. She squeezed them tight, by way of apology, as she remembered with a flush of shame how hard she had fought her mother's love when she was a child.

When Connie was a child, it was her mother's watery voice that woke her for school every morning. Her mother's anxious face was the first thing she saw at the school gates every afternoon. Her mother's fussing hands helped her into her pyjamas at night, and brushed her hair, and with every gesture her mother poured out of her a love that was too weighty for one little girl to bear. Love enough for two children, it seemed to Connie now, and it grieved her to think how little of that love she had returned.

"I'm so sorry," she said. Her mother's fingers were grasping hers so tightly that they might have been bound together by a thin, taut piece of wire.

"Sure, you weren't to know," said her mum, mildly.

But that wasn't entirely true either. As a child, Connie was aware that her mother was sad, but she never stopped to wonder why. No more than she stopped to wonder why her grandmother was so eccentric. Or why her aunt Alma was so harsh. That was all just part of the landscape of her childhood, along with the endless catfights between her mother and her aunt, fights that saw Connie forever being thrown into the back of the car to be barrelled away from Alma's house as her mother babbled a litany of petty grievances at the rain-streaming windscreen and other cars beeped at them and her mother started crying, again. Those arguments were always followed by reconciliations, which were followed by more arguments and more reconciliations, until the last, big argument, one as deadly serious as the others had been frivolous. ("I knew you were a fool," said Alma. "I knew you were a jealous little cow, but I never knew you were a treacherous bitch.") Connie never did find out what that argument was about, but those words still play out in her head, all these years later. Looking at her mother now, it occurred to Connie to wonder what else there was about her that she didn't know.

"So, what happens now?" she asked, remembering the letter she was holding in her hand.

"Well, someone will need to type it up," said Connie's grandmother, rising to her feet with a scrape of her chair and moving off into the gloom of the kitchen. A cave-like place of long-exhausted bulbs and unwashed dishes, empty jam jars cluttered the counters along with small heaps of unopened bills and hoarded egg boxes awaiting a new incarnation.

"I could do it," said Connie, turning to her mum and speaking very deliberately. "I could type it up tomorrow."

"Excellent," said Deirdre, her huge voice welling up out of the corner. She was foostering about in a bottom cupboard, withdrawing ancient bottles of gin, and vermouth and crème de menthe. When she straightened up, she was breathless, a bottle of sherry in her hand, grasped by the neck.

"You might want to correct the spellings while you're at it. Your mother always was the most hopeless speller."

She deposited the bottle of sherry on the table with a thump and Connie stared at her, wondering were these little cruelties of hers deliberate, or were they unconscious? Did she even think about these things before she said them? If anything, it seemed to Connie recently that her grandmother was becoming more sweeping in her pronouncements, and more cavalier towards other people's feelings. She reminded her of a big old jellyfish, wafting her way through life, oblivious to the pain that was caused to others by the tentacles that came trailing in her wake.

"Macdara was the best speller of the lot of you," she was saying. "Macdara won first prize in the spelling competition at school, did you know that? 'Trepidatious' was the word that sealed his victory, as I remember."

"How could we forget?" said Alma, inclining her face towards her sister with a slow roll of the eyes.

Lining four crystal glasses up on the table, Deirdre began to pour a small measure of sherry into each. The glasses were so dusty they were almost opaque, the cuts in the crystal as black as soot. Connie took a corner of her scarf and gave the rim of her glass a discreet wipe before she lifted it to her lips. Her grandmother was struggling to untie a small plastic supermarket bag, her fingers wobbling at the knot. Eventually she got it loose to reveal an already opened pack of ginger nut biscuits. Connie stared at the pack suspiciously, thinking, Expiry date? She reached a hand out and took one, dunking it into the puddle-coloured drink. The sherry tasted mouldy, or was it the biscuit? She nibbled at it anyway.

"What about Dad?" she asked, all of a sudden. "Where's Dad in all of this?"

She looked from one to the other of them. Saw the answer on their faces.

"So he doesn't know about the letter?"

"This is women's business," said her grandmother. "Your father gave up the right long ago to have a say in any of this."

And if there was a militant edge to her voice, if there was a touch of bitterness, who could blame her? This was a woman whose husband had left her for a Moroccan man half her age. If Alma was a bit tough, maybe you'd have to be tough if you discovered that your husband was sleeping with every female reporter on the island. If Connie's mother was fragile, and prone to sorrow, well, it was very clear to Connie now why that might be. All of a sudden *everything* seemed very clear to Connie.

"*Sláinte*," said her grandmother, lifting her small glass and puckering her lips to sip from it. The rest of them lifted their glasses briefly in response, and as they did so, Connie experienced a shudder of vertigo. A sense of the future and the past cohabiting with the present, as if the scene in front of her was only the most minute and inadequate manifestation of a vast, non-linear reality, one that her brain could only catch the tiniest glimpse of. It was only then that it occurred to her — amid the creeping spider plants and the dusty books, with her grandmother's distinct smell of never-washed lambswool and chemist-shop perfume hanging in the stale air — it was then that it occurred to Connie that it was not a secret, this thing that her mother had told her. It was not a secret because at some level she had known it all along.

She remembers it.

A smattering of sequential happenings, like numbered dots of ink on a page. It's only now that she realises what it is that she remembers, now that she can join the dots.

She remembers her mother going to London. An unusual trip — even at the time she would have known that it was out of the ordinary for her mother and her grandmother to go to London to see a show. Her father was busy with work so she was sent to stay with her aunt Alma, and her mother forgot to pack a toothbrush for her so Alma had to take her down to the chemist's to buy a new one. Later that day, or maybe it was another day, Alma took Connie and Nora on a carriage

184

ride around Stephen's Green, and afterwards she treated them to lunch in Captain America's. Connie ordered a banana split that came with a purple paper parasol stuck into it, and a long-handled spoon to eat it with. She still remembers the foamy taste of the canned whipped cream and the nibs of roasted hazelnuts that were sprinkled on top. She remembers the sense that Alma was spoiling her; she remembers not understanding why.

It was probably only a day or two that Connie stayed with Alma, but in her memory it seems like a week, a month, a year. When eventually Alma brought her home, it was to her grandmother's house rather than to her own, and her mother was upstairs, resting after the journey. Of course, in retrospect this made no sense. The flight from London was less than an hour, an anomaly that Connie would not have noticed at the time. She would have been distracted by the presents they brought back. She remembers her grandmother opening a suitcase out on the kitchen floor. In it was a Hamleys bag, and out of the Hamleys bag came two baby dolls, one for Connie and one for Nora. Connie remembers Alma's reaction, heard but not understood.

"Jesus, Mother! Isn't that just a little bit inappropriate?"

"Don't be ridiculous," said Deirdre, handing out the dolls.

Nora's doll was dressed in a pink Babygro and Connie's doll was dressed in a blue one, which was fine by Connie because at the time blue was her favourite colour. Connie laid her doll down on the floor and went about the work of undressing it. She had difficulty getting the poor doll's arms out of its sleeves — the arm was fused into a rigid bend at the elbow, so you had to pull the fabric of the suit to breaking point to get it free — but once that was done, all you had to do was pull the Babygro down over the doll's belly and yank it free of the legs. Under the Babygro, Connie discovered, the doll was wearing a cloth nappy, and under the nappy, to her horror, was a small plastic penis. She dropped the doll on to the tiles as if it had caught fire.

Alma let out a squawk.

"Oh, sweet Jesus," she said, dry, rasping laughs coming out of her. Her hand was clasped to her chest and her eyes were streaming silent cartoon tears, tears that had been dyed bright blue by her mascara. (At that time Alma was a great woman for the blue mascara.)

Connie remembers wailing.

"Would you stop that caterwauling!" said her grandmother, moving across the kitchen with murderous intent. "This can easily be resolved."

She came back with a bread knife.

"Pass me that doll."

Alma was retching with laughter. Tears leaving wet blue runs on her white skin, like streaks of toilet cleaner on the enamel of a lavatory bowl.

"No," she was saying. "Please, no. This is too much."

Connie remembers picking the doll up by the arm and passing it up to her grandmother. Her wailing had stopped and in its place was a sticky, breathless curiosity.

186

Her grandmother laid the doll down on the kitchen table and, using a rapid sawing motion, she removed the offending penis, slipping it into the pocket of her voluminous skirt. She handed the doll back to Connie.

"Now," she said. "Problem solved."

Connie shook her head.

"I don't want it."

"Don't be ridiculous. It's exactly the same now as the other doll."

Again, Connie shook her head.

"I don't want it."

And so they stood facing each other in the kitchen, Connie aged seven, and her grandmother aged fifty-seven, and one of them more determined than the other. They would have been standing there all night if the standoff had not been resolved by Nora. Six years old and already a peacemaker, she came forward with her own doll and offered it to Connie.

And so it came to pass that Connie got the girl doll, with her pale pink Babygro and her discreetly featureless plastic bum. Nora took the poor butchered boy doll, with his blue Babygro and underneath it a tiny rough-edged crater where his little plastic penis should have been. But life would have its revenge on Connie, by visiting on her two boy babies, one after the other, as living reincarnations of that poor rejected boy doll.

Connie turned her key carefully in the front door, anxious not to make the slightest noise that might wake the boys. She slipped her feet out of her shoes and picked them up, using her fingers as a prong. With her huge fake fur muffling her movements, she swept through the living room and into the small kitchen at the back of the house. Moonlight was streaming in the back window, throwing a melancholy glow over the dinner dishes that were stacked in the sink where she had left them. A red light flashed on the washing machine where a load had finished but not been unpacked. A carton of milk stood on the counter with a spill leading away from it like a snail trail. The kettle was off its moorings and a bottle cap lay where it had fallen on the kitchen floor. Connie sighed, wondering for the hundredth time how it was possible for anyone to create such a mess heating up a single baby's bottle.

She crept up the stairs, stopping on the landing to peek into the boys' room, where, by the blue light of the nightlight, she saw Oscar asleep in his cot. With his knees pulled up under his chest and his bum in the air, he looked like a Muslim at prayer. Ernie was splayed out in his little bed with the covers thrown off him and his dinosaur pyjamas all a-tangle. His hair was matted with sweat and in his right fist he was clutching a small plastic figurine he had found in the playground — a miniature Woody from *Toy Story*. He had refused to let it out of his hand ever since. Connie stood for a moment in the doorway and watched her sons sleeping. She would have liked to kiss them, but she was afraid of waking them. Softly, she stepped back out on to the landing, leaving the door of their room ajar.

The light in her bedroom was on but Emmet was fast asleep, an open copy of a book about Lance Armstrong slumped face down on his chest — Connie had given it to him for Christmas but he never seemed to be able to get past the first page without passing out. She plucked the book off him, closing it and sliding it on to his bedside table. She shrugged her coat off and then her cardigan, climbing out of her leggings and tossing them on to the chair in the corner. Without even bothering to put on a nightdress, she climbed into the warm bed in her T-shirt and knickers, pulling the bobbin out of her hair and dropping it on the floor before reaching out to turn off the light.

She had only been out of the house for an hour or two, but she felt as if she had returned home from a long journey. The echoes of the evening's revelations lapping over her like waves, a sense of clouds and sky over her head, a feeling of water moving all about her, she could have been lying on a darkened beach, or in the bottom of a boat, instead of in her own bed.

She curled over on to her side for comfort, and Emmet fell in behind her, nuzzling his chin into the curve of her collarbone. Connie was reminded of those fortune-telling fish that you hold in the palm of your hand. The way they curl up is supposed to tell you something about yourself. She lay there trying to remember what it was those fish were supposed to tell you, but she was so tired that she fell asleep without ever remembering.

At some point during the night, Connie wakes to the sound of a small boy calling out in the dark. She cocks her ears and listens out for which of them it might be, identifying the cry as Ernie's. Glancing over briefly at her husband, who is fast asleep (or pretending to be), she leaps out of the bed, anxious to get to the child before he goes and wakes his brother.

Ever since the boys arrived — one after the other in the space of less than two years — sleep has become the dominating force in Connie's house. Sleep, and the lack of it, is what governs Connie and Emmet's relationship. It has become the currency of their marriage — a small stack of casino chips that they barter with each other, exchanging an extra hour in bed for a sexual favour or a night on the town. Like water that has become dangerously scarce, what little sleep that is available is measured out between them with meticulous precision, each of them guarding their own share with a primitive ferocity.

In the four years since they became parents, there has been only a handful of occasions when they have both slept through the night. Between the colic and the teething, between the nightmares and the head colds and the barking dogs and the mating cats and the car alarms going off out on the street, there is seldom a night that one or the other of the boys doesn't wake up. And while at first Connie and Emmet took it in turns to get up — in the beginning, Emmet even helped with the night feeds — now that he is trying to finish his book, on top of teaching full-time, Connie feels in all conscience that he needs his night's sleep. So, tired as she is, when she hears Ernie calling out for her in the dark, Connie hauls herself out of bed and staggers into his room.

The room is sealed off from the world by blackout curtains, the nightlight throwing outsize fish shapes across the walls. Ernie's eyes are wide open, his pupils pinned. "There was a wolf," he says. In Ernie's dreams, there is always a wolf.

"There aren't any wolves in Ireland," whispers Connie, settling herself down on the bare floorboards beside his bed. Her back against the clammy wall, she slides her hand under the duvet to reassure her child.

"It's only a dream," she says, closing her eyes and using her own breathing to still his, her own hand to cool his; whether it works or not she doesn't know, because she falls asleep before him.

Some time later — Connie has no way of knowing how long, but it's still dark outside — she wakes to find herself sprawled on the floor. A crick in her neck; her shoulder hurts where it's been resting on the wooden boards. Her nose and toes are frozen to snapping point. Terrified of waking the boys, she crawls out of the room on her hands and knees, aware even as she is doing so of the absurdity of the situation she finds herself in. Nothing matters so long as she makes it back to her own bed without waking them.

"Mum."

She keeps her eyes closed for a few seconds, maybe even for as long as a minute, as some hopeful part of her brain clings to the possibility that he might go away again if she doesn't open them.

"Mummy," he says. "Mummy. Wake up."

He's pulling at her arm now, using all the weight of his stocky little body to haul on her, as if he were attempting to pull a large boat out of the water.

"Stop it," she says, opening her eyes to glare at him. "Get off me." In her irritation, she sounds like a small child herself.

"Mum, I'm hungry."

"I'm coming." she says. "You go on down and turn on the telly."

As she passes out of the room, she looks back and sees that her husband is curled up on his side. His face buried in a mound of pillows, he is sound asleep. In Connie's head, a stopwatch begins to count the seconds that he remains asleep while she herself is awake. She pads down the steep stairs to the living room, awarding herself a point for every creaking step. With every toy she stoops to pick up, with every movement of her exhausted limbs, her sense of martyrdom grows. When she steps on a small piece of Lego, the pain only serves as proof of her misery.

"Fuck, fuck, fuck," she says as she rubs the ball of her foot. The boys' eyes stare at her sideways from the couch. Another second and their eyes slide back to the TV.

Moving across the room, Connie trips over a phone charger and curses again. She bends down and yanks the charger out of the wall. A temper raging in her, she wants to throw it across the room. Instead she slams it down on the desk, shocked to find herself up against the limits of her own personality. Forbearance, patience, calm — Connie understands these things now. She understands why they are virtues.

In the kitchen, she heats some porridge and serves it up to the boys in front of the TV. She cleans off the kitchen counter and sweeps the kitchen floor. In her mind she's totting up all the jobs she's done in the house already today, measuring her tally of household chores against Emmet's. Every time she puts out a bin bag, every time she bends over to pick up a pair of dirty underpants or wipe the pee stains off the toilet seat, the resentment sloshes around in her heart. Even as she's hating him, she hates this in herself. Never in her wildest dreams did Connie think she would ever turn into this kind of woman.

Connie, who always *preferred* the company of men to that of women. She couldn't wait to get out of school, smothered by that all-girl environment. It was only when she got to college that she found herself in her element. As a student of history and politics, she was one of the few women in a class full of earnest young men, and she revelled in being one of the lads while delighting at the same time in not being one of them. She made a point of sitting in the front row of the lecture hall, taking copious notes in green ink, before swinging her neat little bum back up the auditorium steps, pretending not to notice the effect she was having on the boys. Her shining hour came during a presentation on the causes of the American Civil War, when she set out a complicated analogy likening the countdown to the conflict to a game of strip poker between North and South. And if the mention of strip poker by a twenty-two-year-old Connie — wearing her tight black polo neck and her tartan miniskirt — if the mere mention of the word was enough to cause a rise in the temperature of the room, and a few coughs and splutters from the shyer boys, well that was something Connie would have taken no heed of. At that time she was of the view that there was nothing to separate the men and women of her generation.

"The only difference between the men and women of our generation is that the men pee standing up and the women pee sitting down," she argued at a college debate (even though she and a girlfriend had once managed to subvert this rule at an outdoor concert where the queue for the ladies' Portaloo was unmercifully long). Speaking in support of the motion that "Society no longer has a need for feminism", Connie declared that the women of her generation only had themselves to blame if they failed to take up their rightful place in society. Afterwards, in the college bar, between shots of tequila and the flagrant chain-smoking of Marlboro Lights (when Connie looks back on her college days she sees herself always in a cloud of smoke), she made the same case to her class tutor. While her tutor slid his hand up her skirt, Connie told him how future generations would have no need for special courses on women's history because women would be out there making history for themselves, an argument that seemed only to heighten the tutor's admiration for her, driving his hand further up her thigh and his tongue into her ear.

The boy wonder of the history department, he was just back from Oxford with his newly earned PhD (a study of the Irish chaplains who served in the First World War). With his never-brushed hair and his murky green eyes — eyes the colour of an empty wine bottle with the light shining through — Emmet brought a touch of rock-star glamour into the fossilised atmosphere of the history department. Heavily made-up girls lined the front rows of all his lectures; the same girls were to be found leaning against the wall outside his office, or sitting cross-legged on the floor waiting for him to come out, while back in his rooms Connie lay naked in his bed. That was where she spent most of her final year, smoking cigarettes and reading novels and listening to Emmet's music collection, when she should have been in the library. When her final results came through, she had earned herself not the first she had once hoped for, but a bare 2.1. But by then she and Emmet had moved in together, taking a one-year lease on a small flat above a Lebanese restaurant on Camden Street, and the loss of that elusive first seemed a small price to pay for love.

Oh, Connie, she says to herself now, as she stuffs another load of his dirty socks and knickers into the washing machine, slamming the door so hard that for a minute she's afraid she's broken the catch. Connie, Connie, Connie. How could you have let this happen to you?

"Hey," he says, when he comes down the stairs just after nine.

Freshly showered and wearing blue jeans and a white shirt, with a pea-green lambswool jumper his mother gave him for his birthday, he smells of peppermint toothpaste and suds, his hair wet and dark. He comes into the kitchen and picks an apple out of the fruit bowl for his breakfast. He looks so handsome, and so clean, that Connie can't help but fancy him. In her oversized cardigan and her grubby T-shirt, she feels like a slob. Hair unbrushed, mascara down around her cheekbones, her hands are in the sudsy water, fondling last night's dishes.

"Well?" he says, teasing her with his eyes.

"Well," she says, determined to match him monosyllable for monosyllable.

He comes up behind her and slips a hand under her cardigan, taking hold of her right bum cheek and squeezing it. He snakes the other hand round her waist, sliding it up the front of her chest and taking her right breast lightly in the palm of his hand, with his fingers splayed on either side of her nipple, and his lips worrying the back of her neck. Hands submerged in the warm, wet sink, she's shackled by him. She closes her eyes for a second, breathing in the smooth, clean feel of him.

"How about a ride?" he whispers into her ear.

"How about an elbow in the goolies," she says, pushing him away from her with her hip as she takes another plate out of the sink and stows it on the drying rack. Drip, drip, drip. She hears him laughing as he moves out into the living room. He's gathering up his papers and stuffing them into his laptop bag, in preparation for the day at his mother's house. His mother has created a special workspace for him in her dining room. She stocks up on the coffee he drinks and the biscuits he likes, all in the service of the great book. A book he needs to write if he's ever going to get tenure — if he's ever going to make professor, which is what Emmet fully intends to be.

"You could always take the day off," says Connie, leaning her head back and throwing her voice after him. "It is a Sunday, after all."

Of all the days that she spends alone, it's the Sundays that she finds the hardest.

"Come on, Connie. You know I can't."

And of course, she does know. She knows that his deadline is only six months away. That the book has to be ready for next year's centenary of the start of the war. That it would have been written years ago if it wasn't for her and the boys . . .

"I know," she says. "I know."

He hovers in the kitchen doorway.

"So, what was the drama?" He has his laptop bag in one hand, his bicycle helmet in the other. "Last night, what was the big drama?"

"Oh," says Connie. "It's a long story. I'll tell you later."

As he leaves, she hears him call out a goodbye to the boys. She hears the door close behind him and is overcome by despair. The day ahead of her seems impossibly long. The task of filling it impossibly arduous, a task made all the more difficult by the boys' racing reserves of energy. By her own epic exhaustion.

An exhaustion that lies in wait for her every morning when she wakes up; it follows her around all day, hanging like lead weights off the hem of her clothes, constantly trying to pull her down. She recharges herself with coffee, enjoying a brief burst of energy before she goes flat again. She eats, and experiences a short sugar burst, which dips again after half an hour, leaving her more tired than she was before. Like a woman in danger of being washed away by raging flood waters, she grabs on to any piece of driftwood she can find to steady herself. A mug of tea, a bar of chocolate, a sneaky cigarette. Anything that might give her the strength to muddle through another hour of another interminable day.

Keep swimming, she tells herself, channelling Dory in *Finding Nemo*. Keep swimming, keep swimming. Sometimes it seems like all she has in her head these days are cartoons.

She was folding the washing when her phone rang. Her mother's number on the screen — as soon as Connie saw it, she wondered had her mother changed her mind. Too late if so, the e-mail was already gone — Connie had typed it up and sent it off ten minutes ago.

"So, they rang me."

"Okay," said Connie. "We were expecting that. What did they say?"

"It was a woman. She wanted to know if the letter was genuine."

"Well, that's fair enough. Did she ask you anything else?"

"She asked me if your father knew about it." (Always "your father", never Liam.)

"And what did you say?"

"I said I would prefer if he wasn't told."

Connie had a vision of the news conference, and the discussion that would inevitably take place.

"Was that it?"

"No. Someone else rang me back afterwards."

"Probably a reporter."

Acushla's voice broke through with a question, as tentative as a puff of smoke.

"Do you think they'll print it?"

Connie paused, not quite sure how to answer. A confession from the wife of a former minister that she had travelled to England for an abortion, in contravention of the protection accorded to the unborn by the constitution? *Of course* they would print it. Just try and stop them. She began to wonder did her mum have any idea what she was getting herself into?

"Oh, they'll print it all right," she said gently. "There's no question, Mum, but they'll print it." (They would run a news story too, most likely on the front page, but Connie thought it better not to mention that yet.) "You're not getting cold feet, are you?"

"No," said her mum, with too much emphasis in her voice. She sounded like she was trying to convince herself. "No, no. I want to do this."

Connie wedged her mobile in between her shoulder and her ear so that she could get on with folding the dry clothes while she was talking.

"Okay," she said. "Because it's not too late to pull out if you don't want to."

She was holding a pair of Ernie's trousers up against her belly, running the palm of her hand over them to flatten out the kinks. She folded them over once, twice, and set them down on the kitchen table, taking care to keep them well clear of the jam spill she had failed until now to notice.

"No, I do want to," said her mother. Her voice had a disjointed quality to it, which led Connie to think she'd taken a Valium. "It's just . . . I don't know. It's just that I'm nervous, I suppose."

Connie plucked a T-shirt of Emmet's off the clothes horse as she listened. She pinned it to her chest with her chin. Taking the sleeves, she doubled them towards the centre. Folded the T-shirt over twice and set it down on the table.

"I don't know how people will react," her mother was saying. "I'm a bit nervous, I suppose, about people's reactions."

Connie reached deep inside herself, trying to find the energy to give her mother the encouragement she needed.

"I think you'll be surprised," she said, "how sympathetic people will be. You'll get great support from people once they know."

She picked up a pair of Emmet's boxer shorts, fastening the single button on the crotch before folding them over.

"When are they going to publish it?"

"They're talking about tomorrow. Tomorrow is the day."

"What about Dad? Are you worried about how he's going to react when it's published?"

"No!" said her mum defiantly, her voice skittering off the word. "No, I know how he'll react. He'll hit the roof."

And whereas before it had seemed to Connie that there was fear in her mother's voice, and trepidation, whereas a moment ago she had sensed a pitiful anxiety about how people would react, the mention of her father seemed to have invoked a spirit of brinksmanship in her. It occurred to Connie that perhaps her mother's new-found activism was not about women's rights, or women's freedoms and men's role in suppressing them. Perhaps it was just about one man and one woman, and the endlessly unhappy dance they were leading each other, a dance that would continue, most likely, long after this storm had passed. The thought of it made Connie feel sad and faintly sick.

After her mother had gone off the line, she stood in the kitchen for a moment, with the phone cradled in the crook of her neck. She wondered what to do with the stray sock she was holding. Three times already this sock had gone through the wash, and still Connie couldn't find its partner. Holding it with the tips of two fingers as if it were a dead mouse, she dropped it into the bin.

One thing about living with three men is the amount of socks they have. Another thing is the amount of shoes.

You'd swear you were living with a family of octopuses. Octopi? Whatever. Connie seems to spend her life putting away shoes.

Everywhere she looks there are runners strewn about the floor. A pair of small red wellies abandoned inside the front door. A single sandal peeping out from between the cushions of the couch. There are slippers in the log basket and Crocs in the toy trunk; a pair of Emmet's leather brogues sitting neatly side by side on the floor at the foot of the armchair, as if the person who was wearing them had spontaneously combusted, leaving only their shoes behind them.

In a frenzy, Connie goes around the house piling shoes high in her arms like firewood. When she's gathered them all up, she finds there's nowhere to put them. She stands in the middle of her tiny house, trying to create by sheer force of desire some new storage space where none exists. Walking over to the playpen, she bends down, releases her arms and a cascade of shoes tumbles out.

The idea of the playpen was that the boys would play happily in it and Connie would sit at the table and do some work, but it has turned out the other way around. Often of a morning Connie will climb into the playpen with her laptop while the boys have the run of the house. Her latest innovation is to upend a box of cornflakes on to the kitchen tiles and let them turn the cornflakes into a quarry, running their diggers through them and shunting them around the floor, grinding the cereal into dust with the knees of their corduroy trousers. The cost of a box of cornflakes is less than two euro. The clean-up time, ten minutes of vigorous sweeping or five minutes with the hoover. The time bought, as much as an hour. If she's focused about it, she can get her blog written in the space of an hour.

Connie writes a weekly blog, which she distributes to her modest Twitter following. She produces the occasional feature article for one of the national newspapers, where the editor is someone Alma knows. She conducts potted interviews by e-mail, quizzing minor celebrities about the silliest of things (What items are always to be found in your fridge? What's your favourite smell?). And while it's not exactly the career she once had in mind for herself — a career with a regular pay cheque, and colleagues, and lunch — the cost of childcare makes it unfeasible for her to work outside the home. With a house in negative equity to the tune of two hundred thousand euro, and four people to feed on a junior lecturer's salary, Connie's career is a luxury that, for the moment at least, they cannot afford.

Out in front of the house there's a stagnant river, and between the house and the river there's a green area, and it's there that Connie brings the boys to burn up some time. With a mug of tea in her hand and the sun on her face, she watches them at play, a warm weight settling over her like a mosquito net, creating a thin veil between her and the world.

A dog emerges from one of the houses and the boys make a beeline for it.

"Wait, guys. Be careful," says Connie. But her voice sounds thin and unconvincing, like Willy Wonka. Stop. Don't. Come back.

Already the boys are throwing a stick for the dog. The dog fetches the stick and comes back with it and Ernie tries to wrestle it from his mouth while Oscar tries to mount the animal like a horse. Connie calls out to him.

"Oscar. Don't torment that poor creature."

But her words might as well be thoughts for all the impact they have. They might as well be speech bubbles, floating away in the air. Above the river wall the seagulls are wheeling, letting out heartbroken cries as they plummet. A woman on the bridge is throwing bread for them, and above the woman's head sits the stadium, like a big hairdryer hood. "The bedpan" the locals call it. But then the locals have a name for everything.

"Nice day for it," says Connie's neighbour, stepping out of her house and yanking her shopping trolley over the threshold after her. A birdlike woman with twig-thin legs that end in big bird feet, she is well into her eighties but still as fit as a fiddle.

"Amazing," says Connie, smiling up at her.

"They're saying we're in for a good summer," says the neighbour.

"We don't get good summers."

"I'm telling you. The fella was on the radio this morning. He says the good weather's here 'til September."

"I'll believe it when I see it," says Connie. "After everything we've suffered these last few years, a proper summer is exactly what we need, seeing as none of us can afford to leave the country."

Five years since Connie has had a holiday, and she finds herself craving the heat.

"Well in anyway," says the neighbour, tucking her chin into her neck, "it'll save on the gas bills."

The neighbour trundles off down the road, dragging her trolley after her, and Connie closes her eyes to savour the sunshine. With her eyes shut, the light becomes liquid, pooling around her. From what seems like very far away, she hears wailing. Is it Ernie? she wonders. Or Oscar? It takes her a second to decide. She opens her eyes to see her youngest falling across the grass towards her.

He tumbles into her arms, his skull as hard as a nut under her chin, his tears big wet smears on the skin of her hand. Wrapping her arms around his squidgy belly, Connie feels so full of love for him that she could burst. She pulls him into her, burying her face in the hollow at the back of his neck and kissing him there over and over again. It's only when he's had a fall that she gets to kiss him like this.

"My baby," she says, breathing in the powdery smell behind his ear. The word sends a jolt through him. He stiffens and fights to get free of her.

Connie wrinkles her nose.

"Ah, not again," she says, bending down to inspect the soles of his shoes.

"Shit," she says, without a trace of irony. "Shit, shit, shit, shit, shit."

She prises his left shoe off him and carries it into the front garden. Picking up a toothbrush that she keeps on the windowsill for this very purpose, and holding the sole of the shoe under the outside tap, she begins to work the dog shit out of the grooves of the runners. Her movements are driven by rage. Rage against the faceless dog owners who don't pick up after their dogs; rage against Dublin City Council, who don't enforce the fines against the dog owners who don't pick up after their dogs; rage against her husband, who at this moment is sitting at his desk in his mother's house eating chocolate biscuits. Fucking asshole, she says to herself, as she scrubs the side of the shoe and holds it under the tap, turning her face away to avoid the fine spray of shitty water that bounces back off its surface. Asshole, she says again, addressing her husband in her mind. For some reason, it seems clear to her that this is all his fault.

A beep sounded loud and close and Connie looked up to see her mum's car rolling up to the door.

"I thought we'd get some coffees and go to the playground," she said through the open car window. "I need to find some way of putting in the day."

Not for the first time, Connie was grateful for her company.

"Hang on," she said, dashing into the house to grab her handbag. Keys, spare nappies, baby wipes . . . She pulled the door behind her. Already the boys were scrambling into the back of their granny's car, clambering over the large overnight bag that was there. Opening the passenger door, Connie had to move a leather vanity case that occupied the front footwell along with several pairs of shoes.

"Why am I getting a *Thelma and Louise* feeling about this?" She looked sideways at her mum and saw her eyelashes wobbling away behind her sunglasses.

"I thought it might be best if I stayed with your grandmother for a few days."

She was looking up at the rear-view mirror as she pulled out. Her nails were displayed like pale pink shells along the steering wheel; the large dress ring she was wearing on her right hand threw off shards of coloured light.

"Is that Grandmother's ring?" asked Connie, even though there was no doubt in her mind that it was.

"Oh," said her mum, still looking into the mirror as she answered. "She gave it to me. She can't wear it any more — her fingers are too puffy."

"Right," said Connie, thinking uneasily of the picture her grandmother had given her the last time she visited — a print by a well-known Irish artist. Connie knew it to be of some value so she had tried to refuse it, but her grandmother had insisted. "I *want* you to have it," she had said, in a high, airy voice. "Who knows who might get their hands on it after I'm gone."

"You don't think she's losing her marbles, do you? It's very unlike her to be giving stuff away."

Connie's grandmother had always guarded her few precious possessions so fiercely. Only once had Connie and Nora ever been allowed to play with her jewellery, and even then she had hovered over them making sure nothing went astray.

"I suppose she's just getting old," said Acushla, with a shrug in her voice.

From the back of the car Connie could hear Ernie counting cars. Oscar was pretending to count too, repeating the numbers he'd heard coming out of his brother's mouth but in a random sequence. Connie closed her eyes to quell the sense she had of some nebulous dread.

The playground was swirling with children when they arrived. Connie opened the gate, and the boys disappeared in amongst them. She bolted the gate behind her and followed her mum over to a picnic table.

"So," she said. "I suppose there's nothing for us to do now but wait."

Her mother sat with her shoulders slumped forward, her hands hugging her coffee cup. An oyster-coloured pashmina was draped elegantly over her shoulders. Her eyes were blinking shadows behind her sunglasses.

"I feel a bit bad," she said. "Sneaking out on your father like that."

"Oh, come on, Mum. It's no more than he deserves."

The more Connie thought about it, the more it seemed to her it was the very least he deserved.

Her mum sighed. "I suppose."

"I feel like such an idiot," said Connie, "for taking his side all those years."

She cringes with shame as she thinks of it, what a daddy's girl she was.

"You adored your dad," said her mum with a weak smile. "It was never my desire to come between the two of you."

"I know," said Connie. When the truth was that her mother never could have come between them, even if she had wanted to. There was nobody could have come between Connie and her dad.

In her mother's presence Connie was a serious child, imperious and bossy, but as soon as her father came in the door, he brought a sea breeze with him, whipping Connie into peaks of giddy froth. The less time he spent at home, the more Connie delighted in his presence. On the many, many nights when he was out at some constituency event or other, Connie would insist on waiting downstairs for him, falling asleep on the couch in the breakfast room while her mother moved about the kitchen completing her chores. The next thing Connie knew, her father would be scooping her up in his arms and carrying her up the stairs. As he slid her into her own bed, she would curl up between the cold sheets like a little guard dog who was finally off duty now that her master was home.

In later years her dad used to take her on his rounds of the doorsteps on Saturday mornings. She would hand out election leaflets, and nod and smile as he promised to help someone skip a hospital waiting list, or dodge a prison sentence by grace of his intervention. The evident devotion of his daughter was a subtle vote-getter, and something that would not have been lost on him, not for one moment. When he was appointed to Cabinet for the third time, it was Connie who accompanied him to the start of the new Dáil term. She got a new dress for the occasion and a new pair of patent pumps, and her picture was in all the papers the next day. (Her mother was at home in bed with a sore throat — an excuse that in retrospect seemed a bit thin to Connie, but then in retrospect there were so many things that suddenly made sense.)

"Oh, God," she said. "I was such a little misogynist!"

Remembering how she loved being with her father. How she preferred her grandfather's company to her grandmother's. It was Connie's grandfather who taught her to play draughts, challenging her to epic tournaments that swallowed up entire rainy afternoons, while Sam sat by the window painting. He always had a stash of chocolate in the top left-hand drawer of his desk, and it was he who taught her to dip the end of a Time Out into her mug and use it as a straw. ("I don't normally subscribe to these new-fangled confections," he would say, "but I have to make an exception for Time Out. It's a magnificent addition to the repertoire.") Connie has such happy memories of those lovely, languorous afternoons at her grandfather's dining table, with a large Latin dictionary wedged in under her bum, and her shoes hanging like lead weights off her dangling legs, with her grandfather's old-time music swirling in the air and his smirking blue eyes watching her as she huffed him. A sense of comradeship between them, as if they were on the same side in the game of life.

And they *were* on the same side, that was the truth of it. Before she even knew there were sides, Connie had sided with her grandfather. Treacherous little girl that she was, she had sided with her father. She had sided with the entire male population over the female. Because women, it seemed to Connie, were always complaining about something. They were always bickering with each other, or bitching, and if they weren't crying about something they were mounting a silent protest, one that only they knew the logic of. And it seemed to Connie that there was some disposition to unhappiness in the women of her family, some determination to be unhappy that must be located somewhere on the second X chromosome. The men seemed so much happier than the women, and so much more fun to be around.

"Mum—" she started to say, but she was interrupted by the sound of a child calling out to her.

"Mum!" It was Ernie, from the top of the slide. He was standing gripping the handrails with his little fists. His solemn face searching out hers for approbation. Connie gave him a circus smile and a thumbs-up.

"Ah, God," she said as she turned back to her mum. "Wouldn't that melt your heart."

"He's a darling," said her mum, and it seemed to Connie that in their love for the boys they were in perfect tune with each other. All the little things that mattered to Connie — the visceral fear of a fever, the momentousness of a newly glimpsed tooth, the joy in kissing the velvety sole of a baby's foot — her mother understood all these things. Her mother supported her, slipping her small gifts of cash to pay for make-up or a haircut. She helped her with babysitting, taking up the slack wordlessly whenever Connie needed her, whereas her father seemed to be talking to her in another register, about all the things they used to talk about before she had babies, things that were so remote to Connie now that she could barely hear him . . .

"You know you've been a great mum to me," she said, leaning forward to search out her mother's eyes behind her sunglasses. "You do know that, don't you? Nobody could have been a better mum."

Her mother tilted her head to one side and sighed.

"I do my best," she said. "Just like you do, darling. You try to be the best mother you can be . . ."

And Connie was about to answer her when something occurred to her.

"Hang on," she said. "Where's Oscar gone?"

A moment of playground panic; a second went by, and then another second, before she located him, waiting for a little girl to vacate a swing. He had his hand down the front of his trousers to fondle himself. ("Captain Elastic" Emmett liked to call him, because he seemed never to tire of stretching his little penis out like bubble gum, to see how far it would go.)

"Oh, Jesus," said Connie, covering her mouth with her hand. "Would you look at my son."

Her mum took in the sight of Oscar, and bit her lip and smiled. As she turned back to Connie, the smile turned into a laugh, tears forming in her eyes as she shook her head helplessly from side to side. Connie began to laugh with her, the two of them shaking with speechless laughter so that at first neither of them noticed that Connie's phone was ringing. It was hopping up and down on the surface of the picnic table. The screen displayed a photograph of Connie's father's face. A red receiver icon and a green receiver icon, inviting her to accept or reject the call. Still breathless from laughing, Connie reached out to reject it.

It was early afternoon by the time they got back to the house.

"Can we bake?" asked the boys as soon as they were in the door.

"Jesus, lads. We're only just back from the park. Would you not think of having a nap?"

Their two little faces turned up to hers in expectation of disappointment. For weeks she'd been promising them they could bake. For weeks she'd been postponing the promise. Maybe later, she would say, maybe tomorrow. Hoping they would forget about it, but of course they didn't.

"You promised us we could bake."

"All right," she said wearily. "Let's bake."

So here they were, standing precariously on a pair of kitchen chairs, with adult-sized aprons tied twice around their bellies and wooden spoons in their hands. Flour in their hair, and in their eyebrows and their eyelashes, flour in every crevice of their clothing. With their cheeks flaming and their eyes wide and serious from the task at hand, they were blithely unaware of the spectacle they presented.

Connie was just about to put the tray of cookies into the oven when she saw a sudden movement in the corner of the room. She froze with the tray in her hand. She saw, but did not react. For a second, maybe two, she stood and stared at the rat. The rat sat and stared back. Connie dropped the cookie tray and screamed.

In one swooping movement she hooked a child under each arm and climbed up on to the couch. She managed to reach for her mobile, which was on the table. Stabbed at Emmet's number; the phone rang three times and went through to voicemail. She rang his number again, and again the phone went through to voicemail. Again and again she rang, picturing the tally of missed calls mounting on the face of his phone, a measure of her growing hysteria. Seven calls she made, and still the rat sat in the corner of the kitchen, picking away at a stray crumb of cookie dough.

Connie decided to make a run for it. She hefted a child on to each hip and made for the door, her bare feet barely touching the floor, as if she was running through a pit of flames. She slammed the front door behind her and threw the boys into the back of her little car, climbing into the front seat herself and starting it up. The soles of her feet naked on the pedals.

On the way to Emmet's mother's house, she kept trying his number. With each unanswered call she chalked up another black mark against him. By the time she had pulled up outside the house, she had scored twenty-seven unanswered calls. She rang on the side door, but again she got no answer. She bent down and retrieved the spare key from under the mat, letting herself into the dark hall. Turning the boys loose on their granny's fridge, she made her way up the stairs to the first floor, driven now by fury. The interconnecting reception rooms were deserted, sunlight streaming in through the back window, throwing a lopsided rectangle of light across the pale carpet. The dining room table was piled high with Emmet's books, but there were no signs of recent industry. No coffee cups, no loose notes, no uncapped pens. With something approaching relish, Connie crept up the stairs to the second floor. Past the framed portrait of Emmet in his graduation robes, his parents standing proudly on either side of him. Past a mosaic of family wedding photographs. She took in her own with a single withering glance as she charged by.

She found him in his old room. The bedroom door was ajar, and through the opening Connie could see the bottom half of his body lying on top of the single bed in all his clothes. She could hear the television, with a sound coming out of it like a swarm of angry bees; she recognised it as the drone of racing cars looping a track. Gingerly, she stepped around the open door and saw that he was fast asleep, the remote control lying on his belly and his hand placed protectively over it.

"At least he was on his own," said her friend Orla, palm clamped to her chest with relief. "I thought you were going to tell me there was another woman in the bed with him."

A pale dream of a girl, Orla's skin was stretched so thinly over the fine bones of her face as to be almost transparent. Delicate colours moved beneath the surface. At one time a coral-pink flush would show, high up on her cheekbones; another time it was the blue veins you would notice, marbling her eyelids and her temples, and again, the purple shadows under her eyes.

"But that's the worst of it!" said Connie, putting her daiquiri glass down on the low table for a moment and looking around at her friends. (It seemed clear to her that the only thing to do under the circumstances was to get drunk.) "I think I'd have preferred to find him in bed with another woman. For all the action he gets these days, I'd have *understood* if he was sleeping with another woman. I'd have understood if he was sleeping with another *man*. I swear to God, I'm so knackered, I wouldn't care. It's the fact that he was sleeping alone, that's what I can't forgive. The thought of all that delicious sleep. I don't see how I'm ever going to forgive him."

"Hard to see," said Rachel, shaking her head. The only one of them who was still single, Rachel could be relied upon to take a hard line against male trans-gressions.

"I'd kill him," said Trish. "If Ross did that to me, I'd murder him." (Ross who can't keep his hands off other women when he's had a few drinks. Ross who once asked Connie did she like it up the ass. I'd want to kill him too, thought Connie. If I was married to Ross, I'd happily kill him.)

"The only problem with killing him," said Orla, in her reedy voice, "is that you'd be left minding the boys on your own, which would be a bit of an own goal."

"Oh, I've no intention of killing him," said Connie, with all the command of a hanging judge. "The punishment I have in mind is much slower and more painful. I intend to make him pay me back for all the sleep he's been stealing from me."

Bending down to pucker her lips over the tip of her straw, she drained the last of her frozen daiquiri in one long slurp, sending a glacier at breakneck speed through the cavities of her skull. Even as she was gasping with the pain, she was raising her hand to order another round.

"There should be some kind of warning," she said, after they'd moved on to the next bar. They were standing outside on the street, smoking Rachel's cigarettes, even though the rest of them were supposed to have given up. "They should have a public health campaign," she went on as she lit up. "People should be warned about the dangers of marriage."

"It's not possible for men and women to live together happily," she said to Rachel in the nightclub. The others seemed to have disappeared, leaving just the two of them slumped side by side on a velvet couch. "I don't know a single couple who manage to cohabit happily."

She was stunned by the clarity of this thought.

"I swear to God, I can't think of anyone I know who has a happy marriage!" (Her grandfather was the only person Connie could think of who was in a happy relationship, which said something in and of itself about relations between men and women.)

"What about your parents?" asked Rachel, confused. "I thought your parents were still married."

"Ah," said Connie, thinking of the reams of newsprint that must even now be reeling off the great printing presses in the west of the city. Corralling her slurred thoughts into line, she made a mental note to buy the newspaper on her way home. She imagined how she would wobble into the Spar while her taxi meter ticked away outside. She would squint at the small print in the dark back seat of the taxi, not sure if it was the darkness or the drink that was preventing her from reading it. Already she could imagine exactly what it would say.

FORMER MINISTER'S WIFE BREAKS SILENCE ON ABORTION

Liam

Liam endured a night riddled with dreams.

Normally he tended to dream only when he was travelling, or when he was sick, but for some reason on this occasion he was assailed by dreams all night long. He dreamt first of his father. A strangely prosaic dream whereby he and his father were tending a bonfire in an oil barrel in the corner of the garden. (Back then you could still light a bonfire, something Liam's own government would later move to ban, relegating one of the great pleasures of his youth to the realm of nostalgia.) Often of a summer evening Liam's father used to make a bonfire for all the packaging waste from the kitchen, tossing it on to the flames with all the absorption of a child playing with matches. In the dream, Liam and his father stood admiring the curious colours thrown up by the melting plastic, and Liam could feel his face being roasted by the flames while at his back the chill crept in from the darkening woods around him. There was no smell in the dream, only swirls of thick smoke distorting the air and the sense of his father standing beside him, solid as a tree, with his boots planted firmly in the gravel.

Without warning, the dream morphed into a nightmare. Liam was turning the compost heap over with a pitchfork when he came across his father's body. A flesh-covered hand in the early stages of decomposition, like the body of the farmyard dog that Liam had encountered in the compost heap one spring morning, warm and steamy after a whole winter of being dead.

"Jesus!"

He sat up in the bed, choking on his own breath. Eyes wide and staring, his brain tumbling through time. He turned towards his wife for ballast, only to find the bed empty beside him. He checked his watch and saw that it was almost three, which was late for Acushla to be home but not so late as to worry him. He rolled the duvet round himself and curled into the comfort of it, falling straight back into a tunnel of dreams that were all about Acushla. When he woke again, it was just before six and her side of the bed was still empty.

His first thought was that she must have had an accident and that he should ring the Guards. He reached for his phone and was about to dial 999, but first he found himself rehearsing what he would say to them. He would be forced to identify himself, and to explain that his wife had not come home last night, and there would follow all kinds of intrusive questions and innuendo as they tried to come up with sordid scenarios to explain her absence. Putting the phone down again, he leaned over and turned on the radio, hoping to catch the news. If there had been a fatal road accident in the city during the night, or some other catastrophe that might explain why she had not come home, it would surely be on the news. He sat up in bed as he listened to the six o'clock pips.

The first headline was about a tornado in Oklahoma. The second concerned an ongoing scandal about penalty points, and the third referred to the wife of a former minister who had admitted to having had an abortion. It took Liam a moment to realise that the former minister they were referring to was him.

Liam's phone started ringing as the newscaster was reading out the weather forecast (another day of sunshine, announced with a mixture of disbelief and delight). He eyed the phone, identifying without answering them calls from every political correspondent in the country. Calls from the news desks of all the major newspapers, and all the broadcasters. He sat on the edge of his bed, elbows on his bony knees and bare feet planted in the carpet, with his phone in his hand. The minutes slipped by, the phone rang and rang and still Liam sat in his pyjamas on the edge of his bed. Like someone who finds themselves at the bottom of a deep well without a rope, or far out at sea without an oar, he allowed himself the luxury of a period of inaction to wallow in his despair. A despair that seemed so absolute that everything that went before it now paled in comparison. The loss of his seat, even that now seemed little more than a common or garden crisis, and one that could have been overcome. But this . . . it was hard to see how there was any way back from this.

Not since he was a child, sitting cross-legged on the bare boards of their bedroom floor as his brother beat him at snakes and ladders — not since then had he experienced such an abject feeling of defeat. It was all he could do not to cry.

His press officer phoned at thirteen minutes past seven. He must have delayed ringing until he'd listened to *It Says In The Papers*. With a sinking heart, Liam accepted the call.

"Jack," he said.

"All right," said Jack, without any preamble. "*The Irish Times* is leading with it and the *Indo* have it shoehorned into their later edition. RTÉ, Newstalk, Today FM — you name it, they're all over it. And I just got a call from the BBC, which means it's about to travel across the water."

Liam could hear the bounce in Jack's voice. After two years in the wilderness, his phone was hopping again. He was back in business.

"I didn't have a clue," said Liam. "I'm as surprised as you are."

"I figured as much."

That was Jack for you, he always had to be ahead of the curve. God forbid anyone would steal a march on him.

"It was an ambush," said Liam, resting his forehead on his hand. "A fucking ambush is what it was."

And the fact that Liam found himself using the F word, that was an indication of how rattled he was. In a world where profanity sometimes seemed to be a language in and of itself, Liam had always prided himself on keeping his vocabulary clean. Often in the privacy of his own head he would unleash a string of obscenities, but seldom if ever did he allow them to escape out of him.

"I hate to be the one to ask you this," said Jack, with most uncharacteristic hesitancy. "Don't take any offence now, but do you think she's left you?"

Liam raked a hand through his hair.

"That would appear to be the case," he said, hearing the note of self-pity that he had tried but failed to keep out of his voice.

"Do you think she's likely to do any interviews?" persisted Jack. "I have a horrible vision of her turning up on *The Late Late Show* on Friday night."

"How would I know?" said Liam, and this time his voice came out more like a bark. A narky, yappy little bark. "I don't know, Jack," he said, in a whine now. "All these things you're asking me, I don't have the answers to any of them."

He clenched his head with his hands, squeezing the bones of his skull tightly between his fingers, as if it was a football he was trying to burst. His mind was empty of everything but the fact that his wife had left him, taking his career with her.

"Fuck, fuck, fuck, fuck, fuck," he muttered to himself. It was only when he heard Jack's breath on the other end of the phone that he realised he had spoken out loud.

She had no understanding of politics, that was the problem. She was ignorant not just of the nuts and bolts of political life, but of the impulses that drove it. The sense of a big picture, the call to public service, all of that was incomprehensible to Acushla. She was like a peasant living in a medieval village. Her life revolved around a small circle of relationships that were confined within her familial walls. The world outside might as well not have existed, so little did it concern her. She was a creature of the microcosm.

When Liam first ran for public office, in a constituency that was hers by birth rather than his own, his wife was no help to him. She seemed to have no knowledge of the terrain, no insight into local issues, and no contacts worth speaking of. She resisted any suggestions that she take part in the canvass, on the basis that she wouldn't have a clue what to say. On the one occasion that she agreed to hand out election leaflets outside Sunday Mass, she found the experience humiliating and resisted ever doing it again. Absorbed at that time in the potty training of Connie, and in painting the kitchen cupboards a sunflower yellow — a task she insisted on undertaking two weeks before the election, despite Liam's pleas for her to hold off — Acushla made it clear from the start that his political career was nothing to do with her, and if at first she did nothing to hinder it, she did nothing to help either.

Alma was a mighty help, enlisting at his kitchen table amid the paint fumes and the endless cups of instant coffee. Together they worked their way through the electoral register, the way you might work your way through an old orchard, trying to shake every last vote out of it. Alma had a masterful command of the facts and figures, spitting out strings of numbers representing first-preference votes from elections before she was even born, recalling the patterns of transfers and the vagaries of each electoral area; she remembered exactly how many ballots had been cast in each election, and how each of those ballots had played out for each candidate along the magnificent if somewhat eccentric path of the single transferable vote. Late into the night she would wax lyrical about the beauty of the PR system. The wonders of the tally. The drama of the five-day count. Many years later, when Liam became Minister for the Environment and was foisted with the unenviable task of introducing electronic voting to a country enamoured of the paper ballot — a task that would turn into a career-defining fiasco — it was Alma who warned him against it.

"You're making a mistake," she said. "You'll ruin all the fun — surely you of all people would prefer a paper ballot to a bloody machine?"

"You might as well ask the lobster whether he prefers a slow death or a fast one," he said dolefully.

She laughed that laugh of hers that was like a pigeon cooing, and often afterwards she quoted it back to him. "How's life in the lobster tank?" she would ask whenever she ran into him around government buildings. When Liam lost his seat, Alma sent a courier round with a live lobster packaged in a Styrofoam box, thick elastic bands wound around its claws. At the time, Liam failed to see the funny side of it.

"Well," said Mick, with a chuckle in his voice. "Never a dull moment."

226

Instantly Liam was sorry he'd come. He was tempted to turn away again rather than suffer his brother laughing at him. It was infuriating to Liam how Mick managed to find the humour in everything.

His brother's text had caught him at a weak moment. He was standing in his kitchen in the aftermath of the crisis meeting Jack had pulled together. Empty mugs strewn about the table, and half a digestive biscuit languishing on a plate. His phone had for some reason stopped ringing, and while the endless noise had jangled his nerves, the absence of it was almost worse. The sense of something happening behind his back, that was something Liam had always hated. He was standing staring at the phone, waiting for it to ring — he was almost willing it to ring — when he saw a text message come in from Mick.

I'm here if you need me. M.

He was so touched by his brother's gesture of support that he could have cried. Acting on impulse, he grabbed his car keys and drove straight over to Alma's. A house he'd only ever visited on the canvass — standing on the doorstep shooting the breeze with Alma about the latest polls. He had never actually been inside.

"Come on in," said Mick, and reluctantly Liam stepped into the blood-red hall. Framed watercolours of roses on the walls, and on the floor a pale pink carpet. He had the uncomfortable feeling that he was venturing into a strictly female domain.

"Shhh," said Mick, finger to his lips. He led the way down a short flight of steps into the kitchen. "Alma's asleep upstairs."

"Is she all right?"

Mick closed the kitchen door behind them before he answered.

"She's a bit shook. Your man being let out on bail, it was the last thing she needed. She hasn't been sleeping well since."

Liam nodded in reply, but he was having trouble concentrating on what Mick was saying, so preoccupied was he by his own troubles.

"What can I offer you?" Mick was asking. "Coffee? Tea?"

Barefoot and wearing nothing but a pair of jeans and an open-necked shirt, he looked mightily at home.

"I'm all right," said Liam, shaking his head. With his hands in his pockets, and his fingers stroking the inside seams, he walked to the glass-paned back door and peered out into the garden. He turned to see Mick watching him.

"You could at least say something," he said, angry all of a sudden with his brother, although he hardly knew why.

"What do you want me to say?"

"I dunno. That you're surprised, maybe? That you're shocked? Say anything, but don't just stand there looking at me like that."

"I'm not going to pretend to you that I'm surprised," said Mick. "I knew about it already. I've known for a long time."

"Of course. Alma would have told you."

Mick shook his head.

"Actually, it was Acushla told me. A very long time ago, Acushla told me about it."

Liam couldn't believe what he was hearing. A landslide started in his mind, the ground under him falling away.

"When was this?" he asked, grappling for some facts to steady himself.

"About a year after it happened. I bumped into her in town. The poor kid was upset. She needed someone to talk to."

Liam narrowed his eyes as all kinds of images unfurled in his brain. He imagined Acushla in a flood of tears, with Mick bending to comfort her. The next thing he had an image of his wife in his brother's arms. He forced his eyes tight shut, his paranoia spinning out of control. He didn't know what to be thinking.

"What are you doing here?" he muttered under his breath. (That's what his counsellor had told him to say to the negative thoughts. Ask them what they're doing there, said the counsellor, and tell them to go away.) "What are you doing here?" he said again, spitting the words out through gritted teeth. His attention had turned backwards into his own head, and he was only barely aware of his brother standing in front of him.

"Jesus," said Mick, throwing up his hands in a gesture of surrender. "Don't blame the messenger."

Liam stared at him, trying to remember what else the counsellor had told him. Don't get yourself into negative spirals. Don't go over to the dark side.

"I'm sorry," he said, swallowing hard and drawing his hand down over his face, as if he was holding a hot cloth that he could use to wipe away his thoughts and start afresh. When he took his hand away, he saw that Mick was looking at him with alarm.

"Sorry, Mick. I'm a bit upset."

Mick nodded, and this time Liam was glad he didn't say anything.

"It's been a shitty time," he said, hearing the whine come through in his voice again. How he hated that whine; no matter what he did, he couldn't keep it out of his voice. "It's been such a shitty, shitty time," he said. "Do you know, Mick? There are times when I despair of things ever getting better."

"It's the anger," he said. "I've never come across anything like it."

The two of them were sitting in his car outside Alma's house. Mick with his towel and togs rolled up on his lap. Liam with his car keys primed to start the engine. ("Would you not come for a swim?" Mick had asked, offering him the loan of a pair of togs. "You're all right," said Liam. "But I'll drive you out there if you like.")

"Nice jammer," said Mick, as Liam started up the engine. "What is it?"

"A Skoda," said Liam ruefully. "Not that that stopped them from having a go at me."

COLLINS SPLASHES OUT ON FLASH NEW CAR was the headline in one of the tabloids. As if he had any choice but to go out and buy a car. What did they expect him to do, walk everywhere? Gone was the infamous "car with a star"; the Garda driver was also, obviously, gone. Liam was forced to dig out his old driving licence, which had lapsed in the years since he had become a minister. He had to resit the test, a humiliation the tabloids devoured with glee, mocking up pictures of him wearing L plates plastered to his chest and a dunce's cap on his head, under the headline **COLLINS GOES BACK TO SCHOOL**.

"The anger that's out there," he said, as he reversed carefully out of the square. "You've no idea, Mick, what it's been like. It's like they take pleasure in abusing us. The last time I went to a match in the Aviva, I had a pint thrown over me." (Liam was careful always to use the new name of the stadium, in deference to its corporate sponsor.)

"I suppose you can understand it," Mick was saying. "There's a lot of people out there having a tough time."

"Yeah, well that's fair enough, but they act like they had no hand or part in it! The very people who were buying those houses they couldn't afford, the same people who were buying brand-new cars on the never-never, and apartments in Bulgaria, they're the ones who are shouting the loudest!"

Liam could hear his own voice, thin and high-pitched with indignation.

"Yeah, well," said Mick. "It's always easier to blame someone else for your troubles, isn't it?"

He was bent over in the seat, rummaging around in the glove compartment. Liam was about to tell him to take his nose out of his bloody glove compartment when Mick straightened up, brandishing a CD case.

"Dire Straits," he said, and his shoulders were wobbling with laughter as he opened up the case and took the disc out. He shook his head and let out a long sigh of pleasure as he slid the CD into the player. "Oh, Liam. That could not be more fucking appropriate."

Liam steered the car through a roundabout. Taking the two o'clock exit into an industrial wasteland, he peered out at a row of travellers' caravans parked on the verge. A fire burning on the ground. A child wearing nothing but a sagging disposable nappy. Further along the road they drove past a scrapheap, old cars piled high and ready for flattening. A repository for shipping containers; they were stacked one on top of the other like giant Lego bricks. Round the next corner they came upon the sewage plant and then the electricity generating station, and on the other side of the road, the flat blue sea.

"I have to hand it to you," said Liam. "You sure know how to pick a scenic spot for your swim."

Mick laughed.

"I wouldn't mind, but it's your constituency. You're supposed to love every square inch of it."

The fucking cheek of him! This was the guy who had stolen their father's seat out from under Liam's nose. A seat that should by rights have been Liam's. After all, it was Liam who had taken a course in auctioneering with a view to taking over his father's practice in town. It was Liam who took the bus home from college every weekend to help out on the farm. Liam who took an interest in the local news, while Mick rarely bothered to make the trip down from Dublin. When their father died — of a heart attack so sudden that he fell and cracked his head on the tap in the farmyard — it was Liam who found him. There was so much blood on the ground that Liam's first thought was that he'd been stabbed; it was only when the doctor arrived that they discovered the truth. Throughout the three days of the funeral, Liam was so shocked that he hardly knew where he was. And by the time his father was buried and the grave covered over, Mick had it all sorted that he'd be the one to defend the seat in the by-election, on the basis that he was the firstborn, and that was the end of that.

Mick bought himself a house in town and pretended to be living there, not that anybody was fooled. Especially after he married Alma, there was hardly a weekend a month that they spent there. He retained the seat all the same, buoyed up by his youth and the rumoured promise of a junior ministry, rumours that he and Alma had themselves started. During his first term, he managed to secure a brand-new public swimming pool for the constituency, and an investor to come in and put up a gleaming new shopping centre on the outskirts of town, sinking its foundations right on top of an ancient burial site despite the objections of a handful of local poets and tree huggers. Once the tills started ringing in the shopping centre, Mick's seat was safe for as long as he wanted it.

By that time Liam was living in Dublin and the farm was leased out to a neighbour. When eventually their mother died, they sold the house, and the farm along with it. And while Liam did nothing to save the farm — he did think about it at the time but ruled it out as impracticable — he mourns the loss of it still. He imagines himself walking out of a summer evening to count the cattle, with the darkness gathering in the trees and the river like a strip of tin foil in the moonlight. He sees himself turning to walk back across the damp grass to the house, pausing at the stile to smoke the last cigarette of the day; the vision is so real to him that it's almost as if some shadowy version of himself is still there, living the life that he always assumed was his to live. The life his father and grandfather lived before him. In many ways it is more real to Liam than the life he has ended up with, a life that was never of his own choosing.

As the long, slow notes of an electric guitar sounded the start of "Brothers in Arms" — a track Liam had always loved, never mind his brother's derision — he found himself enveloped in a fog of homesickness. He was homesick for the land. Homesick for the fields, and the trees. For the one-word exchanges that said more than a thousand when you moved among people who spoke the same language as you. He was homesick for home, which was always and forever the place where he was born. No matter how long he lived in the city, Liam had never been able to call it his own.

Liam parked the car up at the base of the South Wall and watched as his brother set off for his swim. He was heading for the Half Moon swimming club — a whitewashed area halfway along the sea wall, with iron steps leading down into the water. Normally it was only the regulars who swam there, but the sunshine had brought out the fair-weather swimmers. Young men taking running jumps off the sea wall, legs pedalling for a moment in the air before they hit the water.

Mick negotiated the uneven surface of the wall in a gentle waddle, his shoulders tilting from side to side as he went, his head bobbing up and down like a nodding dog. Towel under one arm, he raised the other arm in greeting to everyone he passed. Not a care in the world; it was maddening to Liam to watch how he had reinvented himself.

If you'd been offering odds a few weeks ago on the chances of Mick turning himself around after the pepper grinder thing, you'd have been looking at 100/1, maybe even 1,000/1. And yet Liam had opened his paper the other day to see that Mick had signed himself up for the summer season of *Celebrity MasterChef*. He was pictured wearing a white apron and brandishing a wooden spoon at the launch of the RTÉ summer schedule. Liam could just see it now, how his brother would charm his way back into public life, landing like a bruised plum into the soft heart of the nation's affections.

"Don't bother waiting for me," Mick had said. "I'll find my own way back."

But instead of driving away, Liam sat on in his car. There were half a dozen others lined up on either side of him in the car park, all with their engines turned off. Some of the drivers had their doors open, with their legs stretched out to catch the sun. Summer sounds in the air. From one car he could hear a ribbon of jazz. From behind him, the hum of an ice-cream van, and the patter of children's voices. From out of the babble, one sound isolated itself so that all the others disappeared. Opening his eyes, Liam saw that what he was hearing was the radio, streaming through the open window of the car next to him. He leaned forward to turn the dial on his own radio, and there she was. The sound of her voice familiar but different, like the sound of your own voice played back to you. Liam could tell by listening to her that she was nervous.

"We're talking about twenty years ago," she was saying. "There was no internet back then. I had no way of finding out any information, no way of getting in touch with other women who'd had similar experiences."

Her voice, as fragile as a tune played on a tin whistle.

"I was utterly alone," she was saying. "As far as I knew, I was the only person this had ever happened to."

There were long, empty spaces between her words and Liam found himself listening to her as he had never listened before. Listening to her as a stranger would, with nothing to stand in the way of his sympathies.

"When I came back, I couldn't tell anyone about it, which made it all the harder."

The interviewer's voice broke in on tiptoe.

"Can I ask you where your husband was when all of this was happening?"

Another pause, and it seemed to Liam that the world turned on her answer.

"Well," she said at last. "I can't really speak for him. I can only speak for myself."

"But he knew about it," said the interviewer, pressing her ever so gently. "Your husband knew at the time that you'd had an abortion?"

"Oh, yes," said Acushla. "He knew. Of course he knew."

"And yet he subsequently opposed the legislation to introduce abortion information in this country, in line with the 1992 referendum."

"That's right."

"That must have been very difficult for you," said the interviewer.

"It was," said Acushla. "It was absolutely devastating."

The presenter allowed a few seconds to go by before breathing in heavily, for effect.

"Acushla Collins. Thank you so much for joining us."

Liam closed his eyes and let out the breath he was holding. His shoulders collapsed and his head fell down on to his chest. Like an inflatable doll with the air gone out of it, there was nothing inside of him to hold him up. Nothing whatsoever in his head for a minute, perhaps even two — for the entire duration of an ad break, and then a piece of music, Liam thought of nothing at all. It was only when he heard the presenter preparing to read out the comments of the listeners that he came back to his senses.

He sat up in his seat, afraid for Acushla now. He of all people knew the bile that was out there. The unholy vitriol this interview was liable to bring down on her.

He was bracing himself for it, but to his amazement the comments were overwhelmingly positive. There were one or two, of course, who condemned her for the action she had taken — one listener in particular said that she would have God to answer to for her actions — but by and large the response was sympathetic. Caller after caller praising her for her courage, and sharing similar stories. As Liam listened to them, he was aware of the tide of public opinion slipping out from under him. He felt stranded and alone.

And what he wanted to say — what he wanted people to understand — was something he had tried to explain to Acushla a number of times over the years, something she never seemed to be able to grasp. What he wanted people to know was that it was his sorrow too, the fact that they lost that baby. It was his sorrow too.

Liam always wanted a big family. As a young man, he always pictured himself surrounded by multiple offspring, an older version of himself stalking the fields with his sons and walking his daughters up the aisle of the small church where he himself had been married. In those visions he wears his age on the surface, like the lead actor in a family saga who has had talcum powder combed through his hair in the make-up department, and skin-coloured putty applied to his face to denote the passage of time, even though the audience knows that he's still a young man underneath. His wife is in the garden gathering flowers for the table, and she too has talcum powder in her hair and a layer of putty on her face, but underneath everyone can see that she's still the same girl he fell in love with all those years ago.

When Liam married Acushla, he was blinded by the beauty of her. Blindsided into believing that she fitted the part, he wrote her into the story of his life, ignoring his mother's running commentary in the background. (His mother made no secret of the fact that she would have preferred him to marry a local girl.) "She's very pretty," his mother said, when Liam first brought her home. And Liam knew what she meant by that; she meant that Acushla was too pretty. "She's a jittery little thing," said his mother, again implying that this quality was enough to make her unsuitable for the life Liam had in store for her. "I can't see her getting the hang of it," by which she meant that Acushla would never master the uneven temperatures in the kitchen range, or learn how to set the fire at the back of the grate so as not to smoke out the front room, or how to drape her clothes over the upstairs banisters so as they wouldn't be damp when she went to get into them in the morning. It had taken Liam's mother years to get the hang of all these things, and it wasn't that she doubted Acushla's ability to do the same; she doubted her willingness. And she'd have been right.

"I can't seem to get warm," whispered Acushla, that first night she stayed in Liam's mother's house. Wearing the diamond he had bought her on the ring finger of her left hand (Mick had already given their grandmother's old ruby ring to Alma), Acushla was curled up in a shiver between the cave-damp sheets in the single bed in the guest room. Liam crept across the bare creaking boards and she scooted over in the bed to make room for him; he had to put his fingers in her mouth as he made love to her, to stop her from giggling. To Liam's surprise, Acushla was a very noisy lover.

That night was the making of Connie, a fact that was not lost for one moment on Liam's mother. "She's fierce healthy-looking, for a premature baby," his mother remarked, when Connie landed in a Dublin maternity hospital barely six months into their marriage. Acushla had insisted on having her baby in Dublin, and when she left the hospital three days later, it was to her own mother's house she went, ostensibly for a few weeks; those weeks turned into months as Liam drove up and down every day to tend the farm. Eventually he found a fellow to take care of the day-to-day running of it and he rented a house in Dublin, leaving the drawings for the new bungalow he had planned to build gathering dust on the desk in his father's study.

There was no bungalow built. No more babies born, although there were two miscarriages within the space of as many years, by which time Liam had managed to capture the fourth seat in Dublin south-east on the basis of a bare four thousand first-preference votes — it was the transfers that clinched it for him. And if Acushla's last, disastrous miscarriage was not his finest hour as a husband (always in his mind he thought of it as a miscarriage, unable to bring himself to use the word "abortion"), it wasn't fair to say that it was his fault either. There were rumblings of another election when it happened, and if there was one word you didn't want to encounter on the doorsteps it was the word "abortion".

Afterwards, they went for marriage counselling, attending a number of tortuous hour-long sessions in a windowless room at the top of a Georgian building that housed an Indian restaurant in its basement — for ever afterwards Liam would associate this phase of his marriage with the smell of tikka masala. The therapist Acushla had chosen was a middle-aged woman with undyed hair. She always wore the same smock top and the same fat-person jeans. The same pair of lace-up leather sneakers. As soon as Liam saw her, he knew he didn't stand a chance.

"Your wife," she said to him, using the word as a stick to beat him with. "Your wife — and I'm using her words, not mine — feels that her needs are being sacrificed on the altar of your political career."

Liam nearly choked with indignation when she said that. He crossed and uncrossed his legs in an attempt to disguise his impatience. The therapist was watching his every move with a knowing look in her eyes, as if she knew exactly what he was thinking. As if she knew exactly what he was going to say before he even opened his mouth.

"What my wife fails to understand," he said, looking unblinkingly at the therapist as he tried to ignore the sound of Acushla's sobbing, "what she seems determined not to understand, is that I am not a free agent. I'm a member of a government that has been elected by the people to do a job." (He was Minister for Defence at the time, a fact he assumed the therapist was well aware of.) "I have a most sacred job to do, and while I understand that Acushla and I have had our personal difficulties recently, I am nonetheless obliged to rise above them and look at the bigger picture."

The therapist dipped her head a little and rested her chin on her knuckles, without ever taking her eyes off Liam. Not since he was seven, and he and Mick had been called into the local priest's office to answer for the theft of some candles from the shrine in the church (which of course Mick was guilty of), not since then had Liam had the sense that someone could see right through him, right through to the wrinkled little walnut of guilt at the centre of him, a guilt he had no sense of ever having warranted. How to explain to this woman the injustices that had assailed him his whole life?

"I'm just doing my best here," he said, appealing to her for some sympathy. But he should have known better.

"Has it ever occurred to you that you might be abdicating responsibility for the personal, and using your political duties as an excuse? It sounds to me like your public persona provides you with a pretext to distance yourself from what's happening at home."

"Ah, now," he said, taking a hold of the armrests of his chair and raising himself up tall. "I'm not going to sit here and listen to you filling my wife's head with those kinds of ideas. I won't have you handing her ammunition to use against me. I won't stand for it."

The therapist looked up at him with a vicious glint in her eyes.

"Oh, really?" she said. "You and whose army?"

They were all against him.

That's how it seemed to Liam now. Starting with his own mother, who had always sided with Mick. His twin brother, who had always delighted in putting one over on him. Even his wife never once took his side in anything. It seemed to Liam that the whole world was against him, and through no fault of his own.

He was always a good son. A good brother. A good husband. A good public representative, but still and all the voters had deserted him. After twenty-five years treading the footpaths of their bloody constituency, trampling in their dog shite and picking up their discarded crisp bags, they had cast him out. A quarter of a century, during which time there wasn't a single night of the week but he was attending the removal of some constituent who had died, or a residents' association meeting. Not a Saturday morning but he was at a school fair, his arms full of cling-filmed banana bread and freezer-bagged fairy cakes, and the ear chewed off him about the need for a new classroom, or an extra resource teacher. After twenty-five years of this slavish community service they had dumped him, and for what?

As Liam drove back past the power station, past the sewage works and the scrap metal yard and the abandoned shipping containers, he began to talk to the radio, mounting a calmly reasoned defence of his record in government; it was a defence he had rolled out a hundred times in the past few years in interviews with print and broadcast media, but he continued to pursue it, because in his mind every word of it was true.

"We brought about the greatest period of prosperity this country has ever known," he said, cocking his head to one side as he spoke in his most patient and reasonable voice. "We tripled child benefit. We banned smoking in public places. We brought peace to the island."

"Well that's all very well," the interviewer would say. "But you also brought the country to ruin. You beggared the banks. You sold our sovereignty down the river. Generations to come will end up having to pay for the mess you made of things."

"No, Séan," said Liam, furrowing his brow as he spoke to the windscreen. "You see, that's where you're wrong. Yes, we suffered an economic crisis, yes, the effects of it have been the cause of much hardship for a great number of households, but the Irish people are nothing if not fair, and it's simply not fair to place the blame at the door of one party. What happened was not the fault of any one government. What happened here was the result of a global economic crisis . . ."

So engrossed was Liam in the argument he was making, so determined was he to finally convince his imaginary audience of the reasonableness of what he was saying, that he failed to observe the yield sign at the approach to the roundabout. He failed to check the traffic coming from the right, and sailed straight into the path of a Louth-registered BMW. The BMW swerved to avoid him, letting out an angry beep. Heel of the hand on the wheel, Liam beeped back at him, three long defensive wails. As he drove on, eyeing the BMW driver warily in his rear-view mirror while at the same time checking ahead of him in case a Garda had witnessed the incident, it seemed to him that he didn't have a friend in the world.

It was only when he stopped at the traffic lights on the Beach Road and indicated to turn left for home that he thought of one last port of call. Indicating right, he pulled on the wheel in preparation for a last-minute change of lane.

"Dad," said Connie, when she answered the door.

She was wearing dark glasses and her face was pinched and pale, her lips set in a grim straight line. Liam's hopes of a fair hearing plummeted at the sight of her.

She took a step back, pulling the door in on herself. The hallway was so small that she had to press back against the coat rack to let him through. A huge flower arrangement was balanced precariously on a side table at the bottom of the stairs; the vase wobbled precariously as Liam brushed by it and Connie went to steady it.

"Nice flowers," he said. And as a joke, "What did he do?"

"Don't go there," she said, in an ominous voice.

Liam ducked his head to pass into the living area, plastic toys crunching under his shoes as he went.

"Boys," said Connie. "Are you not going to say hello to your grandfather?"

The boys were playing on the floor behind the couch, blankets and quilts draped over the dining chairs to form a den. One by one they emerged on their hands and knees.

"Hiya, lads," said Liam. He bent down from the waist to greet them, shaking hands with them as if he was on the campaign trail. They stared up at him, not quite sure what to make of him. He had his hands in the pockets of his sports jacket, and nervously he jangled the coins that were in there. The boys waited to see if this was a prelude to a gift. A conjuror's trick that would end in him producing a coin from his pocket, or better still a chocolate bar. Once they realised it wasn't going to happen, they ducked back into their den.

"Will you have tea?" asked Connie, going to put the kettle on without waiting for an answer.

"Sure," he said, and he followed her into the kitchen, his hands still in his pockets. With the chairs all in use for the den, there was nowhere for him to sit. He paced down as far as the back wall and turned round.

"It's a bit cramped for you all here, isn't it?"

Connie stared at him with a puzzled look on her face.

"What do you mean?"

She had pushed her sunglasses back on her head and Liam could see that her eyes were washed-out-looking. He found himself wondering had she been crying, and if so why.

"You must be very tight for space. The four of you."

Connie shrugged.

"People raised ten kids in these houses. I think we can manage with two."

246

He turned to peer out into the back yard, where a pair of garden chairs occupied the small patio area, leaving barely enough room for the boys' trikes and scooters.

"It would be nice for the lads to have a garden," he said, craning his head up to search out the sky.

"We do have a garden." She was lining a pair of mugs up on the kitchen counter, and dropping tea bags into them. "It's small, but it's still a garden."

Looking out the window, Liam saw where Connie had installed creepers along the side fences. She'd planted shrubs and a maple tree, with a bird feeder hanging from its branches.

"I reckon the market might be bottoming out," he said, turning away from the window. "It mightn't be the worst time for you to think about trading up."

"Hang on," said Connie, standing in the middle of the kitchen with a milk carton in her hand and an expression of disbelief on her face. "Is that what you came here to talk to me about?"

He paused, not sure what to say.

"You're unbelievable."

The way she looked at him, they might as well have been strangers.

"Mum's left you. She's camped out in Grandmother's house, doing back-to-back interviews about the abortion you somehow neglected to tell anyone about. The nation's up in arms at the thought of your blatant hypocrisy, and you're standing here talking to me about property prices. Are you completely mad?"

Listening to her, it did seem to Liam that he wasn't handling this particularly well.

"I think I'm in shock. I wasn't expecting any of this, Connie. I had no idea it was coming. Your mother didn't think to warn me about it."

"You still don't get it, do you?"

She put the milk carton down on the kitchen counter and took a step towards him. Her face was all screwed up as she spoke, as if she'd been sucking a lemon.

"It's always someone else's fault, isn't it? That's the thing with you. Everything that happens is someone else's fault."

"Ah, now —" he started to say, but Connie wouldn't allow him to speak.

"I don't want to hear it," she said, throwing her hands up in the air. "I've no interest in hearing it. Don't you see? There's nothing you can say that will make it okay."

Liam stared at her, struggling to understand what she was saying, this daughter of his who had once been such a great little friend to him. When did Connie stop being his friend? he wondered. It seemed to him that everything had changed between them once she started having babies.

"Come on, Connie. Don't you go turning against me now. You and me were always such great pals."

Connie shuddered, and closed her eyes. When she opened them again he could see that she was full of tears, her mouth open like a bird so she could breathe.

"Yes," she said sadly, nodding her head and wiping her nose with the back of her hand. "We were great

248

pals. But I'm not taking sides with you against my mother any more. I can't do it."

"So everyone's against me."

"It's not that everyone's against you," said Connie, and there was a whistle of urgency in her voice now, like the sound the old kettle used to make on the Aga in Liam's mother's kitchen when it was gone past the boil. "It's just that you're in the wrong and you won't admit it. If you could only acknowledge it, then maybe there might be some hope for you."

She turned away from him and placed her hands on the kitchen counter, letting her head hang down on to her chest, like an athlete resting after a long run. Their two mugs of tea sat untouched on the counter beside her. Liam stood for a long time and watched her, his head slowly churning all the things she'd said.

"So what should I do?" he asked her at last.

"What should you do?" she repeated, turning her face to look at him.

He nodded, and she stared at him.

"I don't think I've ever heard you ask anyone for advice before."

And come to think of it, Liam hadn't either — he couldn't remember ever seeking anything other than professional advice, in the sanctity of a consulting room.

"Would you believe me when I tell you I'm asking for it now?"

Connie paused, and it seemed to him that she was weighing up whether to help him or not.

"One word. That's all I have for you."

"Okay."

"You might want to try saying you're sorry. Say it like you mean it. If you say it often enough, people might even start to believe you."

"Sorry," she repeated as she pushed him out the front door. With the flat of her hand on his back, she pounded him a few times with what could almost have passed for affection.

So, here he is again outside Acushla's mother's house.

He's standing underneath the acacia tree in the front garden, where he spent many a night when he was courting her, and the only thing that's missing is the cigarette. He finds himself wishing he never gave them up.

He bends to pick a stone up from the gravel, tossing it against the window pane, but the noise it makes is hardly audible and there's no response. He takes another stone, tossing it harder this time, but this one bounces off the wooden window frame. The third stone he throws strikes the centre of the bottom pane, shattering it instantly.

"Oh, shit!" Liam doubles up, chest to his knees with his hands clutching his head as two startled faces appear in the top half of the window.

"Oh, shit," he says with a lurch of despair, as he comes to terms with the fact that things are still getting worse instead of better.

"Sorry," he calls out as the front door opens and Acushla and her mother appear in the doorway. Wearing long nightdresses and backlit by the bright hall, they have the appearance of two welcoming saints with the light of heaven shining behind them. Liam experiences a strange sensation of weightlessness, as if he has died and is about to enter the afterlife.

"I'm really, really sorry," he says, taking the steps two at a time so that before he knows it he is standing before them. Acushla's expression is stony but Liam has the impression that Deirdre is trying to suppress a smile.

"Can I come in?" he asks, appealing to his mother-in-law rather than his wife.

"I suppose you had better," says Deirdre with great gravitas, pulling on the heavy old door to admit him. Acushla turns without so much as a glance at him and leads the way down the back stairs to the kitchen. Deirdre rolls her eyes and follows her daughter down, leaving Liam to bring up the rear. Past the empty spaces on the walls, spaces Deirdre has preserved for thirty years so that everyone can see where her husband removed those paintings that were his on the day he left her. "Excuse the cold," she likes to tell her visitors, "but it's not worth the cost of heating the whole house for me *alone*." (Whereas Acushla's father's flat is always as warm as the toast he likes to burn and scrape before he eats it.)

"Tell her I'm sorry," says Liam, addressing himself to Deirdre rather than Acushla.

Acushla won't even look at him, so Deirdre has agreed to act as a conduit between them. With the three of them sitting round the large table, the low-hanging light casting shadows on their faces from above, the scene has all the appearance of a seance, except that the communion is between the living rather than the dead.

"Tell her I'll do anything to get her back. Anything she wants, I'll do it."

Deirdre repeats this to her daughter and Acushla listens, her eyes resting with great composure on her mother's face. Liam can see that she's thinking about it.

"You heard him," says Deirdre. "He says he'll do anything."

"Tell him I only have one condition," says Acushla, after a pause.

"No problem," he says straight away, addressing his wife's impassive profile.

He turns to Deirdre. "Whatever it is, tell her I'll do it."

Deirdre waits, alert as a croupier, for Acushla to show her hand.

"I want him to give up his place at the head of the table."

With the crown of her head high and proud, and her hands still in her lap, she enunciates every word with gentle precision. "Every day for the rest of his life, I want him to sit across from me at the table."

Deirdre blinks at her as if to say, *What? Is that all you're going to ask for?*

"That's all I want," says Acushla, and she turns her head slowly to face Liam. Liam looks her in the eyes, and in them he sees something that he never knew was there. All these years, and never did he have the faintest inkling that Acushla had in her the stuff of political genius.

"You're on," he says, nodding slowly and looking at her with a new respect.

There were dozens of screaming teens gathered outside TV reception when they arrived.

"One Direction are on after you," explained the young woman with the clipboard who emerged to greet them. She led them up the stairs and ushered them into the green room, offering them tea or coffee, which they both declined. She guided them towards a sofa, waiting for them to sit down before she spun away again. Never had Liam been so aware of them as a couple as he was now, sitting nervously upright on the unyielding sofa like a pair of immigrants; all they had with them was their story.

"Liam," said the producer in greeting, "Acushla, thanks very much for coming in to us."

"Thanks for having us," said Acushla, her face tilted upwards in a practised smile.

"Now," said the producer, his head spinning round as he looked for the young woman with the clipboard. "We need to get Liam and Acushla down to make-up."

The way he said it, Liam had the feeling that he was talking in code. The young woman came and led them away down breeze-block corridors, up bare concrete stairwells and down more concrete stairwells until they arrived in the make-up department. They were put sitting side by side facing a huge mirror, the two of them draped in hairdresser's capes.

"You've gorgeous skin," said the woman who was doing Acushla's make-up. "If only everyone had your skin, my job would be a lot easier."

253

Liam could see that Acushla was pleased. She was shining with all the attention she was receiving. A divine grace settling over her like a bridal veil, he was reminded of the day he married her. He remembered how she had appeared in the doorway of the church on her father's arm. With her head bare and her golden hair adorned only by a single white camellia, she made her way down the aisle with glorious ease, her head bowed with pleasure under the weight of all the admiring attention. Suddenly Liam felt very sad at his failure down the years to give Acushla the attention she needed. It seemed to him now that it would have cost him nothing to give her a bit of attention.

"Nervous?" he asked her, talking through the mirror.

"No," she said, with a smile. And considering this was her first time on TV, her level of calm was incomprehensible to him. He still developed a pit of fear in his stomach every time he prepared to go on air. Just as bad now, if not worse than the first time, despite all the media training he'd had over the years.

"If you're going to apologise, the trick is to do it properly," said the communications strategist he had hired to prepare him for this interview. "No excuses, no whining. Just say that you were wrong, that you regret the way you handled it, and that you wish you'd done it differently."

Liam was still repeating those instructions to himself when the host popped his head in to make-up to greet them.

"Liam," he said, pumping Liam's hand up and down. "Good to see you."

"So brave of you," he said to Acushla, leaning down to bump his freshly made-up cheek against hers. "Don't worry, I'll be gentle with you." And with a slow wink he was gone.

As Liam and Acushla waited hand in hand in the wings (make sure you walk on stage holding hands, the communications strategist had said), their host was straightening his tie and firing a quip into the waiting studio audience to warm them up. The newsreader on the nine o'clock news was wrapping up the bulletin with one late-breaking headline. Liam could see her face on the backstage monitor, he could see her lips moving and the measured movements of her head, but the volume on the monitor was turned off so he couldn't hear what it was that she was saying.

"Two minutes to air," said someone as the ads started rolling. Liam took a deep breath and squeezed Acushla's hand tighter while they waited for their cue.

Breaking news . . . Three Irish human-rights activists are to be deported from Israel. Tarquin Kilpedder (73), Emer Barry (37) and Nora MacEntee Collins (28) were arrested in the Gaza Strip on Wednesday morning and taken to Givon Prison in the Israeli city of Ramla, where they've been held ever since. The three activists were in the area as volunteers with an international organisation that provides solidarity to fishermen and farmers in Gaza.

Nora

The first thing Nora saw when the electric doors slid back was her parents, standing side by side at the welcome rail, like something that happens to you in a dream, when people from different parts of your life converge on you without explanation — you might find your dentist and your first boyfriend together in your mother's kitchen, or your grandmother and your yoga teacher sitting in the front seat of a car while you sit in the back. Her brain gave a lurch as she tried to construct a narrative that would explain their presence here together. Her mother stepped out from behind the railing, bizarrely colourless with her undyed hair. She looked like an unpainted plaster model of herself.

"Nora," she said, looking down at Nora's feet. "What in God's name happened to your shoes?"

Three days in an Israeli jail and the only thing her mother was worried about was her shoes. Nora looked down and saw the unpainted toenails, the smear of toe jam in the curve between each toe. The patches of raw skin where her feet had repeatedly burned and peeled while she was working in the fields.

"They never gave them back to me," she said, watching for her mother's reaction. "They knew we'd look like nutters without our shoes."

"Well," said her mum, coming forward to hug her. Nora expected to be released from the hug immediately, but instead her mother hung on to her. For what seemed a very long time she did not let her go, and Nora was forced to settle into the hug. With her cheek lying against her mother's soft cashmere shoulder, and her eyes open on to the bright colours of the juice bar at the arrivals gate, she had a sense of what it must have been like to be a baby.

"It's good to have you home," said her mum, and Nora could have sworn that she had tears in her eyes.

"Nora," said her dad, coming forward to lift the backpack off her shoulder. He gave her an awkward squeeze, the backpack bumping against the both of them. "Is that all the luggage you've got?"

A white light assaulted her, and a fraction of a second later there was the sound of a camera shutter. Her dad whirled round with the deep swing of a shot-putter, to confront the photographers.

"Now, lads," he said, putting up a stop hand.

Nora's mum put an arm around her and went to bundle her past the cameras.

"Wait a minute," said Nora, slipping out from under her arm. "I haven't done anything wrong."

She turned towards the snappers, peeling off her jumper as she did so, and veterans of the media though they were, neither of her parents had the presence of mind to step out of the shot. The next day the papers would all publish different variations of the same photograph. A picture of Nora standing proud in the arrivals hall at Dublin airport, wearing a Free Gaza T-shirt, with her parents lurking behind her like common criminals.

The house was smaller than she remembered it, and more cluttered. The smell inside impossible to conjure up until you stepped back into it, but once you did, it was hard to imagine how you could ever have forgotten it. A smell of lingering peat dust and her mother's old-rose bath oil, with a base note of cheese that's been left for too long in the fridge.

Nora stood in the hall. Hemmed in between the bulging coat rack and the Mrs Delany prints on the wall, she felt as if she was caught between two worlds. The world she was about to enter seemed unreal to her, or maybe she was unreal to it. A distance between them, like an encounter with a friend you haven't seen for a long time. She was reluctant to move any deeper into the house.

She was aware of a terrible sense of loss, but what it was that had been lost she could not have said. She felt as if she had left her body behind her in that hot little cell in Givon Prison. The memory of the dead air was still on her skin, the struggle to breathe in enough oxygen. "Breathe shallow," Emer had said to her. "Try to breathe shallow." For three days she and Emer had lain bunk over bunk, silent sometimes and sometimes talking, banging on the steel door of the cell for water, shouting out for Tarquin and waiting to hear Tarquin shout back. She could still hear the sound of his jaunty old voice, heard through the walls like a snatch of dialogue from an opera, in all its exaggerated bravado. Nora missed Tarquin already. She missed Emer too, and the simple meals they had been served, on blue plastic trays, of rice and cucumber and tomato. (Nora was a vegetarian and could not eat the chicken her captors offered her.) She missed her prison cell, she realised with surprise. While she was there, she had thought of nothing but the desire to get out. Now, given the choice, she would almost have gone back.

There were five plump silver fish lined up on a chopping board on the kitchen counter. Five dead eyes staring up at the kitchen ceiling. The presence of five raw fish in her mother's kitchen was only slightly more bizarre than the presence of Nora's father, a presence that had still only partially been explained.

"*Celebrity MasterChef*," said Nora again, not sure she had understood him correctly.

She was looking suspiciously at the fish.

"What are they?"

"Sea bass. According to the fella in the fish shop, they're a bugger to bone."

With a tea towel slung over his shoulder and a grubby apron strung under the overhang of his belly, he was brandishing a long, thin filleting knife.

"The skills test," he said, eyeing the fish dolefully. "That's the thing I'm most scared of. You wouldn't know what they'd throw at you."

"Will you've tea, Mick?" asked her mum. She was taking china cups out of a cupboard underneath the counter and setting them on the table.

"Pour it out for me," he said, "and I'll drink it while I'm doing this."

Nora was struck by the normality of their conversation. The way they spoke to each other was entirely normal; that was what was so weird about it.

She looked around the kitchen and saw all the familiar things on the walls — the Edward Hopper print her mother had bought in MoMA, the Clinton/Gore election poster she'd brought back from Washington, with a Hillary flier wedged in between the glass and the frame. The china cups they were drinking from were part of the set Alma had been given as a bride — as a child, Nora had broken one of them and hidden it in the bin rather than confess; as far as she knew, her mother had never noticed.

Nora sipped at her tea. Jet lag swirling around her, she still had the noise of the plane's engines in her ears. The chill of its air-conditioning system was still in her, and the smell of airline meals heating in the galley. A yearning for home that had not been satisfied by her return.

"Tell me about Acushla," she said, in an effort to anchor herself. Her voice sounded a false note, and she hardly recognised it.

"Oh, yes," said her mother. "You missed all that."

There was something different about her mother but Nora couldn't put her finger on it. Something strangely rigid in her demeanour. Even the way she was sitting, perched like a schoolgirl with her hands tucked under her thighs, it was not like her.

"I've just been reading about it on the plane."

"Yes," said her father, lifting a fish spine by the tail and flicking it into the bin. "I'm afraid she's usurped my place as the country's media darling."

"She's shown great courage," said Nora's mum solemnly, and Nora looked at her closely, not sure if she was being sarcastic or not.

"Unbelievable," said Nora, shaking her head.

For years Nora had despaired of her family's cynicism. For years she had tried to stir them to action, urging them to join her campaign against the use of Shannon airport by the US military. ("And watch all the American multinationals pull out of Ireland?" said her father.) She had tried to sign them up to petitions in support of Falun Gong. ("I would," said her grandfather, "but I'd be afraid it might prevent me getting a visa for China.") To join a vigil for the release of Aung San Suu Kyi. ("How does she always manage to look so *elegant*?" said Acushla.) That her meek and pampered aunt should become the figurehead of a protest movement, this seemed to Nora a most unlikely turn of events.

"How's Liam?" she asked.

"Oh, he's trotting around after her like a wee lamb," said her father, with no attempt to disguise his pleasure. "She has him by the bollicks, and she knows it. Now," he said, straightening up and looking at the clock. "When would you ladies like to eat?"

"Why don't you have a bath?" said Nora's mum. "I'll run you a nice hot bath and then we'll all sit down to dinner."

Under cover of the sound of gushing water, Nora slipped up to her old bedroom and closed the door quietly behind her. Like a guest in a stranger's house, she was desperate for a moment on her own. She sat down on her bed, pulling her knees up to her chest and resting her chin on them. Taking stock of her belongings, she searched for a pattern that would allow her to stitch herself back together again. The dream catcher in the window. The patchwork quilt on the bed. The snow globes she had collected as a child as mementoes of her parents' travels. The inspirational verses she had copied out and pinned on to her bulletin board. *Do not go where the path may lead, go instead where there is no path, and leave a trail* (Ralph Waldo Emerson). *We must not fight injustice, we must make it invisible* (Gandhi). Above her desk there was a framed portrait she had painted of herself in junior school, with oversized round eyes in a big round head. As she looked at it now, it seemed to her that she had captured something of herself in that self-portrait, an aloneness that she had not been aware of at the time.

Nora was fourteen when her parents split up, and at first she didn't notice that anything was wrong, because she was so used to her dad being away. It was the height of the peace process and her dad was Junior Minister at the Department of Foreign Affairs, so he spent more time in Belfast than he did at home. ("Up there riding anything in a skirt," her mother told her later, and all Nora could think was, What kind of a person tells her daughter that?) Nora used to see her dad every night on the TV. Walking into Stormont buildings, walking out of

Stormont buildings. Standing outside Stormont buildings with a ragbag of other politicians and officials. To Nora they had the look of a band of puppets about them. Some muppetry quality in the strange assortment of shapes and sizes, all clumped together. Nora's dad was easy to pick out because he stood a head and shoulders above everyone else.

The peace talks regularly went through the night, and often they went through the weekend, so it was no surprise to anyone if Nora's dad wasn't home much. But even after the peace process had ended, after the historic conclusion, for which the nuns led tentative prayers of thanks at Nora's school assembly — after George Mitchell had flown home to New York and Tony Blair had gone triumphantly back to London, and the hotel rooms of Belfast had emptied themselves of reporters and camera crews, and the news bulletins had gone back to reporting other things that were happening in other places — even then there was no sign of Nora's dad. It was only when she went through his wardrobe and discovered that his clothes were gone, only then did Nora figure out that he wasn't coming back. The final confirmation came not from either of her parents, but from a tabloid newspaper that Nora caught sight of one day in the Spar. She was on her way home from school and she had stopped to treat herself to a bag of popcorn with some coins she had found in her pocket when her parents' wedding photo caught her eye, looking out at her from the front page of one of the papers. "The Good Friday Disagreement" the paper had dubbed the split.

Nobody thought to tell Nora. There was never a day when her parents sat her down and explained to her what was happening ("We both still love you . . . It's not your fault"). At no point did either of them outline a plan to her ("You'll spend weekdays with your mother and weekends with your father"), let alone ask her how she felt about it. She was just another thing to be divided between them, at their convenience.

As Nora lingered in the slowly cooling bath her mother had run for her, with the slither of rose oil on her limbs and a scented steam misting up the windows and mirrors, she felt as if nothing had changed. Her parents had not asked her permission before they broke up her family; it seemed equally unfair to her now that they had not asked her permission before putting it back together again.

Her mother's voice trilled up the stairs calling her down to dinner and Nora closed her eyes. She slid her bum along the oily base of the bath, pushing her knees into a deep bend. She arched her spine and craned her neck backwards, allowing her head to sink down below the surface, where no further sounds could reach her. Just the sound of her own breath, amplified by the water and eerily alien.

"Habeas corpus," said her father, continuing a conversation that had begun in the car. "I think we definitely have them on habeas corpus."

He was hunched over the kitchen counter, putting the finishing touches to his potato dauphinoise.

Blowtorch in hand, he was carefully scorching the scales of scalloped potato that formed the surface.

"I still haven't worked out if you're pulling my leg," said Nora, turning to her mother for help.

"Oh, it's no joke," said her mum, looking up for a moment from setting the table.

"Were you even informed as to what they were charging you with?" asked Nora's father. Poised on his toes like a jewel thief, he settled a perfect square of creamy caramelised potato into the centre of each plate.

"You're missing the point," said Nora as she watched him.

With great care he leaned a naked white fillet of fish up against each potato square. Armed with a squidgy plastic bottle, he began to pipe small blisters of red sauce around the edges of the plates, dropping a sprinkling of crispy bacon crumbs on top of each blister.

"No bacon for me," said Nora, holding up her hand to stop him, but she was too late. She had not eaten meat since she was fourteen, but her dad seemed incapable of retaining this simple fact about her. The last time she visited him in Brussels, he suggested they go out for a steak.

"Okay," he said, throwing his hands up to beat an imaginary clock. "That's it."

Before serving up the plates, he insisted on photographing them from every angle, muttering to himself as he went.

"They're going to get me on the presentation. I still haven't nailed it on the presentation."

Nora carried the first two plates over to the table and he followed with the last one.

"Well," he said, raising his glass of wine as he fell into his chair. His forehead shining with sweat, his face flushed from his efforts. "To the two most important women in my life; it's good to have us all round the same table again."

Nora looked across nervously at her mother, expecting a snide remark, but instead her mum smiled, her eyes moving from Nora's dad to Nora before settling back on him. And again Nora saw something curiously unsure in her demeanour, something she had never seen in her before.

"They refused to allow you to make a phone call," her dad was saying. "That's another grounds for complaint."

"You're missing the point," said Nora again, turning to face him. "This isn't about me. This is about the people of Gaza. They're the ones who are being denied their rights, on a daily basis. They're the ones who are living in an open prison. That's the thing that matters here, not what happened to me."

How many times had they had this conversation? Or another one just like it. It was a well-worn path they liked to tramp along together.

"It's *wrong*, what's happening in Gaza." She put her fork down and fixed her eyes on her father.

He looked at her as if he could barely contain his amusement.

"You agree with me," she said. "I know you do! When it comes down to it, you believe in all the same things I do. But you keep coming up with excuses not to do anything about it."

"You're right," he said, with a maddening smirk, and she was reminded of the way he used to tickle her when she was a child. On weekend mornings, when she came into their bed in her pyjamas, he used to catch her by the legs and tickle the soles of her feet. The more she wriggled and squealed, the harder he tickled her; he wouldn't give up until she begged for mercy.

"I'll tell you what," he said, serious all of a sudden. "Once I've been crowned *Celebrity MasterChef Ireland*, I might consider lending my support to one of your crusades. I could go back to Gaza with you, we could do a Gaza version of *I'm a Celebrity . . . Get Me Out of Here*."

Nora stared at him, not sure whether to laugh or cry.

"Ah, Nora," he said, choking on his own suppressed laughter. "I'm sorry, I just get such a kick out of winding you up . . ."

"I can't deal with him," said Nora, turning to her mother for support. "How can you deal with a person who refuses to take anything seriously?"

Her mother seemed not to have been following the conversation. She was holding her fork with her left hand and her right hand was lying limp on the table, curled into a loose fist.

"Mum," said Nora. "What happened to your *fingers?*"

"I can't believe you didn't tell me."

They had moved into the living room after dinner, taking their wine glasses with them. The evening was too warm for a fire, warm enough even for Nora and her mother to remain bare-shouldered and bare-footed. The sash window was open as far as it would go, a deepening blue sky outside. The stadium had absorbed all the glory of the summer night into its fish-scale skin.

Nora and her mother were curled up in opposite corners of the huge three-seater couch. Nora's dad was in the kitchen, practising how to debone a chicken. ("Is there no cleaver in this house?" he had asked, before realising his mistake.) Nora closed her eyes, unable to shake off the image of a huge square blade. She hugged one of the couch cushions to her chest so as to still her shuddering.

"I can't believe I didn't *notice*."

Now that she had noticed, it was impossible to take her eyes off them. Those poor maimed fingers.

"Why didn't you tell me?" she asked quietly, even though she knew the answer. Maybe if she had been in the habit of getting in touch more often, maybe then she would have been told.

Her mother's eyelids fluttered momentarily, untold clouds passing behind them as she let the question go unanswered.

Nora sighed from deep down in her chest as it dawned on her that everything that had passed between them over the years had been leading to this moment. Every instance of neglect on the part of the mother (deliberate or accidental, it didn't make a difference, not at the time). Every act of revenge on the part of the daughter (noticed or unnoticed by her mother). Every step they took away from each other had in fact been bringing them closer to this. A moment that was always going to come. Perhaps not necessarily in this room, on this couch — it could just as easily have been in a hospital ward with one or the other of them coming round to consciousness again after a road accident. It could have been at a funeral, the two of them standing over someone's grave. It could have played out in a hospital mortuary, with one of them laid out on the slab — but it was always going to come. Nora experienced a great wave of relief that it had not come too late, this moment of reckoning.

"I would have come back. If I'd known, I would have come back."

"I know. That's why I couldn't tell you."

Her mother's stockinged feet were knuckled up under Nora's bum, her mother's toes wriggling endlessly. Nora would have liked to change her position, to get away from the toes, but she did not want to appear to shy away from this awkward intimacy.

"It must have been terrifying," she said, treading oh-so-gently. She was trying to feel her way into the story, like someone venturing into a dark room, afraid of knocking something over.

Her mother frowned the question away.

"I didn't think they were going to hurt me. I thought they'd just take whatever they could find and go. It never occurred to me that they would be prepared to hurt me."

Nora squeezed her eyes half shut and covered her mouth with her hand, unable to contain the images she was seeing in her mind.

"I can't bear to think about it. It's horrific."

Her mother answered her in a matter-of-fact voice.

"These things happen to people," she said. "And we are people."

"Oh, Mum," said Nora, and the way she said it, it sounded like she was pleading with her. Tears in her eyes, she didn't trust her voice to speak, so instead she reached out for her mother's hand. Cradling it between her own, she began to stroke it very gently, taking care not to avoid touching the poor wounded fingers.

There was a question Nora wanted to ask, but she didn't know whether to voice it or not.

"Mum," she said carefully. "The people who did this to you. Did they catch them?"

Her mum reached out for her glass of wine.

"Oh, yes," she said, and her voice had changed. The tone of it was more brittle now, and more brusque. "Yes, they've charged one of them. But the trial won't be until next year. He's been released on bail in the meantime. He's probably out there right now, breaking into someone else's house."

"Will you have to give evidence?" asked Nora, as her father appeared in the doorway, his apron still on and smeared now with chicken guts. He placed the palm of his hand on the crown of her mother's head. Resting it there with great solemnity, as a priest might when giving a blessing.

"I thought we said we'd cross that bridge when we came to it?"

Nora's mother stretched her neck back so that she was gazing up at him, and the look she gave him was one of such trust and dependence that Nora couldn't help but be touched.

"It's good to have you home," he said to Nora, using the word without a hint of self-consciousness. She thought of what she would have given over the years for the three of them to be together here like this, in quiet harmony. Now that it was happening, it was hard to know what to make of it.

On her way up to bed, Nora stopped to peek into her mother's bedroom and saw, with one slow sweep, her father's shoes under an armchair, one of his shirts hanging off the curtain rail, and a copy of *The Economist* on what used to be the unoccupied side of the bed.

As a teenager, Nora was a spy. A dedicated listener at doors. A rifler of drawers. She always made it her business to know what man her mother was seeing. What woman her father was sleeping with. In her travels between her parents' separate residences, she was ever alert to the appearance of a new toothbrush beside the sink in her mother's house, or a man's sock behind the bedroom door. She took note of any face creams she found in her father's bathroom, or herb teas in his cupboards, using every detail to construct a picture a criminal profiler would have been proud of. And while she never stopped to consider the ethics of what she was doing while her parents were philandering with other people, now that it was the two of them together, she had an acute awareness of their privacy, and a desire not to violate it.

Waking up on her first morning home, she lay in bed and listened as her father pottered about downstairs. She heard the stairs creaking as he carried a tray upstairs for her mother. She heard the springs groan as he climbed back into bed beside her. The sound of their voices through the wall; she couldn't make out what it was they were saying, just the sweet trickle of their conversation, like a nearby stream. Listening to it made her feel lonely all over again.

"Well," her father said, when finally she came downstairs. "The dead have arisen."

He was standing at the cooker stirring a pot of custard for his ice cream. Barefoot and unshaven, he was wearing the peony-print kimono Nora had given her mum for her fiftieth birthday. When he turned towards her, Nora saw that the kimono was unbelted and hanging open on to a T-shirt and a flabby pair of boxer shorts. She was assailed by a mental image of her father's penis under there, sticky with sex.

"Here," he said, holding out a spoon to her. "Taste this and tell me what you think. I've infused it with rosemary."

Nora turned her face away in disgust.

"There's no doubt about it," she told Connie. "They're definitely sleeping together."

She had arrived at her cousin's door without warning. Walking across the bridge in the cool of the morning, she had skipped down the short flight of steps to the green area in front of Connie's house. A terrace of tiny red-brick houses, like something you might see in an English soap opera; every evening on the dot of half seven the *Coronation Street* signature tune rang out down the row, followed by the *EastEnders* sig at eight.

Nora peered through the front window, expecting to see the boys tumbling towards the door, but all she saw was Connie coming down the stairs. Long legs first, then a sage-green baby-doll nightie trimmed with black lace, until finally Connie's startled face appeared. She lit up when she saw her cousin.

"Nora!" she squealed, throwing open the door.

"Did I wake you?"

Connie flung her arms around her. "When did you get back?"

"Only last night. You're the first person I've visited." Nora stepped inside the door.

"Where's Emmet?" she asked, looking around the empty room. "Where are the boys?"

"They've gone to the playground," said Connie. "It's all part of a new regime. Every Sunday morning, come hell or high water, he has to take them to the playground."

"Oh?"

"This is what I do while they're gone," said Connie, holding up a copy of the IKEA catalogue with a TV smile. "I lie in bed reading the IKEA catalogue. That's how sad my life is . . ."

She stopped herself and stood staring at Nora as if she'd only just noticed her standing there.

"I can't believe you're here! Come on into the kitchen. I'll make you coffee. I'm so happy to see you!"

They settled on low stools in Connie's kitchen, surrounded by the smell of washing powder and soggy cereal. The sound of the tumble dryer stopping and then starting up again in the opposite direction. Connie had tucked the hem of her negligible nightie between her thighs and crossed them, to hide her knickers. Her hair was falling in loose spirals from the crown of her tiny head, and the shadows round her eyes were darkened by her day-old eye make-up. It seemed to Nora that Connie was getting more beautiful, if anything. She could never but be aware of Connie's beauty, with a tribal brew of jealousy and pride in equal measure.

"So," said Nora. "It seems that my parents are sleeping together again."

Connie wrinkled her nose.

"Can we be sure about this?"

"There's no doubt about it. They're definitely sleeping together. Last night I heard sounds coming from their bedroom. At one stage I heard her give a kind of a squeal."

"Oh, Jesus," said Connie, baring her teeth.

"I can't get my head around it. They're getting on so *well*. It's like the divorce never happened. It's really weird."

"I don't find that weird at all. Your parents always got along well together. Way better than mine did. You got the feeling that they actually *liked* each other."

Nora nodded as she acknowledged the truth of this.

"Your house was such a happy house," said Connie. "Before your parents split up, it was a really happy

275

house. Whereas the atmosphere in *my* house — do you remember? It was like Berlin before the wall came down."

"Well, now we know why."

"Yes," said Connie with a sigh. "Now we know why."

They stared into each other's eyes, and it was as if the music had stopped and the parcel of family history they had been passing back and forth between them was being opened. One layer at a time, they were moving closer and closer to the nugget of truth that lay at the centre of their lives.

"He used to bully her," said Connie, in a voice that was little more than a whisper. "Do you remember? He used to bully her in front of us."

"I know," said Nora. "I remember."

"He was a pig to her, and I did nothing to stop it. I feel so bad about that now. Especially now that we know what she was going through. I feel so bad for taking his side."

"Ah, Connie, you were just a kid."

"Still."

"She seems to be getting her revenge on him now."

Connie smiled.

"I *almost* feel sorry for him. He had to beg her to take him back."

"Do you think they still love each other?"

"I don't know. I don't think love has much to do with it. I've reached the conclusion that relationships between men and women are all about power. It's all about the balance of power, and if you can't get that right, then it's a fight to the death."

And it seemed to Nora that Connie wasn't talking about her parents any more — it seemed to Nora that she was talking about herself.

"Is everything okay between you and Emmet?"

Connie bent her head and looked down into her lap. She sighed, and for what seemed like a long time, she didn't speak.

"You don't have to talk about it if you don't want to."

"It's not that. Part of me does want to talk about it. I'm just afraid that if I start, I won't know where to stop."

She looked up at Nora and smiled an apologetic little smile, and Nora didn't know what to say to her. What could Nora say to Connie about husbands, and babies? Nora, who had never even had a proper boyfriend.

"Is it that bad?"

"Oh, I don't know. I'm so tired I can't tell. We're still talking to each other, which is something, I suppose. We're still sleeping together, whenever we have the energy. But basically it's more like a war than a marriage."

"For all I know, that's normal."

Connie burst out laughing.

"Oh, Nora. I missed you!"

"I missed you too," said Nora, even though strictly speaking that wasn't true. When Nora was away, she missed her creature comforts all right. She missed her Barry's Tea and her Walnut Whips and she missed the salmon avocado rolls she and Connie craved from the sushi place on Capel Street, but curiously enough, she did not find herself missing people. She didn't miss her grandparents, even though she adored them both. She didn't miss Connie's boys, or Connie herself, even though Connie was the closest thing she had to a sister. Of all the people in the world, it was Connie who Nora loved best, and yet she did not miss her, not even for a moment, when she was away. Like a hot air balloon, the stays that tethered her to her family had to be severed every time she went away. And it was only when she returned that she felt herself being reattached.

"I wish you wouldn't keep disappearing off like that," said Connie, sticking her bottom lip out in a show of petulance. "I don't like you being away so much."

"I always come back."

"Yeah, but not for long. I bet you're planning your next escape already."

Nora decided not to mention the e-mail she'd received from Amnesty last night — an e-mail about the human-rights situation in Syria, it had her thinking of her next move already.

"My boys hardly recognise you, Nora. Every time you come back, I have to explain to them who you are."

How to say this without hurting Connie's feelings?

"Don't take this the wrong way, Connie, but sometimes I feel like there isn't much for me here."

"But this is your *home*."

That word again. Nora kept hearing it, and every time she heard it, she wondered what it meant.

"This is where your family are."

And of course Nora couldn't say it, but that was the very thing that kept her away. The fact that they all

278

lived within a square mile of each other, it was claustrophobic to Nora. She wondered how they could bear it.

"I know, Connie. I know, but . . ."

How to explain it? The feeling she had when she was away of being free. Whereas here she felt so *unfree*. Unfree of her parents and her past, unfree of her feelings, feelings she had been trying for so long to get away from.

"Nora," said Connie, looking at her with the kindest of expressions in her beautiful eyes. "Whether you like it or not, this is always going to be your home."

Nora's mother was not doing well.

At first she had seemed to everyone to be coping magnificently with what had happened to her. Like a building that has withstood the force of an earthquake, or a tree left standing after a storm, everyone was so relieved that she had survived it, they just assumed she would go on surviving it, day after day, into the future. But the cracks began to show over time, and the more time went by, the more she seemed to be struggling.

Nora would wake in the night to hear her padding about the house. The next thing, she would hear the sound of Eckhart Tolle's voice filtering through the walls; it reminded her of a Speak & Spell, with the cadences in all the wrong places. (It was Acushla who had suggested that Alma listen to *The Power of Now* — in a bizarre role reversal, Acushla was now giving Alma lessons in survival.) In the mornings Alma was groggy with the effects of what Nora suspected were sleeping pills, and in the evenings she was wakeful and anxious. She was getting headaches too, with increasing regularity. Incapacitating migraines that left her incapable of working for days at a time. Nora never remembered her mother suffering from migraines before.

"How are you doing?" Nora asked, as she leaned into the darkened bedroom. The curtains were scrunched tight against the bright evening, the daylight outside rendering them luminously transparent. Her mum was lying fully clothed on top of the covers, a silk scarf draped over her eyes as a blindfold.

"I'm okay," she said, speaking in a tremulous whisper, as if there was a sleeping baby in the room and she was terrified of waking it.

Carefully Nora perched on the edge of the bed, laying her hand on her mother's thigh.

"Can I get you anything?" she whispered.

Her mum shook her head, moving with the utmost care. The sense of some explosive substance that would detonate if disturbed.

"I brought you some water," whispered Nora. She held the glass up to her mother's lips for her to take a sip.

"Delicious," came the whisper. She mimed a thank you that was audible only as a series of little puffs of breath. Nora took the glass away and set it down on the bedside table, careful not to make a sound as she was doing it. She let her eyes wander over the room, falling on shapes that were strangely unfamiliar in the shadows. A large mirror that gave the illusion of a door opening on to another room. A white sequinned evening dress hanging from a cupboard door in a plastic dry-cleaner's sheath; it looked to Nora like a ghost about to rise up for a haunting. A black satin nightdress coiled on the floor; in the darkness it could have been a crouching cat.

She listened to her mum's breathing, shallow and deliberate, and she tried to follow it with her own breath. From outside the room came the sound of an ice-cream van. The jingle stopped abruptly and then started again just as suddenly. Nora listened as the sound of it receded into the distance, and when it was gone, she sat on in the silence. There was something restful about sitting in the stillness of her mother's illness. It was like being in the presence of a big drugged bear.

Three days Nora had been home, and in all of that time nobody had asked her a single question about the month she had spent in Gaza. Oh, her father had asked her about the conditions inside the jail, and Connie wanted to know whether she'd met a man while she was away (which she hadn't), but nobody had expressed the remotest interest in the work she'd been doing, not until she visited Macdara.

"Now," he said. "I want to hear all about it."

He was smiling at her with his eyes, letting his gaze rest on her the way very, very old people do, even though Macdara was only in his late forties. Macdara's ways were at odds with his appearance, which was curiously youthful. ("What do you expect from someone who has nothing to do all day but take long baths?" Nora had once heard Acushla say. "No wonder he has no lines. He has nothing in the world to be worrying about.")

Nora and Macdara sat at a wonky wrought-iron table that had been set into a small sunny patch in the corner of Nora's grandmother's garden. A garden that her grandmother kept untended as a testament to her husband's abandonment of her. From the ravening creepers to the perennially unpruned trees, everything pointed to the absence of a man in the house.

When Nora and Connie were children, they used to spend hours acting out elaborate games in this garden. They played Sleeping Beauty here, with Connie the sleeping princess and Nora the valiant prince cutting his way through the brambles to reach her. They played Snow White, using Macdara's studio as the cottage of the Seven Dwarfs. They played Hansel and Gretel, with their grandmother cast (unbeknownst to her) in the role of the witch. For Nora, the garden still held the echoes of all those childhood games.

She had come to visit her grandmother, but found only Macdara at home.

"She's gone to the charity shop," he told her. "For some reason she's taken it upon herself to bring all her old clothes to the charity shop."

"Really?" said Nora, struggling to take in this information. Never once in her whole life did she ever remember her grandmother throwing anything out. (She's a Womble, Nora's grandfather used to say, forgetting that Nora was too young to remember the Wombles.)

282

"She's taken to decluttering all of a sudden," said Macdara. "I've no idea what prompted it, but it's most out of character."

He led Nora outside, offering her a glass of lemon barley water, which he fetched from the gloom of the studio. They sat side by side, with their chairs turned to face the sun, sipping at the cloudy drink. Nora closed her eyes and allowed the silence to swarm round her as she waited for Macdara to say something. You wouldn't know what Macdara might say. He might just as easily say nothing.

She set her glass down on the slanting surface of the table and stretched her legs out in front of her to catch the sun. She slipped her feet out of her flip-flops, enjoying the wormy squelch of soil between the blades of uncut grass. She was aware of the sound of a train scuttling along the track behind the garden, aware of the cloying scent of the honeysuckle that had been allowed to run wild along the walls. She was aware of Macdara's presence, as tenuous as the company of a wild hedgehog, or a hare that had ventured into the garden. You were afraid to move in case you might scare him off.

"Lemon barley water is a good thing," he said eventually. "I'm not sure whether people appreciate what a good thing lemon barley water is."

"It's delicious," said Nora. "It reminds me of being a child."

Macdara looked at her curiously.

"I keep forgetting," he said, "that our little Nora's all grown up."

And it might have sounded creepy coming from anyone else. If you didn't know Macdara, you might think this was a creepy thing to say. If you listened to Nora's mother talking about him, you might assume that he was handicapped perhaps, or an invalid of some sort. If you saw him in the midst of his family, silent and watchful where everyone else was so noisy, you would know there was something not quite right about him. But Nora had grown up with a child's view of her uncle, and that view of him had never left her. She saw the slight figure bulked out by cardigan on top of cardigan, turning from his desk as she and Connie pushed open the door of the studio. She saw the childlike man who would gracefully receive the tea they'd made for him from weeds they'd found in the garden. She saw the solitary audience member, sitting on a chair in the studio while she and Connie acted out their shambolic plays for him.

"What was it like?" he asked her. "What was it like, this place you've just been to?"

Nora paused before she answered. There was something about Macdara that made you want to choose your words very carefully when you spoke to him. You had the sense that you were holding an instrument in your hands and that Macdara was listening out for the sound you would make with it; you had the feeling that he would know if you sounded an untrue note.

"It's a sad place," she said. "I think it's the saddest place I've ever been."

"I'd like to hear about it," he said.

284

And there was something wistful in his voice, this middle-aged man who had only once in his life been out of Ireland. He had been to France, many years ago, on a scholarship that was supposed to last a year but ended after just a week. A trip that was the butt forever afterwards of many a family joke. It was Alma who suggested he write an account of it entitled "A Week in Provence". Macdara smiled with good grace every time that joke was rolled out, but he never ventured off the island again. Talking to him about her travels, Nora felt like an ancient adventurer who brings back tales of distant lands, along with a trunk full of strange trophies, with which to mesmerise the people at home.

"It should be a beautiful place," she said. "That's what's so sad about it. At one time it must have been the most beautiful place, this ancient city beside the sea. But there's almost nothing left of it now, only rubble and sand."

Macdara had his head inclined towards her, his pale eyes endlessly patient.

"I can just picture it. You describe it well."

"The people have no way of making a living. They try to fish, but their fishing boats are taken away from them. They try to farm, but the snipers shoot at them while they're working in the fields. Even the olive trees," she said, and in her own voice she could hear a shrill note of indignation. "The settlers break the branches off the olive trees to spoil the harvest."

"But that's terrible!" said Macdara. "That's just terrible." He was shaking his head as if he found it hard to believe what she was telling him.

"Yes," she said. "It is terrible."

And she wondered, if Macdara could see this so clearly, why did everyone else find it so hard to see how terrible it was?

When the Garda came to the door, Nora's first thought was that it must be something to do with her deportation from Gaza.

A Friday morning, her dad had left at the crack of dawn for another day of filming. Acushla had just arrived for coffee, along with Connie and the boys, bringing with them a box of small cakes. Instead of leading them straight into the kitchen, Nora's mum took the boys out into the back garden to show them the nest of newly hatched robins in the crook of the wall. The boys were more interested in the cakes than they were in the robins, but they were too polite to say so.

"Do you know a funny thing?" said Alma, as she stepped back into the kitchen, closing the glass door carefully behind her. "I've spent my entire adult life talking about politics and the economy and the state of the nation — but I find that none of that's of any interest to me any more."

Connie was setting out the cups, but she paused and looked up at Alma, waiting to hear what her aunt was going to say.

Alma was still standing at the kitchen door. She was gazing into mid-air as she spoke, while the rest of them stopped what they were doing to listen. Nora had a queer sense that they were all of them actors on a stage, waiting for Alma to deliver a key soliloquy before the action could resume.

"The thing is, I find I've no interest whatsoever in what's happening in Iraq, or Afghanistan," Alma was saying, as she walked over to the fridge and took out a carton of milk. "I couldn't tell you who's in power in Israel. Or what's happening in Libya. It's like I've no space in my mind for any of those things any more."

"Welcome to my world," said Connie with a snort. "What you're describing is the state of my brain ever since I had children."

Alma filled the milk jug and paused with the carton still in her hand.

"The only thing that interests me now is when those little robins are going to take flight. It's the only thing that seems real to me."

She had her head tilted to one side. A wistful note in her voice, as if she regretted the insight.

"I know it sounds mad, but I could quite happily sit here all day waiting for those little birds to fly away."

Acushla stared at her, and Nora could see that she was still adjusting to this new incarnation of her sister.

"When can we have the cake?" asked Ernie.

His brother was beside him, springing up and down on the spot.

"When can we have the cake? When can we have the cake? When can we have the cake?"

"Now," said Acushla, coming to attention. "Now is the time for the cake. Come and help me put them out on the plate."

The kettle boiled and switched itself off and Nora poured some water into the coffee pot to warm it. She was just emptying the water out into the sink when the doorbell rang.

"It's probably Grandmother," she told Connie. "Would you mind getting it?"

But instead of her grandmother, it was a female Garda who stepped into the kitchen (Nora's dad would have called her a ban-Garda). She had her hat in her hand, and her hair rolled into a neat little bun at the nape of her neck.

"Sorry to disturb you," she said, stepping forward tentatively with one navy-trousered leg. "I can see that you're in the middle of something."

"Not at all," said Acushla. Best girl in the class, she was already extending an arm to usher the Garda forward. "Will you have some coffee?"

The little boys stood staring at the Garda, the cake for the moment forgotten.

"Honestly, I'm grand," said the Garda, looking at Acushla only briefly before turning her attention to Alma. "I just wanted to have a quick word with Alma. There's something we need to bring to your attention."

The movement of air in the room was suspended as they all waited for the Garda to explain.

"A woman was killed in a house in Blessington last night. The state pathologist is only arriving at the scene now, so we've no official comment as of yet. But we believe she was killed by an intruder."

Nora became aware of her own breathing, hard and slow. Connie's breathing, and Acushla's breathing, and

288

the little boys' and her mother's — it seemed to Nora that they were all of them doing nothing but breathing. Breathing the Garda's words in.

"We've arrested a man and we're holding him in Blessington Garda station. But we thought you should know, it's the same man who's been charged with the attack on you."

In the pause that followed, the sound of the doorbell rang out, much louder than it had been before. Connie slid sideways out of the room, and a moment later she returned with her grandmother following behind her. Hair falling loose over her shoulders, Deirdre was wearing a magenta beret and holding a bunch of lavender that had clearly been stolen from someone's garden along the way.

"Did I miss something?" she asked, in her huge billowing voice.

Briefly the Garda explained the sequence of events again, while Nora watched her mother's face.

"Well," said Deirdre, addressing herself to Alma with her startled eyes wide and bright. "It would appear that you had a rather lucky escape."

And really, it did seem to them all that this was the case.

The crisis came the next morning.

Nora slipped downstairs to get herself a glass of water and found her mother sitting in the chair by the back door. Her mouth was turned upside down in a carnival mask of a sad face. Her eyes, dripping heartbroken tears.

"Mum!" said Nora. "What's wrong?" She sank to her knees on the cold tiles, one careful hand on her mother's arm. Through the glass door, the sky was a cocktail of oranges and reds, but the garden was still steeped in darkness.

"What is it?" asked Nora, but instead of replying, her mother just stared at her. In her eyes Nora saw a dull glint of catastrophe, as if she had caught sight of something so terrible that she could not put it into words.

"Oh, Mum. There's no need to be afraid. He's locked up now. He won't be allowed out again for a very long time."

Her mother shook her head as the tears slid out of her.

"It's over, Mum. I know it doesn't feel like it, but it's over now." (They had been through all this last night. Time and time again they had talked it through. How the murder charge would take precedence. How Alma's case would be adjourned. It might never even come to court.)

"It's not that," said Alma, shaking her head vehemently. But what it was, she could not bring herself to say.

Nora sat with her and waited, looking at the lurid sky while her mother cried herself out.

It was the baby robins, she explained eventually. A cat perhaps, or a fox — who knows what it might have been, but they were all gone. All that was left of them was some blood and feathers, and she couldn't bear it.

Of all the things that had happened, this was the one thing she could not bear. The poor little baby robins.

"Right," said Nora's father, his hair sticking up in a tuft at the back of his head, his eyes wild with incomprehension. He had come down to find Nora and Alma wrapped up together, one seated in a chair and one on the floor, the mother's head resting on the daughter's.

"I don't understand," he whispered to Nora when she came back down after putting her mother to bed. He was assembling a breakfast tray for her, but he was so addled that he couldn't get the sequencing right and the toast popped before he had even turned on the kettle. "Did something else happen?"

"Yes," said Nora. "Something else happened."

Her father stared at her in genuine confusion and not for the first time, Nora found herself wondering how her parents had managed to live for so long in the world, while learning so very little.

Nora runs.

Waking before everyone else, she slips out of the house. She runs to the lighthouse and back, a route that takes her on a path along the edge of the strand, and past the electricity plant, and out on to the sea wall. She runs the surface of the wall, aware even as she's doing so that she's taking a risk with her ankles on the uneven surface. At the end of the wall a handful of Poles and Lithuanians are to be found fishing from the rocks behind the lighthouse — before they came, nobody ever fished there. Nora turns and runs back without stopping, past the morning strollers and the dog walkers; on her right, the car ferry keeps pace with her as it ploughs its way into the heart of the city.

She is halfway back down the wall one morning when she sees her dad sauntering towards her, a pair of Ray-Bans on him and his towel under his arm. It's his walk that she recognises first — the ungainly waddle of him.

"Good morning!" he calls out, once they're within earshot of each other. Nora raises her hand to greet him, but it's a few long seconds before they draw level.

"Well," she says. "No filming today?"

"Not today," he says cheerfully. Not a word has he said to them about the outcome of the contest, but there is no concealing the fact that he's at liberty again after only two days. Nora and Alma have drawn their own conclusions.

"If you'll wait for me, I'll treat you to a cup of coffee afterwards," he says with a nod towards the coffee van at the base of the wall.

Nora sits and waits for him while he swims; once he's dressed again, they walk the last section of the wall together.

"What'll you have?" he asks her, and Nora can't help but notice that he doesn't know how she takes her coffee.

"A latte," she says. "Full-fat milk."

As he queues for the coffees, Nora takes a seat on a low wall in the sunshine. She closes her eyes and hears, but does not see, two women sitting down beside her.

They start up a conversation, and it takes a moment for Nora to realise that they're talking about her dad.

"Is that your man?" says one woman. "What's his name, Collins."

"The fella who had the wife had the abortion?"

"No, no. That's the brother you're talking about. This one's the fella who was out in Brussels. The one with the pepper grinder."

"Oh, that's right," says the other lady with a chuckle.

Nora opened one eye and saw her dad standing patiently in the coffee queue, his coins clutched in his hand like a child about to spend his pocket money. She felt a rush of affection for him, and a desire to protect him.

"He'd be on a good pension," said one of the women.

"Ah, he would be, yeah. He'd be on a grand pension."

"I wouldn't be worrying about him."

"No, he won't starve, that's for sure."

Nora smiled and closed her eyes again, surprised by the comfort it gave her to find herself among people who know who you are.

"What about this weather?" said one of the women.

"It's miraculous," said the other. "It's nothing short of bloody miraculous."

The weather was all anyone was talking about. Weather the country had not seen the like of in a generation, day after day broke to clear blue skies, and no end to it in sight. All round the coast, people took to the beaches, while in the midlands they headed for the lakes and rivers. In the cities, children in discount wetsuits leapt joyously from buildings and cranes into any patch of water they could find. On farms and building sites, working men stripped off their shirts as telephones rang out in empty offices. The city parks turned yellow and dry as savannah, the citizens lazing on the parched grass so tanned and happy as to be barely recognisable even to themselves. A smell of barbecued meat hung on the air; hosepipe bans were put in place and reservoirs ran dry. A summer with the power to change everything: after year upon year of austerity, it was just what the country needed.

To celebrate this miraculous summer, it was decided that a party should be held in the square. The party was scheduled to coincide with the screening of the first episode of *Celebrity MasterChef*. Nothing would do the neighbours but to have a ritual screening. Coloured bunting was strung from the lampposts. Barbecues were borrowed and kegs of beer bought. They'd even erected a gazebo, out of old habit, in case of rain. Maurice the neighbour rigged some electrical cable out through the open door of his house to where a large screen had been set up in the centre of the square. ("Say nothing," he said. "Me son nicked it from his office.")

By the time the programme went on air, they were all of them stuffed with charred sausages and shop-bought coleslaw. Half drunk on draught lager and warm white wine. While the kids played hide-and-seek among the bushes (Connie's boys included), the adults drew their chairs in close to the bonfire someone had lit in an empty-bellied barbecue. There was a huge cheer as the title sequence appeared on screen, showing Mick standing in line with the other contestants. "I'm just hoping not to make a complete eejit of myself," he said in the soundbite, and again everyone cheered.

Connie gripped Nora's arm and whispered something into her ear, but what it was Nora couldn't hear. "Have some more wine," whispered Maurice, leaning across to top up their glasses. His hair had started to grow back, giving him the appearance of a fledgling chick. Nora looked over and saw her parents sitting huddled side by side on foldout chairs in the grass, both of them swathed in picnic rugs. Her dad had one arm around her mum's shoulders and with the other he was smoking a fat cigar. Nora couldn't help but think how content they both looked.

She turned to say this to Connie, but Connie had turned towards Emmet, who was sitting on the far side of her. Her face nestled in the crook of his neck, she had her fingers tucked inside the waistband of his jeans. Nora looked about her and saw children sitting in parents' laps. She saw teenagers flirting awkwardly with each other as they rolled a sneaky joint. Even the old lady from across the square had a small dog on her knee. It seemed to Nora that she was the only one who was alone.

She leaned her head back to search out the sky, but what she saw instead was the stadium. Lit up from within, its great steel girders looked as fragile as balsa wood, its glass panels as thin as rice paper. In the sky above it, birds were flying. Dozens of seabirds, picked out by the stadium lights; they glowed like paper lanterns. As she watched the magical flight of those beautiful birds of light, it seemed to Nora that everything was possible, even for her.

"Come for tea," her grandfather had said. But it wasn't her grandfather who answered the door. It was a man Nora had never seen before. Slender as a girl, he had tight brown curls and brown eyes like conkers. He was wearing a Che Guevara T-shirt and a pair of crumpled linen trousers, and Nora noticed that he was in his bare feet. For a moment she wondered had she rung on the wrong door.

From somewhere inside the apartment came the sound of her grandfather's voice.

"Nora! You haven't met Nando."

Her grandfather stepped into the corridor. Backlit by the flood of daylight from the living room, he looked like he was standing on stage at the start of *The X Factor*.

"Nando's from Argentina," he said, as if that explained everything.

"Oh!" said Nora in surprise. The only Nando she'd ever come across before was the Nando from *Alive*. Nando, the hero who walked across the mountains for help.

"Nando's a reiki healer," Manus went on to say. "We're hoping that reiki might help to ease some of Sam's symptoms."

Nora stepped forward to plant a kiss on her grandfather's scratchy old cheek.

"Forgive my apparel, but I have a bit of a cold." He was dressed in an Aran sweater and Thai fisherman's pants, a pair of knitted slipper socks on his feet. He had a blue Tuareg scarf wrapped around his neck and head, leaving only his endlessly startling blue eyes uncovered.

"You look like Lawrence of Arabia," said Nora.

"You wouldn't be the first person to remark on the resemblance," he said, with some delight. "Have I ever told you the story about the lady who came up to me in a supermarket in Los Angeles?"

"The lady who thought you were Peter O'Toole?" Nora glanced behind her to see if Nando was still there, but he had disappeared.

"Oh, I did tell you." He sounded a little disappointed that he wasn't going to get to tell the story again.

He stepped into the kitchen and Nora followed him.

"We'll have tea," he announced, and moved across to the sink to fill the kettle from the tap. He set it into its cradle and switched it on. As the kettle began to creak, Nora was listening out for other sounds, in other rooms. A feeling like being in a field at night, she was aware of the presence of other living creatures around her, heard but not seen.

"I want to hear all about your trip," announced her grandfather, turning his magnificent eyes on her. "But let's wait until we're sitting down. I want Sam to hear it too."

He pulled at the coils of his scarf to loosen it a little about the chin. Small beads of perspiration were gathering along his forehead.

"Is that not a bit hot?" asked Nora.

"On the contrary. It's actually very comforting. Plus I'm anxious not to pass my cold on to anyone. In particular I don't want Sam to get it. Although I must say, his immune system is in better shape than my own. He's as healthy as the proverbial butcher's dog."

As her grandfather equipped a tray with mugs and milk and sugar and fig rolls, Nora studied the various newspaper clippings he had pinned to the doors of his kitchen cupboards with thumb tacks. A letter someone had written to the paper calling for a nationwide campaign against stickers being placed on apples. A list of all the foods you should eat to counter memory loss. A review of a biography of Patrick Leigh Fermor.

"I was never in Israel myself," he said, "or Palestine for that matter. But I was in Beirut, you know, in 1964. Beirut was quite something."

The kettle had boiled while he was talking.

"Wait, now," he said, as if she had been the one speaking. "I have to concentrate on the task at hand. I'm like my car — I can only do one thing at a time." (Driving anywhere with Nora's grandfather was a hair-raising experience — if it was raining, you had to choose between using the indicators or the windscreen wipers.)

Moving with painstaking concentration, he poured water into the teapot, swirling it around before tipping it out again into the sink. With all the care of a scientist stooped over a laboratory bench, he transferred a heaped teaspoonful of Earl Grey tea leaves from a tin on the kitchen counter into the heated pot. Then another spoonful, and a final one before pouring in the boiling water. The smell of orange peel filled the kitchen.

"Now," he said, closing the lid. "I'll carry the tea if you follow with the tray."

"Sam!" said her grandfather. "Nando! Tea is served."

With the great glass windows magnifying the heat of the afternoon sun, it was as hot as a boiler room, but Manus didn't seem to notice. Nora set the tray down on the table and slipped her cardigan off. Her arms were pale where she had kept them covered all the time she was in Gaza. Only her hands and face were tanned.

"Sam," said her grandfather, looking up at the door. "Come and say hello to Nora."

"Nora," said Sam, delight dawning on him with the memory of her name. He walked towards her with his hands down by his sides. Behind him, Nora could see Nando hanging back. She was acutely aware of him watching her as she greeted Sam.

"Oh, Sam," she said as she hugged him to her. "I'm so happy to see you."

"Nora," he said again as they pulled apart to face each other. He was working his lips over her name.

Nora smiled into his dark-lashed eyes, lashes that were so black they always looked wet. Eyes the colour of coffee beans; at one time there had always been a sheen on them, a glinting hint of his buoyant good humour. Now there was only a worried stillness. As he chewed at his bottom lip, Nora saw that his teeth were nicotine-stained. His face was unshaven, but he was wearing a freshly ironed shirt and a pair of clean jeans, evidence of her grandfather's devoted but imperfect care.

"Come on," said Manus. "Let's have the tea."

Nora and Sam sat down side by side and Nando took a seat opposite them. Nora tried not to look at him too much. She tried not to look for too long, but a jigsaw was forming in her head all the same. A series of fragments that came together to form a composite. The sugary brown eyes, the hair that curled behind his ears. He wore a signet ring on his right hand. A frayed leather bracelet around his slim wrist.

"How's your father taking his disappointment?" Manus asked. He was holding the teapot protectively in his hands but he had paused in the pouring of it while he asked the question.

"Oh," said Nora. "He's blaming the sea urchin. Apparently it's all the sea urchin's fault."

Her grandfather resumed his tea-pouring with a smile.

"Have a fig roll," he said. "You haven't lived until you've tried a fig roll." The way he said it, in his huge old voice, he made it sound like a voice-over on an ad. (How *do* they get the figs into the fig rolls?)

"Whereabouts in Argentina are you from?" Nora asked Nando. She was thinking, Buenos Aires. She was picturing darkly lit cafés with white tablecloths, and people dancing the tango.

"I'm from Baroliche," he said. "It's in the south." And she had the feeling that he wanted her to ask him another question. She had the feeling that she could ask him anything and he would answer her. There was something wide open about him, something that made you think of deep oceans, big skies.

"Nando is a ski instructor," said Manus. "In another life."

So that was it. Altitude. Snow.

"Is that what brings you here? The summer?"

"Well actually, it's winter now in Argentina."

"Of course," said Nora, feeling like an idiot. She flipped the world over in her head. Tried to imagine skiers traversing upside-down mountains, inverted penguins strutting around on upended icebergs and ships sailing along an upside-down sea. She thought of snow, and found herself wishing she could scoop up a handful of it and bury her face in it. She was so hot! Her cheeks felt flushed, her armpits sticky, her dress was clinging to her thighs. She would have liked to slip out to the bathroom and wash her face. Put on some deodorant, slap some powder on her nose. Instead of which she picked a magazine up off the table and began to fan herself with it in the hope that she could regain her cool.

"Now," said her grandfather. "You promised you'd tell us all about your travels."

RELATIVE VALUES

In today's *Sunday Times*, the writer Manus MacEntee and his granddaughter, the human-rights activist Nora MacEntee Collins, talk about passion and pride and the joys of an unconventional family.

Manus

Nora is the quintessential Scorpio. She's brave and calm but under the surface there's plenty of passion bubbling away. Ever since she was a little girl, she always had a built-in radar for injustice of any kind.

Nora was born during the era of glasnost and perestroika. It was the time of the famine in Ethiopia. A time for brave souls, and Nora is without a doubt one of them. It was a good day for the world the day Nora was born. Sometimes the world manages to deliver of itself precisely the kind of people it most needs.

I tried to teach Nora to play draughts when she was a little girl but she was absolutely hopeless at it. No matter what I said to her, I could not induce her to huff me. But that's Nora for you, she's not capable of taking anything if it's at a cost to someone else.

Nora's an only child and I think her parents' divorce hit her very hard. For years she lived this nomadic existence, moving back and forth between two different homes in two different countries. What impressed me most was how

302

she managed to remain loyal to both her parents throughout that time. She never once took sides, which says a lot for her strength of character.

I'm so proud of the work that Nora does. She's a warrior for justice and I can't think of a better way to use the life you've been given. If everyone was like Nora, we would have something close to heaven on earth.

My dearest wish for her is that she will meet someone who deserves her. Nora is such a very fine person, it will be hard for her to find someone to match her, but when she does find such a person (and I do believe she will), he or she will be a very, very lucky sod.

Nora
I love the look on people's faces when I introduce my grandfather to them. I tend to forget that other people have grandfathers who spend their days on the golf course, or doing the crossword. My grandfather is more likely to spend the day on a sunbed and the night out partying. I have friends who live in the flat below Grandad's, and whenever they have a party, he appears in his dressing gown in the small hours and joins in the dancing.

I remember one time when I was a kid, Grandad picked me up from school in his Jag, and all the other kids in my class thought he was a rock star. It was like having one of the Rolling Stones as your grandfather.

When I was born, Grandad and Sam had already been living together for years. It never occurred to me that there was anything strange about your grandfather living with another man. A boy in school told me once that my grandad was queer, but I didn't know what that meant so I took it as a compliment.

The most important thing Grandad taught me was the

importance of kindness. He always says that the only thing that matters, in the end of the day, is how we've treated one another. I try to remember that.

I'm convinced that Grandad is going to live for ever. He seems to get younger and younger as time goes on. If you asked me his true age, I'd say he's about seventeen. Forever seventeen.

When I was a little girl, Grandad used to read the death notices out of the paper to me — he said there was a story in every one. When his death notice eventually comes to be written, it will make some story.

Manus

It's true that Manus is a great fan of the death notices. They're the first thing he turns to every morning when he sits down with his newspaper, a pot of tea in front of him and a single slice of toast (burned and then scraped, just the way he likes it) with a spoonful of his famous home-made marmalade. Manus makes marmalade every year from tins of canned oranges that he orders on the internet. His marmalade is rough-cut and heavily spiced, in deliberate defiance of the wimpish excuse for a thing that you find in the shops these days; it was the disappointment of factory-made marmalade that forced him to start making his own. A joyous ritual that he carries out once a year to a soundtrack of the Andrews Sisters, or Bing Crosby, singing along in his tuneless voice as he stews the fruit in a huge catering pan that he keeps for this express purpose. Using the empty Hellmann's mayonnaise jars that he hoards all year round, and the jam jars his ex-wife stockpiles for him, he makes gifts of his marmalade to everyone he knows for Christmas, holding back half a dozen for himself to see him through the year.

He and Sam are in the habit of having two breakfasts. The first, which they consume in bed with the radio on, consists of small earthenware cups of black coffee and little bowls of granola heaped high with Greek-style yoghurt and pebbled with blueberries. It's Sam's job to make this breakfast, a task he carries out with great seriousness but increasingly erratic timing. Some days it could be eight in the morning by the time he wakes Manus with the tray. Other days it might be five or six.

On this particular morning, Manus was woken at three by noises in the kitchen and the smell of coffee brewing. By the time Sam appeared, heartbreakingly boyish-looking in nothing but his pyjama bottoms, Manus was sitting up valiantly in the bed with his pillows stacked behind him and the clock radio turned to face the wall so that Sam would not see his mistake. There was chamber music playing instead of the morning news programme, but Sam didn't seem to notice. There was so much now, that Sam didn't notice. Invisible shutters falling down around his mind, blocking out bits of the world without him even knowing it.

Side by side and with hardly a word spoken between them, they ate their breakfast in the dead of night. Through the gap in the curtains Manus could see the sky outside, an unfathomable black. He was aware of a longing in him for the cold discomfort of early-morning flights, overnight train journeys, late nights that turn into early mornings. Somewhere on their travels they had come across a bakery that served coffee and hot buns to the revellers coming out of the nightclubs.

"Where was that bakery?" he asked Sam. "The bakery with the hot buns."

And Sam seemed to know just what he was thinking, as if the thoughts flowed freely between their two minds.

"Barcelona," he said. "They were cinnamon buns."

Sometimes Sam remembers things that Manus doesn't. Things from long ago, they are as real to Sam as things from yesterday. More so, perhaps.

Manus had the smell of cinnamon in his nostrils now, and the taste of treacly coffee in his throat. A memory of those black-tobacco cigarettes with no filter, their butts littering the ground. From the radio, the announcer's voice sidled in among his memories like smoke.

"Well, that was Schubert's famous string quintet for two violins, viola and two cellos. That piece of music, written just before the composer's death at the age of thirty-two . . ."

Once they had finished their pre-dawn breakfast, Manus shifted his empty bowl and cup on to Sam's tray and stacked it over his, allowing Sam space to get out of the bed. Sam picked up the trays and carried them out to the kitchen while Manus slipped down under the covers again. He closed his eyes in the hope of going back to sleep, but the coffee had done its work and his mind was too alert. He lay in bed and listened to the strange, sucked-up silence of the night. He heard the soft, padding sound of Sam, foostering around in the living room

307

like a fox, then the sound of a lighter sparking up a cigarette. Now Manus knew for certain that he would not be able to go back to sleep, for fear that Sam would leave the lighted cigarette on the arm of the couch, for fear that it would fall down into the couch cushions and smoulder. Your sense of smell fails to function when you're asleep — Manus had read that in the paper recently, and ever since he has feared a fire in the night, imagining himself slipping into a smoke-induced coma as the flames lick at the foot of his bed.

"Burned alive," his death notice would read, which would at least be some consolation. For years he and Sam had made a play of coming up with ever more sensational storylines for their death notices, in keeping with the colourful ends they delighted in envisaging for themselves. "Eaten by a crocodile," Sam might say as he and Manus made their way along a rickety rope bridge above a flooded river in Cambodia. And Manus would add cheerfully, "As he would have wanted."

It was what each of them wanted, to go out with a bang. A plane crash would fit the bill, they were agreed upon that. And there was a time when they travelled so much that it seemed almost a likelihood. Another distinct possibility was a bus crash — those ravines in Peru, they were almost begging you to take the plunge. Malaria would be glamorous, or even dengue fever. ("Succumbed to a fever," the death notice would read, with deliberate poetic flourish.) Kidnapping was always in the running, especially when you insisted on taking a road trip through Colombia in the 1990s. "Under no circumstances is anyone to pay a ransom for us,"

Manus had told his family before they left. "If you do, I'll haunt you." Of course there was always an outside possibility that they would be taken by cannibals and made a human sacrifice of — why else would anyone undertake to go on a walking tour of Papua New Guinea but out of a desire to be eaten? ("Slowly, in Papua New Guinea," the death notice would read.)

Slowly. That was what they had feared the most. Your faculties taking leave of you one by one, leaving only layers of indignity in their place. A humbling that you had no choice but to succumb to. And of course they had always assumed that it would be Manus who would suffer this humiliating decline, with Sam as the witness. Never once did it occur to them that it would be the other way round. Manus smiled at the thought that life was playing this little joke on them. For all the times they had tempted fate with their talk of crocodiles and ravines, for all their bravado in the face of death, life was determined to have the last laugh.

Manus fears death now, not for and of itself, but because he fears what will become of Sam when he's gone. A quarter of a century between them — it is too much to hope for that Sam will go before him. Sam is only fifty-eight. Manus is eighty-two. When first they met, those numbers seemed like mere diversions — they were nothing but fireworks lighting up the sky, talking points for other people to ooh and aah over, but now ... now the numbers have taken on a deadly menace. No matter how he goes at them, Manus cannot make of them anything but what they are. A formula for disaster. An equation that cannot be resolved. He retreats into binaries, taking the days as they come, one by one.

Never does Manus let a day go by without reading the death notices. As soon as he has their second breakfast laid out on the table, as soon as he has his toast buttered and his tea primed with milk, he opens the paper to the inside back page and, with an almost sensual pleasure, begins to read.

Working from top to bottom, he scans the columns, searching out certain key words, like "tragically", or "suddenly", for closer reading. He makes a point of skimming over any notices that allude to grandchildren, or great-grandchildren, as being too dull to bother with. Similarly the deaths of religious do not merit his attention, unless there's a mention of time spent on the missions. He has a particular distaste for the self-satisfied death notice, with its reference to a career spent in the higher echelons of the civil service perhaps, or an association with a particular golf or sailing club. Snippets of verse he finds vulgar in the extreme, likewise epitaphs in the Irish language (the deceased probably didn't speak a word of Irish). Manus respects brevity in a death notice, with a particular eye to the intriguing detail, like the mention this morning of a solicitor's firm in Mallow, with a telephone number supplied for "any enquiries".

"What on earth could that mean?" he asks aloud, looking up at Sam, without really expecting him to answer.

Sam is lost in the task of assembling his breakfast. Like all Moroccans, Sam is a hopeless sugar addict. Even now he is dumping spoonful upon spoonful of sugar into his tea; if Manus didn't stop him, he would empty the whole bowl into his cup. He pours a long lick of honey on to his bread, concentrating so intently that he is not aware of Manus watching him. He picks up the bread and eats it, humming to himself as he chews. What it is that he's humming Manus cannot make out.

"What are you humming, Sam?" he asks, speaking with great gentleness so as to mask his irritation. The humming has a bad effect on him, so he tries to divert Sam. Even humming along with him is better than listening to Sam humming to himself. Anything is better than listening to the humming.

Sam looks up, confused.

"You were humming something. I was trying to make out what it was."

Sam looks back at him with desperately serious eyes.

"It sounded to me like it might have been the Ink Spots. Am I right?"

Manus begins to hum, and after a bar or two, Sam joins in. The words singing themselves in their heads. Would you look at us, thinks Manus. Two old queens sitting here over our breakfast, humming away like halfwits. If anyone could see us! There's an absurdity to it, he thinks; it's like something out of Beckett. But there's a certain beauty to it too, with the smell of burnt toast hanging in the air, and the sunlight tumbling in on them through the giant window. What there is, despite everything, is love.

⋆ ⋆ ⋆

Sam was the most beautiful creature he ever saw.

The first time Manus set eyes on him, he was walking down Grafton Street as Manus was walking up. A bitterly cold day at the hard end of winter; there was a frost on the ground even though it was past midday, but Sam was wearing no coat. His head was bare and he had no scarf or gloves on him, just an Aran jumper and a pair of threadbare tweed trousers. He had a pair of huge black dogs with him and they were straining on their leashes, pulling him along as if he were a chariot. His chin was raised and his head leaning back on his neck, and the way he walked, it seemed to Manus that his feet hardly touched the ground. Manus was just approaching the corner at Weirs when Sam swept past him. He turned to watch in his wake, arrested by love as by a thunderclap; he had no idea if he would ever see him again. All he knew was that he would never forget him.

At that time Manus was forty-eight. He had been married for nearly thirty years to a woman he liked very much and with whom he had three wonderful children. He had achieved literary superstardom with a novel that was generally considered to be the finest work of Irish fiction since *Ulysses* (although nobody suggested it was in quite the same league), and this astounding and unexpected critical success had been crowned with a most gratifying commercial triumph when his book was made into a movie, starring Peter Finch and James Mason. On the day the cheque for the movie rights arrived, Manus went out and bought himself a brand-new Jaguar saloon. The car he chose had pale

312

blue paintwork, with leather seats and a walnut dashboard, and Manus had been driving it ever since, with a fierce, undying loyalty that only increased with age. The older the car got, the more alarming the smells and sounds that it emitted, the more loyal Manus became to it. They were growing old together, Manus and his car. Both of them creaking and groaning and farting and belching (although the burning smell of oil that the car emitted was a thing of fragrant beauty compared to the smells that escaped from Manus these days). No matter how much trouble it gave him, Manus would not give up on that car, no more than it would give up on him. What passed between them was nothing more or less than love.

In the years that followed the release of his book, and the film of the book, Manus rested on his laurels, eking out a comfortable living from the largesse that had so unexpectedly dropped into his life — a largesse that grew miraculously over the years as the result of a series of canny investments. And while he did on occasion make further attempts at writing, mapping out an idea for a novel or scribbling down a single passage of prose, he always returned to the conclusion that with that one novel, he had reached the limit of his abilities. For the most part, he was content with what he had achieved.

Dublin at that time was a place of empty spaces. The great Georgian squares that had once been the light and life of the city lay dark and derelict, their roofs stoved in so as to escape paying rates. Anyone who could get out of the city did get out, moving their families to the newly built housing estates in the suburbs, where shopping centres began to spring up, and schools and playgrounds, and if they weren't beautiful they were at least warm and clean, and nobody who made the move regretted it. Those few people who chose to stay behind had the city to themselves, and it took on the atmosphere of a small town, or a village, so intimate was the sense of community among those who remained. Manus couldn't walk down Grafton Street without bumping into a dozen people he knew, and at night he and his friends huddled in the snugs of a handful of pubs in the dark back streets, pubs that felt more like the front parlours of people's homes than they did public houses.

It was only when they had children that Manus and Deirdre began to entertain at home. This was the mid-sixties, and people in Dublin had begun to drink wine. Often of a Friday Deirdre would make a big stew, and Manus would buy in a case of cheap Italian red, and people they knew and people they didn't know would come to eat and drink and, mainly, talk.

It was at one of these Friday gatherings that Sam appeared, several weeks after Manus had first sighted him. He arrived in the company of an obscure scion of the Guinness family whose dogs he had been employed to walk. The moment Manus saw him standing there by the fire — wearing the same Aran jumper and the same paint-splattered tweed trousers he had been wearing that day on Grafton Street — as soon as Manus saw him he realised that he had known all along that he would come, and that now he had come, they were both of them on a trajectory that could not be altered, or avoided, any more than it could be regretted.

Now in his late fifties, Sam still has the jet-black hair he had as a young man, but it's coursed with white, as if he had dipped his fingers in wet paint before running his hand through it. He still has the bockety teeth he had then, teeth that stand apart from each other like tilting dominoes. Stained with age and tobacco, they lend him a perverse attraction, hinting at something dangerous and disreputable in his past. The hazelnut eyes are streaked now with confusion in place of the seductive humour that once danced across them like the flames and silhouettes of a James Bond title sequence.

When the doorbell rang, Sam was sitting at the window. With the iPad on his knee, he was working at the screen with a stylus, looking up every so often at the vast view. He was looking not at the clusters of red-brick houses down below him, nor at the strip of sea in the distance, with the sails of the yachts out of Dun Laoghaire splintering the blurry horizon line; he did not see the church steeples peeping up like weeds above the trees, nor the office blocks with the workers moving about within their windows. He didn't even glance at the stadium, slouched in the landscape in the form of a huge sleeping S — all he had eyes for was the old Victorian gasometer with its red wrought-iron pillars and its pointed peaks. When Sam paints the gasometer, what appears on his screen is a series of minarets, set against the clear blue sky of another place, at another time. For it is the minarets of Tangier that always appear in Sam's paintings, against ever-changing skies. The skyline of home, always present in his memory.

He never went back after he met Manus. There was an arranged marriage waiting for him at home, and a place in the family business, and he was afraid that if he did go home they would not allow him to leave again, afraid that something might have reached them of the life he was living. If that was the case, it would not have been beyond them to force him to stay. He caught sight of the city of his childhood only once in all the years, from a promontory beyond Tarifa as he and Manus were driving across the south of Spain. They got out of the car and stood and stared over the straits to where the sunlight flashed off the tips of the minarets, and they sat there until nightfall so that Sam could see the lights of Tangier in the dark. Ever since that night, Sam has been painting the same sight over and over again, in every light. Manus suspects it will be the one thing that remains when everything else is gone.

The doorbell rang while Manus was preparing the lunch, mashing smoked mackerel with mayonnaise and lemon juice to form a pâté, which he planned to serve with slivers of brown soda bread and unsalted butter. (Manus minds his own health as well as Sam's, because he knows that he must stay alive as long as is humanly possible in order to care for Sam. It is the centrepiece of his existence, this need to stay alive.) He dropped the fork he'd been using into the sink and wiped his hands on a tea towel to rid them of lemon juice before making his way down the corridor to the intercom.

"I've a parcel for you," said the voice at the other end.

"Can't you leave it downstairs?"

"It's registered, you'll have to sign for it."

"All right. I'll be down in a minute."

It was probably a book to be reviewed. *The Irish Times* was in the habit of sending him books, and occasionally he obliged, just to keep his hand in. There again, it could be a gift. Acushla was in the habit of ordering gifts for him on the internet. Thoughtful things for the winter, like flannel pyjamas, or cashmere socks. Yes, it was probably a present from Acushla. By the time the lift reached the ground floor, Manus was as excited as a child at Christmas at the thought of what the parcel might hold.

When he saw the size of it, when he took it from the postman and felt the weight of it, it was clear to him that this was not a pair of cashmere socks, or a book for that matter. Unless it was an encyclopedia, and encyclopedias didn't exist any more, did they? Not since Wikipedia. This bloody thing weighed a ton and it was as hard and unyielding as a slab of stone. Manus signed the postman's console and lugged the parcel back to the lift, holding it down by his knees with two hands, like a builder shifting a paving block.

"What the devil?" he asked himself as he heaved it down the corridor and in through the door of the apartment.

"A parcel," he told Sam, hoisting it on to the table. He was in the habit of speaking to Sam as you might speak to a dog or to a baby, without ever expecting an answer.

He examined the parcel, looking for any indication of who might have sent it, but there was none. Just Manus's own name and address, hand-written in bold capitals with a black magic marker. He turned the parcel upside down, looking for a return address, but all there was, in the top left-hand corner, was the number of a PO box in Dublin.

"Let's see now," he said as he tugged at the plastic wrapping the parcel was encased in, trying to rip a hole in it. The plastic stretched and thinned where he tugged at it but it would not rupture. He was forced to go into the kitchen to fetch a knife, making a stab in the parcel as if it were flesh and pulling the skin away in one long strip. What this revealed was a stack of loose-leaf low-grade printer paper, as thick as an old Dublin phone book; it was held together in the old-fashioned way with a Bridget's cross of twine. On the title page were two sparse lines of printed script, in 12-point Times New Roman: *Untitled, A Novel.*

After he and Sam had finished their lunch, Manus cleared the table, leaving the dishes in the sink water to soak, a slovenly habit he had adopted recently in order to lessen the monotony of the task (all he had to do later was take them out of the water and prop them on the dish rack to dry). Afterwards, he set Sam up in front of the TV and put on a DVD for him, selecting at random an episode of *The Waltons* from the box set that Acushla had ordered for him over the internet. Sam found *The Waltons* soothing. Something about the pace of it, and the tranquil setting, seemed to instil a peace in him. When the end of each episode came, he would join in the voices bidding good night to each other as the lights went out around the old wooden house.

"Good night, Elizabeth. Good night, Mary Ellen."

Manus would join in too, although it was not clear to him whether Sam knew they were just playing along with a TV programme or whether he was under the illusion that they too were tucked up under the eaves of that darkening house as the crickets cheeped and the wind chimes sounded and the signature tune swung up out of the darkness with its cheery trumpet and its rolling guitar, sounding its way into yet another episode. Sam was capable of watching three or four of them, back to back, of an afternoon. And Manus would take the opportunity to retreat to the far corner of the living room with a book, with the soft tones of John Boy's reminiscences adding a nostalgic undertow to whatever it was that he happened to be reading.

With Sam absorbed in the soft glow from the television, Manus slipped the twine binding off the manuscript and eased the great hunk of paper out of it. Picking the title page off with a licked finger and laying it to one side, he leaned down over the opening paragraph, with only the faintest stirring of curiosity. He was fully expecting to be disappointed. He had been sent so many books over the years, embarking on each

319

one with great hope only to be let down. But he only had to read the first line to know that this one was different. By the end of the first page, he knew that this was the book he had been waiting for, the book that had existed in his imagination ever since the day he had packed his own novel into an envelope and sent it off. Always he had known that there was a book like this out there, and it was this knowledge that had stopped him from ever attempting to write again himself. Because unless you could write something as good as this, there was no point in even bothering.

What this writer had achieved was something Manus had lusted after and longed for all his life. Not as a writer but as a reader; he had begun to wonder did it even exist, other than in his own longings. A book that rips a seam through the earth, throwing up out of the torn ground the beating wings of the human soul. What this writer had achieved was nothing other than the sublime.

When Nora came by the next morning, she found him sitting at the dining table. Upside down in front of him, in a higgledy-piggledy pile, lay the seven hundred and eighty-seven pages he had spent the night reading. Seven hundred and eighty-seven pages and not a page too long! Not a single word wasted! Manus had spent the morning trying to compose his response. He had started draft after draft that he discarded in disgust, wasting page upon page of expensive headed paper before finally happening upon a formula of words that did some justice to the masterpiece he had just read.

Posterity clanging in his ears, he was as certain as he could be that whatever he chose to say about this book would live on long after he was dead.

He was just signing his name to the letter when the doorbell rang. He looked round at the scrunched balls of paper that littered the surface of the table, at the empty coffee cups and the biscuit crumbs, at the Anglepoise lamp, still burning although it was nearly eleven. He folded his letter in three and slipped it into an envelope. Hastily, he inscribed the address of the post office box on the front of the envelope before rushing to open the door.

"Hi, Grandad."

Nora appeared to be dressed for a jog, in a T-shirt and leggings and a pair of battered old runners. Her hair was freshly washed and smelling of lemon grass. Her lips glistened with a slick of pink gloss. She had a pair of rolled-up yoga mats under her arm, and the sight of the yoga mats reminded Manus that she had promised to take him through a meditation practice. Nora was convinced that meditation would help him cope with the stresses of caring for Sam, even though Manus had tried to assure her that he didn't find it stressful caring for Sam.

"Hi, Sam," she said, raising her hand towards the window, where Sam was sitting in a chair in his pyjamas, gazing out at the view. For once there was no cigarette in his hand.

"He hasn't had a cigarette all morning," whispered Manus. "Normally by this hour he would have smoked half a dozen. Say nothing, but I think he may have forgotten that he's a smoker."

Nora was looking at him strangely.

"You look like you've been up all night!"

"Perhaps," he said vaguely, looking into her rather than at her. "You see, I've happened upon something quite extraordinary."

She looked about her, as if the thing he spoke of might be an object, or an animal that was lurking under the table.

"What is it?"

He paused before he answered.

"A book," he said at last. The word came out all consonants, like a single note sounded with a guitar pick. "A most extraordinary book."

Nora looked back at him with her big owl eyes.

"Did *you* write this book?"

"Lord, no! That's the whole point. Someone else did."

Nora was still staring at him.

"I don't understand."

"This," he said, patting the pile of pages on the table. "This is the proof I've been waiting for."

Nora's eyes were wider now, if that were possible.

"Proof of what?"

"Proof of everything!" he said. "Proof that I was right not to write a dozen mediocre novels. Proof that we are human, and that someone else has witnessed the lives we have lived. This book," he said, pausing for effect. "This book is proof that we existed!" (A phrase Manus had seen carved into the wooden wall of a reading nook in Shakespeare and Company in Paris; it had come back to him repeatedly as he was reading this book.)

Nora was smiling.

"That's perfect!" she said, as if he had just pronounced the magic word. "That's what meditation's all about. It's all about cultivating a deeper awareness of our own existence."

Her smile was gently indulgent, like the smile of a good fairy. Not for the first time, Manus had the sense that Nora was actually much, much older than him, that she had lived for centuries and centuries and had a clear sight of things that he could only catch the most fleeting glimpses of.

"Now, are you ready?" she asked.

Already she was rolling the mats out on the floor.

"I thought we'd start with some breathing exercises," she said, sitting down on the edge of a chair and propping her ankle on her knee as she removed one sneaker and the sock underneath it to reveal a broad, flat foot with blue-painted toenails. Swapping sides, she removed the other sneaker and the other sock and set both feet on the floor, her hands on her knees; the hands too had stubby blue nails.

"You might want to start by lying down."

"Easier said than done," he said as he looked at the ground. It seemed like a long way down.

With considerable creaking, he managed to lower himself slowly until he was crouched with his knees on the floor, the knuckles of his hands out in front of him to steady him, like a sprinter about to take off. Snatching his hands up off the ground, he allowed himself to fall to one side, landing heavily on one hip. From there it was an easy rollout to a horizontal position. The feeling of the hard floor under his back was surprisingly pleasant; it reminded him of his youth.

"I'm going to give you an eye pillow," said Nora. He had a sense of her hovering above him, and next thing he felt a soft weight on his eyelids, and a smell of dusty lavender.

"Now, I want you to start by taking a few really deep breaths. In through the nose and out through the mouth. In through the nose, out through the mouth . . ."

He heard her voice moving away from him, and for the first time in a very long time, he forced himself to empty his mind of everything but the most basic mechanics of life. In through the nose, out through the mouth. In through the nose, out through the mouth . . .

He was aware of thoughts darting out like little fish from behind the rocks in his brain. Something Sam had said in the middle of the night, coming back to him now. The drip from the kitchen tap — he must find someone to fix it. The book he had just read was a noise in his head, like the roar of a nearby waterfall.

"If your mind wanders, just bring it back to your breathing."

But he had lost the rhythm of it. The breath was stuck in his chest and he had to release it in a clumsy stumble out through his mouth. This breathing thing, it was trickier than it seemed. He made a fresh attempt, harnessing all his powers of concentration to control it.

In through the nose, out through the mouth, he chanted silently to himself, thinking ruefully of old dogs and new tricks as his thoughts marched off in a new direction. He made a half-hearted attempt to catch them, like a man chasing along a city pavement after a scrap of paper or a sweet wrapper that has been picked up by the wind and is dancing away from him, always just out of his reach.

He left Nora and Nando minding Sam while he went out to post his letter.

Nando had arrived early for his session. Nora seemed in no hurry to leave. When Manus left, they were sitting over a pot of tea while Nando told her all about his plans to convert an old shipping container into a home. Any other girl would have run a mile at the thought of such a plan, but much to Manus's amusement, Nora seemed charmed by it.

The meditation had rendered Manus curiously elated. He floated his car to a stop in a loading bay outside the post office and clambered out. He wasn't in the habit of parking his car so much as abandoning it anywhere it would fit. Generally a bus stop or a taxi rank, as the average parking space would not suffice.

He was inside the post office for five minutes perhaps, increasingly aware of an uncomfortably full bladder as a woman at the top of the queue arranged for a number of enormous parcels to be weighed and franked for posting to Latvia. The man ahead of him was buying savings stamps with the contents of his coin jar, and Manus waited with growing exasperation as the single post office worker counted out the coins. At last it was his turn. He approached the hatch and purchased a book of ten local stamps, fixing one carefully on to the front of the envelope before he moved away from the counter to hover in front of the postbox. With all the gravitas of a man voting in a historic election, he deposited the letter into the mouth of the box, listening out for the small thump from inside as it ended its fall.

Buoyed up by the safe execution of his errand, he stepped out of the post office into the startling sunshine, only to find that his car had been clamped. The clampers were still on site, a black man and a white man wearing matching uniforms. The white man was already climbing back into the truck, while the black man was straightening up after applying the clamp to the Jaguar's wheel. Poor sod, thought Manus, imagine the abuse he gets. He determined to be especially courteous to him.

"Gentlemen," said Manus, stepping forward with his hands up, to indicate that he intended them no harm. "If you would be so good as to wait a moment until I've paid my fine, then you'll be free to take that contraption away with you again."

It was his full bladder he was thinking of, and the need to conclude this matter expeditiously. Taking his credit card out of his wallet, he handed it to the black man. The man had shiny ebony skin and a large, wide forehead. His bloodshot eyes were dull with the expectation of abuse.

"I wonder would you be so good as to do the honours for me?"

The man furrowed his forehead, not sure what to make of what he was hearing.

"I don't carry a mobile phone," explained Manus apologetically. "Generally your colleagues are kind enough to make the call for me."

Manus was on first-name terms with most of the city's clampers, and by and large they allowed him free range of the parking spots in town. This pair he had not encountered before. This pair must be new.

"It's all right," he said, nodding encouragingly. "Just dial it in."

Shoulder up to his ear to hold the phone, the clamper put the call through. As he was reading off the credit card numbers, he kept glancing up at Manus, afraid that he was falling victim to some scam.

"Marvellous," said Manus, when the clamper came off the phone and returned the credit card. Once he had removed the clamp from the wheel, Manus handed him a ten-euro note, folded over lengthways so that it formed a taper.

"You're crazy," said the clamper, staring at the banknote he was being offered as if it were a lit fuse. "You're completely crazy."

He was still shaking his head from side to side as he walked back to the truck. Manus pulled away from the kerb, giving the clampers a long, low honk of his horn. The clampers beeped back, two jaunty beeps. That was another team that would never bother him again. For eighty euro, plus the ten-euro tip, he would enjoy free parking for the foreseeable future. For all of his eccentricities, Manus could be surprisingly sane when it came to money.

On the way home, he stopped to drop his already read newspaper in to his ex-wife and to use her lavatory. Deirdre claimed she couldn't afford a newspaper of her own, so Manus was in the habit of dropping his around to her once he'd finished with it. Even though the alimony he paid her was more than sufficient to finance the purchase of her own paper, it would have been less fun that way. It gave Deirdre such satisfaction to live off his hand-me-downs.

"Do you have time for a cup of tea?" she asked him, without waiting for an answer. "Here," she said, fanning a pile of what appeared to be takeaway brochures out on the table in front of him as he sat down. "Have a look at those."

"What is it I'm looking at?"

He opened one brochure to find lists of canapés. According to the lists, you could have ham-hock terrine and tuna sushi rolls and smoked salmon blinis with horseradish crème fraiche. You could have mini-beefburgers and wild mushroom arancini and miniature onion and gruyère tarts, all at what seemed to Manus an eye-watering price. And the most surprising part of the whole thing was that of all the people in all the world, his ex-wife seemed to him the very least likely to splash out on a raft of wildly expensive canapés. There was something about this that didn't add up.

"They're from the caterers," she said, with a girlish lilt to her voice. "For my party."

Like a bell ringing in a far-off room, Manus had a faint recollection of this topic being raised before.

"Ah," he said, "your party." Hoping this would prompt her to offer up some more clues. But she was busy ferrying china cups and saucers to the table. Then a matching milk jug and sugar bowl, and a shop-bought Swiss roll. There was something faintly comical about the way she went about assembling her quaint little tea party. She reminded him of a character out of Beatrix Potter — an upright cat, or a hedgehog dressed in human clothes. With her great white eyebrows spilling down over her eternally surprised eyes and her two loops of white hair hanging like long ears on either side of her face (there were a few white hairs visible on her upper lip that he couldn't help but notice), she could even have been a very large old rabbit.

She set the teapot down on the table and sat down heavily in front of it. Lifting the lid, she gave the tea a stir with the handle of a knife.

Manus turned his cup right side up to reveal layers of tannin build-up on the tender white china inside. The tea set had belonged to his mother, but he had left it behind when he went, thinking it petty to claim it. Clearly, it hadn't been washed since. Deirdre did not believe in washing teacups, or teapots (or salad bowls, for that matter, or omelette pans). She believed it destroyed the flavour to wash them. She was adamant on wiping only.

"Remind me," asked Manus. "When is your party?"

"Well, my birthday's on the Friday," she said. "So I thought we'd have the party on the Saturday."

She had never been a birthday person before. All the time he'd been married to her, she had refused to celebrate her birthday. In an attempt to overcome this prohibition. Manus had once made the mistake of throwing a surprise party for her. She had turned on her heel and walked back out of the room, furious that her friends had seen her without her make-up.

"You never cease to surprise me," he said. (She never ceased to *amuse* him, with her childlike passions.) "Why now?"

She looked at him for a long time before she answered, her hands cupping the hot teapot as if it were a crystal ball.

"I'm going to be eighty. And the closer I get to it, the lighter I feel in my heart. For the first time in my life, I have a great desire to celebrate."

Never had it occurred to Manus to envy his wife, but it occurred to him now. It occurred to him that she had nothing in the world to be worrying about. Her work on this earth was done.

"I've spent so many years worrying about Macdara. I've worried myself sick about Acushla, because she's so soft. I've even worried about Alma — her hardness was such a worry to me. But a funny thing happened to me recently. I realised they're not my responsibility any more. Their lives are their own to live and their troubles are their own, and there's nothing more I can do."

Manus didn't like to tell her this, but he had had the same thought many, many years ago.

"Their lives will go on," he said, "long after you and I are gone."

"Yes," she said, "I can see that now. Funny how I could never see that before."

"Let me offer you another comforting thought," he said. "In a hundred years' time, nobody will even remember who any of us were."

He knew this would amuse her, and it did. This was the secret of their friendship, it seemed to him. The fact that they were amused by the same things.

"They'll remember you," she said, "because of your book. Whereas my art was, by its very nature, transient."

He shrugged. He had never placed the same value on his book as other people had. He couldn't really see what all the fuss was about, couldn't see what made it stand out from anything else. The book he had read last night, now that was a different matter. The shadow of it stretched across his day like the shadow of a mighty mountain. He kept going back to it in his mind . . .

Deirdre lifted the teapot and Manus held his cup out to her to receive the tea. He poured himself some milk and gave it a stir, leaning down to slurp the first mouthful, even though he knew this would annoy her. The annoyances were a part of it, this imperfect intimacy that existed between them. Like fond siblings, they were familiar with each other's every foible.

"After everything that's happened," she said, "I feel it's an opportune time for a gathering of the tribe."

"What exactly do you have in mind?" he asked, with some suspicion.

"Just a little family get-together. I thought it would be nice to gather the four generations together under the one roof. A meeting of the clan."

They lined up in front of Manus's eyes, two by two, as if they were boarding the Ark. He pictured himself and Sam coming up the front steps, then Alma and Mick, arm in arm and laughing, followed by Nora, who he saw walking alongside Nando. Now Connie and Emmet and the two boys, and after them, Acushla and Liam, side by side but not touching. At the back of the line was Macdara, all on his own. Why did the thought of it give him a shivery sense of foreboding? He felt as if someone was walking on his grave.

"We'll open up the double rooms," Deirdre was saying, her eyes sparkling with an intent that was almost sinister. "We'll have champagne first, and canapés, and then everybody will have to perform a party piece, even the little boys."

Manus found his suspicions growing, a feeling of unease that he could not explain. For a moment he wondered if perhaps Deirdre was planning some kind of ritual massacre? He had a vision of his entire family lying in lifeless puddles on the floor of her drawing room, while a toxic gas hovered in the air and she stood by the fireplace and sang "The Last Rose of Summer". That had always been her party piece. Even now he could hear her singing it in her huge voice, a voice that could fill every inch of any room, no matter how large.

"Why am I getting a bad feeling about this?" he asked her.

She stared at him with pantomime innocence, her spiky eyelashes blinking away at him.

"Why would you say that?"

"Because I know you," he growled. "And I know when you're up to something."

"I am not!"

"Oh, yes you are."

"Oh, no I'm not."

"Oh, yes you are," he said, determined to have the last word. He knew her well enough to know that she was up to something. But what it might be he could not for the life of him have guessed.

They were always great friends.

They were friends before ever they were married and they remained friends afterwards, strange as that might seem to some. "Isn't it funny the way we've ended up being such good friends?" she said to him once. It was the day of Connie's wedding and he had insisted on walking her out of the church behind the bride and groom, leaving Sam to trail behind with Macdara. "Well, lass," he had said, holding out his arm for her to take. "We should present a united front as grandparents." When the truth was that he wanted to save her the indignity of walking down the aisle alone. "You're a good friend to me," she said to him later that evening, when he sat down beside her to take a rest from the dancing. "You might even be my best friend," she added with mild disgust. "God help us all."

He was twenty when he met her. A medical school dropout, he had managed to find a job with an advertising agency to tide him over until he fulfilled his dream of becoming a writer, a dream he never doubted would come to pass. Deirdre was seventeen and fresh out of Ennis. With her elocution-lesson accent and her thick black hair worn loose down her back, she was on the run from her mother's small-town ambitions for her, ambitions she was hell-bent on frustrating. They met in McDaids on a wet summer Saturday and Manus offered to buy her a drink. "I'll have a brandy," she said boldly. He used to tease her about that afterwards. Who drinks brandy on a summer's afternoon? Only a girl just up from the country!

"Your mother and I always had great affection for one another," Manus told Acushla when she came to him once looking for answers. She was wondering, not for the first time, whether to leave her husband. "The secret to my relationship with your mother is that we never took each other too seriously," he told her. "No matter what happened, we were always able to laugh about it." Looking at Acushla, he could see that laughter was the last thing on her mind. You would think, by looking at her, that she had forgotten how to laugh.

"Macushla," he had said, resting his hand on her thin arm. "Macushla, my blue-eyed Macushla." (It was Manus who had the naming of her, and he had named her with that song in mind, a song he sang to her often when she was a child.) "Macushla," he said. "Macushla," and with his words he was deliberately evoking that beautiful old melody in both of their heads. "Do you think you might try, for a change, not to take everything so very seriously?"

She had smiled at him then, through her tears, and she had promised him that she would try. But Manus didn't hold out much hope for her. He had seen too much of life to think that there was any hope of a person changing their colours once they were cast. Acushla had been born with a deadly appetite for battle, a battle that she had waged first on her sister and then on her husband. Now at least it seemed to Manus that she had found a fight that was worthy of her. It was highly amusing to Manus, if not to Acushla, to think of her as a feminist icon. He was very much cheered not just by his younger daughter's belated blossoming, but by the notion that life still had it within its power to spring him the odd surprise.

It was one of the more unwelcome things about getting older, the sense of certainty that had begun to plague him. The stories of people's lives seemed at times so obvious to him, it was as if the whole world was a book that he had reached the end of, while everybody else was still reading. A sad and lonely feeling; there was nothing that gave him more pleasure than encountering a last-minute plot twist.

In Alma and Mick's wounded reunion Manus saw a beautiful logic, and it seemed to him that in his failure to foresee it, he had neglected to factor in the virulent strain of monogamy that affected all the women of his ex-wife's lineage. In Acushla's reconciliation with Liam, he recognised the same fatal strain of loyalty, one that he suspected Connie had inherited as well.

"I'm afraid we're one-man women," Deirdre said to him once, stating it as a sad fact, when he had asked her whether she ever saw herself marrying again. He was reminded of a story she used to tell the children when they were small. A story from her own childhood, about a swan whose mate was shot by a poacher; the widowed swan spent the rest of her days going up and down the river alone. "Swans mate for life, you see," Deirdre would say. "If a swan loses its mate, it will live out its days alone rather than ever mate again." Only now does Manus see that in leaving Deirdre, he doomed her to spending the rest of her life alone. A fate she bore with silent dignity, just like the swan in her story. It seems to Manus very sad that he never saw that until now.

Of all the surprises that lie in wait around the corner, Manus prays that one of them is reserved for Macdara, but he fears that this is not the case. He sees Macdara living out his life alone, and he understands that Macdara's self-imposed celibacy is the result of his own highly publicised sexuality. If Manus has one regret, it is the hurt that he caused to Macdara. That's the one thing he would like to be able to go back and change.

"It wasn't you that put Macdara off sex," Deirdre said to him recently. "It was all that rugby."

They were walking along a country lane, the hedgerows spilling over with life and colour. Ahead of them the coffin of an old friend was being borne along the road from the church to the graveyard by a slow-moving hearse. The friend had been a contemporary of Deirdre's at the Abbey. He had stood best man to Manus at their wedding. Now he was dead and they were walking after his coffin.

"Poor Macdara," said Deirdre. "He never recovered from being forced to play all that rugby."

Manus smiled at the comfort his ex-wife never ceased to find in these tangents of hers, tangents that for all their whimsy still contained somewhere within them the seeds of some grain of truth. It was true that Macdara had been traumatised by the smelly, sweaty-fleshed contact of the school scrum; it had produced in him a distaste for physical intimacy of any kind.

"Do you think he's lonely?" asked Manus, looking down at his shoes as he walked, one foot appearing in his line of vision, then the other. He was trying to keep step with Deirdre, walking deliberately slowly in order to do so.

"Oh, no more than any of us," she said. "Perhaps even less. Don't forget, Macdara chooses to be alone."

As they took their places round the open grave, a very old priest recited an inaudible prayer.

"Hypocrisy of the highest order," hissed Deirdre into Manus's ear. "Sure, he always held that the notion of God was a nonsense."

Manus turned his face in order to whisper back.

"Hypocrisy, my dear, is the medium in which we move."

A non-believer himself, Manus was nonetheless a great fan of Christian pageantry. In particular he was a sucker for a rousing Christian hymn. There was nothing quite so comforting to Manus as a good Protestant hymn.

"Well, lass," he said, as they began to move away from the grave. He held his arm out for her to fall in

337

step with him, noticing with surprise that she had tears in her eyes. For a moment he thought that perhaps it was the sun that had made her eyes water, but when she spoke, her voice was affected too.

"Do you know what just occurred to me," she said, reaching out to grab his arm as she stumbled on the uneven ground.

"What?"

She gazed up at him with a fierce look on her face. "Now that Donal is gone, you're the only one left who remembers me for the girl I once was. And I'm the only one who remembers what you were like when you were young."

The funerals were coming hard and fast. Hardly a day went by but Manus spotted someone he knew in the death notices. Today it was Freddy Noble whose death was being announced. Beloved husband of Margaret, said the death notice. Deeply regretted by his devoted daughters Michaela and Ursula, his sons-in-law Arthur and Alan, granddaughters Isobel, Amy and Emily, and his many nieces and nephews. *Ar dheis Dé go raibh a anam dílis*.

Manus laughed.

"No mention of poor Patricia," he said to Sam.

"Patricia," said Sam. He appeared to be giving the name great thought. "Patricia and her cassoulet."

"Forty years," said Manus. "Freddy's been living with Patricia for forty years, and not a mention of her in the death notice."

As he spread a thin layer of marmalade on his toast, he was smiling to himself at the endlessly bizarre turns of human behaviour. He was wondering to himself, fleetingly, whether Deirdre might expect a mention in his own death notice. Surely not, he thought, although technically she was still his wife. Manus had no doubt that Deirdre would outlive him. He was always telling her she would live to be a hundred, and for some reason this seemed to irritate her. She took it as an insult, which was why he persisted in mentioning it.

Manus would have liked to go to Freddy's funeral. He and Freddy had been in boarding school together, and when Manus sold his book, it was Freddy who had looked the contracts over for him. Often over the years he and Sam had been invited to eat with Freddy and Patricia in their little house down by the Dodder. (Manus and Sam could of course be counted upon not to be judgemental about Freddy's domestic arrangements.) Patricia was a terrific cook and a priceless mimic, and Manus had many a happy memory of nights around their table, replete with Patricia's famous cassoulet. Yes, Manus would have liked to be at Freddy's funeral, if only to see how the wife and daughters would handle the presence of Patricia. That would certainly be worth seeing, only Manus had to bring Sam to a doctor's appointment.

"Sam," he said. "We should start getting ready. We have to be at Dr Boylan's by eleven." Manus had been careful not to mention the appointment until now, aware that it would only rattle Sam to know of it too far in advance.

"Dr Boylan," said Sam, flustered already. "What time do we have to be there?"

He rose from the table, unaware that his shirt was still open, the buttons unbuttoned and his white vest visible underneath.

"Eleven," said Manus. "Don't worry, we have plenty of time."

He came around the table and drew Sam's shirt closed. Fastening the buttons, he took care to keep his hand movements as brusque and businesslike as possible. Sam had developed a tendency to mistake some of Manus's more innocent ministrations for sexual advances, with the result that Manus was wary of touching him. He was afraid to put his hand on Sam's arm, lest Sam take this as a come-on, afraid to stroke Sam's hair lest this should lead Sam to stroke him back. Sam's illness seemed to have had the effect of stoking his sexual appetite and freeing him of his inhibitions, whereas on Manus it had the opposite effect. Manus didn't like making love to Sam any more, or being made love to by him. It didn't feel right, not when he couldn't be sure that Sam knew what he was doing. This wasn't something Manus felt he could talk to anyone about. Just another of the many little lonelinesses he had acquired since Sam first started to get sick.

"It's hot out there," said Manus. "You'll hardly need a jacket."

Selecting for himself a battered panama hat from the shelf in the cupboard, he set it on his head and checked for his keys and his wallet before ushering Sam out into the hall and closing the door behind them.

As they waited for the lift, Sam was anxious, impatiently watching the numbers on the display above the door.

"What time do we have to be there?" he asked.

"Eleven," said Manus. "We've loads of time."

"We've loads of time," said Sam, as if Manus was the one who needed convincing.

When the lift arrived, there was someone already inside. A very obese young man, Sam and Manus only just about managed to squash in beside him. The lift doors closed and Manus noticed that Sam was humming the Oompa Loompa tune from *Charlie and the Chocolate Factory*; he prayed the young man would not recognise it. Painstakingly slowly they moved down through the six floors, arriving at last on the ground floor. The lift doors opened and Manus and Sam were forced to step out into the lobby to allow the young man to emerge. They got back in for the last leg of their journey, down to the basement car park. Sam was still humming as they stepped out of the lift and walked towards the car.

"Now," said Manus, opening the passenger door for Sam. He waited until Sam was safely in, then went round and climbed into the driver's seat. He started the engine, checking the petrol gauge to see if they would need to stop. The needle showed the tank a quarter full. That would get them to the doctor's surgery and back, if not much further. Turning the radio on to a classical music station, Manus swung out of his parking place (the spaces on either side of him were empty, because no one could fit their car in beside his for fear of scraping it). He put his foot to the floor so as to make it up the ramp, and an unholy noise erupted from the back of the car, as if tin cans had been attached to the bumper.

"Damn it," said Manus, and he stopped the car at the top of the ramp, wrenching the handbrake up and hauling himself out. He went round the back of the car, stooping to look underneath it.

The fender was hanging off. It was clinging by one dull and neglected chrome arm on to the round rump of the car. When Manus touched it, it clattered to the ground, skittering away down the ramp. He inched down the slope to retrieve it, moving sideways and with great care, like a skier caught in deep snow. As he bent down to pick up the fender, he heard a noise that surprised him, a noise like something snapping. The last thing he saw was his car rolling backwards down the ramp towards him. The last thing he heard was the orchestra of St Martin-in-the-Fields, conducted by Sir Neville Marriner, with their beautiful rendition of "Sheep May Safely Graze". The last thing he thought as he lay on the ground with the weight of his own car rolling over him was how curious it was that he of all people should be brought back into the fold in this way at the end.

MacENTEE, Manus (Dublin, and formerly of Kildangan, Co. Kildare) — 26 June 2013 (tragically), in his 83rd year. Deeply regretted by his partner Sam, his wife of many years Deirdre (née O'Sullivan), his daughters Alma and Acushla and his son Macdara, his sons-in-law Michael and Liam Collins, his granddaughters Constance and Nora, his grandson-in-law Emmet and his great-grandsons Ernest and Oscar. Requiem Mass at Star of the Sea Church in Sandymount on Friday at 11.00, followed by a cremation service at Mount Jerome Cemetery.

Macdara

"I always thought he wanted to be buried at sea," said Acushla.

"You can't be serious," said Alma.

"That's what he always said he wanted," said Acushla, her words rising up and down the scale like notes on a piano.

"He said to it me too," said Deirdre. "Many a time he told me he'd like a sea burial."

They were waiting for the undertaker, the four of them sitting in the hush of the waiting room — they had turned down the offer of a home visit in favour of neutral ground.

"I did hear him mention it once or twice," said Alma, "but I always assumed it was a joke. He used to say he'd like to be eaten by a crocodile, but I think it's safe to assume that was a joke too."

Nobody replied. Alma looked from one to the other of them, her eyes wide and unblinking as if to say, *surely* you agree with me?

Macdara coughed, to break the silence.

"I don't remember him ever showing any interest in sailing," said Acushla. "Does anyone remember him ever showing any interest in sailing?"

"No," said Deirdre quickly. "Just sailors."

Macdara leaned forward.

"If it's what he wanted, we could always ask."

The sound of his own voice was a surprise to him as much as it was to anyone else.

"We could always ask them," he said tentatively, "whether it's possible?"

As soon as he'd finished speaking, he sank further into his chair, pulling his chin down on to his chest and his shoulders up to his ears. Alma leaned her head back against the wall, closing her eyes with a sigh, while Acushla propped an elbow on an elegantly crossed knee, wobbling her head encouragingly. His mother gave him a discreet wink, as if they were bridge partners and she was communicating something to him about their next move. Macdara was just on the point of venturing to speak again when the undertaker came into the room. He advanced with his arm extended to greet the grieving widow, who was already rising from her chair to accept his condolences.

"She's describing herself as his *wife*," Alma hissed as they were leaving. Her mother had disappeared back into the dark recesses of the funeral home in search of a bathroom.

"Well, technically she *is* his wife," said Acushla, moving through the door Macdara was holding open for her. "They were never divorced."

The three siblings formed a loose circle out on the pavement, assailed by a barrage of light and heat, along with the smell of chips from the takeaway next door.

"Sweet Jesus," said Alma. "This presents us with a bit of a diplomatic situation."

"What do we do?" asked Acushla, reaching up with a perfectly manicured hand to pull her sunglasses down over her eyes. "You don't think she'll want to sit in the front pew in the church, do you?"

"I don't see any indication of her taking a back seat. As far as she's concerned, she's the grieving widow."

"So, where does that leave poor Sam?"

"Right where she always wanted him," said Alma. "At the mercy of her generosity."

"Oh, pray," said Acushla. "Pray she doesn't use this as an opportunity to get her revenge on Sam. I wouldn't put it past her to pull rank on him now that she can."

"I'm afraid we'll just have to make sure that doesn't happen," said Alma.

And they all fell silent again as they contemplated the rocky path that lay ahead of them. Macdara turned to see the undertaker ushering their mother out the door of the funeral home. Her hair had come loose of its moorings and her cape hung lopsided off her stooped shoulders. As she squinted into the glare of the sunshine, Macdara was struck for the first time by how old she had become. She had gone and got old without him even noticing.

It was always his mother Macdara was closest to. Ever since he was small, his mother had been his silent ally, the champion of his every idiosyncrasy. There was no aberration Macdara could adopt, no whim of his that his mother would not indulge. From his refusal ever to eat meat that had any bones in it, or fruit that had any pips in it (apples, pears, grapes — Macdara had an unnatural fear of their offspring growing inside his belly), to his insistence on wearing wellies every day to school, his mother bent to every turn of his personality. Macdara's clothes had to be washed a dozen times before he wore them because he hated the feel of new fabric. He had to have flannel sheets because he found cotton too scratchy. His shoes had to be weathered by the shoemaker, and his hair had to be cut at home because he would not go to the barber's. On the rare occasions that Deirdre resolved to trim his fingernails, she would always have to ring the neighbours first, to warn them not to call the Guards when they heard the screams. When Macdara was sick, as he often was, his mother never forced him to go to school, allowing him to spend the day in her bed instead, reading detective stories. Some days he was allowed to stay in her bed even when he wasn't sick. Some days he was allowed to stay in her bed just because it was raining, or because it was cold, or because he didn't want to go to school.

"It's very hard for Macdara to go to school," his mother used to say, a phrase that his sisters pounced on and repeated ad nauseam. "It's very hard for Macdara to go to school," they would mimic, bobbling their sleek little heads from side to side as they performed the imitation. And Macdara would skulk away, withdrawing further and further into his own silent world, a world that only his mother seemed to understand. Because the truth was that it *was* very hard for Macdara to go to school. There were days when it was hard for Macdara to go out of the house. He was like a soft-shell crab, or a turtle without a shell. He seemed to have been born without any of the body armour that other people use to survive in the world.

Macdara's father was baffled by him. With his boyish enthusiasm for life and his eternally optimistic view of human nature, Manus was at a loss to understand Macdara's fears, fears that were born not of experience but of some pathological sensitivity his father was not wired to comprehend. But while another man might have forced him to engage in blood sports and eat spare ribs with his bare hands, while another man would no doubt have argued that Macdara's weaknesses were all due to his mother's indulgence and that it was his duty as a father to provide a counterweight, Manus was happy to let Macdara off. Like a dog and cat who are forced to share the same house, Manus and Macdara managed to live alongside each other quite happily for years, while ignoring each other almost entirely. When his father moved out, Macdara was surprised by the size of the hole he left in the house, a hole that was filled by the sound of his mother shouting, and Alma slamming doors and Acushla's heartbroken sobbing.

Macdara had pitied his sisters then, because their loss was so much greater than his. And he pitied them again now, because they had lost the parent they loved more. For his part, Macdara couldn't help but be relieved that it was his father and not his mother who had been the first to go.

It was his sisters who told him.

They appeared at the studio door, Alma with her head hanging down and Acushla hovering behind her.

Macdara noticed straight away how pale they both looked.

Alma took a deep breath in through her mouth. She had a strange half-smile on her face, more of a grimace than a smile, and her eyes were all red.

"Macdara," she said. "I'm afraid Dad's had an accident."

"Oh, dear," said Macdara. And he pictured the scene. He saw his father's car standing at a jaunty angle in the middle of a major intersection with smoke coming out of all its orifices as a distraught woman motorist inspected the damage to her new Mercedes. "I hope there isn't too much damage."

His sisters looked at each other and it occurred to Macdara that they did seem afraid. They seemed afraid of *him*.

"Why are you *afraid*?" he asked, seizing on that one word Alma had used, over all others. A word with the implication of something that was still to come, something that could even now be prevented. "You both look like you've seen a ghost."

Neither of them spoke, and all of a sudden Macdara too was very afraid.

He held up his right index finger.

"Don't tell me," he said, taking sudden command of the situation. "Whatever it is, this thing that you were about to tell me. I don't want you to say it."

He turned away from them then, and walked back into the studio, leaving his sisters standing in the open doorway. Into his bedroom he went, and sat down on the end of the bed, with his hands cupping his knees.

His mind was blank but his breath was coming hard and fast. He concentrated all of his attention on getting his breath back.

After they'd been to the undertaker's, they returned to Macdara's studio to draft the death notice. Leaning their upper bodies in through the open door with their feet still planted outside in the garden, they called to Macdara's mind a pair of explorers surveying the interior walls of a cave.

"Come on in," he said to them, gathering his papers up off the table and removing stray clothes from the chairs. "Sit down. Make yourselves at home."

He filled a jug of water from the tap and poured some lemon barley cordial into it. He set three tumblers on the table, and out of the kitchen press he took a pack of Nice biscuits, arranging a generous supply of them in a wide fan on a willow-pattern plate.

"Why do I get the feeling we're in an Enid Blyton novel?" said Alma, slipping her shoes off as she sprawled in a chair. "I feel like I'm one of the Famous Five."

"The Secret Seven," said Macdara, and despite the circumstances, he was aware of a feeling of great pride bubbling up in him, pride at having his sisters as guests here in his little house. "I think the Secret Seven are the ones you're thinking of," he said happily. "They were the ones who had a den." (When Macdara was a kid, he used to read those books over and over again — it was the Five Find-Outers and Dog who were his favourites.)

"I was a Nancy Drew girl myself," said Alma, and to Macdara's great pleasure, she reached out for a biscuit and began to nibble at it. Her face was puffy with what Macdara recognised as the effects of medication. Her figure plumper as a result of all the gourmet meals Mick had been feeding her. A softness to her that had not been there before. For the first time in his life, Macdara was not scared of her.

Doyenne of a hundred fund-raising committees, Acushla took a pad of paper out of her handbag and a freshly sharpened pencil. Flipping the cover of the pad back on itself and positioning the pencil expectantly over the blank page, she looked up at the others.

"Okay, where do we start?"

"MacEntee," said Alma, settling back into her chair and closing her eyes as she began to dictate the copy. "Manus. In his eighty-third year. As the result of a tragic accident . . ."

Acushla's head was bowed down sideways over her page, the tip of her tongue probing the corner of her mouth. The sound of her pencil scratching away at the surface of the paper.

"Deeply regretted by . . ."

Macdara waited to see what Alma would say next.

". . . his loving partner Sam."

Scratch scratch scratch went Acushla's pencil.

"His ex-wife Deirdre . . ."

Acushla looked up.

"She's not going to like that."

Alma threw her hands out in exasperation. Her poor fingers made Macdara wince. He couldn't look at them without feeling pain.

"We can't say 'wife', as if they were still married," said Alma.

"We can't say 'ex-wife' either," said Acushla back to her.

"I've a suggestion," said Macdara.

They both turned to look at him, as if they had only just become aware of his presence.

"How about 'wife of many years'?"

Acushla froze as she considered it. Alma dipped her head like a conductor guiding an orchestra into a quiet section of a symphony.

"Do you know," she said, raising her head again. "That could work."

"It's brilliant," said Acushla, scratching away furiously at the page. "Absolutely brilliant."

"It's beautiful," said Alma. "Although since we're being such sticklers for detail, I'm not sure it's entirely accurate to use the word 'tragedy'. It seems to me that 'a tragedy in his eighty-third year' is a bit of a contradiction in terms."

Macdara brought his shoulders together to make himself smaller, and leaned in over the table.

"But it *is* tragic," he said, fixing upon it as a point of fact.

Alma raised her eyebrows as she waited for him to explain.

"By its very definition it's a tragedy. The death of a man because of a fatal flaw is defined as a tragedy."

"I don't understand," said Alma. "What's the fatal flaw?"

"Don't you see? That stupid car was the fatal flaw."

Alma smiled and nodded. Something dawning in her eyes, something almost like respect.

"So we're sticking with 'tragedy'?" asked Acushla, anxious to move on.

"Absolutely," said Alma. "A tragedy it is."

A tragedy was what it felt like to Macdara at times. The enormity of it taking him by the throat and tightening its grip on him until his eyes were watering and he could hardly breathe. It was in those moments that it seemed to Macdara that the world had stopped its turning, and it was hard for him to imagine that any other human being had ever been bereaved quite like he had been bereaved. That anybody else's death could ever have had quite such a profound effect on the physical world, altering the taste of all the foods in it, distorting the look of a room when he walked into it, and bending the scale of the streets and the buildings outside so that everything he looked at appeared strangely but inexplicably wrong. Only the sounds of the world were unchanged, the noise of the traffic and the exploding roar of the crowd from the stadium, the babble of the football fans gathered outside the pub after the match had finished. Macdara felt like shouting at them as he walked past, "What are you laughing about? Did you not hear? My father *died*."

At other moments, it seemed to him the most ordinary thing in the world that his father should have died. Doesn't everybody die, after all? Why should his father be any different? In those moments it seemed to Macdara that it was a mistake to make too much of a fuss of this one ordinary old death. It seemed unseemly to make too much of it.

"At my age you don't get sad when someone old dies," said his mother. "At my age you see it as a cause for celebration when someone of Manus's age dies."

They were all sitting around his mother's table, eating an Irish stew that a neighbour had dropped in. Nora had heated it up while Connie set the table. It was only when he began eating that Macdara discovered how hungry he was.

"You don't really mean that," said Acushla, looking at their mother with brimming eyes. Connie too had tears in her eyes. The expression on Nora's face was more like disappointment. Even Alma appeared shocked.

"Manus lived a long and rich life," said Deirdre, speaking with slow emphasis. "He had the good fortune to be whisked away before falling prey to decrepitude. Something you should all get down on your knees and give thanks for, since you're the ones who would have ended up looking after him."

Blinking her dry eyes, she stared brazenly back at them all, and for the first time in his life, Macdara saw something in her that he did not like. A ruthlessness that he'd never seen before. He found himself wondering when it had crept in.

Macdara's father's death was reported in all the papers, as you might expect, and the TV news even ran a pre-prepared obituary. How long had it lain in wait? Macdara wondered, before experiencing a pang of something not unlike jealousy at the thought that there would be no obituaries to mark the passing of his own outwardly unremarkable life. Unless? Unless. Macdara still harboured an intermittent but ardent hope that he might yet achieve something remarkable with his life.

It was in this spirit of hope that he had sent his book off to his father. Taking every care to preserve his anonymity, he had printed the manuscript off and parcelled it up, despite the clamour of voices in his head telling him he was a fool. He had walked to the post office, tormented by those voices. Even as he was standing in the queue, they would not fall silent.

He's going to hate it. This rubbish? Sure it's hardly even literate . . . Self-indulgent crap . . . What kind of delusional freak would think this worth publishing? What a shameful waste of paper and ink . . . You'd have been better off using the paper to wipe your arse . . . And to think, you could have been out doing something useful with your time, instead of writing this pathetic crap. Pathetic, pathetic, pathetic.

Ten, twelve times a night Macdara woke in the grip of a sickening panic, remembering with a physical lurch of his heart his wildly reckless act. What on earth had he been thinking, sending the book to his father? He would roll over on to his tummy in agony, burying his face in the pillow to smother the thought. He would contemplate for one wonderful moment the possibility that he had only dreamt that he had posted it, abandoning that fantasy with a despair that was almost hysterical. He would bang his forehead off the pillow over and over again, punishing himself for his own foolishness. Eventually he would turn over on to his back again, talking himself back to sleep with a flock of familiar reassurances, like sheep you might count.

At least he had not put his name to the book, that's what he told himself. There was no way his father could have known that he was the author. His father probably hadn't even had time to read the book before he died. If there was any comfort to be found for Macdara in Manus's sudden death, it was in the realisation that in all likelihood he must have died before he got a chance to read his book.

They decided to wake him in the funeral home. It was not the custom to wake people at home any more, not in the city at least.

"That's a country thing," said Alma.

"I don't like the idea of having the body in the house," said Acushla. "It gives me the creeps."

"Think of all the tea we'd have to make," said Deirdre. "We'd have to give people *sandwiches*."

Macdara agreed that on balance it was best to wake his father in the funeral home.

In death, his father looked like somebody else. A generic dead person, all barely covered bones and waxy skin. With his eyelids closed forever on his magnificent eyes, he could have been anybody.

"Who *is* that?" asked Ernie, eyes wide with awe as he was led up to the coffin.

"That's your great-grandfather," whispered Connie.

Macdara could hear Ernie sucking this information into his chest in a raspy asthmatic wheeze.

"Here," said Connie, rooting around in her handbag, "have a puff of your inhaler."

Oscar was up on tiptoes, trying to see over the rim of the coffin. Connie pushed him and his brother towards their grandmother and stood for a moment by herself at the head of the coffin. Macdara noticed her hands fluttering loose by her sides. It occurred to him that she was wondering whether she dared touch the corpse or not. As he watched, she placed a hand on the edge of the coffin for a moment before snatching it away.

"I can't believe he's gone," she said, sitting down beside Macdara. He could feel the swell of her sorrow rising and falling in her. She allowed herself to tilt a little to the side, so that her shoulder rested against his. He reached out a hand and patted her on the arm. He couldn't think of a thing to say.

"It's okay," said Connie. "There's nothing you can say."

On the far side of the coffin, Connie's children had settled themselves on chairs between their grandparents, while Deirdre sat alone at the end of the row. Acushla was feeding the boys wine gums, dispensing the sweets straight out of her handbag one by one, while Liam tapped at the face of his phone. It occurred to Macdara that Connie's children would forever after associate the taste of wine gums with their great-grandfather's funeral. Those were the kind of things that children remembered.

The door of the room opened and out of the patch of day-light Mick and Alma materialised. Macdara noticed how Mick moved with practised ease, working his way along the row of chairs to greet Acushla first, then Liam and finally Deirdre. Coming round the base of the coffin, he gave Connie a kiss on the cheek.

"Macdara," he said. "I'm so sorry." He took Macdara's hand and grasped the flesh of his upper arm.

"It's all right," said Macdara, sitting back down again too quickly. No sooner was he sitting down than the door opened again and Nora came in. She had Sam with her, along with some other fellow Macdara did not recognise. He felt a stirring of anxiety at the presence of this stranger.

"Sam," he said, getting up and moving towards the door. He shook Sam's hand, taking care not to stand too close to him. He was worried, as always, about his breath. Worried there might be a smell off it, he liked to keep his distance from people in case this was so. (In school once, someone had made a comment about his breath, and he had been worrying about it ever since, despite his obsessive use of mouthwash and mints.)

"Sam," said Mick, closing in from one side. "I'm so sorry." He pulled Sam into a half-hug, gripping his arm with one hand while the other went round Sam's shoulder. Sam was wearing a highly unsuitable burgundy velvet smoking jacket and a silk cravat. On his bottom half, a pair of jeans and runners. Acushla hovered beside Mick, waiting for her turn with him.

"Sam," she said gently. "Do you want to come over and see Dad? He looks so nice, I think you should see him."

Sam allowed himself to be led over to the coffin. All eyes on him, he stood looking down at the face of the

358

man he had lived with for more than three decades. Acushla stepped back a few paces to give him space.

"Do you think he knows what's happening?" whispered Connie.

"Maybe it's just as well if he doesn't," Macdara whispered back.

"I'm not sure it's fair," he heard Alma say, her voice coming from somewhere behind him. "It's not fair to have him here."

Mick's voice came in reply to her, somewhere above a whisper.

"Poor bugger. He looks like he doesn't have a clue what's going on."

And still Sam stood beside the coffin. The twin candles that flanked it flickered and puffed breaths of white smoke out into the dark air. A door opened and closed. A child tumbled off a chair. Macdara watched as Sam reached his hand into the coffin and fumbled with the clothes Manus was wearing. It looked like he was trying to undo the buttons of his jacket.

"Oh, sweet Jesus," Macdara heard Alma mutter. "What's he doing?"

They all watched as Sam slipped his hand inside Manus's jacket, resting his palm on the place where his lover's heart had ceased beating.

Macdara experienced a terrible rush of sorrow. For a moment he couldn't bear the weight of it and he let his head fall down on to his chest. When he looked up again, Nora and the stranger were on either side of Sam. Putting an arm gently around his shoulders, Nora led him away, guiding him past Acushla and Liam and the little boys, past Deirdre (who reached out and grasped his wrist without rising from her chair) and around the foot of the coffin to a chair at the end of the opposite row. He was sitting directly across from Deirdre now, with the coffin in between them, a discreet white satin sheet obscuring Manus's legs and feet. Was his father wearing shoes under there? wondered Macdara. Or was he just in his socks, or even his bare feet? Macdara's mind roamed these corridors with curious abandon, like a dog off its leash.

That was a good analogy, he thought, and he would have liked to write it down. But he had no notebook with him, no pen. No way of taking notes. Instead he sat studying the faces of his family lined up opposite him. He listened to their voices swirling around him. With his niece's melon-scented perfume fighting against the heady smell of candle wax, and his grandnephews aiming surreptitious kicks at each other's shins while their grandmother turned to talk to her husband — with his mother and Alma sitting side by side now and absent-mindedly holding each other's hand, and the curly-haired stranger bending down to say something to Sam — Macdara found his head flooded with thoughts. Thoughts that swooped down on him like birds gathering in a great oak tree. Words, sentences, whole paragraphs of prose settling around him like crows at dusk. He had a desperate urge to hold on to them, to grab them and stuff them into his pockets, these maddening little morsels of inspiration. And it was then that it came to him. As he sat by his father's coffin, wishing uselessly for a scrap of paper, or a sharp object that he could use to scratch words into the skin of his hand, it popped into his head. A sequence of words as beautifully jarring as it was perfect. As soon as it formed in his mind, he knew that he had found the title for his book. He knew also, with a crashing sense of defeat, that he would have forgotten it again by the time he had left this room.

You always think you'll remember these things, but you never do.

The letter arrived the following morning.

It was the day of the funeral, and Macdara recognised his father's handwriting immediately. He recognised the slanted, spiky script, executed as always in black ink with a thin-nibbed fountain pen. For one mad moment Macdara thought that his father was communicating with him from beyond the grave.

Cradling the letter in his open palms the way you might hold a wounded bird, he walked it over to the kitchen table and propped it up against a box of Alpen, taking a few steps back from the table to gain some distance from it. He needed time to think.

The address that had been handwritten by his father on the front of the envelope was the address of the PO box Macdara had hired at the local sorting office, at a cost of four hundred and seventy euro. The scheme for the hire of the PO box had been brewing in his mind for months. He had looked at it from every angle and it seemed to him that it was the only practical way to resolve the impasse in his head. The book was finished, had been finished for months, but there was no way on this earth that Macdara could even contemplate sending it to anyone until his father had read it. His father's opinion was the only opinion that mattered to him. His father's scorn was the only thing he feared. Because Macdara had written the book with only one reader in mind, and that reader was his father. It seemed to Macdara that there was something mystical about the way the letter had arrived on this of all days. He decided that he would shower first, and then he would get dressed, and only then would he open it.

The whole time he was in the shower, he was thinking about the letter. His mind like a wobbly weighing scale, one minute he was high on the hope that his father had liked the book, the next minute he had tipped over into the despairing certainty that he had hated it. As he dressed himself in his only suit — a suit he'd had for more than thirty years — it seemed to Macdara that he would be taking a great risk in opening the letter. If it was bad (as of course it would be), if it was as bad as he feared it would be, it would sully the day of his father's funeral. And Macdara wanted to keep the day of his father's funeral free of all worldly things.

He decided not to open the letter.

The book was three decades in the writing.

You do hear about this, don't you? You hear about people for whom it took thirty years to write a book. Macdara comes across these stories from time to time and he finds them comforting. What he hates hearing are stories of prolific writers, people who turn out a book every year for forty years. In Macdara's case, the writing is painfully slow, every sentence something to

362

be worked and reworked, until eventually he is happy with it. Macdara has often spent a week on one sentence, a month on a single paragraph. And of course there have been mishaps. At one point a decade's work was wiped out when the old laptop he was using died — it took him another year to recreate what was lost, and even then he couldn't be sure it was quite as good. Other times it seems to him that perhaps the rewrite was better, and he wonders should he destroy all his work and reconstruct it from memory, the way his father burns his toast and scrapes it?

The desire to write has been in him for ever. He remembers riding around in the back of his father's car — he was six years old, or maybe seven — and there were trees going by the window, and Macdara was trying to find the right combination of words to describe them. Not to describe *what* they were, that was something that didn't need describing. He yearned to describe *how* they were. Like the pilot of a plane who traces words across the sky with puffs of smoke, or a graffiti artist armed with a fresh can of spray paint, all of Macdara's earliest instincts told him to carve out a place for himself in the world using nothing but words.

The first person to encourage him was his secondary-school English teacher. Macdara had landed into the school in fourth year, a refugee from the wreckage of his parents' marriage. It was thought that a bit of distance might put him out of harm's way, but the school was only a hundred miles from Dublin, and news travelled fast. By the time Macdara had unpacked his suitcase and stowed it under his bed, his story had done the rounds of the school, and by some unquestioned homophobic logic that was traded around the locker rooms along with ten-packs of Carrolls cigarettes, he had been labelled a bender. His English teacher encouraged him to pour what he was feeling out on to the page, which he did.

"Macdara is a great man for the use of the mixed metaphor," said the English teacher, closing in on Macdara's father at the parents' day at the end of the year.

The English teacher was most interested in Macdara's father. In particular there was the matter of a creative writing competition, which he was hoping Macdara's father would agree to judge.

"Macdara is very *earnest* in his writing," he said, with a nudge in his voice, one eyebrow raised to suggest a shared joke. "Sometimes a little *too* earnest," he said. "I'm trying to introduce the concept of creative restraint."

Macdara's father fastened his famous blue eyes on the teacher and stared at him glacially as the mechanics of the proposed creative writing competition were explained to him. To Macdara's infinite relief, his father had dressed for minimum effect, in an almost-normal single-breasted tweed suit and a silk cravat, worn inside his open shirt.

"I wouldn't give you much for our smarmy friend," he said to Macdara afterwards.

"He's an idiot," said Macdara, using great heat to disguise his colossal sense of betrayal. "The guy's nothing but an idiot."

He was mortified that his work had been ridiculed. Sick with shame that his most solemn efforts had been made fun of. It would be more than three decades before Macdara dared to show his work to another human being, and even then it was under a thick cloak of anonymity.

"The word 'paradise' comes from the Persian word for garden," said the priest. "In ancient Persia the greatest honour the king could bestow on one of his subjects was to invite them to walk with him in his garden in the cool of the evening.

"This is how we imagine Manus now," said the priest. "Wandering the gardens of heaven, deep in conversation with the Lord. And Lord knows, they must have *plenty* to talk about."

Laughter broke out in the church, along with a gurgle of delight at the subversive nature of the joke. The priest was an amateur poet and a fellow Kildare man. An old friend of Manus's, at the end of the Mass he led his coffin out of the church with great pomp, holding the huge gilded cross high for all to see. Propping up the front right-hand side of the coffin with his left shoulder, Macdara fixed his eyes on the shuffling ruffle at the bottom of the priest's vestments, so as to avoid looking the mourners in the face as he passed. There was something touching and sad about the priest's sensible rubber-soled shoes, walking along under all those ruffles. Macdara always found people's shoes very touching and sad.

From the balcony, the soloist was singing "Nearer, My God, to Thee", which made Macdara even sadder.

Outside the church, the sun fell down on them in warm yellow flakes. The little boys ran wild loops of the churchyard, like horses turned loose in a paddock, while the adults in the family were islanded by well-wishers. Macdara shook hands until his arm ached, and eventually the crowd began to thin. He could see his mother now, arching like a pergola over another old lady. His sisters, heads held high and laughing; they were both of them dressed up to the nines. He could see Sam being led to a car by Nando. (Macdara had been introduced to Nando outside the funeral home, and had judged him on the face of it to be a most trustworthy person.)

His father was to be cremated right after the funeral. The sea burial had turned out to be too complicated. To carry out a burial at sea, you had to have a special licence from the Department of the Marine. You had to modify the coffin, by inserting a zinc lining and drilling holes into it, otherwise it would only float; there was even a question of weighing the body down. All things considered, it had been decided that it would be wiser to have Manus cremated, and to scatter his ashes at sea.

Macdara sat beside his mother in the crematorium. Sam was with Nora and Nando, while Acushla and Alma sat side by side at the edge of the pew. As the curtains closed in on the coffin, they clung to each other, sobbing audibly. Macdara found their sudden outpouring of grief puzzling. It seemed like only a moment ago that they had been laughing. From some unseen speaker high up on the wall came the sound of music. Louis Armstrong, singing the mourners out into the sunshine.

After the cremation, they all went to the pub. Acushla had wanted to put on a reception for everyone in her home and Alma had argued for a hotel, but Deirdre had insisted on going to the pub. She had insisted on the pub where she and Manus had met all those years ago, and where he and his friends had held court on so many a night. Nothing would do Deirdre but to have the reception upstairs in McDaids.

There were trays of sandwiches laid out on the bar when they arrived. Yellow light coming through the stained-glass windows. On the walls, black-and-white pictures of Manus and his cohort as young men. Macdara ordered a pint for himself, and one for Sam and Nora. Nando would only agree to having a half.

"I'm a useless drinker," said Nando apologetically.

"An excellent quality in a person," said Macdara. "I whole-heartedly approve."

He raised his glass, making sure to catch Nando's eye before drinking from it — someone had told him that it was deeply offensive to other cultures not to make eye contact while toasting. Macdara felt shy in the presence of Nando, as he often was in the company of anyone other than family. He began to long for an opportunity to escape the circle he found himself in, an opportunity that came soon enough with the arrival of a steady trickle of his father's various acquaintances; in twos and threes they came, clattering up the rickety stairs. From literary compatriots to country relations, from genuine friends to phoney hangers-on, they kept coming until the little room was heaving, the noise gathering like fumes under the glossy ceiling as the extractor fan in the wall whirred away inadequately. The temperature in the room was such that the men began shedding their suit jackets and ties, and opening up the buttons of their shirts. The women bared their tanned arms, giving the gathering a most un-funereal aspect. After three pints, Macdara could feel himself getting drunk, but that didn't stop him going to the bar to order a fourth. It wasn't often he had the opportunity to get drunk.

He found himself standing facing Acushla. Her face flushed from the heat, she wore her cardigan draped elegantly over the shoulders of her sleeveless black dress, and she was holding her glass of white wine out in front of her like a model displaying some kind of kitchen product in an advertisement. Her husband was standing beside her with his arm wound around the small of her back. Liam had his face turned to one side while he talked to someone behind him.

"You know that Daddy loved you," Acushla was saying, her voice pitched higher than usual.

"Of course," said Macdara, stumbling forward as he leaned in towards her. She put the palm of her free hand flat on his chest to stop his fall, leaning in to shout into his ear above the noise of the room. "I know you weren't as close to him as me and Alma were, but that doesn't mean he didn't love you."

And Macdara was about to tell her that he had never imagined this to be the case when he stopped himself. Acushla's reassurances had raised a question in his head, a question that had never existed before. He frowned as he contemplated it, swaying a little on the spot where he stood. Stepping to the side, he set his half-drunk pint down on the bar and made for the loo, aware only of a desire to get away from the noise and the people so that he could think.

The men's room was empty, but even so Macdara made for a cubicle. He had never been able to bring himself to use a urinal in a public toilet, preferring to lock himself into a cubicle so that he could sit down. Letting his suit trousers fall towards the wet tiled floor, he sat on the toilet, half closing his eyes to bring the graffiti on the back of the cubicle door into focus. There was a burst of noise as the door outside opened and closed again. In the conversation that followed, he identified his brother-in-law's voice, along with another voice that he didn't recognise. Desperately, Macdara strained to restrain his bladder, unable to bear the indignity of being heard to urinate.

"Well, we won't see his like again," Mick was saying, with drunken emphasis.

"You said it," said the other man. "They broke the mould when they made old Manus."

Macdara heard a stream of piss, and then another. He listened out for the sound of the taps being turned on for them to wash their hands, and the warm-air hand drier being used to dry them, but those sounds never came. Instead he heard the door hinge opening, and a burst of noise from outside as they left. Only when the door had closed behind them again did Macdara finally let go of his bladder. He washed his hands carefully outside before emerging furtively from the men's room. Grabbing his suit jacket from the hook in the hallway, he left the pub without saying good night to anyone.

The letter was waiting for him where he'd left it. Like a small stone that finds its way into your sock, or a scratch on the lens of your sunglasses, he had been acutely aware of it all day. He had been forced to apply great concentration to the ignoring of it. Now here it was, sitting patiently on the table. Another moment and he would be sitting down, reading its contents.

He took two steps back from the table and turned towards the fridge, postponing the decision momentarily while he searched for something to eat. There were two cold sausages that he had stowed earlier on the top shelf; they were glued to the china saucer by a pool of their own congealed fat. Macdara withdrew the saucer from the fridge and put it to rest on the kitchen counter while he dropped two slices of bread into the toaster. He peeled the sausages off the plate and split them each lengthways with a knife, revealing the globby sausagemeat inside. When the toast popped, he buttered it generously. He tiled one slice of toast with the cold sausages, using the other slice as a lid. Taking the sandwich in both hands, he began to eat it, marvelling at the deliciousness of this thing that he had made. For a moment there was nothing in his mind, only the deliciousness of the cold sausage sandwich. But then the letter caught his eye. He realised that he did not want to open it.

As long as the letter went unopened, Macdara's world remained unchanged. But once he had opened it, once he had read its contents, he would be brought down one of two paths. Either his father had disliked the book (and the likelihood of this was very much uppermost in Macdara's mind), in which case Macdara would have to live for ever with his father's disapprobation, a burden that would weigh heavily on a father-son relationship that had up until now managed to remain miraculously unconfrontational. In the unlikely event that his father had *liked* the book (and it occurred to Macdara that this outcome was almost as terrifying as the prospect of his disliking it), well, that brought with it a whole new set of problems. If his father had liked the book, then there was never any reason for Macdara to have feared his scorn, and no need to have kept his writing a secret from him. If his father turned out to have liked the book, then Macdara would see that he had squandered the opportunity of a friendship with Manus, one based on mutual respect and the pursuit of a shared craft, rather than the pact of mutual misunderstanding they had observed with each other since Macdara was a child.

It occurred to Macdara now, as he licked the last bit of melted butter out of the corner of his mouth and burped a dry bubble of sausage-scented Guinness fumes out of his belly, it occurred to him that there was nothing to be gained by opening the letter. By not opening the letter, he could maintain forever the equilibrium that had existed between him and his father. An equilibrium that had lasted until the final whistle (or the final

371

gasp of a dodgy handbrake). There was no point in revisiting it now. Revisiting it would only bring trouble.

With this thought in mind, Macdara took his father's letter and tore it in two. Observing glimpses of black ink where the envelope and the letter inside it had been rent, he resisted the temptation to peek, tearing those halves in two again, and those halves in two, and those halves in two, until all that remained were small flakes of writing paper and small flakes of envelope, like home-made confetti. Macdara swept them off the table into his cupped hand and dumped them into the rubbish bin.

As he climbed into bed in his vest and underpants, having given himself a special amnesty from flossing and brushing his teeth, his head was spinning from the drink, his stomach unsure about the sausage sandwich, but his mind was untroubled by worries of any kind. He was asleep within seconds.

The letter!

Oh, Jesus, the letter. Macdara sprang out of bed and lurched through the kitchen, head first into the bin. Fingers scrabbling through butter-smeared paper and coffee grounds and melon pips, he began fishing out the scraps. There were fewer of them than you would imagine, and they had found their way further down into the bin than he would have thought possible. He had to turn the contents out on to a newspaper on the floor, pawing his way through a soggy potpourri of eggshells and breadcrumbs, a melon half-shell with its reduced sticker still clinging to it, a toilet roll tube that he had neglected to recycle. Somewhere amid all this waste were his father's last words to him.

Macdara laid the fragments out on the kitchen counter like pieces of a jigsaw. But what he had before him was more of a mosaic. Tiny shards of paper stained with ink that was no longer black but all the colours of an oil spill. Whatever it was that was wet in the bin, it had made of his father's script a watery batik. As his hangover swarmed noisily around his head, as the fact of his father's death uncoiled itself inside his belly, it became clear to Macdara that it was not going to be possible to reconstruct the letter.

He closed his eyes and let the tears slowly squeeze their way out of him. Tears that had been years in the forming. It was a surprise to Macdara what a relief it was to let them finally seep through.

It was a few weeks before they got round to going through his father's things.

In that time, it had been agreed that Nando would sleep in the apartment at night, so that Sam would not be on his own. The meagre resources of the state would be called upon to provide carers for Sam during the day, with the family filling any remaining gaps between them. On the whole, it seemed to Macdara a most satisfactory resolution of the rather precarious situation Sam had been left in by Manus's death.

Sam seemed largely unaware of Manus's absence, and when on occasion he did comment on it, he seemed to absorb without emotion the explanation that Manus was dead. He showed no signs of being distressed, expressing only vague regret, as if it were the death of someone he hardly knew. "Oh, dear," he would say, whenever he was reminded of it. "Oh, dear," he would mutter, with mild surprise. "That's very sad." It was only when Acushla went to clear out some of her father's things, only then did Sam become upset.

"We'll have to do it behind his back," she told Macdara. "The next time the carer takes him out, we can all go round. It will be nice for us all to do it together."

Macdara arrived first, followed within the space of a few seconds by his sisters. Wearing their sunglasses on their heads and carrying empty wine boxes and rolls of bin bags, they looked like ageing film stars who had been sentenced to community service. One silver-haired, the other crowned a pale wheaten gold.

"Why don't we make a start on the clothes," said Acushla, tearing off a bin bag and handing it to Alma. "Three piles," she said, pointing out spaces on the bedroom floor with a manicured fingertip. "One for the bin. One for the charity shop. One for things we might want to keep."

Alma nodded, and it occurred to Macdara how odd it was to hear Acushla telling Alma what to do. Stranger still to see Alma doing it.

While his sisters worked their way through his father's wardrobe, Macdara made a start on his desk. Into a bin bag he tossed all the old matchbooks and swizzle sticks that he found in the middle drawer, all the paper clips and leaking batteries and dried-up pens. Chequebook stubs going back decades and business cards belonging to publishers long swallowed up by conglomerates, all of them went into the bin too. His father's much-stamped old passports he put aside as a memento, along with a box of slides that appeared to have been taken at somebody's wedding. Macdara held one of them up to the light and saw a clutch of women wearing sixties-style clothing; the images were too indistinct for him to recognise any of them.

In the side drawers, Macdara found his father's correspondence. Folders of documents relating to bank accounts and insurance policies. His father had filed and labelled them all meticulously, for fear of anything falling by the wayside. The documentation relating to his work was limited to a single drawer containing a sheaf of annual statements from his publisher. (The manuscript of his father's book, and most of his personal correspondence, had long since been donated to a university archive.) The previous year's royalties amounted to less than a hundred euro, something Macdara found very poignant. But his sadness was banished in an instant by his discovery in one of the drawers of a Time Out bar. Macdara laughed out loud at this joke from beyond the grave.

In the left-hand bottom drawer, he found what he was looking for. His own unbound manuscript, held loosely together by its original twine binding. On the first page, his father had inscribed in slanting capital letters his suggestion for a title. Turning the pages, Macdara could see that his father had peppered the margins with handwritten notes. As he breathlessly leafed through them, he was aware of the invisible dust of his father's final movements falling out from between the pages.

Before he left — with the manuscript of his book carefully stashed in a supermarket carrier bag and his father's passports tucked away in the pocket of his jacket — Macdara helped himself to a small selection of his father's more flamboyant clothing. Now that his father was gone, it seemed important to Macdara that his heirs adopt a little of his eccentricity. Otherwise the family would only sink back into the ordinariness whence they came, something Macdara was determined not to allow to happen.

you are hereby invited to join

Deirdre O'Sullivan

in celebrating her 80th

birthday at her home on

Saturday 5 October at 6.00.

Strictly no presents.

Each guest is asked to

prepare a short party piece.

R.S.V.P.

Deirdre

Deirdre woke on the morning of her party and noticed, for the first time in months, a chill in the air. A chill that registered first on the tip of her nose, and then in the cool intake of breath coming into contact with her warm lungs. A newborn feeling, brought on by the change of season. She felt nostalgic already for the summer that was gone. Eager at the same time for the joys of winter, she found herself thinking with longing of log fires and beef stew. Freezing-cold water straight from the tap. She was surprised how strong a pull was exerted on her by these temporal things.

She hopped out of bed and put on her robe — a sensible purple fleece Acushla had bought for her in Marks & Spencer, it was undeniably comfortable, and Deirdre found herself wearing it more and more recently, despite the loss of self incurred. To her horror, comfort had begun to be more important to her than style, which was exactly what she had always feared from old age. She belted the robe loosely around her waist and slid her feet into her Chinese slippers — slippers Manus had brought back for her from Hong Kong a hundred years ago. They were duck-egg blue with brocade birds on them, and faded though they were, Deirdre loved them.

Stopping off briefly at the lavatory on the return, Deirdre proceeded down two flights of stairs, alighting in her vast bare entrance hall just as a slab of ruby light from the stained-glass fanlight over the door fell in a diagonal across the bare floorboards, spotlighting the two wooden crates of champagne that were stacked against the wall. Veuve Clicquot, Deirdre had chosen, with a flush of pleasure at the thought of how Manus would have appreciated the reference to her widowhood. But of course Manus wasn't here to appreciate it, something Deirdre kept having to remind herself of, over and over again.

It wasn't that she had forgotten that he was dead. Only in her dreams was she under any illusion that he was still alive; during her waking hours she was fully aware of his absence. It was the nature of that absence that she was struggling with. The obstinately finite nature of it. It seemed unreasonable to Deirdre that death should claim Manus so absolutely. That his absence could not be alleviated by the occasional visit, the way someone living down the country might pop up to Dublin for a day, dropping in for a quick cup of tea before disappearing again. That he might not pass by in his car one afternoon with a beep and a flutter of the hand. In particular, it seemed unreasonable to Deirdre that he could not make even a brief appearance at her party. "For One Night Only", as the ad in the newspaper might say of an old-time crooner coming out of retirement. She found herself frustrated by the fact that this was not going to be possible.

Deirdre very much wanted Manus to be at her party. His presence had been her central motivation for having the party in the first place. In conceiving it, she had imagined herself putting on a final display of bravura, largely for his benefit. One last magnificent performance that he would chuckle over afterwards, wondering at her capacity to surprise him even after all these years. With a crushing sense of anticlimax, Deirdre realised that she was throwing a party for someone who wasn't going to be there.

It was not part of Deirdre's plan that Manus would die before her. She had her letter to him written already, a letter that was to be given to him after her death, and in that letter she had said the one thing she had never said to him before, the thing she had been holding out on saying to him all these years. It was her last card, and one that she had delighted in hoarding, but she had always planned to lay it face down on the table when the time came. The fact that she forgave him.

When her children came to break the news to her that Manus had died, Deirdre was sitting in an old wing-backed chair in the breakfast room at the back of the house. A tray in her lap, she was busy licking the envelopes for her invitations. The dry taste of glue on her tongue — a taste that reminded her of the Holy Communion wafers she had not received since she was a girl — she was just licking the last of them when something made her look up at the window.

Through the wobbly glass she saw her three children making their way up the garden towards the house. Solemn-faced and single file, they weaved along the overgrown path, ducking their heads every so often to avoid the overhanging roses. Deirdre put her tray aside and stood to receive them. When they told her what had happened, explaining it to her several times before she understood what it was they were saying, she sank back down into her chair. She looked up at her children's faces, seeing the same expression of alarm in all their eyes.

"I don't believe it," she said in a tone of genuine wonderment. "He's gone and done it to me again."

When Manus left Deirdre, she was in her late forties. Menopausal and wretchedly mercurial with it, she was just struggling to come to terms with the loss of her youth when she was faced with the loss of her husband too. An event that gutted the household like a fire. In the aftermath of it, Deirdre was forced into survival mode, for the sake of the children. That first night without him, they sat in front of the TV in the breakfast room and ate greasy chipper chips straight out of their wrappers. A treat that Deirdre had thought up because she couldn't bear the thought of them all sitting round the kitchen table without him, it failed miserably to alleviate the gloomy pall of his absence.

The children were all in shock, of course, although it manifested itself in different ways. Whereas Alma took to a round of aggressive serial dating, punishing any man who dared come near her for her father's act of faithlessness, Acushla cried herself to sleep every night, soaking her pillowcase with bitterly disenchanted tears. And while Macdara gave no obvious indication of having been affected by his father's defection, Deirdre would come down in the mornings to find the washing machine mid-cycle and his sheets inside. Macdara was fourteen years old at the time, and he had stopped wetting the bed when he was seven; the return of the habit was a clear sign of his distress. When Deirdre found a vile little note in the pocket of his school trousers — a note that had been composed by a number of his classmates, judging by the varied handwriting — she decided to send him off to boarding school, a decision she was forced to make alone because Manus and Sam had embarked on an extended tour of South America. From then on, Manus seemed always to be away whenever there was cause for either crisis or celebration.

It was while Manus was in India that Alma announced that she was getting married; he was in Indonesia when Acushla got engaged. When Acushla dropped out of college, he was on a road trip across Spain, and when Macdara had to be got home from France, Manus was on a remote Greek island and could not be contacted. When Deirdre accompanied Acushla to England to have the abortion, Manus was in Japan. When Mick and Alma broke up, he was wintering in South Africa. All the time Manus was gallivanting about the world, sending swashbuckling postcards from ever-more-glamorous locations, Deirdre was manning the home front. Like the survivor of a nuclear disaster, she was foraging about in the supermarket shelves for food that was past its sell-by date, dressed in second-hand clothes and Alma's cast-off Doc Marten boots. Although in fairness Manus never failed to meet her alimony payments, Deirdre never stopped worrying about money.

And whereas Deirdre was forced to live out the rest of her life in the dark, creaking old house they had bought when they were first married, Manus settled like a soap bubble into his weightless glass apartment above the treeline. The lightness of his life — the gliding, ethereal quality to him as he got older — it seemed to Deirdre in such sharp contrast to the merciless gravity that weighed her down. Stocky as a stevedore, with arms and legs as thick as tree trunks, she was the product of all the years of heavy lifting she had done in his absence. What she wanted now more than anything was something of the lightness he had so effortlessly achieved. And just when she had found a way of achieving that, just when she had come up with a way, at last, of setting herself free, Manus went and pulled the rug out from under her again. In dying before Deirdre ever had the chance to implement her plan, he had stolen a march on her, and here she was, for the second time, left with the task of carrying her children through their grieving.

Deirdre saw no reason to cancel the party. Acushla wanted to call it off, for fear of what people would think, and Alma suggested postponing it, at least until after Christmas. Even Macdara was in two minds.

"I don't know," he said, when he came into the kitchen with his invitation in his hand. (Deirdre had held off on posting them for a few weeks, in order to give things a chance to settle.) "It's hard to see how we'll be in the mood." He turned the gilt-edged card over to study the back of it, even though there was nothing written there.

"On the other hand," ventured Deirdre, "maybe it's just what we all need, to cheer us up."

Macdara frowned, looking at the ceiling as if he was trying to add something up in his head. Ever since Manus had died, Deirdre had noticed this curious focus in him; his mind seemed very busy all the time, but elsewhere. She had the feeling that every word she said to him went unheard, like snow falling in the darkness. She tried speaking very softly, to get his attention.

"If anything, your father's death underlines the need for the rest of us to live for the day."

Like a child who is jealous of a sibling's birthday, Deirdre was anxious for the attention to shift to her. For weeks they had spoken of nothing but Manus. And while at first Deirdre had borne the weight of their grief with good grace, the protracted cycle of mourning had started to irritate her. Acushla in particular had not stopped crying since Manus died. They only had to mention his name and she was off again. It seemed to Deirdre a profoundly unoriginal response to what was essentially a perfectly natural occurrence.

"At my age, you don't get sad when someone dies," she said, repeating once again what she had said to

384

everyone at the funeral. "When someone our age dies with all their faculties intact, it's a cause for celebration."

How many times over the course of those first few days, had she delivered those lines with her customary swagger to a mildly shocked audience. And while it was all part of a script she had spent a lifetime honing, to her own ears it had started to sound somewhat unconvincing. Like a priest saying prayers to a God he had come to doubt the existence of, or a mathematician following the rules of a formula he had come to question, Deirdre could not escape the unsettling feeling that she was talking nonsense.

"Everyone has to die sometime," she said as they left the church after the month's mind for Manus. They were all standing in the churchyard in the evening sunshine, and it seemed to Deirdre an opportune time to inject a little buoyancy into the proceedings. But no sooner had she said it than Acushla's eyes began to well up again. Her sister took her arm to steady her.

"Mother," said Alma, fixing her eyes on Deirdre. "That's enough."

Deirdre looked around at her family, seeking support from some quarter, but none of them would meet her eye. Connie had bent down to tuck Ernie's shirt into his trousers and Nora had turned to see where Nando had got to with Sam. Liam and Mick had their heads down, muttering something to each other. Even Macdara would not look at her, choosing to stare at his shoes instead. Deirdre found herself marooned by her own doing.

In the aftermath of Manus's death, Deirdre was forced to consider the possibility that she had underestimated the resilience of her family. She had counted on them taking his death in their stride, treating it with a minimum of sentimentality and a heavy dose of black humour. What she had not counted on was their grief, a grief that was as profound as it was genuine; the effect it had on her was discombobulating. And while she never once considered the possibility that she too was grieving, she found herself looking out the kitchen window every so often, half expecting to see his car sliding up to the pavement. A dozen times every morning she found herself putting on the kettle and warming the teapot for a ritual that no longer took place. Over and over again she emptied the water out of the teapot without ever having made the tea, and still she could not admit, even to herself, that she was missing him.

Deirdre was going to invite some friends to her party, but then she realised she didn't have any. She had managed to divest herself of them all, semi-deliberately, as the years went by. She had come to the conclusion that it was not possible to maintain multiple friendships; it required far too much effort. It required you to do things that you didn't want to do, and to go to things you didn't want to go to, like other people's drinks parties, and their children's weddings. Like their dreaded retirement dinners, or the launch parties for their ghastly self-published memoirs. "I can't imagine anything I'd like less," she began saying, because she had decided that she was too old for making excuses. "If you don't mind me saying so, I'd prefer to have my toenails pulled out," she would say, in response to an invitation to a golden wedding anniversary, or a ladies' lunch, thinking that surely people would be amused by her honesty and appreciative of it. But they weren't a bit amused. It turned out that people were very easily offended, something that surprised Deirdre enormously. It baffled her to see how thin-skinned people were. You'd think they'd be a bit more hardy.

"I know this isn't your kind of thing," said Acushla when she stopped by one day with the newspaper. (Ever thoughtful, Acushla had taken upon herself her father's habit of bringing Deirdre the paper.) "You don't have to do it if you don't want to," she went on, and Deirdre couldn't help but be irritated by her overly apologetic tone. "It's just this thing I've been invited to. They give out awards to women who've done something during the year."

"Are you telling me that you've won one of these awards?"

It was as Deirdre had feared.

"There's a dinner," said Acushla. "I can always bring Liam, but I thought I'd ask you first, on the off chance that you might like to be there."

Deirdre was just about to make her excuses when something in Acushla's expression gave her pause for thought.

"You don't have to answer now," said Acushla, cutting her off before she had a chance to say anything. "Why don't you think about it and come back to me closer to the time?"

And Deirdre nodded, even though she knew with absolute certainty that she would never in a million years feel like getting all dressed up on a winter's evening only to sit through three courses of mediocre food in a hotel ballroom with a gaggle of silly women when she could be at home in her warm bed with a TV box set.

It was Alma who was responsible for getting her hooked on the box sets, with a gift of *Downton Abbey* that Deirdre found indecently enjoyable (even though Maggie Smith's performance made her ill with envy).

"I had lunch with her the other day," said Mícheál MacAoda, when Deirdre bumped into him on Baggot Street. She was on her way to the off-licence to order the champagne for her party, and thankfully she had dressed for the occasion, choosing to wear a wine-coloured silk blouse, pinned at the neck with the antique cameo brooch her mother had given her as a wedding present. She wore a long tweed skirt with deep pockets, and instead of her usual lace-up leather ankle boots, she had on a pair of soft brown leather brogues that she had long ago stolen from Manus, she and he having precisely the same-sized feet. Her suede gloves were one yellow and one brown, their partners lost long ago; it seemed to Deirdre they provided exactly the right note of eccentricity. When she saw Mícheál walking towards her on Baggot Street, she realised that she had been expecting to meet someone.

He stopped a few feet away from her and pointed at her. Deirdre was reminded of the famous poster of Kitchener: WANTS YOU!

"Deirdre O'Sullivan," he said.

"Michéal MacAoda." She stepped forward to kiss him on both cheeks, a sense of her own long-lost glamour returning to her as a result of this encounter. It was Michéal who had directed her in *The Cherry Orchard* at the Gate, and at the wrap party he had made a fumbling pass at her. A pass that Deirdre had gently deflected, the memory of it was nonetheless fond to her.

"Isn't that funny," he said, gazing at her. "I was only thinking about you the other day."

"Oh?" said Deirdre, opening her eyes wide and plumping out her mouth.

"Yes," he said. "It was after I met Maggie Smith. I had lunch with her the other day, and she planted the idea in my head of putting together a stage production of *Downton*."

And of course, Deirdre knew what he was going to say next.

"I thought of you immediately."

"Oh, Michéal. Don't be ridiculous. I haven't set foot on the stage for thirty years!"

"Nonsense, Deirdre. You could do it in your sleep. The more I think about it, there's no one else who *could* do it. It's got your name written all over it."

"All I can promise you is that I'll think about it," was what she said as they parted.

"You'll do more than think about it," he said, holding his finger up in the air in a parting shot.

As Deirdre sailed across Baggot Street, she was aware of an irresistible energy rising in her, an energy that signalled the advent of a new and most inconvenient lease of life.

The storm came on the afternoon of the party, with heavy rains and a high wind that sounded like a swarm of police sirens converging on some daring heist, or a dreadful car accident occasioned by the rain. Listening to the wail being carried on the air, Deirdre found it hard to believe that it was only the sound of the wind.

"Would you listen to that?" she said. "It sounds like the end of the world."

She had been planning on draping a string of candles in jam jars along the railings that bordered the front steps, but clearly that wasn't going to be possible now.

"I wonder would we put them inside? We could set them up inside the fanlight — that way people would be able to see them from the outside when they arrive."

Macdara came and stood beside her, looking up at where she was indicating.

"You'll need to use the stepladder," she said.

Again he hesitated, waiting for her to say more.

"It's in the cupboard under the stairs."

And where any of the other members of the family would have been exasperated with Macdara for not knowing this, where the girls would have wondered whether he kept anything in his head but pure air, where his father (when he was alive) would have marvelled at his ability to move through the world without accumulating any knowledge of the nuts and bolts of life, Deirdre did not entertain any of these thoughts. She had long ago accepted Macdara for what he was, and expected nothing else of him.

Deirdre had arranged for Macdara to receive her guests for her. Not because she wanted to make a grand entrance, but because she very much wanted to watch them arrive without them being able to see her.

She put the finishing touches to her outfit, using her cameo brooch to fasten the long purple velvet cloak she had chosen to wear over her silk evening dress (a cloak she had worn when she played Gertrude in a 1983 production of *Hamlet* on the Abbey stage; she had liked it so much that she couldn't resist filching it). She adjusted her satin headband so that the feather she'd attached to it rose dramatically from just behind her left ear. Then, turning out the light in her bedroom, she pulled a low upholstered chair up to the window and sat down. With the curtains partly drawn, she peered down into the empty street, waiting for her family to arrive.

It had stopped raining momentarily, but there was still a lot of water on the ground. A taxi swept to a stop at the gate, spreading great wings of water out on either side of it; it was lucky there was no one walking along the pavement or they would have been soaked. Mick appeared on the far side of the taxi and, coming around behind it, opened the door for Alma. She stuck one foot out first, letting it dangle rather inelegantly above the pavement. Then, getting a hold of herself, she managed to rise quite gracefully out of the taxi, with the help of the arm he offered her. She winked at him mischievously, and muttered something to him. They brought the best out in each other, those two, no question about it. As they climbed the front steps of the house, they were wobbling with laughter, but what it was they were laughing about Deirdre could not discern. She watched from above as the front door was opened from within and a handful of light was thrown over them. From below, she heard Macdara's voice.

"The animals came in two by two, hurrah, hurrah."

"Ah, Noah," said Alma, picking up on the joke.

"What a God-awful night," said Mick, stepping inside. The front door closed behind them, cutting off the sound of their voices. Deirdre sat very still for a moment, wondering would she be able to hear them downstairs now, but she couldn't. All she could hear was the low, buzzing static of the air in her room, and the sound of her own breathing, slightly faster and shallower than usual because of her excitement. She rolled her shoulders in their sockets, one by one, moving her head in a slow circle on her neck, with her eyes closed, to ease up the tension. These were things she had learned to do before going on stage.

She heard a sound outside and opened her eyes again just in time to see Nora and Nando coming through the gate. Nando had a guitar case slung across his back and Nora was carrying a wet paper bag in her arms, which Deirdre identified instantly as a gift. (It was just like Nora to flout the no-gift directive, even though she was the one who could least afford it.) They had no coats on them, no hats or scarves, no umbrella. Their hair was plastered to their heads and their faces were damp with rain, as if they'd been crying happy tears. As they flopped up the steps, Deirdre was thinking how nice it was to see Nora so happy. How odd it was that it should be this man — a man who had landed in their lives from the other side of the world — to finally tether her to home.

Liam and Acushla were coming down the street. It had started raining again and Liam was holding a large black umbrella over their heads, Acushla struggling to keep up with him in her high heels. Oh, wouldn't you think she'd wear more sensible shoes on a night like this? But then Acushla never had an ounce of common sense. Poor Acushla.

When Deirdre saw Connie and Emmet and the boys come traipsing up the front steps, she rose out of her chair. Gripping her lower back with her hands for support, she straightened up, allowing herself one last glance in the mirror before she swept down the stairs with the train of her cloak slithering step by step after her.

When Deirdre entered the room, she had a chance to take a quick mental snapshot of her family before they turned to greet her.

Macdara was standing in the centre of the room, holding a bottle of champagne in his raised hand. Connie stood before him with her glass held out to receive it. She was balancing on a pair of platform wedges, with one little boy wrapped around her ankle. His brother was on all fours, disappearing behind the curtains. Liam stood peering out of the window, as if he was waiting for someone to arrive, while Nando was moving round the walls, studying the gallery of framed photographs, with Nora at his side as a guide. He had his arm snaked across the small of her back and she had hers stretched across his, like a pair of figure skaters about to execute some complex move. Emmet was hovering over by the table where the food was laid out. He had helped himself to a canapé, and as he chewed the half he had already bitten off, he was squinting at what remained in his hand, trying to figure out what it was. Over by the fireplace, Alma had settled herself into an armchair with her skirt pulled up over her knees to show off her legs and her face raised as she listened to something Mick was saying. He was standing with his back to the roaring fire, his hands splayed behind him to warm them while he talked to his wife. Acushla stood before them with a plate of canapés, bending from the waist in the manner of an air hostess to offer one to Alma. Oh, why on earth didn't we just let her be an air hostess? thought Deirdre in a flash of clarity. It seemed so obvious to her now that Acushla was born to be an air hostess.

"Mum!" said Acushla when she caught sight of Deirdre.

"Grandmother!" said Connie, turning round. She had to drag her foot along the carpet with the child still clinging to her ankle.

Deirdre felt time speeding up as they all converged on her.

"Deirdre," said Mick, advancing with his arms held wide. "You look magnificent!"

"Happy birthday, old girl," whispered Macdara as he brushed past her.

"Happy birthday, Gran-Mum," said the little boys, and Deirdre found herself wondering was that the moment when she had first loosened her grip on her own life, when she had allowed herself to be called Gran-Mum.

"Happy birthday, Grandmother," said Nora, coming forward to kiss her.

"Where's Sam?" asked Deirdre. She had just noticed that Sam wasn't there.

"Oh, we decided it wasn't fair to bring him," said Nora. "He's not really able to handle crowds, he gets stressed. He's much happier at home with the carer."

For a moment Deirdre was disappointed that Sam wasn't there, until it occurred to her that there had been a time when she and Sam could have been friends — at any time over the years she could have made friends with him — but that time had now come and gone. She had a sense of her life being carried rapidly downstream, of things and people being swept into the past, and herself along with them. A great desire in her to grab on to something. Anything, to still the passage of time.

It was Alma who volunteered to kick off the party pieces. She got to her feet in front of the fire, stepping out of her shoes so that she was standing in her stockings. Without her heels she was smaller, but somehow all the more powerful for it. She pushed the huge satin wrap she wore to the very edges of her shoulders and with her eyes closed she began to sing "Down by the Salley Gardens". Alma was no singer, but she had chosen her piece well, rendering it so low and so slow that it was the words you heard, and not the singing of them. By the final verse she had abandoned any pretence of singing, devoting to those beautiful lines the full glory of her speaking voice.

Before the applause had even died down, Acushla was on her feet. Her choice of a Patsy Cline song was unfortunate. Too raw, too exposed, too high on the scale. As she sang, she couldn't quite hit all the notes. But this imperfect performance brought out only tenderness in Deirdre. She was aware of a fierce pride, verging almost on admiration, for this daughter of hers whose desires always ran so far ahead of her. Deirdre wondered was it too late for her to tell Acushla that she was proud of her. For one dreadful moment it seemed to her that she had left it too late, until she remembered the shy invitation to the Women of the Year awards — an invitation Deirdre had actively considered turning down. She remembered it now with relief and vowed to accept it.

When Acushla finished singing, she looked to Deirdre for approval and Deirdre saw that her daughter needed her still. She needed her now perhaps more than ever. She needed her mother to witness her triumph.

After a short break to fill up people's glasses, Nando played an Argentinian folk song on the guitar. ("He *would* play the guitar," Deirdre heard Mick mutter to Alma.) Next up was Emmet, who told a long and inappropriate joke about a necrophiliac Frenchman. Alma flared her nostrils and narrowed her eyes at him. Acushla looked nervously at Deirdre to see if she was offended, which she wasn't, and Deirdre saw Nora glance pityingly at Connie, who sat ruffling Oscar's hair with her fingers as if she hadn't heard.

For his party piece, Oscar stood in the centre of the room and turned his tongue upside down in his mouth. He was made to go round the room repeating the trick up close for all his older relatives. Then it was announced that Ernie would recite a poem, dedicated to his great-grandmother.

"MASHED POTATO, A LOVE POEM," he said, speaking in a loud monotone. "BY SIDNEY HODDES."

"Stand out into the middle of the room," hissed Connie, giving him a little shove with her fingertips as if he were a small toy boat that she was pushing out towards the middle of a pond.

"Turn around to face Gran-Mum," shouted Acushla.

Ernie repositioned himself to face his great-grandmother, his face flushed as he resumed his recitation.

"Start again," said Alma. "Start from the top."

"Nice and slow," said Acushla.

"Would you leave the poor child alone," said Liam. "He's doing grand. Go on, Ernie. You're doing grand."

Ernie hesitated, looking up at the ceiling with immense seriousness, and it occurred to Deirdre that she would very much like to see this little boy become a man. It would be most interesting to see what kind of a man he would make, this aptly named earnest little boy. Only after he had finished reciting his poem did he realise that he'd forgotten a couple of lines in the middle, but by then everyone was clapping so hard that he retreated gratefully to his spot at his mother's feet.

"Who's next?" asked Acushla, looking round the room. "Macdara?"

Reluctantly Macdara unfurled himself from the shadows. He took a piece of paper from the inside pocket of his jacket and unfolded it.

"This is something I wrote for you," he said, without looking up at Deirdre.

The room fell into silence. Falling with a bump, as everyone became still.

"Shush," said Connie to Oscar. "Shush now."

Macdara prepared to read, with all of them looking at him expectantly, quizzically even; they were not sure what was coming. Once he had started reading, Deirdre noticed that their heads began to bow, as if they were in church. Their faces took on soulful expressions while they listened, and Deirdre saw Alma place a hand on Mick's knee and Mick cover it with one of his. Liam sank down on to the arm of Acushla's chair, and Acushla sagged a little towards him until her shoulder was resting against his arm. Connie propped her chin on top of Oscar's head and absent-mindedly kissed him over and over again. Nora and Nando sat back to back on the floor, each of them looking up at the ceiling, while Emmet watched Macdara with great intent. When the reading was finished, Deirdre understood that Macdara had become a different person in all of their eyes, and that this was his present to her, the answer to a question that she alone had never asked of him.

Macdara's head drooped and his face flushed bright red amid the explosion of compliments that followed his reading.

"Mick," said Acushla, clapping her hands together like a giddy child. "We haven't had Mick yet."

"No better man," said Liam with a dash of malice as his brother got to his feet. (Liam alone had refused to perform a party piece, showing a determination that Deirdre couldn't help but admire. Deirdre had always had a soft spot for Liam. Of her two sons-in-law, he was the one she preferred, perhaps because nobody else did.)

Mick set his wine glass down on a side table and coughed to clear his throat. He lurched his shoulders back and smoothed his hands over his belly.

"Help me out here, will you, son?" he said to Nando, and with a nudge from Nora, Nando took up his guitar. He sat with his hand poised at the strings, his face alert as he waited to hear what it was that Mick was going to sing. Everyone else knew, of course. There was only one song that Mick had ever learned to sing, and that was "Fernando". Before he even began, they were all smiling in anticipation, waiting for that familiar first line. And what Mick lacked in skill, he made up for in passion. He even had the Swedish accent to go with it. Hand on his heart like an opera singer, he held the other hand out to Alma as he sang. She was curled into her chair by the fire as she listened to him. A dreamy look on her face, and a memory there of the young girl she had been when first she met him. When Mick came to the chorus, they all sang along. And silly as it was, Deirdre felt like they were singing the story of their own lives, and each other's lives, in all their glorious imperfection. Mick's party piece was such a success that when it was finished, they launched into another round of the chorus, just for the joy of it.

"Folly that!" said Mick triumphantly as he sat down. And for a moment it seemed that nobody would. But then Nora rose off the floor, dragging Connie with her by the arm. The boys were thrown off her in a tumble on to the carpet.

Of the whole lot of them, Connie was by far and away the best singer, but to Deirdre's infinite irritation she never seemed to know the words of a single song. (Deirdre had told her more than once that it was a sinful waste of her talent not to learn the words of a few songs.) Nora, on the other hand, always knew the words but couldn't sing to save her life. The two of them together, Deirdre dreaded to think.

"Don't look so worried," said Nora. "We've been practising."

She nodded at Nando, who sounded a few notes on his guitar. The two girls stood, shifty and solemn, with their backs to the fire. As Connie's steel-fired voice lit into the first line of their serenade, Deirdre recognised with a smile what it was that they'd chosen, and she realised to her amazement that Connie had even taken the trouble to learn the words. Nora made a husky attempt at balancing the duet, but when the chorus came round, even she couldn't dampen the sound of

Connie's voice, which had the power to fill a cathedral to the rafters. The song they had chosen was an anthem to love, and shamefully sentimental as it was, it did seem to Deirdre, as she listened to her granddaughters singing in glorious disharmony, that she was surrounded by love. The love of her family, there was no getting away from it. There was no getting away from the love she felt for them. And the result of all this love was that it would not be possible for her to leave them. Reluctantly Deirdre reached the conclusion that had always been lying in wait for her — the conclusion that for her, at least, there was to be no easy way out.

With weary resignation, she saw that she would be forced to make that appointment to have her cataracts seen to. She would have to see someone about her hip too, perhaps even submit to surgery to fix it. She would force herself to do her pelvic-floor exercises again, in order to control her bladder. She would get a man in to look at the leaking roof, and the guttering at the back of the house, maybe even get the garden cut back. She would carry on patching herself and her surroundings as best she could, until they could be patched no more. This would be her gift to her family, a gift they would never even be aware of receiving.

"My party piece is a joke," she announced, springing it on them with relish. They would have been expecting her to produce a song. Taking advantage of the element of surprise, she launched straight into her piece at a nice jaunty pace, as befitted her choice of material.

"Now, Paddy Englishman, Paddy Irishman and Paddy Scotsman were on an expedition to chart a previously unexplored section of a notoriously dangerous river, a river that runs through the most impenetrable rainforest in the world, when they were captured by cannibals."

Silence in the room; all Deirdre could hear was the sound of two logs collapsing into each other in the grate. The sound of Oscar's heavy breathing, and Acushla delicately clearing her throat.

"The cannibals tied the three men to a stake and announced their intention to skin them alive, make canoes out of their skins, and eat their flesh."

Ernie and Oscar's eyes widened and their mouths fell open. Oscar shunted himself back a few inches, so that he was tucked in between his mother's legs. Ernie put up his hand, as if he were in class.

"Wait," he said. "How did Paddy Englishman, Paddy Irishman and Paddy Scotsman understand what the cannibals were saying to them?"

"Good question!" said Deirdre. "The thing is, they had a translator."

Ernie seemed to be satisfied with that.

" 'We're going to give you one last request, before we kill you,' said the chief cannibal. 'I'll have a cup of tea,' said Paddy Englishman. So the cannibals gave him a cup of tea, and then they skinned him alive, made a canoe out of his skin, and roasted his flesh on the fire.

" 'What's your last request?' they asked Paddy Scotsman. 'I'll have a whisky,' he said. So they gave him a whisky, and they skinned him alive, made a canoe out of his skin, and roasted his flesh on the fire.

402

"So now it was Paddy Irishman's turn. 'What's your last request?' asked the chief cannibal. 'I'll have a fork,' said Paddy Irishman. Well, the cannibals were a bit confused at that, but since it was his last request, they gave him a fork. And do you know what he said?"

Deirdre paused now in the telling. She surveyed the faces of her family. Then, taking the imaginary fork in her fist, she stabbed herself vigorously in the chest, puncturing herself over and over again as she rolled out her punchline.

" 'You're not makin' no fuckin' canoe out of me.' "

Never before had Deirdre spoken that word out loud, and never again would she. But on this occasion, no other word would do. She had rehearsed the piece out loud, using all manner of lesser expletives, but none of them had quite the impact she desired. She was amazed by the illicit thrill it gave her to use that dreadful, vulgar word. She was gratified by the stunned reaction of her family. For a full second they stared at her in amazement, then, under cover of the raucous applause that followed (with Emmet wolf-whistling through his fingers and Connie shouting, "Way to go, old girl"), Deirdre raised her glass in the air.

"To Manus," she said solemnly, dedicating to him the swan song she had planned for herself.

The room fell silent as they all raised their glasses. In the aftermath of the toast, Deirdre looked out beyond the circle her family formed in front of the fire, through the empty dining room and out the back window to where the night sky lay curiously empty. She could just about make out the stadium, barely visible in the darkness. With all but its most essential lights extinguished, it looked like a great ocean liner out at sea. Deirdre felt all the wistfulness of someone standing on the shore, knowing that the ship she had seen in the night would be gone in the morning, but she would still be here.

PROOF THAT WE EXISTED,
by Macdara MacEntee (Little,
Brown €14.99)

This magnificent debut novel,
an epic study of the human
spirit, took more than three decades to write and runs to nearly
eight hundred pages. Its publication comes less than a year
after the death of the author's
father, Manus, and while the
timing is undoubtedly poignant,
the scale of Macdara MacEntee's
achievement is sure to secure a
place for father and son among
the great dynasties of the
literary world.

Epilogue

Of all the things that happened that year, it was the summer that would be most vividly remembered. Long after people had forgotten all about the horsemeat scandal, and the countrywide flooding, long after the abortion controversy had merged in people's memories with abortion controversies of other years, they would remember that glorious summer. When a popular radio programme marked the turn of the year by conducting a poll of their listeners to identify the highs and lows of the twelve months just gone, it was not the country's exit from the IMF bailout that prevailed. It was not the election of a new pope, nor the visit to Dublin by Michelle Obama. The highlight of the year, as voted by radio listeners, was the long hot summer.

Of course for Manus's family, that summer would forever be associated with his death. Whenever anyone mentioned the long hot summer, they would think not of children leaping joyously from piers, or of young people languishing on their backs in parks. Their thoughts turned instead to the sea of sunglasses that surrounded them in the churchyard on the day of his funeral. The smell of suncream as the mourners leaned in close to kiss them. The taste of the ice creams they had eaten on their way to the crematorium. (Deirdre had insisted on stopping the funeral cortège to treat the children to an icecream, a move that took the undertakers by surprise but would no doubt have delighted Manus.)

They scattered his ashes the following spring, on a dry day at the end of March. They timed the trip for high tide, gathering at midday at a small harbour to the south of the city, where Liam had arranged for the use of a boat. As soon as they arrived, Liam climbed into the back and busied himself with the outboard engine, with Emmet to assist him. Mick stood in the well of the boat, holding a hand out to help the ladies as one by one they hopped down from the pier. Acushla settled the little boys in the bow, while Connie checked the fastenings on their life jackets. Alma and Deirdre took refuge on a bench running along the far side, Alma rooting in her handbag for her sunglasses, while Deirdre struggled to contain her hair in the wind. Macdara stood for a moment, one hand raised to hold his father's fedora to his head, as he enjoyed the sensation of the sea shifting under his feet. The taste of the salt in the air.

"Who are we waiting for?" shouted Liam from the back of the boat. He had the engine started and was keen to get going.

"Just Sam and Nora and Nando," shouted Acushla. "But we can't go without them. They've got the ashes."

No sooner had she said it than they appeared, rushing along the pier carrying rugs and bags and rain gear.

"Sorry we're late," said Nora, as she stood at the edge and looked down at them.

She reached her hand out to Nando and he handed her a cooler bag. She passed it down to Mick.

"Now," she said, "watch out for Grandad."

She dropped a small rucksack down into the boat. Mick caught it with both hands, hugging it to his chest like a rugby ball.

"Jesus," he said. "It wouldn't do to drop that." Carefully, he stowed it under a bench, with his raincoat wrapped around it to protect it from the spray.

"Take care now," he said, sticking a hand out to help Nora down. As they took their seats along the near side, Nando looked around him eagerly, as if he found them all delightful. It seemed to Macdara that it gave the family an added gloss to be seen through the eyes of this new person in their midst. It made them all seem shiny and new.

"Macdara," Acushla called out. "Do you want to sit here?" Already she was moving her handbag on to her lap and sliding her bum along the bench, shunting Alma and her mother further up to make space for him.

"I'm grand, thanks," said Macdara, standing with his feet apart to steady himself as the boat picked up speed. He was enjoying the feel of the wind in his face. The treat of being out at sea. Ahead of them, the chimneys at Poolbeg rose out of a low band of sea mist. A string of white sails appeared as bunting on the skyline. The sunlight fell on the water like splatters of rain.

The little boys were kneeling in the bow, each of them with an arm draped over the side, their fingers trailing the jade-green water. Connie was kneeling between them, with a firm grip on each of their life jackets. The boat turned as it left the protection of the harbour, smacking the waves sideways on now, so that great slaps of spray poured over the side. The little boys squealed with delight. Nando had taken an expensive-looking camera out of his bag and he had the lens trained on Connie and the lads, taking photograph after photograph of them.

The boat climbed the waves, and fell. Climbed, and fell, and Macdara allowed himself to drop down on to a seat beside Mick before he was knocked down. He took his father's hat off before it was blown away. With Dalkey Island ahead of them, Liam guided the boat between the island and the shore. Halfway through the Sound, he let the engine cut out and they all became aware of the seagulls, their screams like a hundred creaking farm gates.

"How's this for the spot?" Liam shouted out.

Mick stood and looked around him. He saw the island, pockmarked by ruined fortifications and rocks and some scraggly goats. A seal popped its head up and disappeared down again under the waves. A slender yacht cut through the water of the Sound like a knife. A yacht with a black sail, it created an atmosphere of great and solemn melancholy, like something out of an Arthurian legend.

"Seems like as good a place as any," he said, looking to Alma for approval. She shrugged, as if to say, Sure. Mick looked to Sam, to check with him, and Sam looked back without giving any indication whether he understood what was going on. Nora put her arm around Sam's back and drew him in towards her, so that their two heads were almost touching. What she said to him could not be heard by the others because her words were carried away by the wind, but they saw that Sam was nodding.

"Let's do it," she said. And she reached her arm out for her dad to pass her the rucksack. Opening up the zip and taking out a small cardboard carton, she paused and looked around her.

"Who wants to do the honours?"

Nobody answered.

"Okay, I'll do it," said Nora. "If that's okay with everyone?"

She got to her feet.

"Don't anyone else stand up," shouted Mick, "or the boat will tip over!"

Nora propped one knee up on the bench and leaned out over the edge of the boat.

"Which way is the wind blowing?" she shouted, looking back towards Liam.

"That way," roared Liam, throwing his arm out the side of the boat, in the manner of an airport groundsman guiding an incoming plane towards its gate.

"Okay," said Nora. "Here goes."

She opened the carton and for a moment nothing happened. Holding it from the bottom with both hands, she pitched it and a small cloud of dust billowed out. Like a swarm of bees suddenly released from a hive, it was picked up by the wind before spreading out and falling down into the sea. Nora gave the box one last shake, just to make sure there was nothing left in it.

"That's it," she said, turning back into the boat. She turned the carton upside down to demonstrate that it was empty.

A seagull overhead let out a single high-pitched shriek. A moment later the rest of the flock followed with a spiral of raucous laughter.

"Well done," said Macdara. "Well done, Nora."

And he started clapping. Whether it was for his father or for Nora, he wasn't sure, but everyone else joined in, even the little boys.

"It's more like coral," said Nora with surprise. "It looks more like coral than ashes."

And it seemed to Macdara that it was just like Nora to inject the moment with a little poetry.

"I think the occasion calls for a song," said Deirdre, and she got to her feet. Moving unsteadily towards the centre of the boat, she swung the loose end of her cape over her shoulder, in preparation for her performance. Fiddling for a moment with the hairpins that so inadequately held her hair up, she closed her eyes as she began to sing. The song she had chosen was a sea shanty, and a great favourite of Manus's. As she sang it, her voice was thrown about by the wind, which gave it an added bravery, and an added beauty.

> Dress me up in me oilskins and jumper,
> No more on the docks I'll be seen,
> Just tell me old shipmates, I'm takin' a trip, mates,
> And I'll see you some day in Fiddlers' Green.

Alma and Acushla were huddled together along one side of the boat, each of them staring down at the wet, shifting floor as they listened to their mother sing. Nora and Nando were sitting opposite them, Nora with her cheek resting on Nando's woolly shoulder and her eyes on her grandmother's face. Macdara and Mick sat facing Connie and the boys, and for once the boys were still, their small, grave faces framed by their huge life jackets as they listened to the singing. Connie's eyes shone with tears that she made no attempt to wipe away. Liam was sitting at the back of the boat, with his arm on the tiller to steady it and his face turned out to sea. Emmet was standing up at the back, a black shadow against the blue sky.

As she reached the final verse, Deirdre stretched a hand out towards Sam. Taking his hand in hers, she held on to it tight while she sang, her other hand stretched out to hold Mick's. For a moment Macdara was afraid that Mick would attempt to further the chain by grabbing his hand, but to his relief he didn't. Macdara was content to sit beside Mick, but not touching. When Deirdre got to the final chorus, they all joined in, and it seemed to Macdara that he had never known a moment of such perfect contentment as this, with the boat bobbing gently on the waves and his whole family in it, singing in unison.

Acknowledgements

The events and characters in this book are entirely fictional, but I have consulted many people in the course of my research. For their expertise on vintage cars, I am grateful to Donal Byrne and Donal Morrissy. Neal Massey advised me on the ins and outs of a burial at sea. Aengas Mac Grianna was kind enough to talk to me about his experiences on *Celebrity MasterChef Ireland*, while Mairéad Delaney's vast knowledge of the Abbey Theatre's history was a great resource — to her and all the staff behind the scenes at the Abbey, my sincere thanks. To the late Garry Henderson, I owe the Hellmann's mayonnaise story as well as the beautiful "Fiddler's Green", a verse of which is included by kind permission of John Conolly. For those readers who have a day-to-day memory of the summer of 2013, I confess that I have bent the weather in places to suit my purposes. The bit about the long hot summer, I did not make up.

My agent Marianne Gunn O'Connor has been a stalwart support, as has her sub-agent Vicki Satlow. My former colleagues in RTÉ have been unfailingly kind. Paul Durcan stepped forward with encouragement when I most needed it. Margaret Daly and Cormac Kinsella offered their wisdom and expertise most generously. To all of them, a warm thank you.

My editors Rebecca Saunders and Helen Atsma worked hard to make this book the best book it could be. I am hugely grateful to both of them. Thanks also to Kati Nicholl, Joanna Smyth and Jane Selley for their valuable input. It has been my pleasure to work with Manpreet Grewal, Tamsyn Berryman, Maddie West and Stephanie Melrose from Little, Brown in London. Breda Purdue and Jim Binchy along with Siobhán Tierney and all the team at Hachette in Dublin have been, as always, wonderful.

Mary Reynolds and Karen Coleman Muldowney helped in different but important ways. So too did Ray Murphy and Margaret Dunne. Hilary McGouran and Valerie Bistany read the book at various stages in its development, and their suggestions were enormously helpful. Áine Lawlor was a valuable early reader as were Sara Burke and Aoife Kavanagh. Finally and most importantly, I am grateful for the support of my family in encouraging me on this path I've chosen. I want to thank my brother Kevin and my sister Meg for their faith in me, and their love. My father Des, for his constant friendship and wise counsel; he also bore with good grace the theft of some of his gentle eccentricities. For Mark and Lucy and Clara, there are not enough words.

Other titles published by Ulverscroft:

YUKI CHAN IN BRONTË COUNTRY

Mick Jackson

Yuki, a young Japanese woman and self-styled psychic detective, tragically lost her mother in the UK ten years ago. After visiting her sister in London, she travels to the last place her mother went before her death: the Brontë parsonage in Howarth, and the snow-covered moors that surround the town. Along with her new friend Denny, a local girl who is keen to accompany her, Yuki goes in search of significant locations and, ultimately, the one person who can explain the ghosts in the photographs Yuki's mother viewed at the Institute of Psychic Studies. Both a pilgrimage and an investigation into family secrets, Yuki's journey is one she always knew she'd have to make.

THE HIGH MOUNTAINS OF PORTUGAL

Yann Martel

Lisbon, 1904: A man named Tomas discovers an old journal that hints of an extraordinary artefact which — if he can find it — would redefine history. Travelling in one of Europe's earliest automobiles, Tomas sets out in search of this strange treasure . . . Thirty-five years later, a Portuguese pathologist devoted to the murder mysteries of Agatha Christie finds himself at the centre of a murder mystery of his own, and is drawn into the consequences of Tomas's quest . . . Fifty years on, a Canadian senator seeks refuge in his ancestral village in northern Portugal, mourning the loss of his beloved wife. He arrives with an unusual companion: a chimpanzee. It is here that this centuries-old adventure comes to its conclusion . . .

ABLE SEACAT SIMON

Lynne Barrett-Lee

Simon is discovered in the Hong Kong docks in 1948 and smuggled on board the HMS *Amethyst* by a British sailor who takes pity on the malnourished kitten. The young cat quickly establishes himself as the chief rat-catcher in residence, while also winning the hearts of the entire crew. Then the *Amethyst* is ordered to sail up the Yangtse, and tragedy strikes as it comes under fire from communist guns. Many of the crew are killed, and Simon is among those who are seriously wounded. With the help of the ship's doctor, the brave cat makes a full recovery and is soon spending time with the injured men in the sick bay, purring and keeping their spirits up. Soon, news of Simon's heroism spreads worldwide — but it is still a long journey back to England . . .

A PERFECT HOME

Kate Glanville

Claire appears to have it all — the kind of life you read about in magazines: a beautiful cottage, three gorgeous children, a handsome husband in William, and her own flourishing vintage textile business. But when an interiors magazine sends a good-looking photographer to take pictures of Claire's perfect home, he makes her wonder if the house means more to William than she does, and question whether home really is where the heart is . . .